PRAISE FOR
wish

"*Wish* is a magical novel, written in a spare and crisp style, plot moving at NASCAR pace, dialogue as true as a first love, and characters real enough to care about, cry over, and mourn. It is that special gem of a book that arrives only so often to reach out and grab for all our hearts. With this novel, Melina Bellows has answered every reader's wish."

—Lorenzo Carcaterra, bestselling author
of *Sleepers* and *Paradise City*

"*Wish* is the story of one girl's life chronicled with humor, hope, and utter exasperation from the 1970s to the present. You will root for Bella every step of the way as she deals with family, romance, and career on the wild roller coaster to adulthood. Fast-paced and funny. Melina Bellows has written a winner."

—Adriana Trigiani, Author of *The Queen of the Big Time*
and *Lucia, Lucia*

"*Wish* is wonderful. Melina Bellows breaks through with a fresh new voice that will carry you blissfully down memory lane. Bella Grandelli is an unforgettable heroine, and when I finished the last page, my only wish was to start all over again."

—Ben Sherwood, bestselling author of
The Man Who Ate the 747 and *The
Death and Life of Charlie St. Cloud*

continued...

Year: 1980
Age: 15
Idols: Charlie's Angels
Favorite Song: "Anticipation" (Carly Simon)
Prized Possession: my virginity
Best Shoes: Candies sandals

I'm sunbathing at the reservoir when my whole entire life does, like, a total one-eighty. It's illegal to swim in the res, so you have to keep an ear out for the police, but as soon as the weather's warm, everyone does it anyway. The fun part is you never know who will show up, unlike our family's country club, where it's always the same old preppies.

I'm just tuning in my transistor radio to "Baba O'Riley," one of my favorite Who songs, when I hear tires crunching on the gravel. I grab my flip-flops and prepare to bolt into the woods, in case it's the cops. But then I hear the car's radio, tuned into my exact station—I mean, Daltrey is blasting, and a hunter green convertible suddenly swings into view. Behind the wheel is Chandler Sumner, a junior who looks exactly like Christopher Atkins in *The Blue Lagoon*. He's with two of his buddies, Brad and Pete. They are part of the popular, jocky crowd who are going to rule Harrison High School in the fall.

Now don't take this the wrong way, because I, like, so totally swear to God, cross my heart and hope to die, that I'm not conceited. But I have to tell you something you are not going to believe: I look like a total fox! I lost twenty-seven pounds and I'm tan. My Dorothy Hamill has finally grown out, and this morning I blew-dry my hair. My wings came out excellent. I mean they, like, totally feathered perfectly.

Chandler and I make eye contact. We are both bobbing our heads and lip-synching. We lock eyes, mouth the crescendo "They're all waaaaa-sted!" and he smiles. At me. My stomach drops, like, ten stories. . . .

wish

MELINA GEROSA BELLOWS

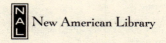
New American Library

New American Library
Published by New American Library, a division of
Penguin Group (USA) Inc., 375 Hudson Street,
New York, New York 10014, USA
Penguin Group (Canada), 90 Eglinton Avenue, Suite 700, Toronto,
Ontario M4P 2Y3, Canada (a division of Pearson Penguin Canada Inc.)
Penguin Books Ltd., 80 Strand, London WC2R 0RL, England
Penguin Ireland, 25 St. Stephen's Green, Dublin 2,
Ireland (a division of Penguin Books Ltd.)
Penguin Group (Australia), 250 Camberwell Road, Camberwell, Victoria 3124,
Australia (a division of Pearson Australia Group Pty. Ltd.)
Penguin Books India Pvt. Ltd., 11 Community Centre, Panchsheel Park,
New Delhi - 110 017, India
Penguin Group (NZ), cnr Airborne and Rosedale Roads, Albany,
Auckland 1310, New Zealand (a division of Pearson New Zealand Ltd.)
Penguin Books (South Africa) (Pty.) Ltd., 24 Sturdee Avenue,
Rosebank, Johannesburg 2196, South Africa

Penguin Books Ltd., Registered Offices:
80 Strand, London WC2R 0RL, England

First published by New American Library,
a division of Penguin Group (USA) Inc.

First Printing, October 2005
10 9 8 7 6 5 4 3 2

NEW AMERICAN LIBRARY and logo are trademarks of Penguin Group (USA) Inc.

LIBRARY OF CONGRESS CATALOGING-IN-PUBLICATON DATA

Bellows, Melina Gerosa.
Wish/Melina Gerosa Bellows.
p.   cm.
ISBN 0-451-21653-9 (trade pbk.)
1. Women journalists—Fiction.   2. Brothers and sisters—Fiction.
3. Autism—Patients—Fiction.   4. Self-realization—Fiction.   5. Twins—Fiction.
I. Title.

PS3602.E6497W57   2005
813'.6—dc22   2005007062

Set in Granjon
Designed by Elke Sigal

Printed in the United States of America

For Suzi and Carl, the best parents in the world

ACKNOWLEDGMENTS

I would like to acknowledge all of my boyfriends, from the jerks to the saints, who loved me, dumped me, and left me no choice but to embark on a joyride of self-discovery. You are the inspiration for this book. A huge thanks goes to my boyfriend for life, Keith Bellows, who, in one sitting, read the first illegible draft and broke out in applause despite its horribleness. In fact, you would probably not be reading *Wish* right now without all of the friends who suffered through drafts, including Deirdre Price and Holly Millea. Three people, however, had the biggest impact. Gloria Nagy was my hand in the dark from the very beginning. Rebecca Ascher Walsh generously edited the horribleness and kept me honest in the process. And Jennifer Gerosa's careful read and shrewd, simple suggestions reinvented the entire ending. (Who says that Hollywood endings don't exist in real life?) The walk down memory lane is courtesy of the tireless research of pop culture vulture Sarah Wassner. I must thank my agent, Claudia Cross, who, despite the babies we each had during the process, was there every step of the way. And of course, heartfelt gratitude goes to the best editor in the world, Anne Bohner, who transformed *Wish* from a wallflower to the Bella of the ball.

wish

Is he *dead?*

I jump off my Vespa and race past a fire engine, an ambulance, and the F.D.N.Y. scrimmage blocking my street.

There, in front of my apartment, is my brother's body, sprawled on the sidewalk.

I barge through the crowd of onlookers gawking, and as I get closer, a frenzy of paramedics descends and starts working on his unconscious body.

"He's not breathing!" yells one of the paramedics.

"Bobby!" I scream, dropping to my knees at his side.

The other paramedic, a woman, pushes me out of the way to strap an oxygen mask to Bobby's face. She pulls down Bobby's chin and begins sliding a silver L-shaped tool down his throat.

"Tube's in," she says. "I'll start the IV."

As she sticks a needle in Bobby's arm, his whole body convulses. His eyes open for a second, then roll back into his head.

The fireman rhythmically compresses Bobby's chest as someone else sticks another needle into Bobby's IV.

"Miss, is he allergic to anything? History of heart attacks? Strokes?" I'm asked as the first drug is injected into Bobby's IV.

"It's complicated—" I stammer, completely overwhelmed by the frantic events in front of me.

I don't know where to begin to explain about my twin. The years of shock treatments, wrong medications, and institutionalization roil in my mind like a sinister kaleidoscope.

How can I lose him now that I've finally found him? My entire life has been a quest for my other half, someone to complete me. My search for a soulmate—which has lead me into intimacy with trust-fund babies, "It" boys, and celebrities—has led me right back to the first guy I ever loved, my twin brother. But life isn't always champagne wishes and caviar dreams when your brother is autistic.

"Get these people back!" says the male paramedic, helping to lift Bobby's lifeless body onto the gurney.

"Can I be with him?" I ask, running alongside the gurney.

"You can ride up front," the female paramedic says. "What can you tell us about his medical history? Who's his doctor?"

I open my mouth to answer, but the only thought that passes through my mind is this: If Bobby's life is ending, then what has been the point of mine?

2

Year: 1974
Age: 8½
Idol: Catwoman weekdays and Cher weekends
Favorite Song: "Me & Bobby McGee" (Janis Joplin)
Prized Possession: purple three-speed Schwinn, with lime green
sparkle banana seat and matching streamers
Best Shoes: red Dr. Scholl's

You only get so many chances in life to make a wish. First stars, birthday candles, fallen eyelashes, and, like right now, when my mom drives over the train tracks and I hold my breath, cross my fingers, and lift my feet in the air—all at the same time.

"Mom, slow down!" I yell as our station wagon passes the Red Hook Bakery, which is a block away from the tracks. Bobby and I are way in the back, facing away from her so we see things going rather than coming. But I've memorized the landmarks: McGrath's Funeral Parlor, Cozy Corner Deli, and the Red Hook Bakery.

"Honey, watch your brother!" my mom calls over her shoulder. She has eyes in the back of her head, beneath her frosted yellow hair. But I wonder if she can see that Bobby has been chucking the groceries we just bought out the back window. There goes her Tab. (Don't worry. I've got the Yodels on my side.)

When my mom says, "Watch your brother," what she really means is "Stop your brother." That's easier said than done, and I'm always the one who has to do it because he never leaves me alone. But with only a half block to go before Wish Time, all I want to do is close my eyes, cross my fingers, lift my feet, and wish so hard my face turns red.

Bobby does things like this all the time. And never gets in trouble. See, we're twins, but I was born first because I cut in line. I think I was so fast and pushy Bobby got stuck coming out of my mom's stomach, so people call him slow. Bobby's like a black jellybean. A lot of people don't like them. But they're not so bad if you give them a chance.

You wouldn't know we were twins because Bobby has straight hair and I've got crazy corkscrew curls that drive my mom crazy when she tries to brush through them. She usually yanks them into ponytails, but sometimes she gives up and I'm left with an afro. The kids at school call me Jimi Hendrix on those days. My grandma—Grandina—said when I was in Mom's stomach I spent all my time curling my hair so I'd never have to curl it again. She's dead now.

That's why I'm wearing her gold heart-shaped locket, because if she were alive, she would still be wearing it. When my mom told me she "went to heaven," I felt like a soda pop exploded in my chest, spraying a messy sadness inside me. I'm not sure about heaven. I mean, look what happened about Santa Claus. Just because you believe in something really hard doesn't make it true.

But anyway, no matter where Grandina is, I want her back. I felt like she was all mine. My parents are always so busy with my brother that they don't have time for me. But I'm trying. Last year I got the lead in *Romeo and Juliet*. But the night of the performance Bobby had a seizure, so they couldn't come. This year I signed up for ballet, which I hate. But so what? It will be worth it if they show up. It's not their fault at all—it's just that sometimes after watching Bobby all the time, there aren't any leftovers left for me. Grandina always had enough love and kisses to go around, even when I'd be scared or sad and need a second helping of hugs to feel full.

Bobby hates hugs. Ever since he was born, he's hated to be touched, even by Mom. Until he was three, my parents also thought Bobby was deaf. But then they found out that his ears worked fine. He just didn't want to listen all the time. He only hears what he wants to hear.

What I want to hear is "Will you marry me?" so I can be a bride. I want that more than anything in the world, including hair as straight as Cher's. Brides are so beautiful, plus they have magical powers. You can see for yourself on TV. If you watch during your mom's programs, sometimes, if you are extra, extra lucky, brides star in the commercials.

My favorite bride (who I really want to be when I grow up) gets to be a bride because of something called a "dooosh." But when I asked my mom if I could get one for my birthday, she just cleared her throat and told me to go outside and check on my brother.

"Bella, did you hear me?" she repeats from the front seat. Bobby has just relieved our family of a frozen chicken. I watch it skid like a frosty bowling ball across the street.

Even though I really, *really*, *really*, *really* want to make a wish, I do what my mother says.

"Hey, Bobby, I'll make you a deal!" I say, taking the Tang out of his hand and rolling up the window. "If you play Bride Practice with me when we get home, I'll buy you a cinnamon cruller."

The smell coming out of the Red Hook Bakery, which is three blocks from our house, is so good that it makes all the spit come to the front of my mouth. One time Bobby went missing and we finally found him down there licking the windows.

"Say your prayers, varmint!" Bobby says. "Prepare to defend yourself, rabbit, 'cause I'm boardin' your ship!"

Great! Bobby has a special way of talking that a lot of people don't understand. I think maybe Bobby's words get stuck in his brain, so he uses other people's words. For example, Bobby loves

Yosemite Sam, so he always talks like Yosemite Sam when he likes something. He hates Bugs Bunny, so if he starts sounding like Bugs Bunny, it means he's about to get mad. It's like a code, and once you get it he's easy to understand. Translation: He'll play Bride Practice.

I help my mother carry in what's left of the groceries.

"Bella, have you seen my Tab?" she says, scratching her head. "And I'm almost sure I bought a frozen chicken."

"Nope," I say and run up to my room and pull the David Cassidy sheet off my bed. Next I run outside and pick a big bouquet of wildflowers from the field behind our house so I can add them to the lime green streamers off my bike's handlebars for my bouquet.

Bobby tags after me and sits in the dirt. He can just sit for hours watching dirt sift through his fingers like it's *The Brady Bunch* followed by *The Partridge Family*. To him, it's *that* interesting. By the time I've picked a bunch of black-eyed Susans, dandelions, and Queen Anne's lace, he's dug up some earthworms and is lining them up in size order. One won't stay straight, and before I can stop him, Bobby picks it up and sucks it down like a piece of spaghetti.

"Gross, Bobby," I say. "If you get worms, Mom's gonna blame me."

"Damn varmint," he says. I drape the sheet around me so it looks just like a perfect gown and veil in one. Together we promenade down our front steps and past the brick row houses that are all stuck together with one long porch. The only way you can tell the difference between homes is when a family puts out a birdbath or light-up Virgin Mary like the Martuccis'. To me, *those* houses have personality.

Anyway, we walk around our block, singing, "Da, Da, Da Duuuum." Starting with our voices really, really low we get louder, one house at a time, so that right exactly by the time we get back in front of our house, we are singing at the top of our lungs. I look so beautiful that people are actually staring at us.

"Oh, are you dressed up as Mother Teresa?" asks Mrs. Martucci, our across-the-street neighbor.

"Yes, ma'am. Mother Teresa on her wedding day," I say, using my manners and adding a fib. "Learned about her wedding in school."

"Oh, my word!" she says, not talking to me. She's talking to Bobby, who has his nose planted between her legs in her private place. He smells people all the time, just like a dog, no matter how much we tell him it's not polite.

"Bobby, quit it!" I tell him. I'm used to him doing this, so I can skip getting embarrassed. I used to get so ashamed that I felt like I was actually the one doing it, instead of my brother. But at this point, it can be sort of funny when it happens to somebody for the first time.

"Ehhh, what's up, Doc?" he says, wrinkling his nose at Mrs. Martucci. "Not polite to sniff like a dog! Not polite to sniff like a dog!"

"Sorry, Mrs. Martucci!" I say, hiding my laugh with a really, really bad sudden cough. I steer Bobby up our front walk, telling him, "Hey, it's time for *Looney Tunes!*"

And what do you know, Bobby forgets all about that cinnamon cruller. Even though I know it's a sin, and the Virgin Mary statue is watching from across the street, I don't remind him. I just run up to my room and put those quarters meant for the crullers back in my glass piggy bank, where they clink me fifty cents closer to my wedding gown and matching veil.

I have to admit, it's not the first time I've pulled a fast one on my brother. And when Bobby has to go to the hospital, for shock treatments and worse, how bad I feel gets caught in my throat like a big ropy knot, and I feel like I am going to choke.

When I'm alone in the house waiting for everyone to get home from the hospital, I usually try to push the feelings down with some Fig Newtons. When that doesn't work, I make bargains with God. I promise I'll bring my piggy bank right down to the Red Hook Bakery and buy Bobby as many crullers as he wants for the rest of his life. Just please, Sweet Baby Jesus, let him get better.

Then when everything goes back to normal again, I pretend I forgot all about the trade. You don't have to tell me how bad this is. I already know, because I think about it at least ten times a day. The Martuccis' Virgin Mary frowns at me sometimes when I walk by, so I know she remembers too.

Maybe God decided that I went too far, young lady, because today something terrible happened. Our principal told our parents that "it wasn't working out" for Bobby to go to school with me anymore. He said that Bobby "disrupts the class" and "disrespects authority." But mostly he's "different."

Every time there is a parent-teacher conference about my brother, it's almost as if a big Gray Cloud barges into our house and rains on our family. I wish my parents would put up an umbrella, but they don't. They just stop talking, and I can take a hint so I do too. The only person who acts normal is Bobby. Well, normal for him, anyway. He'll have as many tantrums as he wants, despite my mother's wet eyes and my father's cloudy face.

"Guess what. I got an A on my composition today!" I announce to my mother, trying to crawl onto her lap with my paper. I try to be really sunny and happy to make up for him. It's the least I can do for shoving past him the day we were born.

"Not now, honey," she says, pushing me off. She doesn't even notice that I'm still in the room when she puts my composition in the wastepaper basket.

I'm not sure what I should do, but I can't take the Gray Cloud anymore, so I go over to play with the Martuccis' dog, Freebie. He looks exactly like Lassie. We're pretending to star in *Courage of*

Lassie (starring Elizabeth Taylor), when the next thing you know I'm flat on my back and Freebie is on top of me. He's so nice, at first, that I think he's roughhousing. Then there's a loud snarling sound and a white flash of fangs in my eyes. Next all I see is blood.

As fast I can, I run home and try to open the door, but it's locked. I ring our front doorbell a hundred times in a row. Bobby answers it and says, "Ehhh, what's up, Doc? I hate people with bloody eyes!" and slams the door. I start ringing the doorbell again a million times, and watch as the blood drips all over the cement steps. Finally my mom comes running and screams, "Robert, come quick! Bella's been hit by a car! Her face!" She hugs me to her, and my blood makes a giraffe shape on her shirt.

"Be brave, Bella," my dad says, driving us to the emergency room with one hand and holding his hanky against my face with the other. I keep my good eye open in case my bad eye falls out and rolls into my lap. I count the red lights he's running. Nine red, four green—then we pull up to the emergency room entrance.

Everyone is in white and rushing around, and there's a weird smell that tastes like someone squirted Bactine right in my mouth. After a really long time, it's our turn.

"We are going to give you a shot of Novocaine so it doesn't hurt," says the doctor, which makes absolutely no sense to me. On top of this, I have to get a shot? As the long needle comes toward my face, I hear a loud clattery bang.

"Mr. Grandelli!" screams the nurse to my father, who is suddenly lying down on the floor. "Doctor, he must have fainted!"

"I'm fine, I'm fine," says my father, propping himself up and putting back on his black-framed glasses, which are now bent. "Just not so good with big needles."

Oh, great, now this is my fault too. I'm so scared about my dad that I barely notice that I survive the shot. As the doctor stitches me up, I don't *feel* the black thread going through my skin as much as *hear* the sound from the inside, like when you pull a Popsicle stick between your teeth. I keep my eyes on the nurse's neat white clogs and imagine wearing them with my bridal gown.

Twelve stitches later, the doctor snaps off his rubber gloves and tells my dad that we were really lucky I didn't lose my eye. But I don't feel so lucky, considering I have to wear a patch for a month. And you've got to be kidding me if you think an extra lollipop is going to make up for that.

When we finally get home I find my mom sitting on the couch staring at the TV, which isn't on. She does this when she's worried about Bobby. When she sees me in the doorway she gets up anxiously and holds my face in her warm hands. She looks to my father and asks what the doctor said.

"Great news! I'm not blind!" I answer for him.

But then there's the sound of glass breaking from the dining room followed by Bobby's laughter. My mother drops her hands and runs toward the china closet, my father right behind her. I'm left standing there alone with my eye patch.

Before they can ask me to clean up another of Bobby's messes, I go up to my room, lie on my bed, close my eyes, and try to imagine my grandmother in heaven. I take off my heart locket and try to open it, which I never can. I give up and play "Gypsies, Tramps and Thieves" and "Dark Lady" on my Close 'N Play record player.

That's when I decide to write Cher a letter. I tell her about Grandma dying last winter, my twelve stitches, and how my brother disappears into an imaginary world all the time. I ask her if she has any advice for people wearing an eye patch.

I'm sure Cher gets a lot of letters, but she will know that I am her biggest fan because I use all of my best stickers on the envelope, and I'm sure we have the exact same favorites. You can tell she has the best taste. Just look at her costumes. I like Catwoman too. She's one of the only people I know who gets to be good and bad at the same time, and not worry about it. And Batman is in love with her, which is a definite plus.

Sometimes, to practice, I make myself face really tough choices. Not just chocolate or vanilla, or Cher versus Catwoman, but worse. Already I'm worried about sharing my ninth birthday with Bobby. When it's time to blow out the candles, am I going to wish for Shrinky Dinks, to be a bride, or for Bobby to get better? My parents say any day he can just grow out of it, whatever "it" is. If he would just wish for himself, I wouldn't have to worry about it. I worry all the more, because he doesn't seem to worry about himself.

In some ways kids have it easy, because people think we don't know the difference between right and wrong. That's the easy part. We do. We just pretend we don't, because making yourself do the right thing, when you don't really want to, is what we need to practice.

3

Year: 1978
Age: 13
Idols: Joni Mitchell and Valerie Bertinelli
Favorite Song: "Stairway to Heaven" (Led Zeppelin)
Prized Possession: turquoise-studded pot pipe
Best Shoes: Frye boots

Something just poked me in the back. I have to make sure I'm not being paranoid, because I smoked a joint during lunch with the cool group. Now I'm in social studies class. I turn around and Heather—she's queen of The Eighth Grade Clique—is nodding toward my foot. I look down at my new Frye boot—God, it looks so beautiful—and see a tiny, wadded-up piece of paper. I drop my pencil so I can bend down and get it without our teacher, Mr. Reep, noticing.

"Spin the Bottle after school?" the note says. *Wow*. This means I am officially in The Clique! Not only that, but now maybe my wish can come true.

Even more than I wish I was flat-chested, I wish, I wish, I wish I had a boyfriend. I have liked boys my entire life. Which is a very long time to be waiting for one to like me back. And at this point I feel like it's showing on the outside, popping out like zits, how badly I want someone to like me. I'm just being paranoid—sometimes pot does that to me.

In sixth grade, cooties were officially over, and people started "going out." No one actually ever went anywhere. Still, to be asked out proved to the whole entire world that you're special. It was only after wasting wishes on about a bazillion first stars that I realized only the short, skinny, straight-haired girls were special enough to get picked.

Short and skinny is definitely not me. I was born with what Grandina would have called "a shapely figure." Shaped just like hers in old photos when she was young. And my mother's too. When my mother first took me home from the maternity ward, she displayed me on the bed for Mrs. Martucci, who took one look at me and said, "Oh, my God. Bella already has hips!" Naturally, my brother's skinny. So, in a way, we both have a handicap.

My whole life I've been bigger than the girls my age, and most of the boys too. Even now I have to take a black Magic Marker and block out the W:32 on the tag of my Levi's so no one can see my waist size. But this year, thank God, the rest of the class is starting to catch up. Even Heather and the rest of the flat-chested popular girls are starting to wear bras, which finally makes it okay for me to wear one too.

Blending in a little better is not the only reason that I like junior high. The other is that my parents sent Bobby to a special school when they found out he was "artistic." This is so lucky, because no way would I be part of The Clique if they knew about my brother. The whole point of The Clique, after all, is to keep the losers *out*. If they knew my own twin still sleeps with a Batman night-light and wears a helmet in case he cracks his head open during a temper tantrum, they'd definitely think that I was a retard too.

I pass back Heather a note that says, "Party up! P.S. I really like your s-chain bracelet."

Getting into The Clique is not easy. It helps if you do one of the following: smoke cigarettes, smoke pot, shoplift, cut class, drink beer, or know exactly when to make a hilarious cut down at the perfect time. I love Marlboro Lights. I also do a little bit of the other stuff, but never enough so that my parents catch on. They have enough problems with my brother without having to worry about me going to jail for smoking on top of it. I always make sure I'm perfect in school and helpful at home so they don't know what I'm really up to.

Heather passes a note back: "I'll trade my s-chain bracelet for your heart locket. P.S. How many kids in your family?"

I would never trade Grandina's locket, so I answer only the second question. "I'm an only child," I write back, adding, "I'm also part Cherokee." I've always wanted to be an Indian. So much cooler than Italian. Besides, I don't have anything in common with my family anyway.

The Clique has Disco Sucks parties at Heather's house every Wednesday, but this is the first time I've been invited. It's eight of us, five girls and three boys, including Zack, Heather's boyfriend, who I know from French class. We meet behind our school and walk together, chucking gravel at cars along the way.

When we get to Heather's, I'm not sure what to do, so I just follow along.

"Let's party up!" says Heather, popping Meat Loaf's *Bat Out of Hell* in her parents' eight-track cassette player.

"Bella, let's use your turquoise pipe," she says, referring to the pipe that she dared me to lift from the head shop when the stoner owner went back to check for a velvet Bay City Rollers poster.

While everyone sits in a circle, I take out my pipe, which I keep wrapped in tin foil, tucked in my little makeup case, in the bottom compartment of my batik pocketbook.

Heather stuffs a bud in the bowl and flicks her Bic to light the pipe for me. I take a hit and pass it around. Then we have really deep conversations.

"Jimi Hendrix died choking on his own vomit," says Heather authoritatively.

"So did Jim Morrison and Mama Cass," I say.

"What are you talking about?" Heather says, giving me a look. Then I feel a bit confused. I think maybe I'm wrong. Mama

Cass choked on toast. Or maybe she was eating toast when she started to vomit. Heather knows a lot more about this than I do. I should have just kept my mouth shut. Oh, no, I'm starting to get really paranoid.

Is everyone looking at me? My mind starts racing. When is someone going to pull out a bottle so we can start playing? I'm terrified but excited at the same time, sort of like how you feel watching *Halloween*—you don't want Michael Myers to pop out, but at the same time you do.

Heather, who wears blue eyeliner and eyeshadow the same exact color of her eyes, gets up and walks over to the stereo. "Zack, this song is for you," she says. "Listen carefully." She puts on "Freebird." When he doesn't get it, she plays and rewinds it three times in a row.

"Thanks, Heather. I love that song," says Zack, who is, in fact, a Lynyrd Skynyrd fan. Zack is very cool. He looks a little like Chachi from *Happy Days*. He has the same middle part, but also wears a rawhide choker. He knows every single word to "Devil Went Down to Georgia." Plus he can play "My Sharona" on his trumpet.

Heather rolls her eyes and comes over to me. "I really need to talk to you," she whispers in my ear. "In private." We go up to her parents' bathroom and lock the door. "Can I borrow your Bonnie Bell raspberry Lipsmacker?"

"Sure. Can I borrow your Visine?" I say. "It would be really beat if my parents suspected anything." I'm starting to come down now, and I'm relieved. I hate that out-of-control feeling.

"Only if you do me a favor," says Heather as she leans into the mirror, running my Lipsmacker back and forth across her mouth. Without turning around, she looks at me in the mirror. "Can you tell Zack that I want to break up?" she says. "He didn't get it when I tried to tell him that he's, like, later much."

This is a big deal, because Heather and Zack have been going out for three straight weeks, and they are, by far, the coolest Clique couple. Now, personally, I think it's really beat to have someone else break up for you. But at the same time, she's definitely not using me. Heather could have asked anyone, but she chose me.

"You're his friend. *Please?*" she says, her blue eyes looking even bluer with the freshly applied Lipsmacker.

Zack is my first boy friend, two separate words. We met in Madame Carroll's French class. We call her Madame Barrel behind her back because she's fat—I mean, rotund, just like a barrel. She's also mean and has a lazy eye. Zack and I speak franglais, which is an English-French mix, to each other.

We go back to the circle and I tap Zack on the shoulder, blow two perfect smoke rings, one right through the other, and say, "Let's parlez." I take Zack up to Heather's parents' bathroom and lock the door.

"Heather thinks you are a really nice person and everything," I say as gently as I can, "but she wants to be friends."

"Pourquois?" he says, surprised.

Now I know for a fact that she's dumping Zack because she heard that a ninth-grader basketball jock wants to ask her out.

"She likes you too much, and she's scared," I lie.

"That's so beat," Zack says, looking away. Then he opens his brown eyes really, really wide and looks at me without blinking for two straight minutes. He's doing the Don't-Cry-Eye Trick. If you don't blink for long enough, eventually your eyes dry out and the tears evaporate.

I have to do something quick.

"Attendez class!" I bellow, puffing out my cheeks, crossing my eyes, and doing my best Madame Barrel impersonation. "Bonjour, Zack! Did you hear ze one about ze cross-eyed teacher?" I say in a crazy French accent. "She couldn't control her pupils!"

Zack cracks up, which makes me crack up, and that's when it happens. A fart shoots out like a cannon. Zack goes silent and looks at me like "Did I just hear that?" Which makes me laugh even harder and fart again, this time like a rapid-fire machine gun.

At this point, Zack is doubling over and gasping for breath. I've never been more embarrassed in my life, but at the same time it makes me feel powerful that I stopped him from crying. Like I'm totally flat-chested or something.

"Make ya a deal," I say. "I'll keep votre secret si vous keep mine."

"Deal," he says, smiling. We share a Marlboro Light and invent our own top secret handshake.

Now that Zack's a free man, we start hanging out after school. I wait for him by the lockers until he finishes trumpet practice, and then we walk to his house. Zack's mom works, so we get to smoke cigarettes. We also play with his boa constrictor, Bernie, and sometimes Zack will give me a little concert on his trumpet, playing my requests like Cheap Trick's "I Want You to Want Me" and "My Sharona," which is by the Knack, in case you didn't know.

Sometimes we Get Comfortable. It started once when we were wrestling around on the couch. He was on top, pinning me down, and then he just lay down on top of me and stayed like that. Our bodies were positioned just right, so we were intertwined, and it felt really, really . . . like, relaxing.

Now we get comfortable all the time. We just lie on top of each other in silence, occasionally asking, "Are you comfortable, mademoiselle?" "Oui, monsieur, are you comfortable?" Sometimes one of us is positioned to breathe on the other person's neck, and this is the most comfortable of all, especially under a blanket with *General Hospital* on in the background. (To be fair, we take turns with an egg timer.) If this is what it's like to have a boy friend, I really can't wait to have a boyfriend, one word.

Then, one day after school, Zack suggests that we hang out at my house instead of his, because his sister, Jaimie, is home from college and would tell on us for smoking.

"C'mon," he says, riding me on the back of his ten-speed. "I've never seen your house."

"All right," I say. But I regret it the second it leaves my mouth. I *never, ever, ever* have friends over, because if they knew how weird my family was, they wouldn't want to be friends with me. What if Bobby has one of his temper tantrums because someone has put his Batman toys out of order? Or if he insists on spaghetti as an after-school snack, which he will only eat one strand at a time with tweezers?

As if it's not bad enough to have a retard for a brother, my dad, an accountant, wears a pocket protector during tax season. (It's tax season.) And you should see his outfits during football season. Let's just say my dad is Notre Dame's number-one fan. And here's the embarrassing part: He didn't even go there.

My mother is the most normal one, but it depends on the day and the state of her "nerves." Sometimes when I go home, she's just sitting on the couch crying or looking into space. On those days, none of my straight-A report cards or Roseanne Rosannadanna impersonations can get through to her. And if that's not bad enough, she has a Florence Henderson hairdo, unlike Heather's mom, who has a shag.

"Let's smoke a joint," I suggest on the way, thinking that if Zack is high he might not notice that my family is stranger than the Munsters. As we pass the Martuccis' light-up Virgin Mary, I make a wish that everyone acts as normal as possible. I know the pot has kicked in when the Virgin Mary shakes her head at me in disapproval.

I cross my fingers as we walk into my house.

"Nice to meet you, Zack," my mother says, stirring the Hamburger Helper on the stove. Her Florence Henderson flip looks even flippier than usual against her Talbots blue blazer. I wish she would wear jeans and peasant tops like Heather's mom, but at least she's not sitting on the couch staring off into space today.

"Hi, Mrs. Grandelli," says Zack. His eyes are beet red. I wonder if my mother suspects anything. She's never met him before though, so maybe she could think that they are permanently like that.

"Bella, have you seen your brother's bus?" she says. "He should be home from physical therapy by now."

On cue, the kitchen door swings open, and Bobby walks in. Although I see him every day, I look at him now with an outsider's eye. I cringe at his helmet, his flannel pajamas (which he insists on wearing instead of clothes), and his *Mork and Mindy* lunchbox. The sensation zaps through me, as if I were chewing on tin foil.

"Holy smokes, Batman, there's a smoky smell in Gotham City," Bobby says, sniffing around us. Oh, no, holy pot smoke, leave it to my brother the bloodhound! I pray to God my parents don't catch on. The last thing I need is Bobby's freaky sense of smell getting me grounded. Zack stares at him wide-eyed.

"We're going to do homework. We have a big French test," I mumble, yanking Zack into the den.

"I didn't know you had a brother," Zack says.

"He's my twin," I say.

"What's wrong with him? He talks like a robot."

"I don't really know. My parents say he's going to grow out of it," I say, dying to change the subject. "C'mon, I'll do your French homework for you."

After conjugating verbs in the past tense, we take a break and Get Comfortable. We are so relaxed, discussing important things, like what a "Sharona" is—"it's a girl," I say; "female body part," swears Zack—that we don't even hear my dad walk in.

He clears his throat. "Bella, it's time for your boyfriend to go home," he says, staring down at his feet.

"Zack's not my boyfriend!" I say as we jump up. I'm not sure which is more embarrassing: my father's purple face or the fact that he called Zack my boyfriend. I swear to God, cross my heart, that we've never even kissed. We were just getting comfortable.

"Well, why don't we give *your friend* a lift home?" he says, jingling the change in his pocket.

We drop off Zack, and on the way back Gary Wright's "Dreamweaver" comes on the radio. Every time this song comes on, it reminds me of the one boy in The Clique that I do wish would notice me, and his name is Matt Dillon. He's the only one who's as tall as I am, and he's sort of a loner, which reminds me of me, even though I always try to be popular by making the perfect cut down at the perfect time.

The only person who knows I like Matt is Zack, because he got it out of me when we were playing Truth or Dare while Getting Comfortable at his house one day. I chose Truth because I was too comfortable to move for a Dare. But I made him swear on his boa constrictor's life not to tell a soul. And then I made him shake on it too.

When Dad and I get home, my mother and father exchange glances and my mother says she wants to talk to me. I'm filled with panic. Does she know about the pot and cigarettes? Did a neighbor see me hitchhiking or coming out of the head shop with Heather? My heart pounds in my chest as I follow her up into my room, where she closes the door and tells me to sit down next to her on the edge of the bed.

"Honey, it's time you and I had a little talk," she says.

I stop breathing completely.

"About the facts of life," she says, her eyes glued to my purple shag carpeting. She pulls out a book, *Growing Up and Liking It*, a box of Kotex, some Tampax, and a one-size-fits-all Maidenform bra.

"So just read this book and let me know if you have any questions," she says.

I almost burst out laughing. I got my period six months ago! I was way too embarrassed to tell my mother, so Heather and I just went shoplifting for Kotex. Besides, I had read Judy Blume's *Are You There, God? It's Me, Margaret* ages ago, so I was already prepared.

"Uh, thanks, Mom," I mumble.

"I'm so glad we had this talk," she says, looking relieved as she stands up. Then she smooths her paisley wrap skirt and leaves me 'n my new friend Tampax to get to know each other six months too late. Sometimes I'm amazed how people living under the same roof can actually be on different planets.

The next day in school I secretly save a seat for Matt at our fifth-period class, which is right after lunch. When the bell rings and he's not there, I know he's cutting. He's *so* cool.

I ask for the girls' room pass so I can look for him. I find him hanging out at The Wall, where The Clique congregates in the hall between periods. He's surrounded by three adults with clipboards and our principal.

First I think he's in trouble for cutting, but as I walk by, I notice that everyone is smiling and talking in that fakey polite way, like how my parents do on the telephone. I want to stay and listen so badly it's killing me, but I make myself keep walking into the girls' room. I open the door a crack so I can watch. I can only catch every few words, but I'm positive I hear "agent," "screen test," "Los Angeles," and "Francis Fold Coppola." Francis Ford Coppola is the director of *The Godfather*, which is a movie where they cut off a horse's head and put it in a man's bed.

After school, I run to the parking lot and break the news to The Clique.

"Matt Dillon's going to be famous!" I announce.

Everyone comes over to listen to me, which makes me feel really important. For some reason, though, this puts Heather in a really bad mood.

"Fuckin' liar," she says, cocking her head.

"Uh-uh," I say. "He's going for a screen test for a movie called *The Outsiders*."

Everyone, besides Heather, starts asking me a million questions, like I'm an expert. Even though I know I'm not lying, I still feel like I'm doing something wrong.

"That's just a rumor," Heather says. She flicks her cigarette ash in my hair.

"No, it's not," I say, my face flushing. "I heard the whole thing. It happened right during fifth period."

"You're such a liar. You're always looking for attention!" she says.

Busted. Getting attention, no matter how good it feels, is a punishable offense in the home and, I guess, outside of it too. But it's too late to back out now, so I keep pushing forward. "I swear to God! Principal Stack didn't even care that Matt was cutting," I manage to say.

"You're just saying that because you like him!" Heather says, flinging her hair over her shoulder.

Everyone gasps.

"You *like* him?" everyone in The Clique says at once. Then they start laughing at me.

"Not really!" I protest.

"Then why did Zack write it in the Slam Book?" Heather says, pulling a folded-up piece of loose-leaf paper from the back pocket of her Jordache jeans. Now everyone is standing around her instead of me. And there it is, on the line across from my name, under the Crush box: "Matt Dillon," in Zack's handwriting. I also see "36 Triple D" under my bra size, which is much less true but more upsetting.

Zack looks at me and sheepishly shrugs. He opens his mouth to say something, but right then, Heather notches a finger around one of his belt loops and whispers in his ear. In that single gesture, I understand everything. I'm beginning to get cliqued out. It's Them against Me, and even though I know Zack really likes me, it's almost impossible to go up against The Clique. I guess things didn't work out with Heather and the ninth-grader.

"I was just kidding," I say to Heather. "We were playing Truth or Dare."

"That's good, because Matt would never like a fat frizzball with big tits like you!" Heather says, pulling a comb out of her back pocket and gliding it through her perfectly straight Olivia Newton John hair.

My face burns with shame. I feel as exposed as if someone ripped off my shirt, and my too-small one-size-fits-all Maidenform right along with it.

"Thanks a lot," I say to Zack.

"Bella, I—" Zack starts, looking really torn, but he's interrupted by Heather.

"C'mon, Zack. I want to make out. Let's go play Spin the Bottle at my house!" Heather says, leading the pack out of the parking lot toward the intersection in front of our school. Not really knowing what to do, I follow a few paces behind everybody.

"Look, it's the 'tard bus," says Heather. "Let's chuck rocks at it!"

Sure enough, my brother's school van is sitting at the red light. Like a target with a bull's-eye, Bobby's helmeted head is clearly visible in the front-seat window.

I hold my breath. Is Zack going to tell my other secret too? We meet eyes, but he doesn't say a word.

Heather picks up a rock and whips it at Bobby's window, saying, "Take this, you 'tard!" The impact of the hit cracks the window, and my brother's head flinches back.

I'm stunned. Throwing a few pebbles at a parked car is one thing, but smashing a window in someone's face is wrong—really wrong. It's almost like hurting people is fun for her or something.

Eddie, Bobby's bus driver, jerks open the door, lumbers down the steps, and starts coming out after us. I'm paralyzed with fear.

"Which one of you threw the rock?" he says sharply, looking at each of us. No one says a word.

"Who threw it?" he demands. "Bella, who threw the rock at your brother?"

"Your *brother*?" Heather says to me, her jaw dropping. "I thought you were an only child adopted from the Cherokee Indians?"

I wish that I could shrivel up and die right there on the spot. But instead something worse happens. I officially get the ax.

"You are just a fat, faggotized retard like your brother," Heather says, wrinkling her nose. She turns on her perfect white Pro Ked heel and walks away.

Zack and I look at each other. He shrugs and turns to follow Heather. I hurl my pipe at him, but he doesn't seem to notice.

"C'mon, Zack." Heather grabs Zack's hand. "And everyone else, except Fat, Frizzy Bella. You're out of The Clique."

At first I think Bobby's staring at me, but it's clear by his glazed, fixed expression that he's looking right through me. He's off in his imaginary world, which makes me feel even worse.

"Want a ride, Bella?" asks Eddie. "No, thanks," I say, and I watch as the 'tard bus takes off.

The Gray Cloud descends as I stand there all alone. Now it's my turn to do the Don't-Cry-Eye Trick. Which doesn't work perfectly every time, for your information.

4

Year: 1980
Age: 15
Idol: Farrah Fawcett
Favorite Song: "Anticipation" (Carly Simon)
Prized Possession: my virginity
Best Shoes: Candies sandals

I'm sunbathing at the reservoir when my whole entire life does, like, a total one-eighty. It's illegal to swim in the res, so you have to keep an ear out for the police, but as soon as the weather's warm, everyone does it anyway. The fun part is you never know who will show up, unlike our family's country club, where it's always the same old preppies.

I'm just tuning in my transistor radio to "Baba O'Riley," one of my favorite Who songs, when I hear tires crunching on the gravel. I grab my flip-flops and prepare to bolt into the woods, in case it's the cops. But then I hear the car's radio, tuned into my exact station—I mean, Daltrey is blasting—and a hunter green convertible suddenly swings into view. Behind the wheel is Chandler Sumner, a junior who looks exactly like Christopher Atkins in *The Blue Lagoon*. He's with two of his buddies, Brad and Pete. They are part of the popular, jocky crowd who are going to rule Harrison High School in the fall.

Now don't take this the wrong way, because I, like, so totally swear to God, cross my heart and hope to die, that I'm not conceited. But I have to tell you something you are not going to believe: I look like a total fox! I lost twenty-seven pounds, and I'm tan. My Dorothy Hamill has finally grown out, and this morning

I blew-dry my hair. My wings came out excellent. I mean, they, like, totally feathered perfectly.

Chandler and I make eye contact. We are both bobbing our heads and lip-synching. We lock eyes, mouth the crescendo—"They're all waaaaa-sted!"—and he smiles. At me. My stomach drops, like, ten stories.

"Sums! Pop the trunk so we can grab the brewskis," yells Brad, ruining our Magic Moment.

Single file, they climb the rocks to get up to where I'm sitting on the levee. My heart is pounding so hard that I can actually see my locket and macramé bikini top going up and down.

"Wassup?" Brad and Pete sort of mumble as they pass me on their way to the shack, the best place to jackknife into the water. Chandler is the last one up, climbing with one hand and clutching a sweating six of Bud in the other.

In addition to, or maybe because of, looking exactly like Christopher Atkins, Chandler Sumner is the most popular guy at H.H.S. Here's proof: He was invited to the senior prom, the junior prom, and he still has a girlfriend from his old boarding school. She's, like, related to the Kennedys, everyone says.

"Nice tan," he says as he hops onto the levee.

"Thanks," I say, sucking in my stomach as hard as I can. "Nice puca-shell necklace." Everyone's wearing chokers made out of those little white shells, but nobody on earth looks as good in one as Chandler Sumner.

"Thanks," he says. "Hey, don't you go to H.H.S.?"

"Yeah, I just finished freshman year," I say, putting on some Johnson's Baby Oil so I look even tanner. I decide to play hard to get. "Do you?" I ask, playing dumb.

"Yeah," he says. "Thought you looked familiar."

Crucial question: Did he recognize the Old Me or the New Me? There's a *gigantic* difference. I've recently starred in my own personal episode of Cinderella. See, I connected the dots between being skinny and having a boyfriend a long time ago, but the being skinny part was always several Twinkies out of reach; therefore so was the boyfriend. It's a vicious cycle.

Then a month before freshman finals, my parents decided to take a family vacation to Florida so my brother could see some doctor who specializes in autism. In addition to Bain de Soleil and Tickle deodorant, I decided to get two packs of Extra-Strength Dexatrim. You're supposed to be eighteen years old in order to buy them, but as I told you, looking older than I am hasn't been a problem for me since, like, sixth grade. Finally, looking old is good for something.

Let me tell you, these pills work like a charm! I lost nine pounds before I even got on the plane, which motivated me to just keep on dieting while I was there. In three months, I've gone from a size sixteen to a size eight, which is life changing when it comes to wearing Sassoons, let me tell you.

The secret to being skinny is simple. Starve! Extra-Strength Dexatrim really helps, but you have to be careful, because if you get up too fast you can faint. Especially if you are lying in the sun catching rays. I learned this the hard way in Florida, when I almost cracked my head open on the pool deck. Thank God my parents weren't around, or I really would have gotten into trouble. They only have enough patience to deal with one head case.

When the pills wear off, you do have to get yourself through monster hunger pangs. Now I'm not psychic like Carrie, or anything, but every time I would get myself through one of those stomachachy-headachy-moments that makes you feel like you are a giant tube of toothpaste, all squeezed out, I'd also feel, well, *excited*! Like I was going to get discovered like Matt Dillon did, or my whole life was going to change or something. And now it has. Chandler Sumner is standing right in front of me, asking what I'm doing for the summer.

"Babysitting," I say. "My mother's helper job starts next week."

"Sums, c'mon!" his friend yells from the shack's roof. "We're thirsty."

"Want to come swimming with us?" he says, mopping his Christopher Atkins bangs off his brow.

"No, thanks. I just went in," I say, knowing my hard-won feathered wings would return to their natural Brillo pad state as soon as they got wet.

Watching Chandler strut away in his Grateful Dead tie-dyed T-shirt, I immediately realize that I made a huge, colossal, gigantic mistake. What if he thinks I don't like him? What if he doesn't walk back this way to his car? What if I have to wait until school starts to see him again? I pretend to read my *Seventeen*, wondering what cover girl Phoebe Cates would have done if she was plagued with frizzy hair that took more than an hour to feather.

After several rounds of cannonballs and jackknifes, Chandler and his friends towel off, and I know I'm almost out of time. "Race ya!" Brad says. The three of them tear down the rocks toward the car. My heart is sinking, sinking. But wait. Chandler is turning around and heading back toward me! Oh, my God, he's coming right my way. . . .

"Duh!" he says, grinning. "Can't get very far without these." He scoops up his keys off the ledge and tosses them in the air, catching them with his other hand. Aside from being perfect, he's also totally coordinated.

As he's walking away, he turns around, so he's walking backward along the ledge's edge. "Hey, tan girl!" he yells over to me. "Got a name? Want to go for a ride sometime?"

And just like that, my wish comes true, and I break my fifteen-year losing streak. Chandler Sumner asks me for my phone number.

I guard the phone for three days so my brother doesn't answer it with his usual "You've reached the Starship *Enterprise*" greeting. Just when I think I don't have one more nonchalant "Helloo?" left in me, Chandler Sumner calls. I do the happy dance right there in the hall while we chat on the phone.

Next thing you know, I'm being picked up for a date! A date! A date! I'm being picked up for a date. "How about Manor Park?" he says, opening my car door for me, which makes me feel totally sophisticated, like I'm one of Charlie's Angels or something. He revs the engine and we're off. The wind whips through my hair (making it even straighter) as I assume the position of copilot and find the best song possible on the radio. It's "Sailing" by Cristopher Cross, and we both say, "Leave it!" *It's a sign*. At every red light I pray someone I know will see me, in case I need a witness later to tell me that I'm not dreaming.

Manor Park is one of the coolest places on earth. It was built by the same architect who designed Central Park in New York City, and it is carved right out of the limestone of the Long Island Sound shore. It's where everyone goes for their first kiss, to break up, or anything else that's, like, really life or death.

As we walk along the slate path together, I'm not quite sure what to do with my hand on a first date. I try to keep it available, in case Chandler wants to hold it. I feel like it's flapping and flopping around like some big fish out of water between us, *begging* to be held. But Chandler doesn't seem to notice. In fact, when we accidentally bump wrists, he just says, "Sorry," and keeps talking.

Luckily the conversation just flows. We talk about the kids we know in common and how much we both like the Grateful Dead and going to the shows while on Magic Mushrooms. Actually, I don't even like the Grateful Dead—it's like an inside joke that I don't get. And I've never eaten 'shrooms. But I want Chandler to think I'm cool, so I listen carefully and bluff along.

" 'Sugar Marigold' is my all-time favorite—" I say.

"You mean 'Sugar Magnolia.' " He laughs, as if I've just made a hilarious joke. I'm about to kick myself for being an idiot, when straight out of nowhere he says, "You seem really mature for a girl your age. Why is that?"

Growing up with an autistic twin, who is called a "retard," "faggot," and "mental case" by the same kids who used to play hot potato at our joint birthday parties can do that to a person. So can having to solve all your problems yourself, because your parents already have their hands full. And keeping a secret like wishing you could snip your brother out of the portrait on your mantel so that you could be a "normal" family. Or the Gray Cloud of guilt for thinking such hateful thoughts that can submerge me in a black abyss of depression for days.

But I don't tell him any of that. I would *die* if he ever knew anything about my brother.

"You seem really mature too," I say, changing the subject to him.

Then Chandler gets really deep. "Yeah, I had to get my head straight," he says. "After I followed the Dead for three months, my parents did an intervention." If there's one thing I've learned from my friendship with Zack, it's that boys like it when you super listen as much as girls do. More even.

"They just totally don't understand me at all," he says. "Anyway, they shipped me off to boarding school for a year, and that's when I got my head together."

"Cool," I say, hanging on his every word like that kitten on the "Hang in There" poster in my room.

"I used to party a little too much, but I have it totally in control now," he continues.

"Of course you do," I say, looking deep into his eyes so he knows I totally understand.

I had heard the rumors about Chandler, who is a trust-fund baby, going to rehab, so I'm glad he's sharing this with me. I don't bring up the Kennedy girlfriend, and I'm glad I don't because before we even pull into my driveway he asks me out for Saturday night. Oh, my, like, God!

I spend the remaining four days getting ready for the date. I decide to take a chance and call Lisa. I don't know her well, but she's a friend of a friend who goes out with Chandler's friend Pete.

"Hey, can I come over and try outfits on for you?" I ask into the phone. What I really want to do is borrow all of her Grateful Dead tapes so I can memorize them.

I can hear her exhale her cigarette, and I wonder if her parents let her smoke at home.

"For my date with Chandler?" I add.

"Cool," she says.

This is what we decide: the white Calvins, my great-grandmother's white vintage lace shirt, and my tan Candies sandals. Sort of hippy, but sort of sexy.

"Could go either way, if he's trying to figure me out," I say as we listen to all of her bootleg recordings. "Should I go buy some patchouli oil?"

"Nah, Chandler likes girls sexy. Wear just enough, but not too much, Love's Baby Soft. There's nothing worse than tasting someone else's smell," she suggests. "And keep your strawberry Kissing Potion in your front pocket so it doesn't ruin the outline of your butt."

"Dynamite!" I say.

I starve all day so I can be super skinny. I lie on my bed, suck in my stomach, and the white Calvins zip up perfectly.

When I see his car pull into the driveway, I try to dart out the front door.

"Not so fast, young lady," my father says. "Your mother and I would like to meet the young man. This is your first date."

My heart sinks. At least it's not football season, so I don't have to worry about the pom-pom Notre Dame hat with the dangling leprechaun.

"We won't keep you, honey," my mother says, smoothing her Florence Henderson. "We just want to make sure he's a nice boy."

Translation: preppy and Catholic.

I bite my lip.

Chandler toots the horn.

"Please?" I say.

"No," my father says sternly. "It's only proper that he should come to the door."

It's my first night date, and my parents are ruining everything.

Just when I start breaking out in a sweat, I hear a car door slam. Out the window I see Chandler bound up the front steps. I fling open the door before he can ring the doorbell, which plays the Notre Dame fight song. He does the handshake thing with my parents.

Just as we are leaving, my brother appears. He is wearing his red zip-up Mork from Ork suit.

"Na-nu-nanu," he says to Chandler.

I would rather have five hundred fathers at this point than one brother.

"Great Halloween costume, Bobby!" I say.

Chandler looks confused. Why wouldn't he be, considering it's July?

"Na-nu-nanu," Bobby repeats like a robotic broken record.

"C'mon, let's go," I say to Chandler as I pull him out the door.

"Who is that?" he asks as we walk down the front steps.

"My cousin," I say. "He's in a play, and that's his costume."

I'm thinking of a million other things to say, but Chandler doesn't even ask any questions. Instead, he whispers in my ear, "Bella, you look stunning."

I'm glad he thinks so, because I took the biggest risk of my entire life—I decided to wear my hair curly. Hopefully I'm tan and thin enough that I can pull it off. Chandler hands me a purple hydrangea, which I place behind my ear. I notice a bottle of Soave Bolla chilling in an ice bucket in the backseat. Classy, right?

"You need to meet the other woman in my life," he says. Before I can flip out, he winks at me and adds, "Her name is *The Horizon*."

The Horizon is the Sumners' forty-foot sloop. It's moored at the Manor Park Yacht Club, and you have to take a launch from the dock out to the boat. The boat is navy blue and gleaming wood, and it rocks like a cradle in the waves. We're sipping Soave, watching the orangey-pinky sky turn purple, and "Sailing" comes on the transistor radio.

And that's when he takes my hand for the first time. He turns to face me.

Oh, my God! Oh, my God! Is he actually going to kiss me now, *before* the date? Did Lisa say my mouth should be open or closed? Do I still have any lip gloss left on? Do I have Soave Bolla breath and need a Binaca Blast? These thoughts race through my mind like stockcars at the Indy 500.

Meanwhile, he's closing his eyes and leaning toward me in slow motion. Just as our lips are about to touch, though, a gust of wind blows a hunk of my frizz into his mouth.

I'm mortified, but he just laughs. "Let's try this again," Chandler says. He puts his hand around my very skinny waist (lost three more pounds!), and then it happens. A kiss so perfect it sends the butterflies in my stomach on a migration south right down into my brand-new bikini underpants.

The entire night is like totally perfect, and on the way home from Le Refuge's, the nicest restaurant in town, Chandler asks if I'm cold. I lie so I can wear his trademark sweater. It's off-white alpaca with a geometric design, and it ties with a sash at the waist. Here's the best part: When he drops me off, he says, "Keep it for a while." And that's when I know it for sure: I have a boyfriend!

That night, I take off all my clothes and sleep in Chandler's sweater instead of my nightgown, despite the fact that it's ninety degrees out. Or at least I try to sleep. But every time I close my eyes, all I can see is Chandler with the sunset glinting on his blond hair. Then I replay all of the good parts until I'm not sure if I'm dreaming or awake. Even in my dreams, I hear the song "Sailing."

We go sailing every day. I am so busy and happy that my appetite just disappears. I don't even need to take Dexatrim. It's as if my heart is so big it fills up my entire stomach. For the first time in my life, I feel perfect. Chandler is the reward for all those weeks of starvation.

The only person who isn't happy about all this is Zack. We are always getting into World War Three about one thing or another. Right now he's yelling at me on the phone because I saw *Caddyshack* with Chandler and not him, as I had promised.

"I can't believe you went with the *Blue Lagoon* guy and not me," he says. "You just don't act like yourself anymore."

"What do you mean?" I say.

"Like all this tie-dye crap you're wearing, when I know for a fact you think the Grateful Dead is an inside joke you don't get," he says.

"Let's just say it's an acquired taste," I reply. "Besides, you wouldn't notice my wardrobe so much if Jersey Jennifer lived closer."

Zack spent the first month of the summer at a kibbutz in Israel, where he lost his virginity to an older woman from New Jersey. He wrote me a letter telling me all about it, in franglais, in case of parental interception. But he got home before his par avion did, so I accused him of not writing to me. We had a fight about that too. I mean, I had written him three postcards from Florida! I even told him about fainting from doubling up the Extra-Strength Dexatrim and my Carrie premonition that something great was about to happen to me.

The truth is, it's hard to find time for a boy friend, two words, when you have a boyfriend, one word. The new me has a new life, and I was facing my next monumental decision, cashing in my V-card.

Losing my virginity is something I think about pretty much all the time. It's the most important decision you make in your entire life, because you only get one chance to do it. So the person you lose it with has to be perfect, because he will be permanently in your memory book. I'm sure Chandler's The One, but I'm not sure I'm ready yet. I'm still sort of amazed at all the doors "thin" can open. If I was still fat, I don't think I would have this huge decision before me.

During a keg party at Chandler's house It comes up. We're lying on a blanket in his backyard listening to Bad Company sing "Feel like Makin' Love." Chandler rests his head on my shoulder and says, "I do, you know."

I shrug and sip my beer. I know where this is going. It's going exactly where he guides my hand when we park at 10:45 before he drops me off at my 11:00 curfew.

"When you go out with an older guy, there are certain responsibilities that go along with that," he explains patiently. "Now you know I love you, right, cookie?"

It was true. We had dropped the L-word on the third date. At this point we have been going out for two months, three weeks, and two days. We've gone to all the bases, so I guess going all the way is the next logical step. Still, I sort of always thought I'd wait until I was sixteen before losing my virginity. The idea of making Chandler wait almost a full year, though, makes me pick my cuticles until they bleed.

A little voice inside me tells me to hold out a little longer, but it gets drowned out by Chandler's persuasive arguments about the responsibilities of dating an older guy. The last thing I want to do is lose Chandler, especially with school starting next week. So I decide to jump off the high dive and end my Summer of Love by taking the next step.

We make a plan: Chandler's parents are taking their Learjet to a wedding on Martha's Vineyard Labor Day Weekend. I tell my parents that I'm sleeping over at my babysitting job, and voilà! we get to spend the whole night together with no interruptions.

The night of nights finally comes. My heart feels like a bongo being played by Ricky Ricardo as we walk up to his room, or floor I should say, since it's the entire attic. Tie-dyed sheets hang on the walls, and he has his own stereo, a bong, and even a mini refrigerator up there. The only thing I hate is the back of his door. It's covered with photographs and love letters from his old girlfriends. I mean *covered*. When I ask him if he can redecorate it, he laughs and says, "Oh, they're all just friends now."

The last thing I want to do is be "just friends," so I tell myself I'm doing the right thing, despite the fact that part of me wishes I could go home.

I'm hoping Chandler will put on "Sailing," but instead he puts on the Dead bootleg with really long drum solos, which I hate. I light some candles and we lie on the bed and start to make out as usual. Then he starts peeling off his clothes and so I do the same. When all of his clothes are off, I notice his tan marks in the dark. He's so tan it looks like he's wearing white shorts. Sort of. His *thing* is so stick straight, I feel scared for a second. Wait! Am I thin enough? I suck in my stomach all the way, which makes me resemble a greyhound because my rib cage looks very exaggerated when I do this lying on my back.

"Promise me you'll never pose for *Playboy*," he says, scanning my body. "Besides, if you get any skinnier, they won't let you."

To me, of course, the ultimate compliment. I am ready.

Then we do it. It hurts in a pinching sort of way, but not as bad as I thought it would. I mean, I've heard some really scary stories about the sheets getting soaked with blood, but for me it wasn't anything like that. If anything, it was nothing. And then it was over.

As soon as we finish, Chandler rolls away from me, and with

his back to me, starts snoring. *That's it?* I think, lying in the pitch-black listening to the drum solo crescendo. Disappointment washes over me and crests in sadness that starts leaking out of my eyes. I feel like the loneliest person in the entire world. If the whole point of sleeping with someone is to feel close to them, then somehow I really screwed this up. I felt like I wasn't even there.

The first day back at school, I tell myself I made the right decision when I see Chandler hanging out in the parking lot with Pete and the rest of the group. I go up to kiss him, but he blocks me and just says, "Hey." I guess this is school, so things might be a little bit different. What does it matter? I mean, I'm dating the most popular boy in the whole junior class! Plus we are racing in a regatta next week. Maybe things will go back to normal on the weekend.

That Saturday morning, I get my mom to drop me off so Chandler can start working on the boat as soon as possible. When I get there, he's already getting high with the guys.

"Hey," he says.

"I wore my lucky bikini," I say, pulling up my T-shirt to show him by new blue tie-dye, his favorite color, that I spent two weeks' babysitting money on.

"Cool," he says, but he's not really looking.

Maybe this is good, because I think I may have gained a pound or two. I've been snacking a lot lately out of nervousness, but I took two Dexatrim this morning and promised myself that I wouldn't eat all day. I want to focus on being the perfect crewmember for Chandler, not on the submarine sandwiches and chips in the cooler.

It's a blustery day, and there are whitecaps on the water. When the flare gun goes off to begin the race, it takes *The Horizon* a while to get into position. Chandler barks out orders, and we all scramble around the deck, pulling in the sails, checking the cleats, hiking out to help her go as fast as possible.

We're about to pass the leading boat when it's time to turn

around the buoy. But suddenly the wind shifts, and Chandler decides to jibe instead of come about. This means I have to switch sides to do the jib, without getting smacked in the head by the beam. I'm halfway there, when suddenly everything starts going dark. I feel myself losing consciousness, which is like going into a nightmare. I wonder if that's what it's like for my brother when he zones out.

Suddenly I'm shocked awake by cold water. Oh, my God, I've fallen overboard!

"Grab the life jacket!" yells Chandler.

I swim to the orange life vest that Chandler has thrown me. As I bob around in the water, waiting for *The Horizon* to come about and pick me up, I start to choke and panic. Not because I can't swim, but because I feel totally adrift. Somehow I managed to come completely unmoored from Chandler. Not only that, but I've lost my bikini top, which proves I can't do anything right. At least they can't tell I'm crying.

Chandler tacks back to me and heads into the wind.

"You okay?" Brad and Pete both say from the edge of the boat.

"Yeah, just throw me my T-shirt," I say. "The boom was coming toward me, and I don't know what happened—"

"You fainted," says Chandler, his voice so cold it could freeze water. He seems really mad.

"I'm sorry," I say, as Pete and Brad pull me up onto the boat. "I know I made us lose the race."

He shrugs. That's all he ever seems to do lately.

The next week at school, Chandler becomes more and more distant. Then he's not even there. We made plans to meet at his car after school, but when I got there, his special parking spot's empty. Since I've now missed the bus, I have to walk all the way home in my Candies sandals. I get blisters everywhere.

If space is what he wants, space is what he'll get, I decide as I stomp home. I also decide that I'd better break up with him, before he can break up with me. The next day I cut my last class and wait by his car. When he sees me, he looks surprised.

"We need to talk," I say. We start driving. He makes the turn, not toward Manor Park but toward my house. Bad sign.

The Gray Cloud of depression comes down and swallows me whole. For the first time in my entire life, I had found complete happiness being Chandler's girlfriend, which is what I deserved for all those months of starvation. Instead, I feel like my future is long lost, along with my brand-new bikini top. I feel like I belong in my family of losers, trapped.

"Well?" I say.

"My last class was canceled yesterday—" he starts.

"I gave you everything," I say. *I threw my virginity away,* I think.

"I just need a little space," he says.

Can't he see that I'm a size six?

"Maybe we should see other people for a little while," he says.

"There isn't anyone else for me," I say, getting out of the car as the tears start to push their way out.

"Hey, Bella!" he says as I'm halfway up my walk. My heart leaps. Maybe, watching me go, he's realized he's made a mistake. I turn around.

"Mind grabbing my sweater?" he says.

My last hope that he'd come to his senses, and he snatches that back too. I had imagined our whole year together, hanging out, going to keg parties, even the junior prom. I'm left with nothing, less than nothing. There's an aching void where my heart used to be, the same horrible feeling I get every time Bobby has a seizure and has to be hospitalized, and there is nothing I can do.

"Hi, honey. How was school?" my mother says to me as I walk in the door.

"Fine," I say, my eyes filling with tears.

"That's good," she says, not seeming to notice. She's got that faraway look. "Would you mind seeing what your brother is up to? I don't seem to have the strength. Oh, and sorry you can't go out with Chandler tonight. Your dad and I need you to watch your brother."

"No problem," I say. "Be right back."

I grab Chandler's sweater and sit on the edge of my bed. I bury my face in it to see if it still has his smell. But I can't smell anything, so I blow my nose in it. Then I throw it down and stomp on it a few times. I vow to never, ever let someone get close enough to hurt me again. I walk back out the front door and head down the walk.

"Catch," I say, using my coldest voice possible and toss the sweater to him.

Chandler does with one hand, and without a word, yanks his convertible into reverse and screeches out of my driveway.

"Jerry Garcia sucks!" I yell as he drives off.

Fighting back my tears, I go into the den, where my brother has moved the furniture around. The couch is right in front of the TV so he can watch *Star Trek* up close and personal. Bobby has himself wedged in between the cushions and the couch frame. Don't ask me why, but that's his way of getting comfortable.

"May the Force be with you," he says to me, and then in a weird Donna Summer voice says, "Bad girls! Hey, hey! Toot toot! I'm talkin' 'bout bad girls!"

"Hi back," I answer and burst into tears. I throw myself onto my father's La-Z-Boy recliner, and let the loud, ugly sobs come out. Bobby turns up the TV really loud, to drown me out.

I can't stand Mr. Spock on decibel ten another second, so I go up to my room and pull the hall phone in with me. When Zack answers, I'm crying so hard no sound is coming out. My breath catches.

Somehow, he knows it's me.

"Blue Lagoon?" Zack says.

"C'est fini," I manage.

"I'm on my way," he says.

A few hours later, Zack comes by and takes both Bobby and me to the movies. We go to see *The Rose* starring Bette Midler. It's really about Janis Joplin, but she couldn't star in it because, as you know, she died choking on her own vomit.

Right as the movie starts, Zack pulls out my turquoise pot pipe.

"Hey! Where'd you get that?" I say. It's been missing for a year, and I've been petrified that my parents found it. I don't want Bobby to see it, but he's mesmerized by the morphing amoebas on the screen.

"You threw it at me during our first fight," he says. "Remember, when you got kicked out of The Clique for having a crush on Matt Dillon?"

"My bra size is not thirty-six D," I say, punching him in the arm.

"World War Three," we both say at the same time. "Jinx!"

When the movie starts, Zack lights the bowl and hands it to me. I take a hit and pass the pipe back. A few minutes later, something really weird happens. I hear this voice. Female.

The second time I turn around to see where the voice is coming from.

Zack whispers, "What are you doing?"

"You guys didn't hear a lady say anything?" I ask them.

Bobby looks at me blankly.

"You're just being paranoid," Zack says, cracking up. It's true, I do get paranoid when I smoke pot. I decide right then and there that I'm not ever going to do it again, no matter how "cool" it is.

As I watch Bette Midler, the voice repeats itself, and I become aware that it is coming from inside me. In a loud and clear voice, it gives me advice I haven't heard since my grandmother died: "Be yourself."

5

Year: 1981
Age: 16
Idol: Brooke Shields in the Calvin Klein commercials
Favorite Song: "Leather and Lace" (Stevie Nicks and Don Henley)
Prized Possession: driver's permit
Best Shoes: white Tretorns with pink stripe

Getting over the love of your life does not exactly happen overnight. Three things help: Zack reminding me that "Blue Lagoon is a tête-de-merde" on cue, distracting myself with tons of Honors English homework and babysitting, and smashing the clock radio against the wall whenever that queer song "Sailing" comes on. It's been over a year since the big breakup and Christopher Cross *still* makes me gag.

It turns out facing death, head-on, can also put things in perspective. I'm babysitting for Dana when we hear this banging, scraping sound outside her window. I pull up the shade, and there's a rapist! Staring right at us! Dana and I look at each other and scream. I yank her away from the window. *Think! Think!* I tell myself. Within a split second, we're flying down the stairs and out the front door, making a run for it to the neighbor's house. Suddenly I trip and fall flat on the ground. Dana laughs. I look down and realize I am covered in daffodil yellow paint.

"It's not funny!" I scream at her. "Run for your life!"

"Stop!" yells a deep voice. It's the scary man! He's dressed in black leather, from head to toe, and he's striding toward us, *fast*. With a knife in his hand.

"Run!" I hiss, trying to peel myself up off the ground. "He's got a knife!"

His long dark shadow drapes over me as he reaches down. Oh, my God, it's *The Shining* and *Friday the 13th* double feature in 3-D all rolled up into one living nightmare.

With one hand, he pulls me to my feet.

"Where's the fire?" he says. "I'm here to paint the house. Didn't Mrs. Daley tell you?"

"Duh!" I say sarcastically. I mean, if Mrs. Daley *had* told me, I wouldn't have made a jackass out of myself tripping over his stupid paint cans, I think. But these days Mrs. Daley was forgetting to tell me a lot of things, like when she was coming home, for example, or how to feed her child when there was no food in the house and I can't drive. I guess divorce can do that to a person.

"I forgot to give you this," says Dana, handing me a note from her mother.

"Oh," I say, reading Mrs. Daley's letter about the painters and instructions for dinner. It's only then that I notice the ladder, perched along the side of the house, and the van parked in front of their house that says PAINTERS PLUS. And that the rapist's knife is actually a paint scraper.

"I'm Jim Mucelli," he says in a calm, steady voice. "Friends call me Mush."

Now that makes me laugh. I mean this guy is, like, six foot four inches of pure muscle, with a handlebar mustache and a Yosemite Sam tattoo on his forearm. The back of his vest says HELL'S ANGELS in red letters. There is not one mushy thing about him.

"I'm Bella, the babysitter," I say. "And this is Dana. She's eight."

"I like your tattoo," she says. "How old are you?"

"Thanks, little one. I'm twenty-four," he says, steering me to the kitchen sink. "Let's clean those cuts." My hand feels like a doll's in his catcher's mitt. Although his hands are big and rough, he washes my bloody palms and knees as gently as if they are flower petals. I get this warm feeling inside, like I'm a little kid and someone, like my grandmother, is taking care of me.

Over the next few weeks, I come to really enjoy Mush's company. Whether he's a Hell's Angel or not, it's nice having a man around the house again. Zack swings by between band and basketball practices to copy my French homework. But, like I said, Zack's my boy friend, two separate words. Sometimes I catch him looking at me, but Zack's skinny, and I have a personal rule about not dating a guy whose jeans I can't fit into.

Besides, the roar of Mush's van or motorcycle vrooming into the driveway gives me a different sort of a rush. He's an older guy, and I have to admit I like the way he always calls me "Miss Bella," like I'm Krystle Carrington on *Dynasty* or something, and the way he always gives me little compliments. I enjoy the contrast of his outer toughness and his inner sweetness. In English class that's called "irony."

Sometimes I invite Mush to stay and eat dinner with us.

"So who's in your locket?" Mush says one night after frozen pizza, nodding to Grandina's necklace. It occurs to me that never once did Chandler compliment my locket, even though I wore it every single time I saw him.

"No one," I say. "My grandmother left it to me when she died. I've worn it ever since."

"So that Zack guy who comes around all of the time isn't your old man?" he asks.

"No, we're just friends," I say. "I don't have a boyfriend."

"That's a shame," Mush says. "A hot mama like you deserves to be worshipped. You look like Cher."

My tight jeans and big hair are hardly intentional, I feel like telling him. Breaking up with Chandler sent me diving headfirst into the Häagen-Dazs. That, plus quitting smoking, has made me go up at least a size. Dieting without help is hard, but after that fainting episode, I decided my Dexatrim days were over. And while the whole world is getting a perm, I already have a natural one.

Although I hate my fat body, at least I can hide inside of it. I'm not even in the mood to be thin yet. Being skinny is a full-time job. The world treats you differently. I'm only learning now that maybe my insides hadn't caught up to the situations my outsides were getting me invited to, like cashing in my V-card before I was really ready.

"Chandler wanted to play the field," I explain. "And do drugs without me bugging him. The truth is I never felt like I was being myself around him anyway."

"How do you mean?" asks Mush.

"Well, I could always figure out what he'd want me to say, and then say it, instead of saying what I really thought," I explain. "I've had a lot of practice with my parents. They have no idea about half the things I think or do."

"Well, anyone who'd dump the real you is a turkey," he says.

"Actually, I'm the one who did the breaking up," I reply. "But it was only a technicality."

"Still, you deserve more respect than that," he says.

"What about your girlfriend?" I ask. An image of Pinky Tuscadero, Fonzie's girlfriend on *Happy Days*, pops into my mind.

"Wife," he says.

"You're *married*?" I ask. The thought had never occurred to me, despite the fact that he's old. After all, Mush's twenty-four.

"Was," he adds quietly.

"Oh, divorced?" I ask. Considering how simply spotting Chandler across the parking lot gives me stomach pains, I can't even imagine going through a divorce.

Mush doesn't say anything for a minute. "My wife died almost two years ago," he says. "Hit by a drunk driver and killed instantly."

What can you say about that? I couldn't think of a single

thing, so I put my hand on his, the way I do with my mom when she's Lost in Space. We sit there like that until the flame on the candle burns all the way down, leaving us in the dark.

Knowing this about Mush explains a few things. Despite the fact that he looks like a serial killer and hangs out with a biker gang, there's something really respectable about him. Like he knows exactly who he is and would always stand up for what he believes in. I always feel safe around him. Instead of a knight *in* shining armor, he's a knight *on* shining armor.

"How did you ever get through that?" I finally manage.

"I'll show you," he says. "What time does Mrs. D get home?"

Half an hour later, Mush is zipping me into a black wind-breaker jumpsuit and strapping a shiny red helmet on me. He instructs me exactly where to put my feet and taps the seat behind him. "This is called the 'bitch pad,'" he says with a sinister laugh. "Hop on."

"Are you *kidding*?" I say.

"C'mon, Miss Bella," he says. "I'll take you anywhere you want to go."

Curiosity gets the best of me. I swing my leg over and put my arms around his waist. I tell him to head to Manor Park, via Chandler's street.

"Ready, jailbait?" he says, revving the engine. In a clap of thunder, we peel out.

Being on the back of a Harley-Davidson chopper going eighty miles per hour feels like fitting into size six white jeans, catching the eye of a cute guy, and being able to fix your brother—times ten. It's the feeling of raw, pure power. Yet, at the same time, you feel alive, vulnerable. It's like electric horseback riding, with the engine throbbing between your legs. I mean, it feels so good that I even forget to look when we pass Chandler's house. (Although I didn't forget to wish when we went over the train tracks, even though closing my eyes, crossing my fingers, and lifting my feet all at the same time was probably not the safest thing.)

But the best part is the complete anonymity. With the helmet on, I don't even have to worry about my parents or neighbors recognizing me as we tear down my town. This must be what it feels like to be Catwoman on a crusade, I imagine as we slice through the night.

By the time Mush drops me off, I'm breathless.

"Better than sex, drugs, and rock and roll, right?" he says.

"Better than size six white jeans!" I say, waving good-bye and running around the corner into my driveway.

In the kitchen, I find both my parents sitting at the table under a large Gray Cloud. I can tell immediately that something is wrong. Not only is my mother Lost in Space, but my father is too. I wonder if I'm going to get in trouble for the motorcycle ride. The thrill of the ride instantly turns into a guilty pit in my stomach.

"What's the matter?" I say, acting innocent.

My dad shakes his head and disappears to the basement so he can perform another miracle of getting a ship inside a bottle, leaving the real problem unsolved. He spends all his time putting together these little models that make people say, "Gee. Wow." Meanwhile, my brother remains as unfixable as ever.

My mother sighs. I call her No Makeup when she's like this. Her pain is all over her face, and she doesn't even try to cover it up with lipstick, even when I offer her my Revlon Fire and Ice.

"You know your father isn't good at dealing with your brother," she says.

I should have known—it's always Bobby. "What's wrong this time?" I ask.

"Well, your father has been going over our finances, and it appears I have to get a part-time job to help pay Bobby's medical bills," she says. "We've liquidated all our savings and investments, his 401(k), and our life insurance policies. At this point we have very little left."

"What can I do to help?" I ask.

"Not much, honey," she says. "The real problem is what are we going to do with your brother after school, since I won't be here for him."

I know what the right thing to say is, but my selfish side tells me to keep my mouth shut. When my parents die, I know I'll be Bobby's full-time caretaker. I was just hoping to find a guy to marry me first. How am I going to manage Bobby, on top of babysitting, homework, and getting skinny again? I'm exhausted even thinking about it.

My mother wipes a tear from the corner of her eye. Watching her get upset over my brother is worse than watching my brother get upset himself. I decide to come to the rescue. My straight-A report cards never seem to get her attention, but maybe this will.

"Don't worry, Mom. I'll take him," I say. "I babysit every day anyway. Bobby can play Atari with Dana."

"Oh, Bella," my mother says, brightening. The Gray Cloud lifts, and the sun comes out in her eyes. She looks at me warmly. "That would be great."

I've never tried hard drugs like heroin, but if it's the same feeling I get as pleasing my parents, I can see why it's addictive.

The following week at the Daleys', I decide to greet Mush at the front door and give him a heads-up the first time he meets Bobby. Mush and I have been seeing each other daily for months now, and over the course of our dinners and motorcycle rides, I've told him about my brother, but the live experience is a little different.

"He's your twin, and he has autism, right?" Mush asks.

"Right. It's a neurological disorder that makes him a square peg in the round hole of life," I explain. Nerditis, I think.

"So he marches to the beat of his own drummer. That's cool," says Mush.

"That's one way of putting it, I guess," I say.

We walk into the Daleys' den, and sure enough, Bobby's in his flannel pajamas doing his Flat Stanley routine, wedged between the couch and the cushions. He's even persuaded Dana to sit on top of the cushion, his favorite. It's really weird, I know, that even though Bobby can't stand to be touched, he still likes the feeling of pressure on his body. Sometimes he even sleeps between the mattress and the box spring.

"Bobby, say hi to my friend Mush," I prompt.

"Knock, knock. Who's there? Land Shark!" Bobby answers in his robotlike speak.

Mush doesn't even blink. "Hi, Bobby," he says. "I see you're a *Saturday Night Live* fan."

I pull Mush into the kitchen and try to explain. "Sorry," I say. "He quotes lots of movies and stuff. His way of communicating."

"That I got," he says. "But what's up with the pajamas?"

"Things that feel normal to us are often really exaggerated for Bobby. Even his skin. Regular clothes are too scratchy—hence the flannel," I explain. "His senses are all jumbled. His eyes and ears function, but he's not able to process the information, because it gets all distorted by the time it reaches his brain. It's, like, lost in translation or something."

"Wow, how have you been able to get inside his head?" he asks. "Is it because you are twins?"

"That's just it. I *can't* get inside his head. But after all these years of watching him, I've figured out a few things about him, like the fact that he thinks in pictures."

"What kind of pictures?" he asks.

"It's like he has a video library in his head," I explain. "He has a picture for everything, especially feelings or concepts, which are hard for him. For example, he hates Bugs Bunny. So when he says, 'Ehhh, what's up, Doc?' I know he's frustrated."

"How did you learn all this stuff?" Mush asks.

"Just being with him," I say. "I've also read every single book that's available on the subject."

"Well, he's lucky he's got a sister like you to care so much about him," Mush says.

Hardly, I think. I don't treat him with half the respect that the Angels treat each other. Hanging around with Mush and his friends, I've come to realize that the brotherhood is thicker than blood. I guess it's different when you can choose the members of your family, instead of being stuck with the ones that God has chosen for you.

"He's lucky in other respects," I say. "You should see the stuff he can do. He's really gifted."

"Gifted how?" Mush asks.

Before I can answer, Bobby wanders into the kitchen, buries his nose in Mush's armpit, and takes a good whiff.

"Whoa!" says Mush, taken by surprise.

"We are on a mission from God!" he says, quoting Dan Aykroyd in *The Blues Brothers*.

"Bobby! C'mon, you know it's not polite to sniff like a dog," I say. I still thank God he didn't do that with Chandler.

"Holy husband, Batman!" says Bobby. "There's going to be a wedding in Gotham City!"

"Thanks for the non sequitur," I say, putting a Rubik's Cube in his hand. "Bobby, can you do this for Mush?"

Within about two minutes, Bobby has flipped all the colored squares into the correct order.

"Wow!" says Mush, genuinely impressed. "That would have taken me about five years. Way to go, little man. Give me some skin!" he says, lifting Bobby's arm to give him a high-five.

"Uh-oh, uh-oh, no, no, *no*!" screams Bobby, backing into the corner, smacking his head again and again. "Book 'em, Dano! Book 'em, Dano!"

Here we go again.

"What did I do?" Mush asks, jumping back. "I'm sorry! I'm sorry!"

For the first time since I've known him, I see fear streak into Mush's blue eyes. A Hell's Angel terrified of a defenseless autistic who can't even count change correctly.

"You touched him," says Dana, coming into the kitchen. "That's not allowed. That's why he's saying, 'Book 'em, Dano.'"

"*Eee! Eeee! Eee!* What's up, Doc? What's up, Doc?" Bobby's high-pitched screeches are louder than a smoke detector.

"You'll get the hang of it," I say, rolling my eyes.

Mush, still looking stricken, has backed himself up against the doorway.

"Okay, Bobby. It's okay. Mush didn't know," I say, steering him around Mush and toward the den. "C'mon, your favorite, *Star Trek*, is on."

"Bella, I'm so sorry!" Mush says. "I would never do anything to harm him."

As we pass him, Bobby stops dead in his tracks. I stop too, to see what he's looking at, and it's Mush's forearm. Namely his tattoo.

"Say your prayers, varmint! Lash your scuppers, ya barnacle-bitten lan'lubber! Come down here and fight like a man!" chirps Bobby happily, suddenly clapping his hands with glee.

Mush flexes his muscles, making it look like Yosemite's guns are going off, one at a time.

"Ha! Yosemite Sam, dancing!" says Bobby, as if this is the most hilarious thing he has ever witnessed in his entire life.

"That's right!" I say, amazed that a disgusting tattoo can suddenly stop a full-blown temper tantrum, even if Yosemite Sam is Bobby's favorite. I've never heard Bobby laugh like this in my entire life.

Seeing Bobby so happy nudges me to ask for something. Sniffing strangers is not Bobby's only doglike trait. He also likes to hang his head out the window when my mom drives us places. I ask Mush if he wouldn't mind giving Bobby the teeniest ride around the block on his motorcycle.

"I just have this feeling that it will be ten times sex, drugs, and rock and roll for him," I say. "All of which he will never experience. Please?"

"Be happy to," says Mush.

I zip Bobby into the windbreaker and put the helmet on him. Then we take the bungee cords from Dana's rat trap and literally strap Bobby to Mush, putting a pillow between them so they don't touch. I pull my cuticles as the chopper slowly rolls down the street, and I really freak out when it disappears around the corner. Why do I push the envelope? What if Bobby falls off and dies? What am I going to tell my parents? What's taking so long? I wish I had a cigarette.

"Maybe they're just having fun," says Dana. "Don't worry, Bella. Mush is nice."

She's right, I tell myself, over and over again until I see them coming up the bottom of the hill.

"Welcome back, cowboy!" I say to Bobby.

"Say your prayers, varmint! And you're gonna be eating lead. I'm a-warning ya, stranger. Oh, yeah? We'll see who'll chicken out first. Ya double-crossing rabbit, you cut down your chances. I'm only gonna count to two and then blast ya. One. Two." He is talking a mile a minute in Yosemite Sam speak.

"Now I'm a huge fan, but I'm impressed. This guy knows, like, even the obscure Yosemite stuff," says Mush, listening carefully to Bobby's joyful rant.

"It all means the same thing," I say. "Translation: He's happy."

I give Mush the biggest hug in the world for treating my brother to a happiness I could have never given him. When I think about it, it's probably the nicest thing any guy has ever done for me in my entire life. Chandler never even asked if I had a brother. Not once.

"Wow. I wish I could drive," I tell Mush, imagining me driving Bobby around with his head out the window.

"Aren't you sixteen?" says Mush.

"Yeah. I have my learner's permit," I explain, "but I never really got around to taking the test."

When I was little, I used to have the same nightmare all the time. I was held hostage in a car driven by Bobby, who is completely out of control at the wheel. The dreams always end the same way, with a deadly crash, and me waking up in such a sweat that I'd have to change my nightie.

Mush looks at me for a while and then says, "I have an idea. Pick you up Saturday morning for a driving lesson?"

Yeah, sure. My parents would freak!

"How about I meet you on the corner?" I suggest. "That way you won't have to make the turn."

That weekend I get my first private tutoring session. Good news: It's a silver 1960s-vintage Corvette. Bad news: It's a stick shift.

"Uh, can't we do this with an automatic?" I say. "I'll crash your car for sure."

"Not where we're going," he says. "Hop in and buckle up."

Mush looks sort of squished in the driver's seat. I can see why he calls cars "crates" and "cages." Whistling along to the Rolling Stones' "Miss You," he steers us to an empty parking lot where he has already set up an obstacle course of orange cones. I'm touched that he has put so much effort into my tutorial.

The biggest obstacle, however, is not the cones. It's getting the frigging car into first gear. Despite his gentle coaching, I stall, and stall, and stall. I start getting really frustrated, but Mush won't let me give up. Finally, I get the car going, but it's bucking like a bronco. After the tenth herky-jerky attempt, Mush leans out the window and barfs.

"I quit!" I say, storming out of the car and slamming the door.

"Wait!" he says out the window. "Why are you being so hard on yourself?"

"Because I'm hopeless and fat and I'll never learn," I say. My eyes start to well. I'm just like my brother, I think. If this isn't symbolic of failing to take control of my life, then what is? In English class, they'd call my loserishness a "theme."

"It just takes practice," he says.

"I *have* practiced," I admit. "I failed driver's ed."

"What?" Mush laughs. "Miss Fancy Honors Classes flopped driver's ed?"

"Don't laugh," I say. It's the only class I haven't gotten an A in, in my entire life.

But Mush is laughing so hard he has to get out of the car to catch his breath. When his giggle fit finally finishes, he comes over and puts his hands on my shoulders. "Look, jailbait," he says. "It's mind over matter."

"How's that?" I ask.

"If you don't mind, it don't matter," he says, smiling. Then he flexes his muscle and Yosemite Sam does a little dance.

"It's 'If you don't mind, it *doesn't* matter,'" I say, correcting him. "And stop doing that with your tattoo. It's gross."

"Only if you get back in the car," he says.

After another hour, I finally get the clutch-gear-gas hang of things. We switch places and he drives us back to his house, which is neat and trim even if it is on the wrong side of the tracks.

"I got a surprise for you," he says. "Wait right here."

A minute later, he reappears on his chopper. He flips open the back compartment to reveal a picnic lunch and a bouquet of red roses. No one has ever given me flowers before.

"I need to make a run, and I want you to come with me," he says, tapping the bitch pad behind him. My heart flickers. I tell it to knock it off.

We cruise on back roads for an hour before Mush pulls into a wide driveway with elaborate gates and a sign that says WOOD-LANDS CEMETERY. Rolling past mausoleums and tombstones, we stop when we get to a large magnolia tree. Mush takes the roses and places them on a white headstone that has a swirly marble angel, wings spread, hovering over it. A little on the gaudy side, I think.

Mush kisses his glove and touches the engraving. It reads: CARLA MUCELLI, 1957–1979. MY BELOVED WIFE, REST IN PEACE.

"Today's the two-year anniversary of Carla's death, and I came to pay my respects," he says. "I appreciate the company. It's still hard to come here alone."

I say nothing. I chide myself for my disappointment that the flowers weren't for me.

To my surprise, he starts spreading out the picnic under the tree.

"Does this bother you?" he asks.

"Not at all," I say. How can I explain that I feel like a third wheel to a *dead person*? I decide to go with it. I mean, after all, we're just friends, right? So I help Mush unpack the pepperoni, olives, and cheeses and ask him to tell me his favorite memories of Carla.

His blue eyes dance as he describes all the little things he loved about her: the way she cried at corny TV commercials; the white nurse's tights that she'd hang to dry in their shower; the rows of red roses, her favorite flower, that she lovingly tended each spring in their garden. He seems so alive and happy reliving all of their Greatest Hits, and I just want to hug him.

So I do, long and hard, when he drops me off. "Thanks for the driving lesson, Professor," I say.

"Thanks for the company. I hope it wasn't too much, about Carla and everything," Mush says. He pulls me close for one last hug. So what if he's a Hell's Angel? I think as I breathe in the smell of his leather. He's the nicest guy I've ever met.

But here's the weird thing. Even though Mush treats me like his date, when we go to the movies or out with his friends or for long drives on Sunday, things never progress beyond holding hands. It's like we are patient stand-ins for each other until the real thing turns up. We never talk about it, but I almost feel like we are both practicing for something else.

Finally, Driver's Test Day arrives. But I'm confused when Mush picks me up at school with his chopper, not his car.

"What about practicing my three-point turns?" I say. "This is my last chance before the test."

"You know your stuff, Miss Bella," he says. "What you need is to quit worrying. Sit back, relax, and enjoy the ride so you'll be fresh."

After a long cruise, he gently pats my leg and motions to the 7-Eleven across from the school. "Soda break?" he says over his shoulder.

I give him a thumbs-up. Mush goes into the store while I stretch my legs in the parking lot. I can't believe my luck when Chandler pulls up, with Pete and Brad, right next to me. I can smell the joint Chandler is hiding under the dashboard.

My heart jumps! Just the week before, Chandler had stopped by my locker, right out of the blue. "Hi, Bella. How are your classes?" he said, looking as cute as ever in his reclaimed alpaca sweater. We made small talk, and I could tell he was checking me out, even though I think I looked really fat that day. It's a long shot, but I'm wondering if Chandler's going to ask me to the senior prom. Maybe he's missed me.

"Brad, hurry up. I've got the munchies," Pete says as Brad hops out of the car. I'm just about to take off my helmet and say hi when I hear them discussing the prom.

"So who ya gonna take, Sums?" says Pete.

"Who cares, as long as I get laid," Chandler says.

"There's always Bella, man. Lisa says she's *still* not over you," he says.

My cheeks start to burn.

"I'm lining Bella up to be my safety date if that hot Cindy chick says no," Chandler says. "But have you seen how fat she's gotten? Like Porky Pig."

"Whoa! That's colder than when you popped her cherry and pretended to be asleep after," says Brad as he gets in the car with a bagful of soda and chips. Their laughter trails behind them as they drive off.

Like a bomb fuse on a cartoon, that hot feeling in my face burns right through my entire body, and I wish I could just shrivel up and die right there on the spot.

On the ride back to Mush's, I realize he can protect me from anything in the world except the thing that hurts the most—the truth. No matter how nice Mush is, we don't have a future together. The problem is I want a future with someone who doesn't even want a date with me.

"What's wrong?" Mush asks as I slide behind the wheel, back at his house. My hands are shaking on the wheel.

"Nothing," I say. *Everything,* I think.

"I've never seen you so quiet," he says. "And why do your eyes look so watery?"

"Allergies," I say. I'm so rattled that I can barely get the car into first gear. The words *Porky Pig! Porky Pig! Porky Pig!* are burning in my brain. I make it out of the driveway and onto the road. Then, out of the corner of my eye, I see a cat dart under the car. To avoid it, I swerve into the opposite lane, right into oncoming traffic.

"Look out!" Mush screams, trying to grab the wheel. A huge moving truck is barreling right toward us, its horn blaring. Just in time, I yank the car back into our lane, but I overreact again. In my panic, I run us right off the road up the curb and into a mailbox, smashing the front fender of Mush's car. In English class they would call this "foreshadowing." My whole life is going to be a disaster.

"Are you all right?" we both ask each other at the same time.

"Yeah, luckily we were only going fifteen miles per hour," he says, turning to face me. "What has gotten into you?"

That's when I blurt out the whole story about 7-Eleven, Porky Pig, losing my virginity to a Grateful Dead drum solo and not "Sailing," the ex-girlfriend collection on Chandler's door, that I'll never love anyone again for the rest of my life, and how I'll have to take care of Bobby when my parents die, if not sooner. I burst into tears.

"Hey, hey," Mush says softly, unbuckling my seat belt and pulling me toward him with his massive arms. I cry until his entire shoulder is soaking with tears and snot.

"When are you going to learn the primary rule of the road? The first person you need to demand respect from is yourself, Miss Bella," he says. "That's the only way anyone else is going to give it to you."

"I *do* respect myself," I say. Especially when I'm thin.

"Not if you're going back for more with that chump," he says, lifting my chin and looking into my eyes. I guess he has a point, but it doesn't make me feel better to admit it. In my heart of hearts, I've been waiting for Chandler to call me up and say he's made a big mistake. I've been hanging on to the idea of him, rather than looking at the reality of how he actually made me feel. Which is like a fat piece of crap.

"Okay, Porky, you'd better get this car in reverse, or we're gonna miss your appointment," he says, flexing his forearm and making Yosemite Sam dance.

"Ugh, I hate when you do that," I say, sniveling. "What about the fender?"

"Nothing that a little body work can't fix," Mush says. "Let's worry about you."

I parallel park and three-point-turn perfectly, and score myself a junior license! But when Mush drops me off, I know our joyride is over for good. He's finished with the Daleys' house and is headed to a biker convention in Arizona. Besides, I've missed Zack and my friends. It's time to give up the role of Biker Girl and return to my regular life.

"It doesn't matter," he says as we say our good-byes.

"Because you don't mind?" I say. "And it's mind over matter: It don't matter if you don't mind?"

He places his finger under my chin and tilts my face up toward him. I think he's going to kiss me, but his hand drifts down and picks up my locket instead. He inspects it silently for a minute.

"No, it doesn't matter that it's not you," he says finally. "What does matter is that I never thought I could care about anyone after Carla. Now I know I can someday. Someday your heart will open again too, Bella," he says, still looking at my locket. His eyes flick up to mine. He adds, "I promise."

Before I can ask him what he means, he claps on his helmet and zooms away. I watch him until he becomes a glint of onyx in the distance.

I think about the last seven months with Mush, and how much more I was myself with him than I ever was with Chandler. It's so much easier when you don't care what the other person thinks of you.

Mush is right about taking control of my own life. I can't wait for Chandler, or any other guy, to tell me I'm okay. It has to come from me.

A few days later I'm slugging through my English homework when I come upon an Eleanor Roosevelt quote: "Where flowers grow, so does hope." It hits me, and I know where I must go for my first drive.

"Mom, can I borrow the car?" I say. "I'll take Bobby with me."

"Sure, honey," she says, handing over the keys.

I help Bobby with his seat belt and slide behind the wheel of my family's station wagon. I hear Mush's words guiding me:

"Buckle up. You never know what the road will bring you." It hits me that I am the one in control when I turn on the radio and can choose any song I want. I spin the dial and stop at an oldies station. Aretha Franklin is singing, "R-E-S-P-E-C-T." *What a coincidence*, I think, as Bobby sings along in a perfect monotone.

Bobby and I clean out Tony's Nursery and hit the highway heading toward Woodlands Cemetery. By the time we finish the errand, Carla's grave is covered with lush rosebushes. When Mush gets back from his biker convention in Arizona, beautiful red blooms will be bursting, in celebration of what Carla loved and the man who loved her. I know I won't be hearing from Mush again, but I don't expect a thank-you note. I did it as much for myself as for him.

On the way home, we're passing Harrison High when Bobby, whose head has been hanging out the window, doglike, the entire time, suddenly becomes agitated.

"Holy ex-boyfriend's car, Batman," he yells, pointing to Chandler's convertible in the parking lot. "Graffiti has struck Harrison High School."

In huge yellow bubble letters on the side of our high school, it says CHANDLER SUMNER SUCKS! Even from here, I can tell by Chandler's body language that he's even more upset than the day he lost the regatta. And no wonder, graduation, not to mention the prom, is just around the corner, and there is no way they'll be able to remove the graffiti in time.

And what a coincidence. The color of the paint is the exact same daffodil yellow as the Daleys' just-finished house.

6

Year: 1983 (spring)
Age: 18
Idol: Jennifer Beals in Flashdance
Favorite Song: "Every Breath You Take" (The Police)
(Anticipated) Prized Possession: college acceptance envelope
Best Shoes: elf boots with leg warmers

Turning down "Tainted Love" on the car radio, I give Bobby the usual heads-up as we pull into the Harrison High School parking lot.

"Coming in for a landing," I say.

"Ten four, good buddy," he says, pulling his head in from the window—he sticks it as far out as he can while still wearing his seat belt. Then, in an order that only he understands, Bobby begins his methodical and thorough routine of putting his new *E.T.* figurines back in his *Incredible Hulk* lunchbox.

It would have mortified me to go to school with Bobby a few years ago, but I don't really care anymore that people know we are related. Although their reaction—"Oh-my-God, you're *twins?*"—really gets a little played out. Like there's anything I can do about that.

I don't see Bobby that much, because he's in a special program. At least he's around regular people in math and science classes. One huge question mark in my life is how is he ever going to fit into the real world? I see high school as practice for that.

The other big question mark is what am *I* going to do in the real world and, more specifically, which college is going to help me figure that out? My first choice is Notre Dame, but I'll need a scholarship because Bobby's health insurance premiums took the majority of our father's savings. I feel bad enough about that—if I get nuked from N.D., I'll feel even worse. It's like my father has a crush on that place, and the weird part is he never even went there. His parents could only afford community college in the Bronx. So the pressure's on because he's living vicariously through me.

The verdict will be in any day now. Most of us seniors are driving home every single day at lunch to check our mailboxes. You don't even need to open the envelopes to know whether you got in or not. If they're big and thick, you're sittin' pretty in Shaeffer City. Skinny and letterlike, you got the shaft. Better start crossing your fingers for your safety school. For extra luck, my father sent away for a mailbox cover in the shape of a Notre Dame football helmet. It's really embarrassing, but who knows? Maybe it will work.

At least there is one certainty in my life: Zack and I decided junior year that we'd go to the senior prom together, no matter what. That was back when Zack still looked like Chachi from *Joanie Loves Chachi*. Now the cheerleaders hang out at his locker, and he's having a torrid affair with the Swedish au pair named Brigitte, who lives next door to him. Whenever I ask him to do something for lunch, he always says, "Can't, babe. Je suis in my prime."

Sometimes I wonder if I hit my prime in tenth grade. I don't even have anyone to have a crush on. Sometimes I think not having anyone to like's more painful than dealing with a broken heart. Because then at least you have a reason for that ache inside, and someone to think about when you listen to all those cheesy Hall and Oates songs on the radio. I just feel sort of lonely and empty, but without the excuse, which makes me feel like I don't even deserve to feel that way.

* * *

I check my Swatch and realize that we're going to be late again. Patience, patience, I tell myself as I sit watching Bobby methodically pack up his figurines. But you can't rush him—no matter how loud you scream, *"What difference does it make if Mr. Spock goes in before E.T.?"* in the silence of your own head.

So I face a choice each and every morning: spend the extra five minutes perfecting wispy bangs, or give the time to Bobby for his toy-packing ritual. It's usually the latter, since I'm the one who makes him hide his toys before going into the building. Looking normal is half the battle in life, and if I could just help him with that, maybe he'd start fitting in.

"Space, it's the final frontier," he says, glancing at me with his peripheral vision.

"Yeah, let's go where no man has ever gone before," I say, as I run/walk him to his class and rush to English. The bell rings, and I get there just as Ms. Fine is closing the door.

"All right, class, let's get started," says Ms. Fine, snapping her fingers and clicking her heels in a mini-flamenco. Ms. Fine is very cool. She lived on a commune in the sixties, and she's always telling us to read *The Feminine Mystique*, preaching carpe diem and letting it all hang out.

"Today we are going to pair up and get started on your big senior project," she continues. "Oral presentations."

The class does a group groan.

"You will have six weeks to prepare, and fifty percent of your grade will be based on your presentation," she says.

More groans.

"Someone please give me a cliché," she requests.

Josh, the class nerd who is sitting next to me, raises his hand, as usual. If you looked up "geek" in the dictionary, you'd see a picture of Josh. Bifocals, Dutch-boy haircut, and high-water pants every day.

"You can't judge a book by its cover," he says.

"Excellent! Class, this is your assignment," she says. "You and your partner are each to come up with your own idea of how to prove or disprove this cliché. But work as a team on the outline. Starting on this side"—she points—"your partner will be the person to your right." Josh and I look at each other.

I would rather have root canal than publicly humiliate myself. So Josh and I decide to get started right away and make plans to meet in the library after school, since I have to wait for Bobby to finish with his life skills tutor anyway.

That afternoon Josh puts down his briefcase next to me. Why can't he use a knapsack like everyone else?

"Hey, how's your brother adjusting to H.H.S.?" Josh says.

"The jury's still out on the new satellite learning program," I say. "Still, I think it's better for him than private school. Bobby's going to have to deal with the real world sooner or later."

"Yeah, well better get to work," says Josh as he heads off into the stacks. I procrastinate by listening to my new Sony Walkman. "American Pie" comes on, and the proverbial lightbulb goes on over my head! I do a lap around the library but can't find Josh. I know he hasn't left because his geeky briefcase is still here.

That's when I look out the window. Oh, my God! It's Bobby getting knocked around by some junior varsity hockey players in the parking lot.

Fury surges up from the pit of my stomach and chokes me around the neck. How dare anyone lay a hand on Bobby, when he's already been through so much in his life—shock treatments, hospitalizations, hours of diagnostics in weird hospitals. Although he definitely bugs me 99 percent of the time with his stupid *Star Trek* lingo and anal-retentive habits, I would kill anyone who harmed a hair on his helmeted head.

With a surge of adrenaline, I sprint out of the building. By the time I get to the parking lot, however, Josh has already positioned his scrawny self between Bobby and the three bullies who have been using Bobby's *Incredible Hulk* lunchbox as a hockey puck.

"What the hell is going on here?" I scream.

"The aliens are attacking! Beam me up, Scotty! Beam me up!" says Bobby in his typical robotlike speak. As embarrassing as Trekkie lingo is, it's an improvement over the hand flapping and "whoop-whoop-whoop" he used to do to relieve stress until about ninth grade. Talk about stress. You should have seen the looks that behavior got in restaurants.

"Shut up, R2-D2," sneers Gonzo, the head bully, shoving him hard. Bobby doubles over. "And that's what you get for staring at me, you freakazoid!"

"Holy nonverbal behaviors, Batman!" says Bobby. "When eye-to-eye gaze exceeds the proper time limit, there's trouble in Gotham City!"

Ugh, he's sharing the social interaction stuff that his life skills tutor's been teaching him. I practice eye contact with Bobby at home. Two seconds is too short, but five seconds is considered aggressive. Stuff that comes naturally to you and me, like eye contact, making conversation, or joking around, has to be taught to Bobby like he's from another planet. No wonder he loves Spock so much.

"Mind your own business!" says Gonzo. "We're just having fun playing with the freak."

"This *is* my business," I say. "He's my brother. And I'll get Zack and the entire senior class to kick your ass if you don't leave him alone."

"This is boring anyway," Gonzo says. "Let's get out of here."

As they walk away, however, Josh blocks their path.

"Not so fast," Josh says, folding his arms across his concave chest.

I hold my breath. It's as if someone has pushed the PAUSE button.

All the action stops, and I'm wondering if I'm going to have to protect Josh from getting beaten up too.

"Apologize first," Josh demands. "And fix the dent in Lou Ferrigno's face."

Gonzo's jaw drops as Josh thrusts the lunchbox into his hands. And just our luck, that's the exact moment when the cheerleading squad saunters by.

"What's for lunch, Gonzo?" they titter, teasing him. "Love your lunchbox!"

The embarrassment on Gonzo's face is so satisfying, I insist on driving Josh home. I mean, the biggest nerd in the senior class coming to the rescue of the underdog against the evil enemies—it was almost like the opposite of an *Incredible Hulk* episode.

"Would you care to come in and play Pac-Man or something?" Josh asks.

"Thanks, but—" I start, knowing how Bobby hates it when his rigid after-school routine is upset. Every day when we go home, he unpacks his figurines, lines them up on the kitchen table, and snacks on cold spaghetti—which he eats one strand at a time with tweezers. Then it's time for *Star Trek* reruns.

To my surprise, however, Bobby's already out of the car. Not only does he love Atari, but it's one area of his life where he's really successful. One look at his mangled lunchbox on the seat next to me and I figure this pitstop is a small price to pay for a little happiness. Besides, I haven't even had a chance to tell Josh about my idea.

"Wow, you're amazing!" Josh says to Bobby as they both work their joysticks.

"I am a Vulcan. I am a Vulcan. There is no pain," says Bobby, nodding his head. "Sir, there is a multilegged creature crawling on your shoulder."

"Great episode," says Josh to Bobby without missing a beat. (Is there a chromosome linking the nerd and Trekkie genes?) "So, Bella, what's your topic?" Josh asks.

"The cliché 'You can't judge a book by its cover' is true, and it can apply not just to books but to music," I say. "The lyrics of Don McLean's 'American Pie,' for example, totally depict the turbulent sixties."

"Wow, that's creative," he says.

"Thanks," I say. "What about you?"

"The dictionary," he says without looking up. "While the cover doesn't give much away, it's truly a fascinating read—which proves that the cliché is true."

"Sounds, uh, deep," I say. Deeply boring, I think. I could never convince anyone, even Ms. Fine, that a dictionary is fascinating.

The following week in class, Ms. Fine takes notes as we all go around the room and reveal our topics.

"Excellent, students," she says. "Now switch topics with your partner. Your mission is to make your outline so crystal clear that your partner will be able to communicate your point as effectively as you can," she says. "And, by the way, you'll be graded by your partner's presentation."

Oh, great! Josh gets to rock out to "American Pie," while I'm taxed with bringing a damn dictionary to life! *As if!* I mean, gag me with a spoon! And Ms. Fine's already recorded the topics so there's no changing it now.

"You have exactly six weeks," she says.

Over the next several weeks Josh, Bobby, and I spend afternoons at each other's houses working on our outlines. Then, one day, Josh, Bobby, and I pull into our driveway and not only is the Notre Dame flag flying but my dad's put Christmas lights all over our N.D. helmet mailbox.

My dad opens the door wearing his pom-pom hat and, oh, God, his kilt.

MELINA GEROSA BELLOWS 70

"Look what I have for you, Bella!" he says excitedly, waving my collegiate fate, concealed in a white envelope. I run up the steps, drop everything, and rip it open.

"C'mon, Bella, win one for the Gipper!" says my father, dramatically quoting Knute Rockne, the legendary N.D. football coach.

My eyes zip along the sentences until I get to the words I never even considered.

"I'm wait-listed!" I wail, sinking to the floor. I don't mention that the letter goes on to say that this is due to my financial aid requirement. Without that, the letter says, I would have gotten in.

My father looks crestfallen. Even the pom-poms on his beret seem to droop. The four of us stand there uncomfortably.

"Emotions are alien to me," says Bobby, breaking the silence. "I am a scientist. 'Fascinating' is the word I use for the unexpected." Whenever anything ever goes wrong, you can always count on my brother to be totally inappropriate.

Bobby wanders off in the direction of the kitchen.

"Well, honey, you tried your hardest," says my father. "Who knows? Maybe you'll still get in."

He gives me a quick hug and disappears into the basement where he is going to perform another miracle of putting a ship in a bottle. I stand there feeling all hollowed out, my hopes drained like the Larios gin my dad empties in the sink so he can launch a ship inside.

"Why don't you join Bobby and go play Pac-Man?" I say to Josh. "I better tell my mom."

I find my mother in the backyard, planting impatiens around the fence. It's amazing how she's kept her Florence Henderson flip all these years. That's a real fashion commitment, if you ask me.

"Well?" She looks from me to the open envelope I'm holding, with the happily raised eyebrows of expectation.

"Wait-listed," I say, watching her brows fall, which feels like the weight of a ten-story building toppling on me. I wait for her to say something encouraging, but once again, those words of comfort don't come. She just gets that faraway look of hers. Now I feel like I've really let down the whole entire team.

"I tried my hardest," I manage.

"I know you did, honey. Everything always works out for the best," she says, but her eyes are back on the impatiens. "How's your father taking it?"

"He's okay," I say. "He's in the dungeon."

"Oh," she says. This is always where he goes when he can't deal with something.

"There's still hope," I add uncertainly. "But I guess I'd better send a deposit to my safety school."

I feel like I'm walking the gangplank as I go down the dark steps to his workshop. When I get there, I notice that he has changed out of his kilt and into his Mr. Rogers after-school outfit.

"I'm really sorry, Dad, for disappointing you," I say, swallowing the lump.

"Honey, you didn't disappoint me," he says unconvincingly. "But what about you? Isn't that what you wanted?"

What I want is all I've ever wanted, for my parents to feel proud of me. I feel like I have to super perform to make up for all the disappointments that Bobby brings them. But getting in to N.D. was the big play, and I fumbled big time.

If my dad could just say something inspirational from Knute Rockne, like winning isn't everything, or he's proud of me for trying, or anything. I wait.

"Bella," he says slowly, his eyes on his work.

I swallow.

"Could you please pass me the pliers?" he continues.

I blink back the tears and look for his stupid tool in its special spot on his workbench, but they are not there. "Um, I guess Bobby took them again," I say. Bobby steals them when it's spaghetti time and he can't find his tweezers.

"I could transfer midyear," I suggest. That's it! Besides, maybe I'll still get in. It's a long shot, but there's still hope.

"It's not important, really," he manages. "What's important is that you tried your hardest, honey. That's what life is all about."

I know he is trying to make me feel better, but it only makes me feel worse that even my best isn't good enough. Not good enough for Notre Dame, not good enough for my father, and therefore not good enough for myself.

Not being able to think of anything else to say, I slink back up the stairs and find Josh and my brother glued to their joysticks. I get a weird pang of jealousy toward my brother. How come nothing is ever expected of him?

"Don't worry, Bella. I'm sure the admissions department will come to their senses," says Josh. "They would be lucky to have you there."

"Easy for you to say!" I spit. "In the last month you've gotten huge, bulging envelopes from Harvard, Cornell, Brown, Princeton, and Yale."

"But I've yet to hear from my first choice, Stanford," he says. "So technically we're in the same predicament."

"Somehow that doesn't make me feel any better," I say.

"You're funny smart, not just book smart like me," he says. "Just look at how you can take a cliché like 'Don't judge a book by its cover,' and make it un-boring."

Just then the phone rings.

"Bella, it's Zack!" my mother calls into the den.

"We have to talk," Zack says, sounding more serious than the day he told me John Lennon had been shot.

"You know you can always parlez avec moi," I say, pulling the phone into the next room. "We're meuilleur amis."

Then he blurts it out: "I'm taking Brigitte to the prom," he says.

"What?" I say incredulously. I was going to make my hair look exactly like Jennifer Beals's in *Flashdance*. I even cut the neck off my sweatshirt for the day-after party at Jones Beach.

"It's just that Brigitte and I have gotten really close——" he says.

"Yeah, between the sheets? She doesn't speak English!" I scream. "Is this so you can get laid? You get laid *every day*!"

"I know I should have told you sooner," he says.

"No shit, Sherlock, considering the prom is Friday," I sputter. "Have a great time in the tux I picked out for you, Chachi!" I say, slamming down the phone.

"Did you have an altercation?" Josh asks.

"This is not the life I signed up for," I say. "First wait-listed and now dumped for the prom."

Then, out of the blue, Bobby points to Josh's breast pocket. The fact that Josh has a breast pocket is a whole other subject.

"Get down, boogie oogie oogie," Bobby says robotically.

Josh starts to blush. "I did buy a pair, but there is no one I really want to go with, except, uh," he stammers, "unless . . ."

"Umm, that's so nice, but . . ." I say.

And just like that, my date switches from Class Stud to Class Geek. At least I'll get to dress up like in *Flashdance*. I guess it's better than staying home and watching *The Love Boat* and *Fantasy Island* with my brother.

The last obstacle remaining between my handkerchief-bottom dress and me is getting through my oral presentation without having a nervous breakdown. Josh and I are the last two scheduled.

I dread every second until the bell rings and the moment is finally upon us.

I hold up *Merriam-Webster's Collegiate Dictionary* and make my way through Josh's outline, until I am finally sliding into the home base of my conclusion, twenty minutes later.

After polite applause, it's Josh's turn. He clears his throat and just stands there. People start to snicker. Why today, of all days, does he have to wear his TAYLOR'S TACKLE SHOP: MASTER BAIT T-shirt? He doesn't even get the joke. Smart people can be really stupid.

He clears his throat again.

"Bye-bye!" I yell out to Josh.

"Miss American Pie," he says, picking up the thread of the presentation we practiced ad nauseam. "Pop songs, as well as books, cannot be judged superficially," he begins. "Take, for example, 'American Pie.'"

People stop talking. This has gotten their attention.

"Don McLean's classic is not just a catalogue of musical events," he explains. "The pop song provides a metaphor for the class of values in America during the sixties."

Josh deconstructs the song line by line, calling out all the references to Buddy Holly, Janis Joplin, the Beatles, and the Rolling Stones. By the time he finishes, the class is giving him a standing O. Shyly he takes his bow, and it hits me: You really can't judge a book by its cover. Josh is a really nice guy. If he could just, just, just . . . Bobby would never, ever let me give him a fashion makeover. But Josh, well, maybe.

"C'mon, Josh!" I say after class, grabbing his hand and running for the parking lot.

Six hours later, our limo pulls up to the American Yacht Club, which has been transformed into Michael Jackson's "Thriller," the theme of our prom.

"Are you sure I look all right?" he asks.

"Promise," I say. "This is going to be awesome."

Josh escorts me out of the limo, and all heads turn. But not to look at me; they want to figure out the identity of my mystery date. Behind his *Risky Business* Wayfarer shades, Josh is unrecognizable. Our mission has been successful, even though we had so many stops to squeeze in that I didn't exactly have time to transform my hair into Jennifer Beals's 'do. I got dressed in a nanosecond at Josh's house.

After analyzing *Seventeen*'s beauty section, we came up with the ultimate makeover. At the optician's, we traded in Josh's black-framed goggle glasses for contact lenses. At the hair salon, he was relieved of his Dutch-boy 'do (or make that don't) and his unibrow (because two eyebrows are better than one). But it was the perfect fit of tails that took him from sort of cute to off the charts.

The verdict?

"Wow!" says Ms. Fine, on hand to chaperone. "Josh, I must say, Bella is a good influence on you."

Zack's blow-up Barbie doll, Brigitte, must have thought so too, because she cut in on our first dance, which was actually good since it gave Zack and me a chance to patch things up.

"Je suis desolé," Zack says, twirling me around to Lionel Richie's "All Night Long." "I was thinking with my little head."

"D'accord, mon ami," I say, giving him a hug. Depending on who's more popular that year, we always seem to be taking turns apologizing to each other. I guess the important thing is we're always friends again.

Josh and I are reunited for "Every Breath You Take." When the song ends, he whispers in my ear, "I've felt that way about you since sixth grade."

You have got to be kidding me, I think. Uncharacteristically, Josh boldly grabs my hand and leads me down to the beach. We slide off our shoes and walk to the far end, where the cabanas end. He pulls me close to him and kisses me passionately.

I gag inside.

Lesson learned: Although liking someone who already likes you makes sense, your head cannot boss around your heart. While I love the feeling of being appreciated by someone smart, I need it to come from someone more confident than myself, not someone who only looks the part of the Cute Boyfriend.

Luckily, we hear the last dance call, which is the perfect excuse to go back and join the group. The band is striking up "Celebration" by Kool & the Gang when Ms. Fine goes up onstage and whispers in the singer's ear. He says something to the rest of the band, there's some paper shuffling, and suddenly they start playing "American Pie."

We're halfway through the second encore when I suddenly see Bobby, who should be home with my parents, scuttling toward me, in that weird, hunched-over, old-man crab walk of his.

"What's wrong?" I say, trying to catch my breath. Why would he be here? Is there a crisis at home? Did someone die?

"Holy special delivery, Batman," he says, pulling a folded-up, crumpled envelope out of his *Hulk* lunchbox.

It was a return address I knew, and a size I liked. I wave to my parents' car, which I spot at the entrance. My parents wave back, and I notice the Notre Dame flag waving from our station wagon's antenna.

"Wahoo!" I rip open the envelope and throw my arms around Bobby and Josh.

"Book 'em, Dano!" screeches Bobby, recoiling from my touch, but so what? I'm too happy to care.

Notre Dame, here I come!

7

Year: 1983 (fall)
Age: 18
Idol: Molly Ringwald
Favorite Song: "It's Raining Men" (The Weather Girls)
Prized Possession: season football tickets (Go, Irish!)
Best Shoe: one penny loafer

*T*hump, *thump, thump.* Before I even open my eyes, I feel the little gremlin banging his sledgehammer on the inside of my skull. It's his job to inform me just how much of the keg I sucked down the night before. By this morning's thump-a-thon, it was gallons, apparently.

Slowly, I crack open my eyes. *Uh-oh. Who the heck's this guy snoring to my right?* And why has he totally redecorated my room with Heineken posters? Wait a minute. Oh, shit, this isn't my room. It must be *his* room. And, and (looking under the blankets), *phew!* Well, at least I'm fully dressed.

Stealing another glimpse to my right, I see the back of a blond head sticking up from the sheets. I rewind the footage from last night. I remember flirting with these really cute guys—juniors, I think. One of them had a lacrosse sweatshirt—ah, there it is, in a ball on the floor. Now, if I could just remember his name . . .

Better to just get out of Dodge, procure some aspirin, and start my life completely over. At Georgetown if necessary. Silently I slide out of bed and look for my shoes. I search everywhere, but I can find only one. Wolves gnaw off their own limbs to escape from traps. A penny loafer is really a small sacrifice compared to a whole limb, I rationalize.

I check to see if the coast is clear and slip out of his room via the window. Thank God I had the foresight—who am I kidding . . . dumb luck—to mash with a guy on the first floor. There are university rules called parietals, including that guys and girls must be out of one another's dorms by 11 P.M. If you're caught, you're out. Of course, rules are meant to be broken, and the brave, horny, or in my case, drunk ones take the chance.

I commence The Walk of Shame back to my dorm. The whole trek I pray I won't be recognized in what's clearly last night's outfit—minus one shoe. In my head I write a letter to my friend Al. This is the last straw.

Dear Alcohol,

I think we need to break up. Sometimes I question your influence over me. See the following.

1. Beer goggles: Why do you have to make everyone look so familiar? Please stop me from talking to the guy with the Flock of Seagulls haircut, acid-wash leisure suit, etc. Why is he so "unique" to me while I'm with you and yet so disgusting to me the next morning after you have worn off?

2. Eating: Why do you constantly suggest that I eat sausage hoagies with cheese fries, along with some "everything" pizza and some stale Cheetos, washed down with orange soda and topped off with a Kudos bar, all after a few ranch Doritos and a pound bag of M&M's?

3. Photo ops: Please stop suggesting the following head gear: football helmets, sombreros, napkins, ties, upside-down cups, inflatable balloon animals, traffic cones, and bras. Especially mine. Photo album's all set, thanks.

4. Phone calls: Why would you so strongly advise me to call Chandler (and every other cute guy) when I know for a fact he doesn't want to hear from me during the day, let alone at 4 A.M.? Furthermore: These hangovers have got to stop. I'm Catholic, so a little penance for last night's debauchery may be in order. But my entire day is going to be shot, and not for the first time.

Please review my grievances above, and get back to me today by happy hour. Otherwise we're quits.

Thank you.

From your biggest fan,
Bella

"Away game?" says my roommate, Carrie, as I fling open the door and dive into bed. Carrie is from New Jersey, a gymnast and catnip to guys. They always love girls who are blond, cute, and little, especially ones they can imagine bending like Gumby into pornographic positions. Carrie has her pick, and because of that, she's really choosy. I admire her restraint, while I'm like a kid in a candy shop with these guys. The ratio is three to one, guys to girls.

"Drink till he's cute!" we both say at the same time and burst into giggles.

"Yeah, but this one was cute *before* the beer goggles . . . I think," I say. "If I only knew his name."

"Don't worry. There's more where he came from," she says. "Worrying about guys at N.D. is like taking sand to the beach."

Easy for her to say. N.D. should really stand for "Non-Dating school." Everyone just gets drunk and "hooks up." The next day, however, you're on your own again. No strolling hand in hand around the campus lakes, no proudly wearing his letter jacket, no mash notes tucked in mailboxes, or any of the other things I'd

imagined that I'd finally experience with a "college boyfriend."
It's the opposite of sixth grade, when it was all title and no action.
Here it's all action and no title.

Most freshmen I know stop short of sleeping around. The
thing about being Catholic is you feel guilty about going all the
way without a "going out" status. For whatever reason, you can
look the other way when you are an official "girlfriend." My personal rule is a little more stringent: In order for me to sleep with
someone, I have to be in love.

Manya, next door, has no such rules. Everyone knows she's an
expert at "speaking into the microphone," and then some. She ad-
vertises her rock-hard body in skintight clothes and has a different guy sleep over every weekend, parietals or not. We call her
"the Professional" behind her back.

Now that I'm a virgin again, I'm definitely going to be more
selective when it comes to making the decision of whom I lose it
to next. (When you don't have sex for a full year, you reclaim your
V-card. For me it's been three years since Chandler, so I'm technically a virgin three times over.) So far this semester I've made out
with two guys—well, last night makes three—but I always stop
at kissing. Or second base.

"Here," says Carrie, handing me two aspirin, a Diet Coke, and
yesterday's mail.

"Thanks for checking the box," I say.

"So I take it you're skipping your first class?" she asks.

"Yeah," I say, but then my eyes come to rest on an official-
looking letter from the English department.

"Uh-oh," I say, sitting up and reading the letter out loud.
" 'Bella: See me immediately after class Friday morning,' signed
Professor Whitford. Why does Oxford-Moron have to see me to-
day, of all days?" I groan, hauling myself out of bed.

Normally, I love my English teachers, but this idiot, a grad
student who's on loan from Oxford, just rubs me the wrong way.

He's thirty and acts like he knows it all. Our feud started when he complained about children playing outside our window during one of his scintillating soliloquies on *Beowulf*.

"Would someone inform those braying billy goats to shut their gobs?" he moaned.

"Actually, Professor Whitford, those 'animals' are learning-disabled children," I informed him, shooting daggers at him with my eyes. "The School of Ed is across the courtyard."

Maybe I'm sensitive because of Bobby, who's still trying to finish high school. He scored nearly a perfect 800 on his math SATs, but any class that requires common sense he has to repeat at least twice before passing.

"C'mon, I'll walk over to the quad with you," says Carrie.

I pull on sweats and a baseball hat and we dash out the door. It's when I'm halfway there that I spill my soda down my chest and realize I only changed one shoe. I'm wearing one loafer and one black pump. I can't take me anywhere, I think.

Propping some proverbial toothpicks in my eyes, I'm barely able to make it until the end of the class, for my tête-à-tête with Oxford-Moron.

"You wanted to see me?" I say as everyone files out of the classroom. My eyes linger on Tim, a starting player on the football team who resembles a walking refrigerator. We've started to become friends, and I've helped him on a couple of papers. His size makes up for his mullet (you know, all business in the front and party round back) and his Members Only jacket. Besides, Carrie says you can always redecorate.

"Yes, Bella," Professor Whitford says as condescendingly as possible for three syllables. "There has been an unexpected opening in the Honors Program of Arts and Sciences. It's a rigorous four-year program in which a small group of students meets with one professor to read, write, and discuss the works of the great thinkers and writers of the ages."

"And?" Long pause while I try to figure out what this has to do with me. "You're recommending me?" Maybe I had this guy all wrong.

"The program is looking for, well, diversity, for lack of a better term. Take this note to the dean's office. While you're far from a perfect student, you're not shy about your opinions," he says, clearing his throat. "Nice shoe combination, by the way."

I look down, then turn fuchsia. Well, at least I won't have to listen to this arrogant jerk anymore, I think as I register and buy a wheelbarrow of classics to catch up on. Our class is held in the Dome building. You can feel the history in the place.

A few days later, I meet my new classmates. Let's just say nerd-o-rama. This crew makes Josh look like Mr. T, and I'm talking *before* his Geek Chic makeover. When the professor arrives, however, I consider hurtling myself through one of the stained-glass windows.

"Students, I trust you've completed Pascal's *Pensees*," Oxford-Moron drones in his arrogant, English prick accent. "Bella, why don't you share your opinions, since you are always so sure of them?"

By the end of the two-hour class, I feel dumb, soap-opera blond dumb. Maybe N.D. was right the first time; maybe I belong on the wait list not in the student body. Anything would be better than writing a ten-pager over the weekend! What about the N.D.–Penn State game? What about all the fun tailgating parties? What about doing the Wave? Beer funnelators at halftime? What about cheering for my new big football buddy, Tim, the walking refrigerator, whom I'd love to redecorate? I realize I have no choice but to spend the weekend right here in the library.

Fate makes it up to me the following week when I bump into Tim in the cafeteria.

"Where've ya been, Bella?" he says.

"Got transferred out of the class," I say.

"The class is not the same without your wisecracks," he says. "Want to have lunch?"

The next thing you know, I'm surrounded by the starting lineup of the Fighting Irish at their unofficial players' table.

"Oh, my God!" Carrie mouths from over at our usual freshman table.

I meet all Tim's football buddies and am having such a good time that I can barely eat a morsel, and that's not like me at all—hungry Hannah that I am. The Dating God notices and tosses me a bone. As Tim and I get up to leave, he says, "Want to study together tonight?"

"Sure!" I say, hoping I didn't sound too overeager. I am so happy that Mexican jumping beans start break-dancing to "Footloose" in the pit of my stomach.

That night I put on my acid-wash jean miniskirt and ruffled shirt, with my favorite leg warmers and scrunched-down boots. I even shave my legs, just in case this is the closest thing I ever get to an official college date.

As I cross the courtyard, I feel totally special, proud even. I wonder if people can tell by looking at me that I'm going to study with one of the up-and-coming stars of our football team.

Nervously I knock on his door and quickly breathe into my hand to check my breath. He swings it open, and I swear to God, his gorgeous body fills the entire frame.

Instead of studying, we procrastinate by telling each other about our hometowns, families, and friends. Tim is an only child who was raised by a single mother in the Eight Mile section of Detroit. The whole time he's talking, I'm trying to detect signs of an H.T.H. (Home Town Honey), but happily I come up dry.

He stops in the middle of his story to say, "Do you hear that?"

What I hear is competing stereo systems. It's "You Shook Me All Night Long" versus "Eye of the Tiger."

"The battle of the bands?" I say.

"No, *that*," he says, pointing to rain gently pattering the window over our heads. "That's my favorite sound."

"Mine too," I say. Our thighs are next to each other, touching. Mine looks like Karen Carpenter's next to his.

"Coming to the game this weekend?" he says.

"Boston College versus Notre Dame?" I say. "Wouldn't miss it for the world!"

"Great! Let me walk you home," he says. "It's dark outside."

Letting myself into my room, I flop onto my bed and pinch myself. There was no good night kiss, but we held hands and *he* initiated it. How lucky can a girl get? He's a football player . . . on the starting line! That's like being a movie star at Notre Dame. The best part is how I feel when I'm with him, absolutely teeny. Make that microscopic.

I cram all week so I can go to the game. Carrie and I make an early start of it, hitting all the different tailgate parties. For the first time I understand why people actually leave the parking lot and go to the game. I especially love watching when they put the players up on the JumboTron with all their vital statistics after they make a great play.

"Bella, there's Tim!" says Carrie, pointing to the big screen. Larger than life, a stiffly smiling portrait of Tim beams, next to a list of his plays.

Then the screen changes, and the little lights zip across and form into words, blinking the question: " 'Bella, how 'bout a real date?' " reads the announcer, in his booming voice. "Whoever Bella is out there, someone has eyes for you!"

"That's the most romantic thing I have ever heard!" swoons Carrie, hugging me.

My insides feel all warm and gooey, like s'mores. Every girl in my dorm suddenly surrounds me and cheers. What are the odds of being asked out in front of fifty thousand people, at a "non-dating" college! The Fighting Irish score a touchdown, trouncing the Eagles, and the entire stadium erupts in applause. My joy is so jumbo I feel like they're clapping for me because I have a date. This definitely makes up for the last two years of high school when the only two guys I knew intimately were Ben and Jerry.

The next day I get home from classes and there's a note under my door from Manya. "Come see me immediately!" it reads and is signed with hugs and kisses. When I go to her room, she presents me with a dozen red roses.

"These are from Tim," she says breathily. "He stopped by earlier."

"You read the card?" I say, eyeing the ripped-open envelope.

"Couldn't help it!" She shrugs again. "It says: 'Looking forward to Saturday, Tim.'"

I float through the week, going to advanced aerobics daily (*Let's grapevine!*) and trying on different outfits for group review. We decide on the Guess? striped overalls with supertapered legs, offset by high-heel boots, in case he takes me somewhere fancy. It's almost as if I'm going on a date for the entire freshman dorm.

When Saturday night arrives, my friends all huddle behind the blinds so they can watch for him.

"Here he comes!" Manya says dramatically. My heart pounds as Tim disappears into my building and everyone scampers back into their rooms.

Suddenly I don't want to go anymore. The pressure is almost too much.

There's a knock on the door. Carrie opens it as I fiddle with a picture of my brother on my desk.

"I'm here to pick you up for our date," says Tim to me. And with that, he *literally* picks me up (*as if I'm a feather!*) and carries me down the hall. I feel like "Yo, Adrian" from *Rocky*.

It's over the Pasta Extravaganza that "He" comes up. I know Tim's father died when he was little, so it takes me a while to figure out who the "He" is. But finally I get it: God.

"Every time I hit an obstacle, He taught me to find a way to steer myself around it," Tim says. "The signs are always there, if you ask for help."

"How do you mean?" I ask.

"When my dad died, it was really hard, but it also provided me with an opportunity to grow up and take care of my mom," says Tim. "And when it became clear I couldn't afford to go to college, He steered me toward football, which got me a scholarship."

To me, God has always been an abstract authority, someone I strive to be a good girl for because I know I'll get a big report card in purgatory. The idea that He's a friend you chat with on the psychic hotline is a radical concept to me. I'm beginning to wonder if there isn't something just a little bit "different" about the boy.

I'm just beginning to put my exit strategy into motion when I remember something.

"The way you talk to God is sort of like the way I talk to my grandmother, who died when I was little," I say, fiddling with my locket. "It sounds like you know Him the way I know her."

"God's right here next to me," he says, tapping his right shoulder. "And right now I'm asking His help to decide the biggest question of my life."

"You mean which pro team to join when you graduate?" I say. I've heard rumors that the scouts are circling.

"No, whether to go to the pros at all," he says. "Or to the seminary."

I choke on my gnocci. "You're considering becoming *a priest*?" I ask. How typical is that? I'm asked out on a date by a clergy wannabe.

"If I go with the pros, the money is really good," he considers. "I'd never have to worry about my mom's finances again."

"Yeah, plus don't you think if God gives you the opportunity, you *have* to go for it. Isn't it your destiny?" I ask.

"No, you always have a choice," he says, a certain firmness to his voice. "It's your choices that define you in the end, not your opportunities."

If Tim wants to become a priest so badly, why does he place my hand on his zipper at every red light on the way home? There's a certain firmness there too.

Over the next few months, we spend a lot of time together, studying, going to meals, partying with his teammates, and having long and meaningful make-out sessions until parietals pry us apart. But, in a lot of ways, Tim remains a mystery to me. For example, I'm not sure if I'm in love or not. But that's beside the point. Why does he never push to go all the way?

Why can't I get closer to him? One night in the library, I say a little prayer to my grandmother and ask her to give me a sign. I'm fiddling with my locket when suddenly I get this flash of female intuition to go to mass. If Tim goes to Him for the answers, maybe I should give it a whirl too.

To be honest, church has always made me zone out. It's like when the adults talk on *Peanuts*, you know, "Wha-wah-wah, wah-wah . . ." But what have I got to lose? I think, as I pack up my books and head to the chapel for the nightly ten o'clock service.

Slipping in the chapel's back door, I'm surprised to find the room already crowded with students. I'm even more surprised to see Tim in the front row, participating in the service as eucharistic minister. Jesus Christ! That's why he always leaves my dorm room so early: to distribute communion! He's been sneaking away to rendezvous with Jesus! I duck out early to avoid having to stick out my tongue in his face.

Two can play at that game. If he's going to cheat on me with religion, I'll just cheat on him with, well, with Honors English! I decide to take Tim's linebacking lead and turn an obstacle (my studies) into an opportunity. When Tim asks me what I'm doing Thursday night, I tell him I'm busy.

Then I *get* busy. Carrie's a little surprised when the keg I'm rolling in is followed by a single file of eight library rats. As my Honors English class opens its study guide, I pour everyone a cold frosty one.

We make up a new drinking game, Shakesbeer, to go along with reading *Richard III*. Six or seven rounds later, we head to the Senior Pub.

Quick learners, I think to myself as I watch my classmates hit the floor and do the worm to "Shout." By the end of the evening, half the class is sucking face with the other half on the dance floor to "Total Eclipse of the Heart."

Since our little bonding experience, my fellow students have rallied around me whenever Oxford-Moron picks on me, which is all of the time. He's always commenting on my outfits. In fact, I got another nasty note to see him in his office.

"I just wanted to let you know that there is a year abroad program at Oxford," he says, his eyes lingering on my high-heel boots. (I wear them on exam days because I think they give me that competitive edge on essay questions.)

"England, fun!" I say. "Maybe I'll have a Princess Di spotting!" Now she married a nerd, but *that* was a wedding.

"It's not just all about fun, Bella," he says. "That's why I think you should apply. A change of scenery would do you good."

"I'll think about it," I say, and I do all the way back to my dorm, where there's a message taped to my door to call my mother.

My heart pounds as I dial the phone. "What's wrong?" I say, because I know that something is. My parents normally call Sunday mornings so my father can discuss every detail of the Saturday night game.

"It's your brother," she says. I can hear the No Makeup in her voice. "Not doing well."

"Bad reaction to the new meds?" I say. They started Bobby on some new drug that's supposed to help his arrhythmia.

"Yes, he's really regressed," she says.

"Bobby's snapped out of it before, Mom," I say. "Just stick to his routines—you know how those make him feel safe."

She's silent for a minute as my mind scrambles for some other words of comfort for her. Then in a tiny, papery voice she says, "We've had to put him in Meadowbrook."

There's been a lot of close calls, but my brother's never had to be institutionalized before. The Gray Cloud comes up and bags me from behind. I imagine myself around the age of ten, doing a Roseanne Rosannadanna routine for my mother. "So, Ma, why do they have a fence around the loony bin? To keep the squirrels from eating the nuts!!" Ba-dum-ba.

I shove these helpless, crazy thoughts aside, clear my throat, and summoning my best in-control voice, say, "I'll be there as soon as I can."

I borrow Carrie's Volvo and drive home. During the two-day journey, I think about how any challenge that I have—boys, books, whatever—is squidildydidink compared to what Bobby goes through on a daily basis. How dare I complain about anything, when the most innocuous stimuli can turn his world into a living nightmare? For him, rain—one of my new favorite sounds—is as unnerving as gunfire. Loud noises are like a dentist's drill hitting a nerve.

I take only a few sleep stops by the side of the road, so by the time I cross the New York border, I can barely keep my eyes open. Still, I drive past home and straight to Meadowbrook.

It's a large building, almost like you'd see on a college campus, but all the faculty wears white. I have to show two forms of ID, even though my parents called ahead on my behalf. I steel myself as I walk to his room, carefully avoiding looking at any other patients along the way. I can't believe he's now officially one of them. When I get to his door, I take a deep breath.

"Bobby?" I say, entering his room. No response. He's just sort of sitting there in a chair, zoning out.

"I brought you something," I say, showing him the *Star Trek* videos. I hate *Star Trek* with a passion but thought the videos might bring Bobby comfort.

"Space, it's the final frontier," he says in his robotic monotone. We watch this one episode where the monster kills one of the "unnamed crew," and Kirk wants to retrieve his body before blasting off. Spock, however, just wants the ship to get away from the monster as fast as possible. I know how he feels. I want to get out of here as fast as possible.

"Go to warp drive. Go to warp drive," Bobby says, repeating Spock's dialogue.

"Yes, Bobby, they are in danger, but they care about their friend, so they want to take him with them," I try to explain.

"That's illogical," Bobby says.

"Yeah, but they're attached to him," I say. "The rule is when you love someone you do things that don't always make sense."

In a way Bobby and Mr. Spock are very similar, all logic and no emotion. But how can I explain love to my brother when I can barely understand it myself?

After a weeklong Spock-a-thon, all I feel is frustrated that I can't seem to help him in any significant way. I'm also furious that my parents are so useless. There must be something somebody can do.

My last night, I go home and have dinner with my parents. My mom makes linguine with clam sauce, a meal that would be stretched out for hours if Bobby were home, with the way he eats his spaghetti, picking up each strand with his tweezers. Maddening, to say the least. Without him, though, the meal is unbearably quick and unsettling.

"Did I tell you that they transferred me into the Honors Program?" I say, trying to brighten the mood.

"Good for you, honey," my mother says distractedly. The No Makeup in her voice is screaming.

"And I'm dating someone," I say.

My mother raises an eyebrow. This has gotten her attention.

"Someone nice?" she asks.

"Yes, and not only is he Catholic but very religious, you'll be glad to know," I say.

"That's wonderful, Bella!" she says. "This is such a special time in your life. College days are so carefree."

Carefree? Is she on crack? Can't she see the Pink Elephant who has crashed our family dinner for the millionth time? My feelings about Bobby, our situation, and my responsibilities start to fester and then overwhelm me. In an instant, I'm erupting like Vesuvius. I can't help it—I smash my fist down on the table.

"Why can't you help him?" I cry.

They both look at me, stunned. No, make that scared.

"Why can't you get a second opinion or something?" I say. "You just let him linger there with freakouts. Why can't you do something?"

"Bella, calm down," my mother says in an uncertain voice. "The doctors are tying to adjust his medication."

"They are always trying to adjust his medication," I blurt. "The one they are trying now really helps, huh? He's practically comatose. I sat with him for about five hours today, and it's like he barely registers that I'm there. I mean, he's so clueless. Does he realize I'm supposed to be at school studying for finals? Of course not. You never notice if I'm there or not, even when his medicine is working."

Shit, I didn't mean to say that. How did that slip out? Maybe they didn't hear.

But it's true. As hard as I strive to achieve, I feel invisible to the members of my family. They don't seem to notice anything beyond my brother. And my brother, he's so much in his own world, I wonder if he would notice if I dropped dead.

"Bella, we are doing everything that we can," says my father, his voice strict and stern. "We are all just going to have to be patient until Bobby rides this out." Then he pushes back from the table and disappears into the basement to perform another ship in a bottle miracle. *Santa Maria* calling, I think.

I watch my mother's cheeks tremble as she scrapes the uneaten linguine into the garbage. The tears welling in her eyes just about put me over the edge. I hate myself. I should have never come home. The more I try to help, the more I add to their problems.

"I'm sorry," I say in a hoarse whisper, taking the plate out of her hands. "We'll think of something."

"Honey, I know you are frustrated," she says. "We all are." I want to hug her, but I feel frozen to the floor. She shrugs and offers a weak smile. Beggars can't be choosers, so I take that as forgiveness.

On the drive back to Southbend, I wonder if I should transfer to a school closer to home. Or farther away. My mind drifts to Tim. "Take adversity and turn it into an opportunity" is his philosophy. Maybe I should pursue the Oxford program; maybe I could learn something. If I could just get into Bobby's head, I know I could make him trust me and lead him back out into the world with the rest of us.

A week or so after I get back, Tim says we have to talk. He's been really quiet lately, ever since this chance for Oxford has inspired me to make my studies a priority and not an afterthought. We go to a bench near the grotto and watch the students rush to and fro in the distance.

"Bella, I'm not sure how to tell you this, but, well," he stammers, "in a way, well, there's sort of someone else."

"I know," I say, patting his hand. "I've seen you two together, and I completely understand." I mean, he might as well have led those ten o'clock masses. Jesus Christ Superstar one, Bella zero.

"You do?" he says, looking surprised.

"There's a closeness there that we'll never have," I say, trying to make it easy for him. It can't be easy to choose God over girls, considering I know the guy gets major wood every time we kiss.

Besides, as much as I've enjoyed the prestige of being a football player's girlfriend, the truth is, I've never felt that close to Tim.

"Thanks, Bella," he says. "I never thought you'd be so understanding."

There's a difference between understanding, and *being* understanding. But what choice did I have?

As freshman year comes to an end, it seems that everyone is partying hearty except for me. I'm going to have to work my tail off to get accepted into the year-abroad program.

Listening to my hallmates blast Eurythmics until the wee hours is one thing, but being held hostage to Manya's sexploits is another. I have no idea who's been in there for the past few weeks, but I can tell by Manya's orgasmic "Big boy! Big boy! Ride me, big boy!" screams that it's a repeat offender, so to speak. I wish the dorm monitor would catch on.

When the head banging against our common wall literally knocks my decorative crucifix onto my pillow, I decide it's time to say something. The next morning I write her a quick note, politely requesting that she keep it down, just until I finish my Honors exams and Oxford application.

Carrie and I are off for breakfast. I bend over and push the envelope under Manya's door. It suddenly swings open, and I'm crushed by a refrigerator that has tripped over me.

"Tim?" I say to the body sprawled on top of me. He must have been so riveted by the sight of Manya, wearing nothing but the *Flashdance* sweatshirt she borrowed from me, that he didn't bother to look where he was going.

The happy couple looks at me in silence.

"So I see you've decided to go pro," I say to Tim.

Carrie's jaw drops. For a moment there is complete and utter silence. And then I can hear the tiniest hint of a choked-back laugh in Carrie's throat. I press my lips together like I'm in church, but it's too late. The most uncouth, nose-snorting guffaw rumbles out.

Carrie and I run off down the hall, hooting all the way.

"Wow!" Carrie says when we can speak again without fear of wetting our pants. "You were soooo cool—ice cold. That remark deserves a celebration. Are you sure you don't want to join me in Nantucket this summer?"

She's renting a house with a bunch of friends from home. Sounds fun, but my brother was just released from Meadowbrook.

"Can't," I say. "I was thinking if Bobby and I got summer jobs together, it might give him an ego boost," I add, not mentioning anything about my own.

I decide to "go pro" myself and pray for a sign that something good will happen.

8

Year: 1984
Age: 19
Idol: Madonna
Favorite Song: "Like a Virgin" (Madonna)
Prized Possession: newfound sense of adventure
Best Shoes: red flats

"You're fired!" says camp counselor coordinator Mr. Howe. He resembles Mr. Potato Head, and he runs the camp where Bobby and I are working. Make that where Bobby *was* working.

"*Sir,*" says Bobby.

We stop and listen. I've never once heard Bobby stick up for himself. This is going to be good.

"There is a multilegged creature crawling on your shoulder," he continues in Spock speak.

Ugh.

"But, Mr. Howe, I thought you said Bobby was a whiz with your computer," I say, hating the pleading, wheedling tone in my voice. "Didn't he organize your database and discover the short circuit, not to mention figure out what was wrong with all the wiring?"

"Yes, but he's too inflexible," Mr. Howe says. "Whenever I change the order of his duties, he resists my authority."

"But he doesn't understand the concept of authority!" I sputter. "He has a strict order for the way things are supposed to go in his mind, and that's his authority," I explain, getting my sarcastic drawl under control. "As long as he gets the tasks done, isn't that all that matters? *Please?* This is his very first job!" I feel nauseous and dirty from all this begging.

Mr. Potato Head shakes his head no. I feel like knocking his nose and glasses off. Or at least breaking an ear. Or telling him Mrs. Potato Head was just mashed or something.

"He's going to have to fit in the real world sooner or later," he says, shrugging. I realize it's a lost cause.

That's exactly what scares the hell out of me. How is Bobby ever going to fit in out there and be able to take care of himself? He needs to learn that doing the task is only half the job, sucking up the rest. If I can just help him figure that out this summer, at least he'd have a shot at a future after high school.

"You can't fire him," I say.

"Why not?" asks Mr. Howe.

"Because he quits!" I say. "And so do I!"

Hmm. Perhaps I should have thought this through a little better, and not quit on a day when my mother's using the car. Today is Circus Day so we all had to dress up in costumes. I took the opportunity to be a lion tamer, so I could wear these fishnet stockings with the seams up the back. They look pretty good with my bathing suit, pumps, and Lone Ranger mask, I thought, although now that we are stomping into town to catch the bus home I'm not so sure. Compared to me, Bobby looks positively preppy in his red pajamas and the clown wig I strapped to his helmet.

I realize this is what those *Glamour* magazine articles mean about stress on the job, when Chandler's convertible whizzes by and toots a few times. Does he recognize me or is he just offering some male appreciation for my fishnets?

At dinner, I watch as Bobby eats his spaghetti one strand at a time with his tweezers, as usual, and try to figure out a way to tell my parents what happened.

"So, Bobby, how was work today?" asks my father, putting down his *Wall Street Journal*. He, especially, loves the fact that

Bobby has a job. I bet he fantasizes about them having father-son chats about making their way up the corporate ladder, the way I fantasize about my next boyfriend.

"Billie Jean's not my lover," Bobby says in a robotic staccato Michael Jackson. "Just beat it."

My parents look at me for translation.

"Uh, things didn't work out so well today," I begin.

"Just beat it! Beat it! Beat it!" Picking up the tempo as if he were singing the refrain.

"Actually, he was fired today, so I quit too," I say nonchalantly.

"Why?" both Parental Units say in unison. I can think of a hundred reasons and they can't think of one?

"Pink Elephant Alert! Pink Elephant Alert!" I feel like screaming. But I don't. I stumble around for a diplomatic way to explain that people don't always cotton to adhering to the strict ritualistic behaviors of an autistic, while said autistic is sitting there toothpicking his green beans without a care in the world. For God's sake, when will they wake up and smell the java?

"Well, Mr. Howe wanted things done a certain way, and Bobby only wanted to do things his certain way," I say. "I guess you could chalk it up to creative differences."

"That's all right, champ," says my father, chucking Bobby in the shoulder, which he clearly doesn't appreciate.

"Eee! Eee! Eee!" says Bobby. "Book 'em, Dano."

"Dad, you know he doesn't like to be touched—" I start.

"Yeah, well, anyway, champ," says my father, continuing, "when I was about your age, they laid off our whole division at the plant and replaced us with a machine. So I know how you feel."

How could my father possibly know how my brother feels, considering he is incapable of communicating his emotions to any of us? But I play along as the Gray Cloud descends.

"I'm sorry," I mumble to my mother as we do the dishes together. "I tried."

"Honey, I didn't think your brother was ready for a job," my mother says, the No Makeup creeping into her voice. "I don't know why you pushed so hard for him to work this summer."

"He *was* doing his job," I say. "It was his social misfit-ness that did him in. And the reason that I pushed for it was because he needs to learn how to fit in. I thought if I could be there to help him, give him pointers . . ." I say, my voice trailing off.

"Well, apparently he's not ready for that," my mother says. "He doesn't need the extra pressure before his last year of school."

"I guess you're right, Mom," I say.

Then what's he going to do? I feel like screaming. But I don't have the energy to dispel the Gray Cloud and point out the enormous Pink Elephant that has been squashing everyone in this house for as long as I can remember.

Just as we are finishing the dishes, Zack calls.

"Voulez-vous go to le cinema, ce soir?" he asks.

"D'accord," I say. "Pick me up, vite! Vite! Vite!"

Anything to escape the gloom in this house! We zip over to the theater, park illegally, get tickets to see *Indiana Jones and the Temple of Doom*.

After the movie, we are discussing whether Zack would rather make a suitable Indiana Jones when we notice that he has a ticket on the windshield.

"Merde!" he says.

"Zack, attendez!" I say, inspecting the pink flier. "It's not a ticket. It's an ad for Greyhound Bus: 'Half Price Tickets to Nantucket.' I should pack my bag," I say in jest. On the way to the movie, I had filled him in on the Bobby 'n' Sis Project Employment gone awry. Now he turns on the car and Madonna's "Holiday" comes on. She is so cool. She just does whatever she wants, and she's Catholic! How does she skip the guilt?

"Why *don't* you go?" he says. "There ain't no jobs left in this town. And don't you have to earn all your room and board for next year?"

"Yeah, the pressure's on," I say. "But I feel like a traitor leaving my brother."

"What more can you do for him now?" Zack says. "Seems to me like you've got nothing to lose. Madonna would do it." The boy does know how to crank up the pressure.

I decide to call Carrie and see if her offer still stands.

"Sure!" she says. "And I heard that there are waitressing jobs at the Chanticleer. You could make big bucks at night and go to the beach all day. Did I mention how cute the lifeguards are?" she says, dangling the bait in front of this little fishy.

Next year's tuition, prime tanning rays, and the possibility of summer love!

I hang up the phone and knock on my parents' bedroom door. "Mom and Dad," I say, interrupting their favorite show, *St. Elsewhere*. I spring the plan on them.

"Is the house chaperoned?" my father asks.

"Don't you trust me?" I say, dodging the question.

"We trust you, honey," my mother says. "But there are a lot of wackos out there, and we don't trust them. That doesn't sound safe."

"Please? I promise I'll make the money I'll need to get me through the semester," I say. "Besides, there are no jobs left in this town."

"Robert, what do you think?" my mother says to my father. Usually they have these conversations in private.

"Please? Please? Please?" I butt in.

"Okay, honey," he says, yawning. "Just promise you'll be a good girl and to call if anything goes wrong."

The day's events, I'm sure, have worn them down, and they

are simply too tired to put up a good fight. It's not that they don't care about me, I tell myself, as much as there are limits to their capacity to worry, sort of like a credit card maximum.

Two days later, Carrie picks me up at the ferry and takes me to the house, which I am imagining to be one of those beautiful estates with a wraparound porch and puffy purple hydrangeas. When we get there, however, it might as well be Sigma Chi. There are dead kegs in the front yard, flies buzzing in the kitchen, and my "bed" is a sleeping bag on Carrie's sandy floor. Still, no Gray Clouds and Pink Elephants, so I'm glad I'm here.

"Can I have a lift over to the Chanticleer later?" I say, a sexy shrew outfit and double-digit tips coming into my mind. "I need to start working as soon as possible."

"Sorry, I just found out they filled the position," she says. "But Mr. Hendricks did put up a Help Wanted sign in the gas station."

"Pumping gas?" I say, the sexy shrew outfit transforming in my mind into icky, greasy coveralls that make me look really fat. With my name in script on a patch over my left breast.

"It's not so bad," she says. "I sorta like working there. Come with me tomorrow, and I'll show you."

"Know anything about gas?" Mr. Hendricks asks the following morning, when I "inquire within."

"Well, I eat a lot of beans," I say, figuring I have nothing to lose at this point.

"A sense of humor's a start," he says. "Carrie can teach you the rest."

"It's easy," she says. "The trickiest part is the neckline of your T-shirt. You need to sport enough cleavage to interest the guys, but not enough so the female clientele will complain about you. If you get it just right, I can guarantee you'll know about all the best parties on the island."

"You're on!" I say. So what if it's minimum wage? I'll work

double shifts to make my tuition money. And maybe I will meet a lot of guys anyway.

After a straight week of pumping gas in the pouring rain without a single party invitation, I decide to cheer myself up by strolling around the cute shops in town. Peering in the window of the Chanticleer, I watch the perfect little families sitting down to their surf and turf dinners. I feel homesick, but for a home even I know I don't have.

Adventures are like volleyball on the beach, I decide. Those Mountain Dew commercials make that sport look really fun. When you actually play, however, you get tired, sweaty, and a terrible bathing suit wedgie. Popcorn is also in that category. Totally overrated. The taste never lives up to the smell.

I'm just about to turn away when I see Blondie, the guy I had the drunken one-night stand with at the very beginning of the first semester! My first Walk of Shame! Gosh, he is cute without the beer goggles after all, I think as I watch him bus tables.

The next day Carrie tells me about last night's date with the Sugar Daddy who took her to a super fancy restaurant, the Galley, for a five-course meal. I tell her about spying Blondie at the Chanticleer.

"That's who you fooled around with?" she says. "I bet it's Grant Stockdale."

"You *know* him?" I ask.

"Of him," she clarifies. "He's a local."

Just then Carrie's date from last night pulls up in his Jag for gas and a good long look down Carrie's cleavage. He's got to be twice her age. I admire her ability to not let it bother her.

"Hi, Carrie," says Paul, aka Sugar Daddy. "I'm off to pick up Bart at the ferry. Can you join us for dinner?"

Carrie leans into his window, tantalizing him with a view of her sinewy curves. "Um," she says, casting a sly glance my way. "I promised Bella we'd go to the Chanticleer and eat dinner at the bar," she says, adding a dollop of mock disappointment. She turns to give me a big, fat wink.

"I have an idea," says Sugar Daddy, playing right into Carrie's plan. "Let's all go."

"Sounds good to me." I shrug nonchalantly from my gas pump.

The second the Jag pulls out, I race over to Carrie and give her a high five. "Chanticleer here we come!" we both say at the same time. It's about as close to a Madonna song as I am going to get!

That evening we wait for our dates on the outside patio. I'm totally nervous. I've never been on a blind date before, but I *had* to seize the opportunity. This will be my first contact with Grant, aka Blondie. But what if he's not our busboy? Or what if he thinks that Bart's my boyfriend? I cross my fingers and hope for the best.

Our dates pull up in the silver Jag. Fossil, I think, as I introduce myself to Bart. So very glad I learned the art of keeping a smile plastered on even when staring death (okay, not death, but forty plus, minimum) in the face.

We arrive at the Chanticleer, and when we walk in my jaw drops. Not only is Grant dressed immaculately in a navy blazer, tie, and khakis, but he's clearly been promoted to maitre d'.

"You look surprised," whispers Carrie.

"I thought Grant was a busboy," I explain.

"Are you kidding?" Carrie says. "His family *owns* the Inn."

Rumor has it that Billy Joel and Christie Brinkley have a house on Nantucket, but the real celebrities here are the locals. Islanders always have the upper hand over the tourists. Doors open for locals that are closed to the rest of the population, no matter how nouveau riche.

We make our way to the hostess stand, and my heart is *thump, thump, thumping*. Grant finishes his phone call, scribbles on the reservation pad, and looks up. Our eyes catch. His gray eyes flick from me to Fossil back to me. Red is creeping up my neck.

"Reservation, sir?" he says.

"Yes, the name is Coleman, party of four," says Carrie's date. "I requested your most romantic table."

I cringe and shrivel inside.

"Of course," Grant says, extending his hand toward the wrought-iron French doors. "Right this way to the veranda."

Sugar Daddy leads and we follow single file, with me second to last and Grant behind me. This is my only chance, or he's going to think I'm really with Fossil. I summon my inner Madonna, and triple dare myself to go for it.

Behind Fossil's back, I turn and wink at Grant.

Does he recognize me? Think I'm a slut? *What am I doing?* Just then, Grant puts his hand on the small of my back in such a way that I know that it is "Ten four, good buddy"—message received.

"Your table, madame," he says pulling out my chair for me.

Three hours and eight courses later, I could almost see how Carrie has made a career out of dating different guys all summer. But it's really not for me. I feel like it's sort of using someone, even if it's just a date. I've also been able to focus on only one person at one time. I never really got that Crosby, Stills & Nash song, "Love the One You're With." As polite as I was trying to be to Fossil, I am completely distracted by Grant.

When we get up to leave, however, there's no sign of him. We walk out of the restaurant, and there he is chatting with the valet. "Ready for your car, sir?" he says to Sugar Daddy. "I trust everything was satisfactory." Secretly, Grant slips a matchbook in my hand.

It's after midnight by the time the trio drops me off. As soon as I get inside, I run down the hall to the pay phone and call the number on the matchbook.

"I'm off in an hour," says Grant. "How 'bout a nightcap?"

Now this is what I call a double date, I think to myself as I count the minutes.

Right on time, pebbles clink against my window. I peek out, and there's Grant, waiting on the sidewalk on a bicycle. There's a bottle of champagne and two crystal flutes in its wicker basket.

"Your chariot, your Highness," he says, bowing toward the bicycle seat. I hop on, grab the back of his shirttails, and he pedals away. After about five or ten minutes we arrive at the windmill, a defunct landmark near the traffic rotary. My you-know-what is totally sore, but I'm not about to complain.

We park the bike in the back and climb up the rickety stairs to the top. Out here in the middle of the Atlantic Ocean, the sky is so inky that the stars look like diamonds spilled on black velvet. They wink at us from overhead. I wink back a thank-you and make a wish.

"To thinking pink, Cinderella," he says as we clink flutes and toast each other. It's only now that I realize the champagne we are drinking is, in fact, pink.

"This time, don't disappear," he says. "All that was left of you was one penny loafer."

"I had a really early appointment—" I start to say.

"Yeah, with a hangover," he says. "I mean, how many beers did we drink that night?"

"Several out of my loafer, apparently," I say, only now getting his Cinderella reference. "I'm impressed your family owns the Inn," I say. "How glamorous."

"Yeah, if you consider it glamorous filling in for the busboy, the dishwasher, or whoever else doesn't show up at the last minute," he says.

"I consider drinking pink champagne by the light of the full moon glamorous," I say.

"Nantucket's got lots of secret pleasures," he says. "You'll see."

"I'll drink to that," I say, and we clink again. After draining our glasses, we move toward each other and lip-lock. Cuisine isn't the only thing French that Grant knows about; he's an expert kisser too. Things get hotter and hotter, and without losing contact we slide down and start rolling around on the hardwood floor. Eventually, we come up for air and Grant rides me home. (This time I sit on the handlebars.)

After a Harlequin Romance month of beach strolls, midnight picnics, and frolicking in unexplored dunes, the first snap of fall in the air gives me a sinking feeling. I've been holding back on going all the way because I'm afraid of our special Nantucket bubble bursting when we return to the reality of school. Thanks to Chandler, I know that not all summer romances are meant to last.

"What's wrong? You look worried," says Grant. We are casting fishing rods into the sea, watching one of our final Sconset sunsets.

"I'm afraid that we'll just be shipboard acquaintances," I say.

"What?" he says.

"Clearly you haven't read *Marjorie Morningstar*," I say. "It refers to a relationship perfectly suited to one environment but not necessarily adaptable to another."

"And that's what you think will happen to us?" he says.

"I hope not, but it happens a lot with clothes. You know, you buy a pair of red lizard cowboy boots on vacation in Texas but never wear them at home. Or once when my dad won a family trip to Jamaica, I had my hair cornrowed like Bo Derek in *10*," I say. "I got off the plane in New York I looked like absolute zero."

He looks at me for a while. Perhaps my weirdness is showing.

"Don't worry about the future so much," he says. "Let life surprise you."

He drops me off and goes to work. I spend the evening eating leftover pizza crusts and watching Johnny Carson until I fall asleep on the couch. Just as I'm hitting REM sleep, I hear, "Wake up, Bella" in my ear. Grant is gently rousing me, and I begin to realize it's not a dream. I jump up, brush my teeth as fast as I can, and in a haze ride on his handlebars back to the Chanticleer, where we slip in the back entrance.

We walk up the steep wooden steps to the top floor, and Grant opens the door and presents me with a maid's room that he has transformed into a boudoir. I love the antique, white chenille bedspread and curtains, wildflowers in a tiny sterling silver vase, and best of all, a window thrust open to let in the sound of the waves crashing on the beach.

"Dinner is served," he says, leading me down to the restaurant's kitchen. While I sit at the butcher's block counter watching, Grant whips up a gourmet feast, with flaming bananas Foster for dessert.

"How do you feel?" asks Grant.

"Like Eloise at the Plaza," I tell him, kissing the end of his nose. I decide right then and there that even if our summer romance doesn't make the transition back to the college campus, Grant has taught me one thing: Some adventures are simply worth having in and of themselves.

9

Year: 1986
Age: 21
Idol: still Madonna
Favorite Song: "Melt with You" (Modern English)
Prized Possession: unlimited Tube pass
Best Shoes: pointy punk boots with lots of zippers

Gamely, I sit in a chair and a girl with a flaming fuchsia Mohawk appears in the mirror behind me. She snaps one of those plastic aprony things around my neck.

"What'll it be, luv?" she says in a thick Cockney accent. I wonder if she's one of Duran Duran's girlfriends or something.

"Um, maybe just a trim," I say, eyeing her coif and losing my nerve. I was lured into Vidal Sassoon by the sign that read STU-DENT DISCOUNT. I'm having a jolly good time reading Charles Dickens, drinking Earl Grey, and tubing into London to see *Cats,* but I feel like I'd fit in better in Oxford if I didn't look so, well, American.

Punk Chick pulls out her shears and starts snipping. Before I can stop her, a six-inch-long hunk of my hair drops to the floor. A few more snips, and she says, "There, that's better."

My once-shoulder-length hair, the same cut I have had since my Dorothy Hamill grew out in ninth grade, is now surrounding me in a dead, furry puddle.

"But aren't you going to even it out?" I say. The left side of my hair stops at my chin, and the right side stops three inches higher, at my ear.

"It's a bi-level," Punk Chick says, yawning. "It's all the rage, luv."

When I show the cashier my student ID, she looks at me quizzically. "For the student discount," I say.

"The *stylists* are students," she informs me. Oh, great, now I have a haircut that's about as cool as a student-driver sign perched on top of my head.

"A *bisexual?*" says Hallie, my Oxford roommate, who hails from Harvard and is witty in a deeply cutting sort of way and actually very nice once you get past the knives.

"A bi-level," I explain, in Punk Chick Cockney. "It's all the rage."

"Hmm," she says, cocking her head this way and that to even me out. "Oh, yes, I get it. When I see your profile from the left you look like a girl, and when you face to the right the short side makes you look like a boy. Very clever. By the way, Grant called." She throws me that candy before she runs from the room so that I don't strangle her.

Grant and I said our good-byes that fall. It was sad, but it was not the violin-accompanied scene I had played out in my mind. When I found out that I got into the Oxford program at the last minute, it was he who urged me to seize the opportunity.

"You're off for your next adventure," he said.

"Promise you'll visit?" I asked.

"When you least expect it," he said, pulling me close and slipping me the tongue. "Expect it."

A lot of girls suffer from the Shop and Return Syndrome. Here are the stages: Intolerable crush on someone unavailable. You obsess, scheme, and plot until you get the guy to like you back. Then, after a few dates, you totally gross out and send him packing. Insert New Crush and Begin Again.

I'm not like that. Having someone who laughs at my jokes

and doesn't mind the ever-swinging pendulum of my weight (and its power to affect my self-worth), keeps me interested. So, remind me, why did I give up spending Grant's senior year with him so I could pursue my studies at Oxford?

The truth is, I've felt as off balance as my haircut ever since Bobby has been freaking out again. Sometimes it's as if my brother and I are on the opposite sides of a seesaw. The better my life goes, the worse his gets. By now I know and almost completely believe that his autism is genetic and has nothing to do with me competitively pushing past him during our birth. Still, I can't help this residual guilty feeling, like I hogged up all the good genes and left him with sloppy seconds.

Then, one Saturday night, the phone call comes. My mother calls but talks briefly, mostly about Bobby and how he's going off the deep end.

In the refrigerator door, the reflection of my haircut looks even more exaggerated, like it would in a fun house mirror. Hallie was right about my haircut. If I turn to the right, I morph into Bobby.

My mother's voice is paper thin and wavery. "This call is expensive, I'd better go," she says before I can even tell her I'm lonely, I'm sad, I'm scared for my brother, and I feel guilty that I'm off in Merry Ol' England having a gay old time. Sometimes, when I should be happy but I'm just not, I want to just blot myself out.

So I do just that with Hallie and some of my new classmates that night. We're in the Bird and Babe, that's Oxford English for the Eagle and Child, and I'm on my fourth half-pint of Guinness when I feel someone tug on one of my last remaining curls. I spin around and am shocked to find myself nose to nose with— *Professor Whitford?*

"Thought that wazzzyouu," he slurs. "But you've shangged into a walking topiary."

"Professor Whitford, what are you doing here?" I ask.

"Some biznesss needed my attenshionn," he says. "I'm finishing the semester at Oxford."

"But what about your Notre Dame Honors classes?" I ask, still amazed to be seeing him. Drunk. And in faded Levi's.

"My colleague from Oxford will be finishing the semester for me," he explains.

Whitford gives me the once-over, and I do likewise. He looks totally different in jeans, smoking a cigarette. His hair, which is normally combed down on his forehead, is pushed back, which for the first time makes him look handsome, in a *Brideshead Revisited* sort of way. I can see why some of the girls in my class had crushes on him. Stop it, I tell myself—it's the ye olde ale spectacles doing my thinking again.

"Your hair," I say.

"*Your* hair!" he says. "Are you going to go back so they can cut the other side?"

"It's a bi-level," I explain. "Vidal Sassoon."

"You're bi? So does that mean you like girls too, Bella? *Hmmmm?*" he says, leaning over and brushing his hand across my bottom.

"Professor Whitford!" I say, mimicking a shocked British accent, only the shocked part is real.

"Call me Niles," he says.

"I can't," I say. "You're my teacher."

"Not anymore," he says.

Hallie, who has been amusing herself with some Argentinian polo players, joins us. I introduce her, and "Niles" puts on the charm, insisting on picking up round after round as we pump the jukebox and listen to "Rock Me Amadeus." When the bar staff rings the bell for orders, Whitford leads us down several back alleys, past what seems like endless rows of tiny houses to an after-hours club.

I don't realize how trashed I am until I attempt my lip liner in the bathroom. My, how this little red pencil really misbehaves after a few drinks. I stumble back to our table and come upon "Niles" on his way to the loo. We bump into each other on the dark stairway.

"What happened to you in there," he says, putting his face close to mine. "Did you get attacked by a big lipstick?"

I lick my hand and try to wipe off my clown mouth.

He pulls out his hanky and says, "Here, let me give it a go." He's so close I can smell the fifteen-year-old scotch on his breath.

But his hand doesn't make it to my mouth. It stops at chest level, where it gives me a quick pinch.

"Ow!" I say, shocked by the fact that he just touched my breast, and not gently either. What strange English custom is this? Is this British foreplay? Or does he enjoy being kneed in the nuts?

"What?" he says, suddenly acting innocent. I may have had a few drinks, but I know what I felt.

"You pinched me!" I sputter, "On—on—on the *nipple!*"

"Well, accidentally, perhaps," he mumbles and shrugs. The Innocent Act again. Then he leans over me and gives me a little peck on the cheek.

Suddenly I am overcome with the nervous giggles.

Whitford starts laughing too, but a full-throated, deep, husky laugh. And then he lunges toward me, pushes me against the back wall, and presses his body against mine. Either he has a pencil (long, thin, and pointy) in his pocket or he's happy to see me.

Before I know what's happening, I'm making out with my enemy. Tongues a-flyin', pencils a-pokin'—and *oh, my God.*

We come up for air, and he takes me by the hand and tugs me up the stairs and into a velvet corner booth where we sit and have our Moment of Truth. His secrets come tumbling out, starting with his first impression of me (he thought I was "zaftig and sexy, like a forties film star"), our year-long feud ("verbal foreplay"), and what he *really* thinks of me ("repressed by that Good-Girl Catholic brainwashing").

"But I've got some ideas on how to cure you of that," he says, resting his hand on my knee.

"Do you?" I ask, borrowing his Innocent Act.

This guy fantasizes about me? My mind swirls with black-and-white, slapstick movie footage of me in a flapper dress, and him, like a horny Charlie Chaplin, chasing me around and around a bed. I'm starting to feel flushed—from the waist down. The funny music stops suddenly with a close-up of the Virgin Mary's disapproving face.

"Professor Whitford—" I start.

"Niles, Bella, Niles," he says, interrupting my home movie. He squeezes my knee under the table and says in a husky whisper, "How about a nightcap at my place?"

"Okay, let me see if Hallie wants to come," I say. Safety in numbers. But Hallie decides to party on with her new polo player pals. What the hell, I think.

Niles's flat looks just like I pictured it, filled with beautiful, leather-bound books and old prints of hunting dogs and geese and stuff. I ask to use his loo while he starts a fire and fixes us another drink. Just what we need at this point.

"Oh, my God!" I say to myself in the mirror, giggling. "I am A Broad Junior Year!"

I rummage through his medicine cabinet (hemorrhoid medicine, *ewww!*) and squirt some toothpaste on my finger, which I use as a toothbrush. I also take some "paracetamol," which sounds from the label like it might be like aspirin or Tylenol, but who knows as the letters refuse to stay still. I already know the Hangover Gremlin has scheduled an early morning visit.

When I go back to the living room, the fire is roaring, but Niles isn't there. I wander until I find him in the bedroom sound asleep, snoring to beat the band. The Clash song "Should I Stay or Should I Go?" pops into my head.

I know I should go, but I don't have the strength. It's like the quiet after the balloon has burst—I suddenly feel very still and deflated and small. Although Grant and I have written a few times, getting him or Carrie on the phone has been impossible. Professor Whitford *is* from home, and he knows me. We talked tonight like I haven't been able to talk to anyone in a while, without having to explain everything. And besides, why should I listen to that little voice? After all, my judgment is clearly off. For two years I've been thinking this man hated me, and meanwhile I've been starring in his fantasies as a femme fatale!

The next morning I wake up to the groping hands of Professor Whitford, who, overnight, has transformed into a human octopus. My what-the-hell attitude has transformed into what-the-hell-have-I-done?

"Bad girl, go to my room," he murmurs. "Oh, you *are* in my room. Oh, you naughty little sausage!"

Then he's kissing me, before I can even brush my teeth. The gremlin is banging, and everything seems fuzzy. I succumb but fend off doing the deed. He seems wryly amused by my rules. Fooling around is one thing, but sex? Even in my confused state, I know I'm not ready for that.

I do my first British Walk of Shame, and I really do feel shameful. I'm not even sure if I like him, but one thing I know for sure: I need to get him to like me, or I'll really be a naïve, stupid slut. It's that same set of unwritten rules that says sleeping with someone is okay if you are in love with each other. I don't think I'll be able to live with myself if I can't get him to like me. If he calls and we go on a few dates, it will mean that I wasn't used, after all. If he shows a little respect, then I'll be able to respect myself.

I then wait all day too hungover to do anything but wait for his phone call, which doesn't come. I eat an entire pack of McVities biscuits, and then order in for Indian food. I decide to call Carrie. Maybe I'll get lucky and catch her for once.

She picks up the phone on the second ring, and my stomach leaps.

"You are not going to believe who I had an Away Game with last night," I blurt.

"Um, Billie Idol?" she guesses. "Are you going to have a White Wedding?"

I hold my breath. Should I tell her? Somehow telling a friend makes it real. If I don't tell anyone maybe it will all go away. But this one is like a burp after chugging a beer—I don't think I can keep it in.

"Oxford-Moron," I hiss and wait for her reaction.

"No!" she says, gasping.

"Yup," I say.

"Bella, I heard he was fired," she says. "There's some rumor going around about him. I don't know what it is, but I can try to find out."

"No, he wasn't fired," I clarify. "They needed him back here for some . . ." My mind goes blank. "He told me. I just can't remember."

"Oh," she says. "What about Grant?"

"You know how carpe diem Grant is. We had a talk about seeing other people while we were apart, you know, 'Dating Lite,'" I explain. "Our agreement is we'd tell each other only if it turned into something serious."

"Yeah, you've taken 'drink 'til he's cute' to the next level, Bella," she says, laughing. "Has he called?"

"No," I say.

"Oh," she says. We both know this is the icky part. We finish our chat with loads of gossip but nothing can really top my revelation.

The icky part lasts two weeks, during which I replay every moment of our encounter and list all the reasons I am gross and unworthy and why Whitford would never call.

Just when I'm about to give up and face the fact that I'm a slut, "Niles" calls drunk from a pub, where he's watching a rugby match on TV.

"Bella, why don't you pop over?" he murmurs into the phone. "I've been tied up in meetings, but I can't get you out of my mind. Really, so'd love to see you."

"Um," I say, not wanting to appear too eager, but relieved that he's called, preventing our encounter from being a one-night stand.

"Let my eyes dance around your forties-film-star elegance," he says, using his poshest accent. I think, all right, just as long as it's your eyes and not your hands doing the dancing.

I let myself be persuaded and meet him at the Eagle and Child, and we discuss philosophy for hours while we watch the rugby matches. He's intrigued by a paper I wrote in which I compared the Age of Reason to a volcano.

"You really have the most unique mind of any student I have ever taught," he says, and we head back to his place to "make a fire."

We get there just before the rain.

"Hungry?" he says.

"Starving!" I say. "Should we order out for curry?"

"Come here," he says from the kitchen. I walk to where he's standing in front of the refrigerator. He's holding a blindfold.

"What's that for?" I ask.

"Come closer," he says in that stern voice he's so often used in class, ignoring my question.

I do as he says. I know it's been done before, and probably better, in *9½ Weeks,* but something lures me in anyway. He ties the blindfold on me and starts kissing the back of my neck. Then I hear him open the refrigerator door and then some paper crinkling.

"Open your mouth," he whispers in my ear.

I'm not sure what the taste is, but it's salty and rich. It takes me a while to figure out that it's smoked salmon. As I focus on the taste, he runs his hand under my shirt. Next he puts something sweet into my mouth.

"Mm, I like this," I tell him. "Valrhona?"

"Very good," he murmurs from beneath my shirt, where he is kissing my breasts. "Would you like some more?"

"Yes," I say.

But the next thing he puts on my tongue has a totally different texture, and suddenly my mouth is on fire! I spit it out on the floor and start grabbing at the blindfold. He grabs my wrists and presses his whole body against me and starts kissing me passionately.

"Now, now now," he says soothingly. "I thought you liked hot stuff. After all, you *are* hot stuff."

I feel foolish for overreacting, but getting a mouthful of wasabi when you are expecting chocolate, while experiencing sensory deprivation and getting felt up, well, it's just weird. Check, please. I'm outta here.

"Okay, okay," he says, sensing my unease. "Our little game is over. Just trying to broaden your horizons, relieve you of your repression."

"I think I should go now," I tell him while moving toward the door. Even if I am a repressed Catholic girl, I like it that way.

"But I have a lovely afternoon planned for you," he says, suddenly becoming very meek and all lovey-dovey. He stokes the fire and brings out an expensive bottle of French wine.

Then the sun comes out.

"Let me take you punting," he says, grabbing a blanket and the wine.

We head to the Cherwell, an almost stagnant river, where we rent a fifteen-foot flat-bottomed boat. Niles works the pole to propel the boat forward by pushing off the river's bottom. As I lie back on the blanket and uncork the wine and take in the scenery, we talk about the books we love.

"Have you read *Zen and the Art of Motorcycle Maintenance?*" I ask.

"Pirsig, brilliant!" he says, his eyes sparkling. "Why do you ask?"

"Because there are themes in that book about stuff that you taught us," I say. "Bits of Pascal and Montaigne."

"Yes, Bella, exactly, you clever girl!" he says. "That novel contains much of what we covered in the nineteenth-century philosophers course."

It makes me feel really smart to be able to keep up with him as we discuss literature and philosophy. He's so confident, and I love how in charge he is. Smart can be even sexier than big, I decide.

As we walk home, he stops in front of the market.

"Wait here," he says in that bossy way of his that I'm really coming to like.

He reappears with a dozen white tulips. "For Oxford's most beautiful mind," he says, bowing down as he presents them. I feel really special, as if he has glimpsed into me and appreciated something that no one else has ever noticed.

When Hallie decides to go to Amsterdam, I invite Niles to our place for the weekend. I'm definitely *not* going to sleep with him, I tell myself. Still, things have gone far enough, and I need to fill Grant in. I'm doing the carpe diem thing here. He should be feeling free to do what he wants too.

I write a letter, explaining everything and walk it to the post-box.

When I return, Niles is already there, singing opera in the shower.

"Hallie, Haddie, what's-her-name, let me in on her way out," he says, popping his head out of the shower curtain. "Care to join me?"

"No, thanks, but take your time," I say. I hate that whole looking at each other naked thing. Some things, like my body in broad daylight, are none of my business, never mind someone else's.

He emerges in my purple terry robe, which grosses me out just the teeniest bit. "When you said your flatmate was going to Amsterdam, it reminded me that I had a stash myself," he says, pulling out a joint.

"I quit that in eighth grade," I tell him.

"What were you, twelve?" he says.

"Yeah," I say. "But it makes me so paranoid that I had a Bette Midler hallucination. She told me to be myself and quit smoking pot, so I did."

"I'll keep you safe," he says, putting the joint in my mouth. I guess one hit won't do much. Or two.

Wow, I was wrong. I feel like I'm in some sort of dream.

After we stub out the tiny roach, Niles says, "Guess I should have warned you—it's laced with hash."

"Yeah," I say. And almost immediately: "I've got the munchies. But promise you won't whip out your blindfold. Let's go see if there's anything to eat."

I go into the kitchen and open the fridge to see the usual suspects—condiments and not much else. I phone the Chinese delivery service. They tell me it will be at least half an hour.

"I don't think I can wait that long," I tell him.

"Perhaps I better distract you," he says, kissing me hard on the mouth. We move it to the bedroom, where he starts pulling off my clothes. It seems sort of rough, but maybe it's just that I'm paranoid. All I know is within no time I'm totally naked.

Suddenly he leapfrogs out of the bed and goes into his

overnight bag. He pulls out two silk neckties. "It's just a silly little game," he murmurs into my ear. "But I brought my Hermès, because only the best will do for you, my dear."

Before I can say anything, he has bound each of my wrists to a bedpost with a tie. He's slithering up between my legs. I can't stand it one more second, and I protest.

"Niles," I start. "This is just a little too weird—" But I'm interrupted by a loud knock on the door.

"Saved by the bell, as it were," he says. "Must be the Chinese food."

When Whitford opens the door, however, it is not the Szechwan beef and moo shoo pork we were expecting, but rather a special delivery, all the way from Southbend, Indiana.

There I am, strapped wearing nothing to the bed, but bracelets made out of Hermès silk ties. My naked professor, holding a twenty-pound note in front of his privates. And Grant, with a bottle of Dom in one hand and a duffle bag in the other.

"Bella, what the hell . . ." Grant says, finally breaking the silence, "did you do to your hair?"

"Long story," I say weakly. "But I'm a little tied up at the moment."

10

Year: 1986 (spring)
Age: 21
Idol: Meryl Streep in Out of Africa
Favorite Song: "Avalon" (Roxy Music)
Prized Possession: portrait
Best Shoes: white pointy boots with gold piping

I feel dirty inside and out. You know Pigpen's dirt cloud on *Peanuts*? If you could see my depression, that's pretty much what it would look like, a big Gray Cloud that follows me around everywhere.

It's been a few months since the silk tie incident, but I still feel like it just happened. As if it's not bad enough that I screwed up everything with Grant, Carrie called back to tell that the reason Whitford was fired was for sampling the coed merchandise. At least three different students came forward to admit that they each had been seduced with his flattery of being "Notre Dame's most beautiful mind." I can't believe I fell for that shit. But I learned one thing. You can punish yourself with men even better than you can with food, if you're feeling guilty enough. Even though I'm a world away, I can't stop talking about my brother.

Speaking of food, I need to take control of my life. If I could just lose a little weight, I'd cheer up. I just need a little snack first. Before I can even stop myself, I polish off all the leftover Chinese food and for lack of a better dessert, eat some frozen hot dog buns doused with maple syrup. Food coma settles in, and I sit on the couch and stare at nothing. God, I'm so full I have to unbutton my pants.

As I wallow in self-disgust, the phone rings. I feel ashamed, as if someone has been watching me and is calling to rat me out.

I don't want to talk to anyone. The phone continues with its stupid, English *bleep-bleep* of a ring. Can't a girl with self-loathing thoughts be left alone?

Bleep-bleep, bleep-bleep. After another five minutes of the ringing I try to zip up my pants and pick up the receiver.

"Say your prayers, varmint!" A loud robotic voice blasts my ear, followed by that familiar gale of odd laughter.

"Bobby?" I say. I can't believe it! Never once have I received a phone call from him. Plus, isn't he locked away in Meadowbrook?

"Holy visits to England, Batman!" he says.

I'm confused. Imagining his unhappiness is what set off my tragic chain of events, but he sounds fine. Meanwhile, I'm a used slut in a food coma.

Suddenly it's my father on the phone. "How's my girl? Great?" he says, not waiting for an answer. "Hey, so are you up for a visitor?"

"Bobby's coming to London?" I say, scratching my head. "Have they released him yet?"

"No, but the doctors thought if he had something to look forward to, a goal to work toward, it would help him," he explains. "He keeps saying, 'Holy Big Ben, Batman.'"

"Wow," I say. "When?"

"If all goes well, about a month from now," he says. "Okay with you, sweetie?" Sweetie, that's a joke. The sweetest thing in me is undigested frozen hot dog buns with maple syrup.

"Sure!" I say, my stomach lurching. I'm in the middle of my own mess—I don't know if I can take on my brother too. "Can I say hi to Mom?" I ask, changing the subject. I've been aching for some TLC, and I could really use a good cry to my mother.

"Uh, she's busy with Bobby's doctors. We'd better go. This call is costing us a fortune. Just wanted to call with the news," he says and signs off.

The next morning, as soon as I open my eyes, I remember that Bobby is coming to visit. For some reason this gives me hope. If he can pull himself out of a black hole, then so can I. A rogue thought crosses over the Gray Cloud's enemy lines and darts into my head: *Anything can happen to you today.*

I heave-ho myself out of bed. *Anything can happen to you today,* I tell myself as I go through the motions of my routine. Think about lunch during morning classes, eat lunch, then think about dinner during my afternoon classes.

The next day I do it again, reminding myself, *Anything can happen to you today.*

The third day, I'm walking down my block toward home, and I see that something *has* happened. The Universe has placed the most beautiful man on the entire earth on my stoop!

"So terribly sorry to disturb you, but it seems I've been locked out," the Greek god Adonis says to me shyly. "Would you mind if I climbed over your balcony to get in?"

"Not at all!" I say, opening the door to my flat.

I lead the way to my room, wondering how fat my butt looks in the pants I'm wearing. We stomp through a minefield of my dirty underpants and cookie wrappers to get to the balcony.

"Sorry," I say, waving to my mess. "Roommate's a total slob."

"Are you American?" Adonis says.

"Yes. I'm over here for school," I say.

"Right. Well, thanks a lot," he says, disappearing out of my window. He pops his head back in, and says, "Saved my life, by the way."

Wait! Wait! Wait! I think. Please come back so I can feast my eyes! But even if he never comes back, something *did* happen. It's a sign to have hope. Hope leads to more hope, I think.

The next evening, Hallie and I are sitting down to dinner when there's a knock at the door.

When I open it, it's Adonis with a bottle of Chianti.

"Uh, hello," he says shyly. "I just wanted to thank you for the use of your balcony."

"How sweet!" I say. "Come on in and meet my roommate, Hallie."

In the kitchen, Adonis introduces himself as Johnner. His beauty stops Hallie in midsentence. Suddenly the atmosphere in the room changes. It's subtle, yet palpable. Hallie's one-upmanship, passive-aggressive put-downs, and strategically flirty comments make it clear that it's a competition and the prize is Johnner. I've never really been good at this, so I keep my mouth shut and listen to them talk.

When she starts asking Johnner questions like how long he's lived next door and what he does for a living, and he divulges that he's doing construction on the flat, she starts losing interest. And then her boyfriend calls from the States, forcing her to forfeit.

That leaves me, the cheese, standing alone. We discuss the Hockney show at the Tate Gallery, and I learn that Johnner graduated top of his class in art college. The construction gig is only to support his habit, which, at the moment, is sculpture.

Speaking of sculpture, luckily for me, Johnner is working shirtless out front the next day when I come home from classes. The muscles in his back are a work of art in and of themselves.

"Excuse me, Bella," he says, stopping me. "Want to go sightseeing in London? I'm off tomorrow."

Oh, my God, he wants to be seen in public with me? Even if this is just part of the thank-you, I am so flattered and excited that I glide through the next twenty-four hours without one single cookie. I mean, not one hunger pang.

The next afternoon we jump on a double-decker bus, head to the very front, and take a seat.

"Vroom with a view," he says.

He points out the sights along the way, personalizing them with tidbits from his past; the pub where he ordered his first pint, the corner where he crashed his Mini Cooper, his favorite bits of architecture.

"This is the Tower Bridge," he says as we pass the mammoth structure. "It was built in the late eighteen hundreds, and it encapsulates the concern for history and modern building technology," he explains. "But in its own topsy-turvy way, it's really a happy marriage."

Suddenly it starts to rain, then pour. Johnner pulls his poncho around me, and we cozily huddle beneath it. As we drive along, I marvel at his sensitivity toward me, the way he attends to my every need, making sure I'm covered with the poncho, asking if I'm comfortable. If I could pay attention to myself the way he does, maybe I would finally understand what all those women's magazine articles mean about "Be Your Own Best Friend."

After the weather clears, we go to feed the pelicans, swans, and ducks in St. James's Park. As we sit on a bench, he perfectly mimics my American accent, and we start talking about music. I love Pet Shop Boys, INXS, and Simple Minds. He loves Flock of Seagulls, O.M.D., and Duran Duran. But we both love the old stuff, Stones, Roxy Music, and Bowie.

"Let's go," he says.

"Where?" I say.

"Everywhere!" he stands up and yells, opening his arms to the sky and spinning around. People stop and stare. Is he crazy?

"Let's go on a scavenger hunt for the best jukeboxes in London," he says, pulling me to my feet. His enthusiasm is infectious, and we are suddenly sprinting through a flock of pigeons hand in hand. As they take flight around us, I feel something open and free inside myself too. For the first time since Chandler, I feel like I'm falling in love.

At the Kings and Cross on Cheney Walk, we sip our pints of

beer surrounded by super trendy London types and punk rockers. My bi-level haircut looks as frumpy as a beehive compared to the rainbow-colored Mohawks and tattooed skinheads around us.

"You go first," he says, handing me some pounds for the juke-box. I punch in one of my Stones' favorites, "Angie."

"Rumor has it that Mick wrote this for his wife——" he says.

"How sweet," I say.

"——after she caught him in bed with David Bowie," he finishes.

"Oh," I say, "No wonder about the line 'I can see the sadness in your eye.'"

We sit, our heads close together, sipping our Guinness, listening to the words.

"Your turn," I say.

Next Johnner punches in one of my favorite Bowie songs, "Heroes."

"What's this song about?" I ask.

"Bowie wrote this about a couple in love who are on different sides of the Berlin Wall, so they can't be together," he says, his lips so close to my ear that they give me a shiver.

"So that's why they want to be dolphins, so they can swim to see each other," I whisper back.

Johnner knows so much about art and music. And with that accent, I could listen to him talk about car mechanics. But before you know it, we have to catch the train back to Oxford.

When our train deposits us at the station, I'm disappointed the night is over, but Johnner is the one who looks worried.

"Bella, I have a confession to make," he says.

He's going to tell me he has a girlfriend, or worse, a wife. Or two Hermès ties he wants me to get acquainted with. I hold my breath.

"I was hoping it would be you," he says.

"Me what?" I say.

"I was hoping you would be the one to let me in the other night," he says.

"But we've never seen each other before," I say.

"Ah, but I've seen you," he says.

He takes me by the hand and we wander home in the pitch-black of night. We go back to his gutted flat, which is not much more than a construction site with a lightbulb hanging from the ceiling. When he switches it on, however, the walls are adorned with huge murals. All of me, lying on my bed.

I stare at the charcoal drawings, blinking hard. Because I can't believe what I'm seeing. I look like Botticelli's Venus. All soft curves, wild hair floating, a beautiful, faraway stare, the very essence of a female goddess.

"Room with a view," I say.

"You've been my muse for weeks, actually," he says quietly from a dark corner of the room. "I hope you don't mind."

"But how could you even see me?" I ask. *Oh, my God, has he watched me pig out in the kitchen too? Eeeek!*

"I couldn't directly, but look," he says, pointing out the back window of his flat. His room is one floor above mine and catty-cornered. If you look down you can see the mirrored wall of my bedroom, which is reflecting my now empty bed.

Now I could have been very creeped out, in that I-wear-my-sunglasses-at-night-so-I-can-so-I-can-watch-you-song type of way. But for some reason I'm not. Even though I know I don't know him, I feel like I do. Second of all, I'm astounded by the way I look in his paintings. I'm wearing the white lace vintage nightgown I bought from the Portobello Road flea market, and my hair is wild. The simple lines really convey my mood, even the way the linen drapes my body looks listless, hopeless, depleted of life. I'm struck by the way he has drawn me from the inside out, as if he really knows me.

We look at the renderings together. "You looked so sad," he says.

"Yes," I whisper. "I was."

"So sad, but so beautiful," he says. From behind, he wraps his arms around me and pulls me toward him. He kisses the nape of my neck and whispers in my ear, "Like a Greek goddess. Stay."

His makeshift bed is no more than some sheets and blankets on a pile of folded-up newspapers and drop cloths. I put on the T-shirt he has worn that day so I can wear his scent and slip beneath the sheets. As he strips all the way down, the candlelight flickers on his corrugated muscles. Maybe this is what all those bodice-ripper Harlequin Romances mean by the word "lust." I've never known that I was capable of having "aching loins" until this very moment.

We stay up until dawn, kissing and talking and touching until the sky turns pinky purple, and we nod off in each other's arms. He doesn't even try to have sex with me, which makes me fall all the deeper for him. When I open my eyes a few hours later, though, Johnner's not beside me. I roll over to find him across the room, sitting in a paint-splattered chair, sketchbook in hand.

"Sorry, but having you right in front of me rather than watching you through the mirror was just too much of a temptation," he says.

I suddenly notice that during my slumber I'd kicked off the sheets. My thunderous thighs totally exposed! Miles of dimpled, disgusting flesh, out in the open! In a panic, I yank the sheets up to cover myself.

"Bella, don't!" he says, flicking his eyes from his sketchpad to my body. "You'll ruin it."

"I hate them," I admit, hiding my face in a pillow. My thighs are hardly worth looking at, let alone drawing. When I catch my reflection in a store window, I visually cut off my lower half and pretend it doesn't belong to me. My face burns hot into the pillow.

Johnner crosses the room so quiet and catlike I don't even know he's next to me until I feel his callused fingers stroking my back.

"But I *love* them," he says.

He said "love." This makes my stomach twinge. Not since Chandler has a guy used that word in a way that had anything to do with me. Not even a part of me.

"How can you call your body horrid names, when all I can see are voluptuous fruits?" he says in a low, totally sexy voice. "Succulent, juicy, exotic fruits."

He nibbles me, and I laugh.

"Okay, okay," I say, pulling him forward to kiss him, grabbing his sketchpad. "Let's see the Horn 'o Plenty."

"No!" he says, shrieking like a girl and jumping up.

It strikes me—he's as self-conscious of his art as I am of my body.

"Johnner," I say. "How about this, for the rest of the time we have together, I'll trust you, if you trust me."

We look at each other for a full minute. Be brave, I tell myself. I pull back the covers to reveal my legs. Tentatively he shows me his drawing.

I gasp. I look even more beautiful than I do in the murals. I realize for the first time that the corny cliché is true: Beauty is in the eye of the beholder. It's the way that Johnner sees the world that makes him an artist. He looks without judgment, past the obvious, to see the latent beauty in everything. My thighs as organic treasures, and his construction job as an opportunity to work with his hands.

Staring at the portrait, I try to burn his Botticellian version of reality into my brain, replacing my fat ugly one. Long, fluid, curvy lines, the very essence of femininity, and they converge to look like me. Then I lead him back to the bed, and I start to make love to him. After a while, he stops and looks at me tentatively. But I show him with my mouth and hands that this is my decision. He makes me feel beautiful, and I want to share myself with him. As our skin rubs together and our sweat intermingles, I've never felt closer to anyone in my life.

Over the next few weeks, I realize that Johnner's uncritical perception of the world is contagious. I start feeling like a unique and beautiful creature, able to inspire great art, rather than like an overweight American with an unfortunate haircut.

But as we fall more deeply in love, I'm aware of the countdown until Bobby's visit. For the fist time in my life, I feel as light and happy and carefree as the pigeons we skipped past on our first date in St. James's Park. Bobby coming is like romance interruptus.

I give myself a strict talking-to: I am going to be in control and make sure that Bobby has a good visit, no matter how badly I just want to be alone with Johnner.

The day of Bobby's arrival, Johnner comes with me to Gatwick Airport. As we wait, I try to explain my brother the best I can—his too-loud voice, his rigid routines, obsessions with cartoon characters, stiff posture, and the funny gaze that always makes him look out of it.

Finally I spot Bobby scuttling out through security, his eyes glued to my feet. He's wearing his Spock ears, which I'm sure gave his fellow riders some food for thought on that eight-hour flight. Here we go.

"No-good bushwakin' barracuda!" he says to me when he finally reaches us. Yosemite Sam. At least we're off to a good start.

"Bobby, this is Johnner. He's my special friend," I say.

I watch as Bobby checks him out with his peripheral vision. "Prepare to defend yourself, rabbit," he says, " 'cause I'm boardin' your ship!" More Yosemite. I start to relax.

The three of us spend the next week exploring Oxford and doing all of London's Greatest Hits: the London Tower, Big Ben, Trafalgar Square. But what Bobby loves best of everything is the London Underground. He has the whole map memorized the very first day.

"If it were up to him, we'd spend all afternoon on the Tube, instead of actually going anywhere," I say to Johnner as the three of us walk to the Kensington station to head to the British Museum.

"Well, why not, then?" says Johnner.

"All right." I shrug. "Bobby, take us away."

"Holy Change at Charing Cross, Batman!" he says excitedly, tracing his finger along the colorful Underground map outside the station. "We connect at Sloane Square."

Bobby swipes his pass and leads us down the escalators. The train comes into the station, we listen to Bobby mimic the automated "Mind the gap" warning, and we jostle in with the other straphanging riders.

As the stops come and go, we eventually get seats, Johnner and I together, and Bobby across the car. Johnner and I pass the time by watching the people, as if we're watching live theater. We make comments to each other about what they're wearing or invent crazy things they might be carrying in their bags. Meanwhile, Bobby stares straight ahead, looking happily stoned. It reminds me of how little babies are soothed by riding in the car.

Then, at Sloane Square, a bunch of punk rockers board the train. One skinhead, dressed in black vinyl, has a face filled with safety pins, and another has a bloodred Mohawk. They have a menacing air about them, and I'm a little nervous that they are standing directly in Bobby's line of sight.

Sure enough, it starts.

"Aye, mate, what would you be looking at?" says the skinhead in black loudly, right in Bobby's face.

I notice the skinhead noticing Bobby's Spock ears, which he has worn every day here. My heart begins to race, and I can feel Johnner tense next to me. But Bobby remains cool as a cucumber.

"Excuse me, sir," Bobby says in a robotic British accent, not Cockney like the Skinhead but upper-crust. "Would you happen to have any Grey Poupon?"

The skinhead bends down so he's eye level with Bobby, who is seated. In fact, they are nose to nose, which I know is too close for Bobby's comfort zone.

"Come again?" says the skinhead.

Without missing a beat, Bobby says, "Mind the gap!" at the top of his lungs.

The skinhead is so startled that he reels backward into his friends, who all start laughing at him. Just then, the doors open and they all tumble out.

Johnner and I are so surprised that we burst out laughing. Johnner is nothing if not nonjudgmental about Bobby. When you accept Bobby for who he is, and don't expect him to be "normal," it really takes the pressure off. I don't feel embarrassed about everything that comes out of his mouth, as if I am responsible for all of his non sequiturs. Through Johnner's eyes I'm able to see Bobby as fascinating—instead of a freak of nature—for the first time.

Bobby's last day we do make it to the British Museum. We're looking at a bronze Henry Moore sculpture of a mother and child. I mention to Johnner how powerful the sculpture's simple lines are.

"That's because sculpture is as much about what *isn't* there as what *is*," he says. "It's the negative space that gives shape to the form."

"Hey, Bobby, come check this out," I say, wanting to share this with my brother. As usual, he has wandered off and is staring at the only thing that isn't a piece of art in the entire room: the red blinking light of the smoke detector.

"No, Bella, let him enjoy what he enjoys," Johnner says gently. "You have to accept him for all the things that he is, and all the things that he isn't."

I glance back at the Moore sculpture and try to let the wisdom of this sink in. He's right, but, but, but, well, it's not that easy!

"Yeah, but what if something happens to my parents?" I say. "Then it's going to be up to me to cure him."

"Cure him or care for him?" Johnner says. "There's a big difference."

"Well, at least find a way for him to be happy," I say.

"How do you know he's not happy?" he asks.

Good question. I had always assumed Bobby was unhappy because of his failure to function in the world. But it's hard to detect his emotions, aside from the basic ones that flare up, like frustration and fear.

"Well, he's always in and out of the hospital and stuff," I say. "That can't make him happy."

"He seems content to me," Johnner says as we walk over to him. "You seem to be having more of a problem accepting his condition than he does."

"Let's ask him," I say. "Hey, Bobby, are you happy?"

"Emotions are alien to me. I am a scientist," he says, quoting Mr. Spock. "Madness has no purpose. Or reason. But it may have a goal."

Johnner laughs, and I do too. "Guess I deserved that," I say.

Before I know it, the visit I had been dreading has sped by. The three of us return to Gatwick to see Bobby off. The visit has gone so well, and I'm feeling so in love and happy, that I spontaneously hug my brother at the gate. It's a mistake.

"Nooo!" Bobby wails. "Mind the gap! Mind the gap!" He recoils as if I have struck him.

"Sorry!" I say. I know I shouldn't have done that. I was just going with the surge of affection I felt for him in the moment. I actually feel a little sad that he's going home.

But my hugging faux pas is not a total disaster. Before long, Bobby stops smacking his head and calms down. Johnner, looking on, says nonchalantly, "So your brother's not a hugger, no big deal."

I try to make myself believe, yeah, it's no big deal and accept who Bobby is without always expecting something more from him. We watch as Bobby, muttering "Fly the Friendly Skies," makes his way down the ramp, never once looking back to say good-bye.

A few months later, Johnny and I have a good-bye scene at Gatwick that plays out a little differently. Let's just say that, well, we are both huggers.

"Get a room!" a rowdy group of American students yells at us as we shamelessly maul each other at the gate. Johnner has tears in his eyes, but I am not sad at all. I am filled with happiness at the thought of our future together. So what if I saw a Speedo bathing suit in his drawer? Other than that he's perfect, and we've made a big decision. As soon as I graduate college, we're going to get married!

11

Year: 1987
Age: 22
Idol: New York Times *columnist Anna Quindlen*
Favorite Song: "With or Without You" (U2)
Prized Possession: my first byline
Best Shoes: black patent leather Joan and David flats with bows

"*B*ella, I've got Steve Guttenberg on line one, Melanie Griffith on line two, and Nora Ephron on line three—all for you," says the receptionist in her usual bored Bronx accent. "Wha-da-ya want me ta do?"

My title is Editorial Assistant. Translation: Slave Girl. My responsibilities include answering phones, faxing, filling out expense accounts, doing research and any other grunt work required of my three bosses. I do the reporting on upcoming film roundups for free. Sounds glamorous, but turns out to be about as glamorous as keeping up a long-distance relationship with Johnner. A lot of phone work with no payoff.

My salary is a measly $16,000 a year, which means I'll be living at home for a while. Carrie, meanwhile, scored a primo job as a media buyer at Chiat Day, a top ad agency, for twice that salary. She's living downtown in a cool Tribeca loft, going to the Odeon every night to meet cute guys on her expense account.

Life for me, however, is more like Bright Lights, Big Suburb. As far as my parents are concerned, it's as if I'm still in high school. Here are the questions I get asked on a daily basis: "Are you going to be home for dinner?" *How should I know? It's 7 A.M.* "Are you really going to wear that?" *Considering I'm late for the train, that'd be a good guess.* And my favorite, "Why don't you take your brother with you? He might meet someone nice." *Um, Earth to Mom. The problem is him, not the people he meets.*

But I'm in a total holding pattern until Johnner gets here. *If* he gets here. Let's just say I'm learning that getting what you've always wanted doesn't always make you happy.

"Having a boyfriend" has made me sort of miserable. Instead of enjoying my senior year, I spent all my time scheming on how to get back to London. I even got a job at Ann Taylor, and after exclaiming "Wow, that makes you look really thin!" about a million times, I earned enough commission to buy a transatlantic ticket on People's Express. So while my fellow classmates were all spring-breaking in Cancun, I was sleeping on the floor of Johnner's latest construction site.

The worst part was Johnner's mood that entire week. Dark and stormy, to say the least. Whenever I'd try to find out what the problem was, he'd just say, "I can't stand being away from you," even though I was right there beside him. The only thing that ever cheered him up was discussing our future together.

I could just picture it: Us living in an enormous loft downtown in Soho, Johnner getting discovered as the next David Salle and being celebrated on the cover of *New York Magazine*. I'll be a famous, oh, I don't know, but who cares? I'll be married to a beautiful, famous artist! And Andy Warhol will show up at our wedding.

But that was six months ago, and *still* no working papers. In the meantime, though, something inside me is shaking its head *no, no no*.

At first I ignore it. *Shut up. You'll ruin everything*, I tell it. *Getting married is what you've always wanted.* Not only is Johnner literally the most beautiful man on earth, but who else is going to make me feel like Botticelli's Venus with thighs like these?

But the inner head-shaking persists. Then a rogue thought

crosses the wedding fantasy firmly occupying the Hopes and Dreams section of my brain: Perhaps there is something that my heart desires even *more* than getting married. I don't have a clue what it is, but I can no longer ignore the gut feeling that's clearly telling me this: *Go find out.*

My plan was to tell Johnner the truth when he comes to visit next month, to meet my parents and have "The Talk" with my father. At this point, my parents have no clue how serious we've become, despite the fact that they know Johnner's planning to move here. The Ostrich Approach. And in this case, it may have worked. If there is one thing I wasn't looking forward to, it was the awkward conversation about their daughter embarking on a life with a struggling artist, not with a perfect Catholic boy from Notre Dame.

"Bella, a package arrived for you," my mother says when I come home from work one day.

"Who from?" I say.

"I think it's from England," she says. I notice she doesn't seem particularly nosy.

I take the large yellow envelope up to my room and unwrap it. First I pull out a letter, which starts, "I just can't do this any-more . . ." Then I extract Johnner's latest work of art, which is a portrait of me getting mounted by a half-man, half-beast centaur creature. From behind. And I'm smiling like the *Mona Lisa*. But the pièce de résistance is a Ziploc baggie filled with something yellow. When it dawns on me what it is, I can't wait until tomorrow morning's Train Therapy with Zack.

Zack and I commute from Westchester into New York City every morning together. We take turns complaining about life back in the nest and give each other parental, career, and dating advice. "Train Therapy" we call it, because it saves our sanity.

The next morning, I grab the Package From Hell and try to light a fire under my brother's butt as usual.

"Bobby, are you ready to leave?" I call up the steps to his bedroom. Every morning I drop him off at his job at RadioShack, which is near the train station.

Bobby appears with a briefcase and his *Murder, She Wrote* lunchbox. "Rock me Amadeus," he says, and we head for the car.

I have a lot more patience now for our morning routine than I did in high school. But I still get the guilts. Here I am going off to pursue a career, while Bobby is barely treading water, as usual. My parents still hang on to this fantasy that any day he'll snap out of it, or meet someone nice, or that some new drug will magically make him normal. I guess part of me does too, because in some ways it's easier to just move over and make room for the Pink Elephant than ask my parents what the hell it's doing in our house.

"Have a good day, Bobby," I say as we both get out of the car and head our separate ways. I remind him, "And remember, when you make eye contact, look away after three seconds. Staring is not polite."

"Nanu-nanu," he says, giving me the Mork from Ork fingers.

I dash for the train, and meet Zack in our usual car.

"You are not going to believe this," I say as soon as we get settled in our usual seats. "C'est encroyable!"

"Oui, mademoiselle?" he says, handing me the Living section of *The New York Times*. He knows how much I love Anna Quindlen's Life in the 30s column as much as I love Hope in *Thirtysomething*.

"Voilà!" I say, pulling out the "Dear Johnna" package I just received from Johnner. I unscroll the pen and ink drawing of me that actually makes Zack put down the Sports section.

"*Whoa!*" he says, spitting out his coffee all over my new stirrup pants. "Talk about doggie style," Zack laughs. "Look at your face! You're like, 'Thanks for the O, gotta go!'"

"That's not all," I say. "His letter says, quote unquote, 'I don't have the strength to continue the relationship.'"

"So *he's* ending it?" says Zack, his eyes still glued to the picture.

"He admits that he never even started the paperwork to move here," I say. "But he sent me something to remember him by." I hold up the Ziploc and say, "Regardez."

"Dude! He sent you his hair?" says Zack, his eyes bulging at the blond locks in the Ziploc bag.

"What am I going to get next, an ear?" I say.

"I gotta say, Bella, I think it's good that Van Gogh took himself out of the game," says Zack, shaking his head. "But you must feel a little strange, considering he was just about to move here and marry you and everything."

"It *is* strange," I say. "But when I look back on things, maybe that relationship was just to get me through a really hard, lonely time. Sort of like a pair of beaded pumps that go perfectly with the prom dress but you never get a chance to wear again."

"Excusez-moi?" he says.

I can talk so easily with Zack that sometimes I forget he's not a girl. "Maybe relationships are like fashion trends," I explain.

"So guys are like shoes?" he says.

"Sort of," I say. "You have to have the perfect fit. A sole mate, get it?" I say, laughing at my own joke. "But in this case, I'm Princess Charming looking for someone to fit the glass slipper. Want to know the really weird part?" I say.

"It gets weirder?" he says.

"When Bobby saw the package, he said, 'Madness has no purpose. Or reason. But it may have a goal,'" I explain.

"Mr. Spock?" he says.

"As usual," I say. "But Bobby was right. Johnner *had* gone mad."

Zack hums the theme song to *The Twilight Zone* and says, "Meet you on the six-o-four?"

"D'accord," I say, pecking him on the cheek.

As I walk down Park Avenue to my office, I feel, well, lighter.

I guess I'm relieved that the relationship's over, in a lot of ways. Despite the seductive fact that Johnner thinks my thighs are not fat but fruits, his dark side makes my Gray Cloud look like a dust bunny. What I'm going to look for in my next relationship is the passion that I had with Johnner, plus the friendship I have with Zack. Once I find that, I know I will have found my true soulmate. We'll be like The Donald and Ivana, Don and Melanie, and Burt and Loni. You know, couples that are built to last.

12

Year: 1989
Age: 24
Idol: Hope on thirtysomething
Favorite Songs: "Brandy (You're a Fine Girl)" (Looking Glass) and
"Straight Up" (Paula Abdul)
Prized Possessions: rent-controlled Manhattan apartment and the Pill
Best Shoes: Guess? cowboy shoe boots

*C*an men and women be friends without the sex thing getting in the way? Zack and I discuss the premise to *When Harry Met Sally* as we walk to the movie's premiere party at the Plaza Hotel.

Taking Zack as my date is the least I can do, considering that thanks to him I'm living in a rent-controlled apartment. Zack's sister, Jaimie, has decided to move to L.A. and become an actress, so I'm subletting her studio on the Upper West Side.

"Ce n'est pas possible to be 'just friends,'" Zack says, shaking his head.

"What about us, then?" I ask.

"We don't count," he says.

"Pourquois pas?" I say.

"Parce que we knew each other *before* I cared about sex," he says. "Bella, guys are friends avec girls pour une reasone. To get inside their pantelonies."

We pass the stretch limos parked outside the entrance and make our way past the paparazzi to the grand ballroom, where the clipboard-wielding gestapo in red pumps looks me up and down and sneers, "Invite only."

I pause, savoring the moment. Ever since landing my monthly Spotlight column, I'm on the A-list for all the movie screenings, industry parties, and premieres. "Bella Grandelli, *Preview Magazine*," I say. We're in!

"Meg Ryan at neuf heure, avec Dennis Quaid!" I squeal to Zack as we make our way to the bar.

Suddenly I feel two hands on my shoulders. Rough. Heavy. Male. Is it Meg's bodyguard?

"Yo, dude!" says Zack to the person gripping me from behind. "What's up?"

It's Matt Dillon, looking pretty much as renegade and James Deanish as in eighth grade. Only now he has a supermodel velcroed to his side.

"Hey! Great to see you guys!" Matt says, hugging us and introducing us to a woman named Uma. "What's goin' on?"

"I heard you got the part in *Drugstore Cowboy*. Congratulations!" I say.

"Thanks," he says. "Hey, how's Bobby doing? I thought about him when I saw *Rainman*."

"You and me both," I say.

Rainman could have starred my brother, because there are so many similarities between him and Dustin Hoffman's character. That movie has made it a million times easier to explain my brother to new people. You say "autism," and people say "Huh?" You say "My brother's like Rainman," and people say *"Really?"*

"Join us in the VIP section?" Matt asks. (Clipboard Nazi inspects her pumps as we pass.) Using my job as an excuse, I introduce Zack and myself to everyone from Billy Crystal to Nora Ephron until the party starts breaking up around 2 A.M.

"Fitzpatrick's?" I say as we leave. Zack flags a taxi.

Fitzpatrick's is the brainchild of some Boston College grads who calculated how much they collectively spent on alcohol and decided to cut straight to the profit by opening a bunch of bars instead of getting real jobs.

What makes the place a gold mine is that it's a total dive,

decorated in grungy college pennants and literally hundreds of bras and ties hanging from the ceiling like corporate tinsel. The music is strictly seventies, and going in there is sort of like *Cheers*— you're guaranteed to run into friends.

"Beau Callahan is guest bartender tonight!" says Zack. Another stroke of Fitzpatrick's genius is keeping things lively by rotating different cute guys as guest bartenders.

"Yo, Beau!" Zack calls out over the blare of "Build Me Up Buttercup," which is getting a drunken backup from half the bar.

Beau makes his way over, we make eye contact, and *BAM!* You know when Batman's doing a fight scene and the word flies out and hits the TV screen? That's exactly what it feels like when we make eye contact.

All right, so I *do* think that everyone is the cutest guy I've ever seen, especially after I've had about ten Bud Lights. But I swear, this is not the Beer Goggles talking. I mean, he's cute, but he's bald. Still, his smile is so megawatt that it lights up his entire face. Like Gray Clouds would just shrivel up in its presence.

"Nice to meet you, Beulah," he says when Zack introduces us.

Ugh, I hate it when guys get my name wrong. Which is all the time. It means that they don't get the real me.

"Nice to meet you, *Joe,*" I shoot back.

"It's Beau," he says with a smile, correcting me.

For the rest of the evening I pump Zack for info on Beau.

"Status?" I ask.

"Not sure," he says. "He's had a really tough girlfriend named Janice for years. She works at Tan Central Station."

"A tanning parlor?" I ask.

"Yeah," he says. "But I heard they were over."

"Hmmmmm," I say. There really is something deliciously leprechaun-esque about this guy.

But here's the thing. In case you don't know, guys in their twenties are basically FOC'd—they all suffer from Fear of Commitment. I thought it was just an N.D. thing, but it's as bad as the cooties epidemic in '76. I literally haven't had one single date in the city in the two years since things ended with Johnner. That's a dry spell that's dustier than the Sahara. No wonder I drink so much.

According to Zack, there's not much I can do about it. If you want to be in a relationship, your best bet is to play hard to get. Never call a guy first and never ask him out. Don't rationalize breaking these rules by telling yourself, "He's just scared." What he's scared of is getting trapped, by you, and his life becoming the sequel to *Fatal Attraction*.

Lucky for me, Beau's bartending so I have a good excuse to talk to him. "Beulah, you're back again?" Beau says the third time I return to the bar to get a round. "You must like me."

"We really should stop meeting this way, Joe," I say.

I'm singing along to the best cheesy seventies song of all time, "Brandy." Beau starts singing too, but he changes the words so he's singing to me.

" 'Beu-lah, you're a fine girl. What a good wife you would be!' Hey, c'mon up here, Beulah!" he says, helping me up on to the bar. He hands me a bottle of woo-woo shots and instructs me how to pour it into the open mouths of the clientele as I dance along on top of the bar.

Everyone's clapping and singing while I'm happily dispensing shots. Suddenly I'm doused with something cold and wet. I look down and realize that my white shirt has been transformed into Saran Wrap. The only body part that isn't totally revealed is my shoulders, thanks to the industrial-sized shoulder pads that I wear with absolutely everything. The entire room goes silent, and I am mortified. The Mortified Moron, dancing on the bar, wiping someone's sex on the beach drink out of my eyes.

"Take it off! Take it off! Take it off!" all the cute, preppy guys start chanting and clapping in unison. Why is getting attention always a punishable offense for me?

"Bitch!" I hear, and my eyes follow the Brooklyn accent to the drink-thrower. It's the tannest girl in the room, despite the fact that it's November, and she has a Pat Benatar haircut and really long frosted nails. Ah, Janice. Getting me back for talking to her man.

As Janice pushes her way in my direction, Zack yanks me off the bar and covers me with his blazer. "We're so outta here," he says, pulling me toward the door.

"But, but, but—" I say, trying to catch Beau's eye. No luck. He's busy fending off Pat Benatar, who is trying to bitch-slap him from the other side of the bar.

"I'm so disappointed!" I wail to Zack in the cab. "We were totally hitting it off!"

"Yeah, until you were winning your own wet T-shirt contest," Zack says, laughing at me.

"I won? Good," I say, getting out at my stop. "Thanks for the blazer. I'll dry-clean it and return it to you this weekend."

"D'accord, babe," he says as we peck each other good-bye. "Au revoir!"

For the next few days, every time Beau barges into my mind, I tell him the bar's closed. So what if I haven't had a boyfriend in two years? The last thing I need is to have a crush on someone with a girlfriend who looks like she has a prison record. Beau's not The One, but he's a sign that cute, funny, nice guys *do* exist in Manhattan. I just need one who's available.

Imagine my surprise when I pick up my boss's messages and find one for me. It says, "Joe called." No number, but the "will call back" box was checked.

I do the Happy Dance all the way back to my desk and call Zack.

"Yeah, he asked me where you worked," Zack says.

"And you didn't tell me?" I howl. "Do you think he'll call back? Do you think he likes me? What about Janice?" I continue, breathless. I have such a good feeling about him—I can't even tell you. It's like sunshine on the inside. It's like, it's like, I know, like a tanning bed for your soul!

"Easy, Princess Charming," says Zack. "Don't crack your glass slipper trying to jam it on the wrong guy's foot."

"D'accord, d'accord," I say.

When Beau and I finally connect the next day, we pick up the banter right where we left off.

"Hey, Beulah," he says. "I have a question for you."

My heart pounds. "What's that, Joe?" I ask.

"Why don't you correct people when they get your name wrong?" he says. "Your entire office thinks your name is Bella."

"The whole world seems to be under that impression," I say. "Really could drive a person to drink, don't you think, Joe?"

"Think you can hold out until the market closes?" he says. "I'll meet you at the St. Regis."

Damn, it's Tuesday! I am not wearing a going-out-after-work outfit. As a matter of fact, my body suit is a size too small and has been giving me a very distracting wedgie all day. But I'll never make it back to my apartment to change into my black stirrup pants and to the St. Regis on time. I know! I'll say I'm busy. Yeah! Play hard to get, like Zack says.

"Six sounds great!" I say. I can't help it! The Mexican jumping beans line up and start doing the hustle in my stomach.

"Gotta hop," he says and clicks off before I can say good-bye.

The hours craaaaaawl by all afternoon, until finally it's time to meet Beau. I get there before he does, so I walk around the block, being careful not to step on any cracks along the way, just for luck. I make a bargain with God. If things work out, I'll really concentrate on finding someone for my brother.

"Beulah, did you have a few rounds on the way?" says Beau, who is patiently waiting in front of the St. Regis. (God, he's cute!)

"No, Joe, why do you ask?" I say, confused.

"I've been watching you walk down the street, and your steps are a little, well, erratic," he says with a lopsided grin.

Busted!

"Just practicing the latest dance craze," I say. "If you are a good boy, I'll teach you sometime."

"What if I'm a bad boy?" he says, opening the door for me like a perfect gentleman.

"Then you get private lessons," I say slyly, giving him a wink.

We settle into a dark corner and continue to banter back and forth as if we have known each other forever. In fact, that evening we realize that we're totally six degrees of separation. We have tons of people in common. Using my crack interview skills, I ferret out the most crucial information. Not only is Beau's career on the rise at Morgan Stanley, where he's about to take his Series Seven and become a trader, but Janice is total history.

When Beau gets the check, he says, "So, Beulah, how about dinner Saturday night?"

"Great!" I say, perhaps with a little too much enthusiasm. Because with that, my body suit unsnaps, and the crotch part suddenly rolls up over my waistline.

We both look down at it, wondering what to say. I'm so embarrassed I think I'm going to die.

"Definitely wear that shirt," he says. "It's even better than the see-through one you wore to Fitzpatrick's."

I pray my face is no longer purple by the time Beau walks me to a taxi. Opening the door for me, he hands the driver a ten and says, "Take excellent care of this lady." He gives me a too quick peck on the lips and says, "Until then."

I literally stop eating altogether for the rest of the week before the date. Because we are not just going on a date—we are going to the most romantic restaurant in the entire city, the Rainbow Room. It's on the sixty-fifth floor of Rockfeller Center and overlooks the entire cityscape. I decide to splurge on a new pouf dress for the occasion.

Beau holds my hand tightly as we step out of the elevator and wait at the maitre d' stand. I look out the window and thank all the first stars I've wished on my entire life for letting me get to be here. Tonight. With him.

As soon as we are seated, Beau is presented with a wine list the size of a phone book. He flips through the pages and tells the sommelier, "The lady and I would like Budweiser. The 1989 vintage will do."

"Pardon, sir?" says the sommelier.

"Two Buds, dude," Beau says.

Isn't that the cutest? While I'm busy worrying how I look, and if I'm acting appropriately and fitting in, he's totally himself. Even on the dance floor he puts me at ease. I don't know how to ballroom dance, but he just twirls me and we laugh when I stumble or step on his toes.

"So, have I been a good boy," he asks, lowering me into a dip. "Or a bad boy?"

"Very good," I say, smiling up at him. "You get an A-plus for such a romantic date."

"Shucks," he says. "I was hoping for some of those private dancing lessons. You know, for that weird dance you were doing along the sidewalk the night of our first date. It looked like—"

"Like what?" I say, choking back my own laughter. What an idiot I must have looked like, hopping and skipping over all those cracks.

"Like you were playing a game that I used to with my little sister, Amy, when we were little, jumping over the cracks," he says.

"Haven't you heard, crack is wack?" I deadpan. "It's the latest craze. Paula Abdul is going to do it in her next video."

After the Rainbow Room, we have a nightcap at Elaine's and

walk back to my apartment, hop, skip, and jumping over all the cracks along the way. We're singing *Partridge Family* songs, making up the words to the ones we don't know.

"I think I love you! So what am I so afraid of?" he sings.

"Afraid of a love there's no beer for!" I sing, taking the next verse.

In front of my building we hold hands and, together, jump over a big, fat crack. And just as we kiss for the first time, the church bells ring at St. Ignatius. It's a sign.

Avoiding all those cracks pays off. Within a month, he's asking to do something Zack made me promise never to initiate: Meet the Parents. I'm really paranoid of being perceived as a ball and chain, so I'd never push this step in a million years. Plus there's the whole twin thing.

I fill him in on Bobby's back story (how many times am I going to have to do this?), and we head through the kitchen door.

"Hi, Mr. and Mrs. Grandelli," Beau says, shaking my parents' hands. "It's a pleasure to meet you."

"Well, well, you must be Bella's boyfriend, Beau," says my father, pumping Beau's hand. It's football season, and my father is wearing his favorite outfit, wide-wale corduroys covered with little leprechauns, and a tie that plays the Notre Dame fight song when you squeeze it.

"Great tie, Mr. Grandelli," Beau says without a trace of sarcasm. "Did you go to Notre Dame?"

My father clears his throat and is saved from answering that question by my mother, who has appeared with a platter of pigs in a blanket.

"My favorite, Mrs. Grandelli. How did you know?" he says, helping himself to the platter.

"Beau, we saw your aunt and uncle this morning at St. Catherine's nine o'clock mass," gushes my mother. "Turns out we've known them for years!"

Bobby shuffles in. He's wearing his latest contraption, a neon orange wet suit with an inflatable life vest beneath it. It has replaced the couch cushions as his favorite mode of relaxation.

"Shake, shake, shake," he says, quoting K.C. and the Sunshine Band. He looks at Beau out of the corner of his eye and puffs into his vest to adjust the pressure.

What makes me love Beau ten times more is the fact that he doesn't even raise an eyebrow.

"Hey, Bobby, I brought you something," Beau says, presenting him with a life-size papier-mâché bust of Mr. Spock that he found at some funky memorabilia shop in the East Village.

"I am a Vulcan, I am a Vulcan, there is no pain!" says Bobby, hugging the bust and shuffling toward the stairs in his usual old-man gait. "There's sixty thousand megabytes in Macintosh City!"

Bobby pauses and steals a glance at Beau from the corner of his eye. Since he got fired from RadioShack, he's back to being gun-shy about making eye contact.

"I think he wants you to see his computer," I say. If you think Bobby's good with a joystick, you should see him work a mouse. I bought him a laptop with the check from my first freelance piece, a *Cosmo* "How Kinky Are You?" sex quiz. Luckily, I found a computer class given as part of a continuing education series at our high school.

After dinner, Beau asks my father about his ships in a bottle collection. "The real question is how do you raise the mast?" he says in complete seriousness.

"I'd be happy to show you," says my father, jazzed that someone has shown an interest in his weird hobby. As they head down to the basement together discussing Notre Dame's latest football record, my mother squeezes my arm.

"Bella!" she says excitedly, looking into my eyes. "This is what you deserve! Such a nice boy, and he's from such a nice family. It really helps to have a common background."

"Mom, let's not get ahead of ourselves," I start to say, but my in-control voice twirls into a squeal. "But I know! Isn't he just perfect?"

We hug. As I breathe in her Chanel Number Five, the same scent she's worn forever, I can't remember the last time I've felt so happy. It's clear that both my parents and Bobby are as crazy about Beau as I am.

The men come up the stairs, and I walk Beau out to his car. I unclasp the locket from around my neck and slip the gold heart off the chain.

"What are you doing?" he says. "You never take off your grandmother's locket."

It's true. I have never once taken it off since the first day my mother put it on me. It's my good luck charm, but a little voice inside me tells me to give it to Beau.

"It's for luck, for your Series Seven tomorrow," I say, slipping it onto his key chain. That's the big test he needs to pass to become a trader.

My good luck charm turns out to be transferable. Not only does Beau pass—within a few months, he's one of the youngest managers at Morgan Stanley.

But here's what I love about him. Instead of turning into a Master of the Universe, he never forgets where he came from. There's this guy named Jim, some borderline criminal who's trying to start his own business, whom Beau has taken under his wing through a mentoring program set up by Morgan Stanley.

"You're mentoring Jim again tonight?" I say, a bit disappointed.

"You've got to respect someone who's not afraid to start over," he says. "I want to help this guy."

"What does that mean anyway, mentoring?" I ask. "Is that code for going out drinking?"

"Just means spend time with him and give him advice," Beau says.

"I didn't know they had guardian angels on Wall Street," I say.

"More like Hell's Angel," he says, shrugging. "It's no big deal."

But it is to me. Even if it cuts into the time I get with Beau, his kindness and his penchant for always helping the underdog makes me slip ten notches deeper for him. For the first time in my life, I decide to go on the Pill.

I know this doesn't make any sense, but I used to think that if I didn't use contraception, then I wasn't really having sex. By not taking responsibility, I was able to stay in denial. But it's different with Beau. For the first time in my life, I feel like I'm doing the right thing by sleeping with him, like we are meant to be together.

My personal rule, based on Johnner's surprise banana-hammock Speedo, is a couple needs to be together for all four seasons before they can really know each other. You need to see the entire rotation of their closet before you can make an informed decision on who you are going to spend the rest of your life with. We're coming up on our one-year anniversary, and so far no major surprises. No Air Supply concert T-shirts, or sandals worn with black knee socks, and he's a boxers not briefs sort of guy. I have to admit, my parents' approval just confirms that Beau is The One.

The night of our one-year anniversary, Beau tells me he has a surprise planned. I wait for him outside my office, and he pulls up in a stretch limousine.

"The Rainbow Room, please," he tells the driver.

The maitre d' takes us to the table we sat at exactly one year ago tonight, and a minute later a waiter appears with one of those silver-domed platters. He lifts it to reveal two Budweiser longnecks.

"Madame?" he says in a stuffy English accent.

I giggle.

"Beulah, you're a fine girl," Beau says, toasting me.

We clink bottles, and I'm just about to take a swig when I see something sparkly tied to the neck of the beer bottle. I give it a little twist and it goes *clink-clink-clink*.

Beau is now profusely sweating. I mean, worse than Albert Brooks in *Broadcast News*.

I start pulling on the ring, which is tied around the bottleneck with a ribbon. Beau gets up from the table and drops to one knee.

"And what a good wife you would be!" he sings as I liberate a three-carat diamond with sapphire baguettes.

As Beau slips the ring on my finger, he improvises the last line of the song, "Make my life and say you'll mar-ry me!"

And with that a trio of violins appears at our table—how they knew the tune to that one-hit wonder, I'll never know.

"Yes, yes, yes!" I say, dropping to the floor to join him. I feel dizzy with happiness.

For the first time in my life, everything is perfect. We set the wedding date for the next summer. My mom and I score at the Vera Wang sample sale, and we book our reception at the swanky Westchester Country Club, hiring a great swing band plus a DJ specializing in seventies music. Beau is making such big bucks that he insists on paying for everything. The fondant icing on the Martha Stewart cake is that I don't even *need* cake. For the first time since my first love, that idiot Chandler, I have returned to the land of size six.

"Honey, we are going to have to take in this dress again. You are losing too much weight," says my mother at my second-to-last fitting. She loves this whole planning thing so much; sometimes I wonder which one of us is getting married.

"I just haven't had much of an appetite lately," I say. In fact, for the past few days I've been feeling downright seasick and felt this stabbing feeling in my side. "Maybe it's just nerves."

"Nerves, why?" she says.

For some reason, the waves of nausea get worse when I think

about my brother. More than anything, I wish I could talk to my mother about it. My whole life when I've tried to tell her how I really feel about anything, she just clams up inside. I feel her click closed, and all that's left is the Talbots shell and the frosted Florence Henderson flip.

"Did you ever have doubts, before you married Dad?" I venture.

"Of course," she says. "I wasn't sure about whether to serve chicken or fish, and the centerpieces were a real challenge, whether or not to go with a lily and rose mix, or—"

"No, Mom," I stammer. "Not doubts about wedding details. I mean, doubts about yourself, or if this is the right person to spend the rest of your life with or what if . . ." I see the Pink Elephant in the corner of the room and lose my nerve.

"You always have to overthink things, Bella," she says, with the pins sticking out of her mouth. "Nothing's ever perfect, honey. You have to accept things for what they are."

Her hands drop to her lap, and I think she's going to elaborate. But it seems like she changes her mind, and she continues on in wedding-speak. "The main thing you have to decide is whether you want the hem to cover your shoes completely, or an inch up, so it's easier to walk. You don't want to be tripping down the aisle on your big day . . ."

Her voice trails off and becomes that unintelligible "Wha-wha-wha" sound when an adult speaks on *Peanuts*.

So if my perfect white-picket-fence future is lying right in front of me, why do I feel like something's missing? Beau is The One for me, even by my parents' standards, yet something inside me doesn't feel all the way filled up. There's so much to do—I probably shouldn't dwell on this. Maybe my mother's right. I do overthink things.

Later that night, Beau notices my worry as we lie on the floor and write thank-you notes for the blue Tiffany boxes that appear daily. "What's wrong, Princess Bride?" says Beau.

"My side sort of hurts, and there's something else: Bobby. It's hard for me to think about the happiest day in my life and my brother at the same time," I say. "I wish there was some way to make it special for him, since it's unlikely he'll ever be a groom."

"Bella, this is really bothering you, huh?" Beau says, putting down his pen and looking at me.

"I know I bring this on myself," I say. "But I just want to make him a part of the happiness as much as I can."

"How 'bout this?" he says. "Let's switch."

"Switch?" I say.

"Yeah, screw Martha Stupid and those books you've been consulting," he says. "How 'bout you get to pick a best man and I'll get a maid of honor?"

"So you'll have your sister, Amy, and I'll have Bobby?" I say, leaping up to hug him. "Thank you, thank you, thank you!"

"Beulah," he says, his tone shifting. "You know Three's Company's okay with me. I *like* hanging out with Bobby."

I gulp. He's given me the ultimate wedding present. My brother can live with us when my parents can no longer handle him, and I didn't even have to ask him for it.

"How do you think the Mr. Spock bust will look on our mantel?" he muses as we return to our note writing.

Beau's act of generosity makes it almost impossible to play Fantasy Virgin. We decide to stop having sex two weeks before the wedding, so that the first night of our honeymoon—at the fabulous Four Seasons resort in Bali—will be like the first time.

With only two nights to go until the rehearsal dinner, however, my bachelorette party weakens my resolve. I found out something miraculous today—I mean, one-in-a-hundred chances—that I simply can't wait to tell him.

"But it's almost three a.m.," says Carrie. "Are you sure you don't want to warn Beau you are coming over?"

"Nah, he'll be thrilled to see me," I say. "Especially when I tell him my big news."

"What big news?" she asks.

"You'll be the second to know," I say, kissing her good-bye and hopping out of the cab at Beau's apartment. "Promise!"

Letting myself in with my key, I find the lights and TV on, but where is Beau? Maybe he's still out, I think, seeing his darkened room down the hall. I go to the phone to call Fitzpatrick's, when I hear a noise from his room. So he *is* home! I run down the hall, and take a flying leap onto his bed.

When I land, I realize that I've landed on a body. With boobs. This can't be. I must be having a nightmare. I just can't believe this. Beau's home, all right. And so is Janice. I peel myself off their grotesque pretzel of limbs. I snap on the light, and the three of us stand there blinking at one another for what seems like an eternity.

Finally I march over to the window, yank it open, and pull the ring off my finger. I curse the first star I see and chuck the three carats with the sapphire baguettes right out the window and onto Lexington Avenue.

My shock at what I've just witnessed starts whirling like a ball of fire in the pit of my stomach. Bracing myself against the window frame, I lean out the window and retch. But the urge to empty my insides gets blocked by my heart, which is stuck in my throat. I swallow my vomit and turn and face them. The stabbing pains in my side are killing me. Janice is hiding beneath the sheet, and Beau is still silent, looking at me wide-eyed. The stabbing feeling in my side is killing me.

Johnner may have been crazy, but Beau? I kicked the tires on this one, took my time before jumping in. Saw every speck of clothes in his closet. Even my parents assured me he was The One. I guess this means I'm the crazy one.

"Had something to tell you, *Dad,* but I can see you're busy," I say to Beau, wiping my mouth on my sleeve. My eyes flood with tears. "I'll fill you in at a more convenient time."

"Bella," Beau stammers. But he's not getting up. And his hand is resting on the white-sheeted lump next to him.

"Don't bother," I say. "I know the way out."

What I don't know, however, is what the etiquette books would dictate to be the best way to inform your former fiancé that you've just discovered you're pregnant.

After not sleeping the rest of the night, I take the first train home to my parents' house. I don't tell them anything, but of course they could tell I didn't come down with a sudden case of pink eye. Sure enough, after I refuse to come to the phone the third time, Beau's car slithers into the driveway.

I hear Beau making absurd small talk with Bobby downstairs, and eventually he comes up and sits on the edge of my twin bed. His head is hanging so low, and his eyes are such apologetic little slits, that I could almost feel sorry for him, if I wasn't so busy feeling so sick and sorry for myself. Now what he did was despicable, but because I believe that we are meant for each other, I'm planning on taking him back after a long, protracted apology.

"Bella, uh, I was really drunk," he starts.

"Yeah," I say, folding my arms across my chest. I wait.

"I'm sorry," he says in a meek voice. "Janice, well, she cornered me in Fitzpatrick's."

"Yeah," I say.

"Bella, I have cold feet, I guess," he says.

I start doing Edvard Munch's *The Scream* in my mind. No, no, he can't say what I think he's about to say . . .

"I'm really sorry," he says, continuing, "but I just don't think I can go through with this."

"Beau, no, we're perfect for each other," I say, weeping. "How could you change your mind about me?"

"It's not you—it's me," he says in a hoarse whisper. "Sometimes I don't think I deserve you, or that I can live up to your expectations."

"And what's that supposed to mean?" I say. So I'm getting punished for wanting things to be the best that they can be?

"It's just that you are so hard on yourself, and you always expect the best out of me," he says.

"So what?" I say.

"Well, Janice, she just accepts me for who I am," he says. "She always has."

"You should have thought of that before we created a child," I spit. "I'm pregnant."

Beau winces ever so slightly. "Bella, of course I'll support the child," he says, looking down. "It's just that I can't . . . we're not . . ." he says, his voice trailing off.

The child, not *our* child. Or even *his* child, for that matter.

If Beau broke my heart the night before, this comment smashes it into two separate pieces altogether. The ache in my chest joins the pains in my side.

"Get out," I say, choking back a sob.

Thinking I actually meant it, Beau does.

It's impossible for me to feel worse, but I manage to find a way. I sob into my pillow until I am too tired to feel anymore.

Worse than telling my parents that the wedding is off, worse than returning all the blue Tiffany boxes, losing the deposit for the band, the photographer, the videographer, and the country club reception, worse than donating my beaded, empire-waist Vera Wang gown to Goodwill, worse than Beau's boss's comment that "Beau'll be a millionaire by the time he's thirty," even worse than imagining my life as a single mother, is this simple fact: I was wrong. How would I ever trust myself again, if I was so dead wrong about this, when I thought we were so perfect for each other? *I* don't even want to be with me anymore.

The next day I call in sick to work, and it's no lie. I feel light-headed, and the pain in my side won't go away. So I go to my gyno to confirm what the E.P.T. two solid lines had already informed me. I tell the doctor about my nonexistent period despite the fact that I was on the Pill.

"They say the pill is ninety-nine percent effective," Dr. Nevin says with a chuckle. "No one ever thinks they are going to be that one percent. Let's first take some blood so I can get a hormone level of pregnancy, and then let's give you an ultrasound."

"I've been having this stabbing feeling in my side for the last week, and it feels worse today," I say as I do what every woman dreads and scooch my naked bottom down to the end of the examining table. "Is that normal?"

"You said your last period was six weeks ago?" Dr. Nevin asks. "Have you had any blood at all?"

"No," I say. "And I feel really light-headed. Is it stress?"

"Hmm, uterus looks normal," he says, working the probe and staring at the ultrasound screen. "But there's a significant amount of fluid in the pelvis. Bella, I think you may have a ruptured ectopic pregnancy."

"What does that mean?" I ask, a feeling of dread coming over me.

"It means you could bleed to death," he says, calling for the nurse. "We need to get you to the OR right away. You're lucky that my office is attached to the hospital."

Lucky? Before the horror of this even sinks in, a resident is pushing me in a wheelchair to the emergency room, asking if there is someone I want to call. Well, I can't call my parents, and I'm not calling Beau. I could call Carrie, but then I think of the one person who would really bring me comfort: Zack.

When I hear his voice on the pay phone in the nurses' station, I burst into tears.

"Slow down, Bella," he says calmly. "Where are you?"

"The baby, I mean, I was pregnant, and Beau, he changed his mind," I sob into the phone, the directions to the hospital and the details of my predicament tumbling out in a big confused mess. "Can you come? I need you."

"On my way!" says Zack as calmly as if he was meeting me at Fitzpatrick's for a brew.

The nurses wheel me into a room, where I change into a gown and a cap. Next they start an IV and wheel me into the operating room. Soon after they move me to the table, the anesthesia kicks in, because the last thing I remember is an oxygen mask being strapped to my face and Dr. Nevin patting me gently on the shoulder.

The next thing I know, I'm lying on a bed in the recovery room, feeling nauseated and woozy. When I open my eyes, I see Zack sitting beside me, "reading" the *Sports Illustrated* swimsuit edition. Something smells really garlicky.

"She's back!" he says cheerfully, holding up a Zabar's bag. "I brought you dejeuner! Pastrami sandwich and pickles."

"I'm going to be sick," I say and start dry-heaving.

A nurse comes in to help me. "Perhaps you should take that outside," she says kindly to Zack. "We need to start her on crackers and juice."

The nurse helps me sit up. "Your husband really loves you," she says, nodding to the doorway where Zack exited with his kosher feast. "He's been a nervous wreck sitting next to you for the past hour."

I don't correct her. In fact, I decide to go with it. "Ring's at home," I say, waving toward my left hand as she leaves the room. "You know, the swelling."

Zack returns and apologizes. "Je suis desole, mon amie," he says, taking my hand. "That's just the way the Jew Crew does it. You know, feed a fever, buffet the flu . . ."

"And what, garlic pickle to death an ectopic pregnancy?" I say.

"What's that?" he asks.

"It means I was pregnant, but it got stuck in the tube," I explain. "I think."

He holds up a plastic cup of apple juice for me to sip. After a moment he says, "They said you had to urinate before you can leave."

"I hate that word, 'urinate,'" I say, taking a sip. "Why can't they say 'pee' like everyone else?"

"Vagina," Zack murmers in a funny voice, saying the other word I hate.

"Stop it," I say, but then I crack up and loudly whisper, "Penis!"

About an hour later, the nurse comes in again and asks, "Okay, do you think you can walk?"

She helps me get to my feet, and unsteadily I step one slippered foot in front of the other and make it across the room, trying not to flash anyone with my backless gown.

"Here she comes, Miss America," Zack sings. "And love the shower cap look. *Très* chic!"

"Actually, no shower for twenty-four hours," says Dr. Nevin, coming into the room. "Bella, you need to take it easy. No exercise for a week. Excessive blood, vomiting, or fever, call us right away. And we need to repeat the hormone test in about a week."

Dr. Nevin and the nurse leave, and I sit down and start to cry. Everything hurts.

"Vagina," Zack says in his funny voice, kneeling next to me.

"Vagina, vagina, vagina." He keeps it up the whole time until we are in a cab, heading back to my place. It makes me crack up occasionally, but then I go back to crying.

"I'm convinced that the baby changed his mind," I admit to Zack. "Just like his father."

Zack wipes my tears with the bottom of his T-shirt. He doesn't say anything, and the truth hangs uncomfortably in the air. If misery loves company, the look on his face shows me that I'm not alone.

Once we get into my apartment, I check my answering machine. No messages. This makes me cry even harder.

Zack props me up on my couch with pillows and hands me the remote control.

"Voulez-vous stay avec you?" he says. "I could skip my cousin's bar mitzvah."

"No, you've done everything a friend could want," I say, blowing my nose. "I just wish I could stop crying."

"I really hate to leave you like this," he says.

"I'll be fine," I say, wiping my eyes. "Don't worry."

"Promise you'll telephonez mon answering machine, if you need anything?" he says, "I'll check mon messages."

"Je promise," I say.

"You're going to be okay, kid," he says. "I know this is really rough, but I promise you are going to be okay."

A few hours later, I'm channel surfing when I hear music. Getting up from the couch, I walk toward where the sound is coming from, which is the window. Looking outside, I spot Zack, standing there in a suit, playing his trumpet. I open the window, and I stop crying for the first time when I Name That Tune. It's our personal version of James Taylor's "You've Got a Friend," all the way from eighth grade, sans the schmaltz. Despite the car crash that is my life, I feel really lucky to have a friend who would do anything for me.

"It's a girl's name!" I shout down to him, the streetlights looking like rainbows through my tears.

"Vagina!" He stops for a second to shout back, before playing the refrain of "My Sharona."

13

Year: 1992
Age: 27
Idol: Nora Ephron
Favorite Song: "Why" (Annie Lennox)
Prized Possession: first cover story
Best Shoes: Billy Martin black lizard cowboy boots

"*T*anqueray martini, straight up, please, with extra olives," I tell the cat-suited waitress at the Temple Bar. It's downtown's coolest date place, thanks to the combination of dark lighting and extra-large martini glasses, which make everyone more attractive, especially to themselves.

"Same thing, but make mine dirty," says Carrie, my date. She's in love, as usual, and as happy as I am for her, it pokes at something sore, deep inside me—as usual.

"Bella, it's been two years since you've gone on a date," she says. "C'mon, cowgirl, isn't it time you got back in the saddle?"

"I don't know," I stammer.

"Miles has a ton of cute friends, older guys," she says. "Some of them even come with their own jets."

But what will I wear over the gaping wound where my heart used to be, a fringe jacket? As jealous as I am that Carrie is head over heels in love with her boss's best friend, which has also had the benefit of catapulting her up the ladder at Chiat Day, this cowgirl still has the blues.

"Thanks, but I guess I'm not really ready to move on," I admit. "Even though I'm coming to realize that Beau wasn't The One."

"But I thought you said he had the perfect résumé?" she says, surprised.

"He did, plus he had the parental approval, which can really brainwash a girl," I say.

"But?" she asks.

"But, well, maybe we weren't so perfect for each other after all. He wanted to have kids and live in the suburbs right away, and, well, the closer I got to that I realized maybe I wasn't ready for full-time motherhood," I say. "Sometimes you want something so badly, you don't stop to check if it really makes you happy."

"I saw them, you know," Carrie says carefully, poking her olive.

A lightning bolt rips down my core.

"You saw Beau and Janice?" I sputter.

"At the Westchester Classic out in Rye," she says. "They live out there, on the grounds of the golf course. Take a sip, Bella."

I do.

"Ran into them pushing a baby carriage," she says tentatively.

A baby carriage! I'm stunned. I had seen the wedding announcement in the church bulletin, courtesy of my mother, but they certainly didn't waste time having a family. It easily could have been me pushing the baby carriage. *If* I didn't come in for a landing on the two of them, *if* I didn't lose the baby, and, well, the biggie, *if* Beau didn't decide I wasn't The One for him. There's not much I can do about the fact that he feels more comfortable with a bimbo.

"Wow," I say.

"Didn't see the baby, but it was definitely that picture of suburbia you say you don't want," she says. "And that's not all."

"Tell me," I say.

"Janice was wearing a shirt that said 'Baby On Board,'" she says.

"Number two?" I say.

"Clearly on the way," she confirms.

Everybody seems to be moving on with their lives, except me. And my brother, of course. Sometimes I feel like I am on a merry-go-round. I keep myself frantically busy with dieting, work, going out with my friends to fun restaurants, obsessing about what I ate, working out to get rid of it, always secretly, desperately wishing that I might meet someone new to pull me out of my slump. Then, occasionally, the ride will stop, and I'll realize that I've been in the same exact place the entire time; it's the rest of the world that keeps moving.

Maybe that's why it's harder and harder for me to spend time with Bobby these days. He's a constant reminder of how stuck I feel. The difference is he doesn't seem to care that he spends his days watching *Star Trek* reruns and playing on his computer, while I get exhausted swimming against the stream of perpetual motion that I create for myself.

Carrie and I pay the check, and she heads off to the Caribou Club to meet Miles.

"Sure you don't want to come? He brought along a friend for you," she teases in a singsong voice. "An Australian gazillionaire with his own airlines."

"Thanks, but I think I'll head uptown in my yellow chariot," I say, flagging a cab. "You have fun, though."

Some girls get the drunken-hornies, but as I whiz uptown, I get hit with a case of the hungry-lonelies. I usually gorge on a pint of nonfat peanut butter frozen yogurt, which I can sort of get away with if I work out a lot. It's worth it, even if I have to go into the bathroom and use the blow-dryer to warm myself up because by the time I'm finished my lips are blue and my hands are numb.

"Tasti D-Lite, on Eighty-sixth and Broadway," I tell the driver.

When we get there, however, it's closed. Then I get an idea. My attention turns to the one guy I really *do* want to talk to.

"Turn here!" I tell the driver. "I've changed my mind."

Should I? Shouldn't I? Maybe he's not alone. I mean, knowing him, he's *probably* not alone. What the hell, it's only eleven o'clock.

I hit the buzzer, lean in, and say, "Bon soir, monsieur."

"Comment t'ally vous, mademoiselle," Zack says, buzzing me in.

He's in his boxers, putting golf balls into a big red Dixie cup, with Letterman on in the background.

I follow Zack, who has followed an errant ball into the sand traps of his bedroom. I plop on the bed and start hopping up and down.

"Stop it. The neighbors downstairs will complain," he says, jumping on the bed and muscling me into submission with a half nelson.

"C'mon, they've got to hear that every single night, Mr. American Gigolo," I say. It's a true fact that Zack rotates women in and out of his sheets with more frequency than he flosses his teeth.

"Dude, no kidding," he says, chortling. "I got a call from the super last week to keep it down."

"Joan the Moan?" I say.

"*You* know *me* better than *I* know *me*," he says.

"That's because we are meilleur amies," I say.

"Oui," he says.

"So, what do you want to be this year for Halloween? Milli Vanilli?" I ask.

"Non, we did that last year. And we're not doing Sonny and Cher again either," he says. "How about pregnant nuns?"

"Ouch," I say. He promised me he wouldn't say the word "pregnant," under any circumstances, until I got over everything. It's been even more verboten than "vagina."

"Je suis desole, pal," he says, giving me a hug. "That was *très* stupid of me. How are you doing about all of that anyway?"

"I know I should be over it by now, but I just can't get excited about meeting anyone," I admit.

"Bella, you are the biggest catch in the city," he says. "As soon as you're ready, guys will be coming out of the woodwork. Je promise. In the meantime, don't put any pressure on yourself."

Then we lie back into the pillows together, and he pulls up his sleeve so I can tickle his arm. We take turns as we yack about his latest conquests, my upcoming interview with Woody Harrelson, and my brother's current lack of progress.

Yawning, I look at my watch. "Yikes, how did we parlez so long?" I say. "It's past two."

"It's pouring rain. You'll never get a cab," Zack says. "Why don't you just stay here tonight and go home in the morning?"

"Slumber party? Okay, give me something to sleep in," I say. "Still got that Cheap Trick concert T-shirt I gave you?"

He laughs and tosses me an extra-large golf shirt, which I change into in his bathroom after helping myself to his toothbrush. It's fun having a slumber party with a boy friend, two separate words.

"You comfortable?" he says as I snuggle up next to him. It occurs to me that men use intimacy to get sex, and women use sex to get intimacy. Snuggling with a boy friend, two separate words, is the loophole.

"Yeah," I say. "I just hope my father doesn't come in again and bust us."

We laugh at the memory, and Zack flicks the remote to a *Seinfeld* rerun.

"Spoon me, babe," he says lazily as we turn to face the TV on his bed stand. I do, and start breathing on his neck, like in the old days.

"C'est mon turn," I say when we get to the commercial.

Zack jumps out of bed.

"Where are you going?" I say, confused.

"To get the egg timer, so you don't cheat like you used to," he says, scampering down the hall. "Voulez-vous some water while I'm up? With lemon the way you like it?"

"Sure," I say.

When he gets back we change places so we can still watch TV as he breathes on my neck. I keep checking the timer, because this feels sooooo good. I don't want it to end. It dings.

But Zack keeps on breathing. At first I'm too comfortable to mention it, but being an upright citizen and all, I dreamily mumble, "Votre turn, maintenant."

"Je sais," he says. "Mais I like looking at the hairs on your arm."

Thanks to his expert neck tickling, I have a major case of goose bumps. This simple act of kindness, wanting me to feel good sans agenda, unbuckles my seat belt and I slip right through the crack. I roll over and face him.

We are nose to nose, blinking at each other in the dark.

He kisses me, and I tumble from the safety of self-imposed dating exile, down, down, down into a warm abyss. The bungee cord around my ankle is my original boy friend, two separate words. Or one?

Zack takes his time and spends hours kissing every single body part. It doesn't feel like sex as much as deep, physical intimacy, like feeling the experience through the other person's skin. Our kissing and touching progresses to sex as naturally as dinner to dessert. Delicious dessert. I have my first orgasm during sex.

"Oh, my God," I say when it's over. "Thank you!"

"You're welcome," he says. "But for what?"

"For making the earth move," I say. "That was my first time."

"No way," he says incredulously, propping himself up on an elbow. "You've been with three guys, right?"

"Four now," I say.

"Well, it makes me mad neither Blue Lagoon, Van Gogh, or Beau didn't take care of you," he says.

"Well, they tried. I always thought there was something wrong with me," I say. "I'm just lucky to reap the benefits of all of your, um, research, Mr. Gigolo."

Before the stomach swirlies of pleasure subside, a wave of panic rips through me. What if I've just ruined the best thing in my life? What if Zack, the original bachelor, '83 Class Stud, is like Harry after he sleeps with Sally and totally freaking out inside?

I screw up my courage and ask him, "Are you *still* comfortable?" I know the insertion of the word "still" will alert him to the fact that my question is psychological not physical.

"Oui, madame," he says, squeezing my hand tightly under the covers. "Et vous?"

More than I've ever been with anyone in my life, I think. How could I not see this tidal wave coming?

Four months go by without anything really changing except the fact that I'm having the best sex of my life. We never have "the talk" about making the relationship exclusive. We don't hold a press conference with all of our friends. But as time goes on, we just become more and more comfortable, until we are one completely compatible couple. Guess that's a by-product of road testing a relationship for thirteen years. After all, we've been saying Je t'aime to each other since eighth grade, not to mention all the default Valentine's Days and New Year's Eves and weddings we've suffered through together. And it certainly takes care of the awkward introduction to Bobby, for one thing. Got that out of the way in 1978.

When Zack and I decide to move in together, we realize that we better come out of the closet. We start big, with my parents. They know that we've been spending a lot of time together, but they never ask questions about us. I think they've taken the Ostrich Approach to my "friendship" with Zack, who is Jewish, because he's not the perfect Catholic boy they envision for their daughter. But who knows, perhaps they've been so consumed with my brother, as usual, that they really haven't noticed that Zack and I have become more than friends.

It's Sunday afternoon, the pot roast is in the oven, and my family is sitting around in the family room, listening to the Carpenters. Bobby is arranging his McDonald's *Back to the Future* collectibles. I decide to be an adult and tell them as straightforwardly as possible.

"Mom and Dad, I just wanted you to know that Zack and I are now together," I say.

They say nothing. All eyes.

"And we've, um, well, we've sort of been, you know, together for, uh, a while," I continue.

Just more eyes. Big and round now, like the Tiffany chargers Beau and I registered for.

"So, um, the thing is, it's, like, we've been starting to talk about moving in together," I blurt out, adding tentatively, "You know, to save on rent?"

"Bella, you know your mother and I don't approve of that," my father says sternly. "Zack's a good friend and all, but——"

"But he's not Catholic, right?" I interrupt, furious. "Well, you're right. He is a nice boy, the nicest boy I've ever known. That's why we're together."

"Honey, have you really thought this through?" my mother says, putting down her *Martha Stewart Living*. "Zack's a nice boy and all, but——"

"But what, Mom? Not the perfect son-in-law you always envisioned for your daughter?" I interrupt again, biting back my fury.

"Honey, no, we're just thinking of you," she says. "And I guess we are a bit surprised."

"Surprised at what?" I spit.

Bobby stands up and throws Doc's Delorean across the room.

"Wheeeeere's the beef?" he yells, offering a usual inappropriate non sequitur.

"This isn't exactly the best time for a Wendy's commercial," I scream at Bobby, losing my temper. My loudness startles him, and he hastily grabs Doc Brown, lunges for the thrown Delorean, and jerkily shuffles up to his room, where he remains for the rest of the night.

Before Bobby's even out of sight, I hate myself for lashing out at him. After all, the people I'm really angry at are my parents. Why can't they just be happy for me?

That night Zack and I are spooning to sleep, but I can't get comfortable. I keep hearing Bobby's weird robotic voice in my head saying, "Wheeeere's the beef?"

I'm also bothered by a couple other things. As a special surprise, Zack took me up to the top of his apartment building, where he had a bottle of wine and a picnic blanket. He pulled out his trumpet, and just as the sun set, he serenaded me with "Somewhere Over the Rainbow." Then he "proposed" for us to move in together.

When I told Carrie the next day on the phone, she was beside herself. "That is the most romantic thing I have ever heard of in my entire life," she gushes. "Oh, my God, if Miles did that for me, I would have dropped to my knees and proposed myself, or at least treated him to a great blowjob. Oh, Bella, I've never in my entire life been this head over heels in love! I can't describe the feeling."

But the truth is I felt, well, nothing. Nothing, nothing, nothing. I knew I should have felt something, but all it was was annoyance that I didn't feel anything.

Lying next to Zack, the awful truth dawns on me. Despite the fact that Zack's my best friend, and I'm having the best sex of my life, I don't have *that feeling*. And I know *that* feeling. I've felt passion a few times in my life, with Chandler, Johnner, and Beau. My brother is right. Where *is* the beef?

When I look into my heart, I admit that if I had to prioritize those three components, my first priority would be the only one missing—the passion. I can't move in with someone I am not in love with. He's safe, but I'm settling.

Gently, I tap Zack on the shoulder.

"Oui, madame?" he says. "Want me to tickle your neck?"

"No," I say. "We need to talk."

He rolls over and says softly, "Hey, pourqois are you crying?"

He holds me as I sob through the night. He just listens and listens as I tell him everything.

"What if we can never go back to being friends, now that we've crossed the line?" I say, weeping.

"Bella, do you want to know what I think?" he says. He reaches for my hand under the duvet.

I nod into his armpit. His Mennen Speedstick is so familiar to me it feels like home. I can't believe I'm doing this. Why do I always have to ruin everything?

"I've known you a long time and have seen you in and out of a lot of relationships," he says.

"And?" I say.

"I think that every time you get into a serious relationship your expectations are so high that it's almost like you are trying to have a relationship for two people." He pauses, then adds, "Because you feel bad that Bobby can't have one of his own. And the way you are so hard on yourself about your weight and your career. It's like you expect yourself to be perfect, to make up for him or something."

And here we have it, ladies and gentlemen. Cue the cheesy circus music, please, and spotlight on Ring One, where tonight's Freak Show act is The Opposite Twins on the seesaw: Weighing down one side we have Dysfunctional Twin, a square peg in a round role, an enigma hidden in a conundrum, gift-wrapped in a Trekkie T-shirt. Riding high on the other side of the seesaw we have the Overachiever Twin, compulsively compensating for their parents' disappointments. In her desperate desire to connect with her own twin, she *fails*! *Not acceptable!* So she searches for intimacy with the rest of the world! She's a slut by day, husband stalker by night. No wonder she's been racing to the altar since leaving the womb . . .

"Bella?" Zack says, gently shaking my shoulder.

"Wow," I say. "That's a concept."

I've been busted for two-timing Zack with my own brother. I'm so used to my heart being pulled in two different directions, one toward the light giddiness of romance, the other toward the dark sadness of Bobby's ever-non-changing situation, that I never stopped to notice how it might affect a boyfriend. Make that boy friend, two separate words.

The next morning, my head is reeling, my heart is aching, and I can't believe I have to go to work. My face is so swollen from crying that I look like the Elephant Woman.

What have I done? I've given up a B-plus for the chance to meet an A-minus, who might not even exist. To make matters worse, the shoulder I've cried on every time I've gotten my heart broken is no longer available to me. I lost my boyfriend and my best friend in one fell swoop. All because of some stupid Wendy's commercial.

"Do you have a cold or something?" says Carrie when I answer her call at work. "You sound weird."

"No, I've just been hysterically crying, that's all," I say, filling her in on the breakup.

"Come to the sneak peek tonight of Nora Ephron's new movie, *Sleepless in Seattle*," she says. "There's no press allowed, but we're doing the advertising so I can get you in."

Talk about cinema therapy! Meg Ryan doesn't marry her fiancé Bill Pullman and instead follows these secret signs to wind up with her true love—Tom Hanks! *Sleepless in Seattle* is a sign: "Don't settle, select!" It might take me a while to get over the hurt, but at least I now have hope that I did the right thing by breaking up with Zack. Perhaps The One still awaits.

I decide to write Nora Ephron a letter.

> *Dear Nora,*
>
> *My* When Harry Met Sally *relationship with my best friend, Zack, just ended. So now I'm at the awful part of my life when Sally is dragging the Christmas tree home all by herself. As a writer for* Preview Magazine, *sometimes I wonder if it's an occupational hazard to expect the music to swell to a crescendo during the big love scene in real life too. Maybe that will never happen. Still, seeing* Sleepless in Seattle *was a sign to have hope. Thanks for a mood-swing evening. I'll tell all my friends to see your movie.*
>
> *Best,*
> *Bella*

Imagine my surprise when I get into work the next day to find this message on my answering machine: "Bella, this is Nora Ephron, you adorable girl. Of course I remember you! I showed your note to the head of the marketing department. It was 'a sign' that *Sleepless* connects with its target audience, girls like you!" she went on to say. "Let's do lunch."

I can't believe this—it's like my life has become a movie! I go from one of my lowest moments ever, having my best friend tell me that I need a shrink because I've been starring in my own freak show act, to power lunching with the hottest female director in Hollywood.

She chooses Michael's, Midtown's primo canteen for the media elite, where we are seated at the very first table. Since Nora's the expert on romantic comedies, I can't help but ask her if I did the right thing.

"First of all, never settle. Select is what I always say," she advises. "If you don't want to be single, you have to put as much energy into your social life as you do into your career," she says. "More, even."

Tough love.

"That means going out every single night, no matter how tired you are," she continues. "And asking every person you know to fix you up."

"Okay, I'll do it," I say. "What else?"

"When anything bad happens to you, think of it as material," she says. "You can use it as a funny story later, because people love hearing about funny bad things happening to other people. Now how about Steve Martin? He's single."

I drop my fork.

"I'm going to call him and tell him about you," she says with a wink. "Waiter, I'll take the check."

Being fixed up by one of Hollywood's most famous directors can certainly take the fun out of feeling sorry for yourself.

✦

14

Year: 1994
Age: 29
Idols: Thelma and Louise
Favorite Song: "All I Wanna Do" (Sheryl Crow)
Prized Possession: Wonderbra
Best Shoes: black and white Jack Rogers sandals

✦

Oh, God, I'm gonna puke I'm so nervous. I'm walking from the jitney to the beach house, about to go on a blind date with fourteen people, and it's going to last from Memorial to Labor Day. All the rich, single, social New Yorkers evacuate to the uberexclusive Hamptons for the summer. Thanks to Carrie, I'm joining them.

I'm on a good-luck streak. Right out of the blue, I get this call from *Style* magazine to be their entertainment editor. My new boss is Blanche, but the staff calls her the Skunk behind her back because she has a jet-black pageboy with this huge white stripe down the front. Plus she bathes herself in Giorgio, despite the fact that it's more eighties than leg warmers and Lionel Richie. There's something about Blanche that makes me feel like a wind-up doll out to get her approval.

It's like the Diva of the Month Club for me. Each month I get to interview a different celebrity for the cover story. The only bad part is the Skunk always forces me to ask the Embarrassing Question. So far she's forced me to ask Jodie Foster to reveal the father of her baby and Demi Moore if she's had a boob job.

But a job's a job, and at least it's letting me afford the Hamptons this summer. As I pull open the screen door to our rented house, I take a deep breath, cross my fingers, and make a wish that I will meet The One this summer. It's been a lonely year since I lost my boyfriend and best boy friend all at once. The few blind dates I've been on have done little to change my single status.

"Hey, Bella!" a voice booms over the din of the blender and the B-52's singing "Love Shack." "What's it like to date Steve Martin?"

My reputation precedes me. I guess I have Carrie to thank for that. The truth is I never officially went on a date with Steve Martin. Nora invited me to a party at her house and forced an introduction. Can you say No Chemistry? He didn't look up from his feet one single time, which turned me into a blithering chatterbox. We finally managed to find some common ground by talking about art. He owns an Edward Hopper, a Georges Seurat, and a Picasso. But when I asked him what it was like to live with an actual Picasso, he said, "I like to keep my private life private."

As much as I love the idea of having a movie star boyfriend, what's the point if the movie star boyfriend wants to keep his private life private? Still, I must admit, Carrie broadcasting that I "dated" Steve Martin does pique the interest of other guys. It's better than saying, well, "She's in a dry spell more parched than the Sahara Desert. Yup, she hasn't had a date in more than a year."

I follow the voice into the kitchen where I find this guy with shaggy brown hair and a wily smirk. He's handsome in a rugged, outdoorsy, J.Crew catalogue kind of way.

"I'll tell you the answer to that burning question if you tell me your name," I say.

"Sorry. Pete," he says, taking a slug of ten-year-old Patrón and pouring the rest into the blender. "I work in advertising with Carrie. She told me to keep an eye out for you." He cocks his head and gives me a hugely exaggerated wink.

He extends his hand, so I do too. But instead of shaking it, he brings it to his lips and kisses it.

Can he smell the Doritos I was eating on the jitney? I *knew* I should have lost weight. Whenever I want something to happen to me, the first thing I do is go on a diet. It's my version of foreplay for life.

Sometimes I tell my shrink, Joyce, that I wish I could be anorexic, but I just don't have the willpower. I say this for shock value, to make her laugh. Joyce then asks me what I really want to control, and we wind up spending the next forty-five minutes talking about Bobby, which is annoying.

If my weekly sessions over the past six months have proved anything, it's that Zack was right: I needed some couch time to deal with my issues. When Joyce starts each session with "Breathe, and tell me what comes up," and I typically answer by saying I wish I had a boyfriend, she always manages to lead us back in time to my childhood, where we go over the Gray Cloud, the Pink Elephant, and the executive producer of both, of course, Bobby.

The good news is at least Zack and I have been able to salvage the friendship. Carefully. We see each other occasionally, but never on a Sunday, the worst day in the entire world to be single, and always sans alcohol. It wouldn't take much to slide right back into the sack—especially now that I know what I'm missing, which is the Sally-in-the-diner scene, but for real.

In a weird way, giving up Zack is a lot like breaking the late-night-munchies habit. Their comforts are similar but ultimately just a distraction from dealing with the painful truth. After Beau, I wasn't ready to move forward no matter how badly I wanted to. And forcing it with someone "safe" like Zack wasn't being true to my heart. Bobby was right about asking, "Where's the beef?" I was settling, not selecting.

But that was then, and this is now.

He hands me a margarita, and I catch a whiff of him. Clean, but with a hint of Coppertone. Just like summer. Suddenly I'm having the fantasy: We'll travel the world, me writing articles for *Vanity Fair*, Pete shooting commercials for Nike. We will become such a team that *Hamptons* magazine will do a feature on us, in our beach house, next door to Kate and Steven Spielberg, who will be the godparents to our children.

"Want to head down to the beach and meet everyone?" he says, extending an arm.

Not really, I think. *Take me to bed or lose me forever!*

"Absolutely!" I say as we interlock elbows. We amble down the sandy path to the beach, and I find Carrie looking impossibly gorgeous in a crop top and cutoffs. Lord, if I can't be skinny, please make my friends fat.

She and Pete introduce me to all the housemates, most of whom are loosely connected through the advertising world. Then this Asian stick figure, who defines heroin chic, comes up and slides her hands into Pete's back pockets.

"Liza!" he says, turning to kiss her. It's subtle, but Liza is brandishing her owner's rights. Fiddling with his hair, leaning into him, giving me the "Gee, your hair smells terrific" by putting her back toward me. What an idiot I am. I've just been on Fantasy Island with a taken man.

My heart sinks into the pit of my stomach. I decide to walk back to the house and look for those Doritos.

"Wait up!" says Carrie, running to catch up with me. "What's wrong?"

"It's just that, well, Pete and I had such chemistry," I try to explain. "But Liza, jeez, she looks like a model."

"She *is* a model," Carrie says. "Pete met her doing one of the Victoria's Secret campaigns. But they're not the perfect couple. They're constantly fighting because she thinks he drinks too much."

"She's just not fun enough for him," I say. "There's no way she could drink a lot and stay that skinny."

For the rest of the weekend, I try to regain the anything-can-happen-to-me anticipation I felt Friday night, but it's no good. Every time the two of them make physical contact it bugs me no matter how sternly I tell myself to get over it.

The next week I throw myself into my work, and it pays off. I land the perfect summer assignment: to interview Kate Capshaw at Quelle Barn, the Spielbergs' East Hampton enclave. Translation: I've just scored myself a week of free vacation!

"Mind if I rent a car?" I ask my boss, Blanche. "I'll need the flexibility (i.e., transportation to the bars at night)."

"No, as long as you ask how that shiksa stole Steven Spielberg from that nice Jewish girl Amy Irving," she says. "Enquiring minds want to know." Ugh, leave it to her to always find a way to insult every person I have to interview from the safety of her own office.

I rent a Mustang convertible and blast old Rolling Stones tapes the whole way on the Long Island Expressway. I'm just going to start my summer over, clean slate. It's mind over matter.

Carrie told me that some people in our share house might be out there taking vacation days. I hope it's some of the singles and not the couples, so I'll have people to party with. When I walk into the living room, Pete appears from the outdoor shower with a beer in one hand and holding a towel around his waist with the other. My heart swoops up, like one of those kiddy kites catching air. I yank the string back. Hold on, cowgirl—the dude's dating a model.

"What are you doing here?" we both say at the same time.

"Jinx!" we answer simultaneously and run around the room trying to pinch each other.

"I'm interviewing Kate Capshaw about her latest movie for *Style* magazine," I say while he says, "R and R."

"Where's Liza?" I venture.

"In Mustique, doing a catalogue," he says.

Immediately, the Mexican jumping beans inside my stomach start doing the macarena.

For the next few days, Pete and I do everything together. At the beach, we put suntan lotion on each other's backs and read the latest Page Six gossip to each other, then later do the dishes after dinner together. It's the little stuff like this, and not necessarily "doing the deed," that I really miss about having a boyfriend, I realize as we head into our separate bedrooms each night.

On the night before my big interview, Pete suggests that I practice my questions on him.

"So, Kate, how'd a shiksa like you manage to steal Hollywood's hottest director from a nice Jewish girl anyway?" I say, impersonating Gilda Radner impersonating Baba Wawa.

"That's an easy one, Baba," says Pete in a super feminine Marilyn Monroe voice. "Great blow jobs. I figured if *Jaws* could make his career, it could make mine too."

I'm laughing so hard that I almost fall off my chair. Well, Okay, I guess the two bottles of Pinot Grigio we polished off with our swordfish steaks made it even funnier.

It's not so funny the next morning when I have to gear up for the Capshaw interview with a huge, colossal hangover. Even though I had really been looking forward to the interview, I was counting the minutes until it was over.

When I finally pull back into our driveway, I see Pete waiting for me on the front steps.

"How did it go?" he asks. "Did you ask Blanche's Embarrassing Question?"

"Yeah, but I phrased it in my own way," I say. "Which was 'How did you know that Steven was The One?'"

"And?" he asks. We are thigh to thigh, looking out at the

waves. I wonder if he is comparing my leg to Liza's, which is roughly the size of a child's forearm in comparison.

"She said, 'I knew it by the way he smelled,'" I say. "So I asked, 'And what was that like?'"

"Calvin Klein Eternity?" Pete cracks.

"Weirder," I say. "She said, 'Like babies when they are born,' quote, unquote. 'Like he was mine.'"

"So did you ask about the husband-stealing part?" he says, riveted.

"Again, I sort of put it in my own words, which was 'Considering he'd just had a baby with Amy Irving, how did you have the confidence to go for it, even if you thought he was hers?'" I explain. "I told her that if I were in her shoes, I would've told myself that the odds were against me, not being Jewish and with the baby, etc." The same way I tell myself that I would never be attractive to Pete compared to a model, I think.

"Whoa! I'm impressed you did it!" he says. "What'd she say, what'd she say?"

"She said that she talks to herself," I say.

"What?" he says, guffawing.

"She said that every time she would hear that negative voice in her head, she'd say, 'No, I am going to *give* to myself, and replace the self-criticism with positive self talk,'" I explain.

"That's so weird," he says.

"Yeah, but it worked," I say. "Look who wound up with the prize? Literally, her thoughts *became* her reality."

I give it a whirl.

Negative Me: Boy, my leg looks fat.

Kate Capshaw Positive Me: My leg isn't fat—it's a luscious fruit!

Negative Me: But Liza's a model. Hello, you do the math.

Kate Capshaw Positive Me: Yeah, but they fight all the time. You are *waaaay* more fun than some skinny . . .

"I have an idea," says Pete, interrupting the private discussion I was having with Kate Capshaw in my head.

"Let's skate over to the Sunset Bar, have one of those killer strawberry margaritas, and then go to the Farmer's Market to buy stuff for dinner on our way back," he says, as excited as a little boy.

"But I don't have Rollerblades," I say.

"I have an extra pair for you!" he says, pulling me to my feet. "C'mon, it'll be an adventure!"

I wonder about the sanity of this plan but rationalize that it's safer than driving drunk. Besides, I'm the Fun Girl, right?

"You okay?" he asks as we make our way out of the driveway.

I'm a little unsteady on my feet, so Pete stays close by me. I'm trying to just go with it, but inside I feel torn. Guilt is gnawing around the edges of the good time I'm having. I would hate to be in Liza's shoes, while I'm literally in her Rollerblades, a fact that Pete did not tell me until after he had laced them up. He assured me that she wouldn't mind. Yeah, right.

Me: You boyfriend-stealing bitch.

Kate Capshaw Positive Voice: I'm not doing anything, I swear! We're just friends!

Me: Good thing you're fat—that'll probably keep you safe.

Kate Capshaw Positive Voice: I'm not fat. I'm fun! We're just going for a drink. What's the big deal? What am I supposed to do, stay home and eat?

"Don't concentrate so hard," says Pete, misreading my furrowed brow. "Just go with it. It's like ice-skating."

We blade the four miles to the bar and perch ourselves on barstools.

"The usual, Pete?" says the bartender, a rhetorical question, as he places a shot of Patrón and a strawberry margarita before him.

"Yes, and the same for our intrepid reporter," Pete says. "Bella's going to be the next Barbara Walters."

I love the attention, but at the same time it makes me totally uncomfortable, so I switch the topic to his career. Currently, Pete's a star on the rise at Grey Advertising where he works on accounts like Victoria's Secret and Heineken.

"Must be really rough, looking at scantily clad lingerie models all day," I joke.

"It gets played out," he says. "My dream is to open up my own shop someday. A small boutique company for nonprofit clients like Greenpeace."

I tell him my dreams of having a screenplay in development and a baby by the time I'm thirty-five, and how I consider the celebrity interviews I'm doing research for the romantic comedy I'll write someday.

"That way if I never get married, I can live vicariously through my female protagonist," I say.

It's really easy to be yourself with a guy when he's not available. And when you've had four or five rounds.

"Oh, you'll get married," Pete says. There's a glint in his eye I can't quite put my finger on. His hand brushes mine, ever so slightly, as he picks up his drink and drains his glass.

"We'd better get back. It's pitch-black," I say, changing the subject. "I guess we missed dinner," I say with a giggle.

Speaking in only Baba Wawa talk, we laugh and stumble on our Rollerblades the whole way back to the house. Once inside the front door, we are sliding around on the linoleum, trying to find the light switch.

"Whoa!" I say, slipping backward.

"I've got you," he says, clamping his hands on my shoulders. We stand there for a minute facing each other, and I can feel it. He is about two seconds from kissing me.

In the dark, I shake my head no. As much as I am attracted to him, I'm not going there. I lean over and snap on the light.

"Let there be light!" I say, breaking the spell.

We unlace our boots, and we head to our separate bedrooms.

"Good night, Baba!" he calls out after me.

"Good night, John Boy!" I call back and dive into my bed, just before I lose my resolve.

If I could pick someone else to have a crush on, I would, believe me. At least Kate didn't have to watch Steven and Amy disappear into their bedroom. But as much as I see the possibilities of a great relationship with Pete, the most I can hope for is a friendship. Talk about a catch-22. It's never been my style to pick unavailable men, but I'm sure Joyce will find a way to tether this to the Pink Elephant too.

When Fourth of July weekend rolls around, I ask Carrie to find us as many parties as possible, so I can avoid Pete and Liza—and maybe even meet someone new.

"Well, you won't have to worry about avoiding Liza," says Carrie. "She's on a shoot."

Absolutely not, I tell the Mexican jumping beans, that are putting on their cowboy hats, fixin' to do a line dance in the pit of my stomach.

I go out of my way to avoid Pete, but, unfortunately it seems to have the same effect as playing hard to get. I feel his eyes follow me around the room, and when the housemates all pile into the car to go hear live music at the Steven Talkhouse, Pete purposefully opens the door on my side.

"Bella, we're going to have to squish," he says, pulling me onto his lap. I'm trying to push up on my toes so my full weight won't be on him, but I'm distracted. In the dark, he has his hand around my waist.

We go into the Talkhouse, and I disappear in the crowd on the dance floor. Loup Garou, this incredible Zydeco band, is playing, and all the housemates are bumping and grinding together in a sweaty frenzy. When the music turns slow, Pete is suddenly next to me. He finds my hand and holds it.

Kate Capshaw Positive Voice: He likes you! He likes you!

Everyone has broken off into a twosome, Pete and I included. With our eyes locked, we are moving to each other's rhythm. Our dance is beyond intimate. The only things touching are our hands, but our eye contact is so intense it feels like we are having sex right there on the dance floor. Then he pulls me toward him and lays the most unbelievable smooch on me. In front of everyone. His friends. Liza's friends. Everyone.

Liza's friends are the ones who find us the next morning intertwined on the couch. Still completely dressed—we had made out for a while until we passed out together. Not that it matters how little action we got. The Hangover Gremlin starts in with his sledgehammer and a banner that reads: "Congratulations, Bella! You've Just Ruined Your Entire Summer!"

I feel like an adulteress. A stupid one. Even if they do fight all the time, Liza's a Victoria's Secret model. He's never going to leave her. No amount of Kate Capshaw Positive Self Talk is going to mitigate this case of the Drunken Guilties.

I try to wake up Pete, but he's totally passed out. I decide to cut my losses, and without saying good-bye to anyone but Carrie, I slither back to the city like the snake that I am.

Late that night, I polish off two pints of fat-free frozen yogurt, and I'm so cold that I have to blow-dry my entire body even though I am wearing a sweatshirt. From the bathroom, I hear the phone ring. It must be Carrie, calling to scrape me up off the floor.

"I know that wearing a scarlet letter is definitely a *Glamour* Don't," I say when I pick up the phone.

"Uh, Bella?" says a guy's voice.

Oh, my God, it's Pete!

"Sorry it's so late, but I just thought you should know . . ." he starts.

That I'm a fat loser who just made a big public mistake? Thanks, I already got the memo.

"Liza and I broke up," he says.

Kate Capshaw Positive Voice: Told you he likes you!

Within a nanosecond I meet him at Rebar, one of his hang-outs. Over a few rounds of martinis, he tells me about ending things with Liza, and I ask him if he's sure he's ready to dive into another relationship. As much as I like him, I know better than to be a rebound romance.

"I've never been able to talk to Liza the way I can talk to you," he says. "Like we can really be best friends." Boy friend. Boyfriend. Thanks to Zack, I've had some practice melding the two. We talk all night and wind up closing the bar. The next day I decide to take a personal day from work, and we don't get out of bed until dinnertime.

Pete and I decide to avoid the beach house drama the following weekend and check into the American Hotel in Sag Harbor instead. The American Hotel is quaint but chic. All sorts of celebrities have been known to hang out in the cigar bar. Often Billy Joel will drop into the bar and play the piano.

After breakfast in bed that Saturday morning, Pete says, "I have a surprise for you." He walks me to the marina and right onto the deck of a forty-foot sloop that he's rented for the day.

"Don't worry about a thing. Just sit back and relax," he says.

"C'mon, at least let me be jib girl," I say.

"You know how to sail?" he says, surprised.

"Enough to know to duck when you jibe," I say.

"Bella, there are so many things I don't know about you," he says, coming over to give me a kiss. "And I'm looking forward to getting to know each and every one of them."

As we turn off the motor and hoist the sails, all that stuff Chandler taught me comes right back. I realize that I am almost twice the age I was when I lost my virginity. As we coast along, I play the Now and Then game in my head. Then: size six. Now:

size ten. Then: My fifteen-year-old self couldn't believe that I was pretty enough to catch Chandler's attention. Now: I am dating the ex-boyfriend of a supermodel.

The rest of the weekend whirls by like one long cocktail party for two, and the only disappointment is when it's time to board the jitney and go back to the reality of our jobs.

But luckily during our start-up months, Pete and I skip all the usual cat-and-mouse games that stand in as foreplay for the majority of thirtysomething relationships. I don't have to present myself as The Challenge, because The Challenge already existed—first it was Liza, and now it's our dueling travel schedules.

Still, after several months I realize that Liza may have had a little, teeny bit of a point about Pete's drinking. Sometimes I'll call his hotel room really late at night, and he still won't be home. And he definitely takes it too far when he's hanging out with his advertising friends.

Like tonight at this rooftop keg party. Granted, I know he's exhausted and jetlagged from coming back from a shoot in L.A., but the fact that it's always him instigating the drinking games doesn't help.

Carrie and I watch Pete and the guys start a rowdy game of Mexican. She can feel me tensing up.

"Try not to overreact—that's what Liza used to always do," she counsels. "Just sort of lure him away, before he goes over to the Dark Side."

"I can see from here that he's on his way," I say. "His eyes turn into little slits, and he gets that dime-slot mouth. Sometimes he actually looks at me like he barely recognizes me."

"Let's you and I check out the tapas bar they just set up on the other side of the party," she suggests. "Boring holes into him with your eyes isn't going to help."

A half hour later, after hearing about Carrie's latest conquest, an investment banker guy, who, of course, is the super responsible type, I can't help myself. I need to check in on Pete. But after doing a lap, I can't find him anywhere.

When I meet up with Carrie again, she says, "Uh, somebody told me he left."

"Left, without me?" I say. "How could he? It's his first night back, and we haven't seen each other in weeks!"

I am in shock. In a fury, I take a cab to his place. Did he leave with someone else? Did he fall off the roof? These thoughts race through my mind. When I can't stand the tension one more minute, we finally pull up in front of his apartment.

"No, I have not seen Mr. Pete," says José, Pete's doorman, who is returning to his post.

Just then, Pete appears, holding a bag from Blockbuster.

"Hi!" he slurs nonchalantly, as if we've just run into each other at the keg.

"High, all right. You're higher than a kite!" I say back sarcastically, ripping the bag away from him, and dumping the contents on the street. *Good Morning, Vietnam* and *Debbie Does Dallas: Uncut Version* stare up at us.

"You might have told me you were going to make it a Blockbuster Night, before you left me at the party!" I say, wild with fury. I mean, so wild I don't know what to do with myself. I feel like I am going to explode. This guy is totally out of control, and he's taking me for the ride with him.

He bends down to pick up his videos, looking drunk and confused.

"Taxi!" I scream. "I'm leaving! Call me when you return to the land of the living."

I spend the entire next day sobbing on the couch, waiting for him to call and apologize. The hours crawl by. I get more and more desolate, but I will not let myself call him. I call Carrie instead.

"Bella, if you want a cowboy, you're going to have to break

him," she tells me. "Pete's always the life of the party, but he's the type who's always going to require a certain amount of cleanup after a big bash."

Finally, finally, finally he calls around five that afternoon. "Work hard, play hard," he says cavalierly, not listening to one word I have to say. I hang up on him and refuse to speak to him for two days.

A dozen long-stem American Beauties arrive at my office. I refuse them, sending them back to the florist. I call Carrie to make her congratulate me three times.

Then, finally, Pete comes over and apologizes in person.

"Bella, I'm sorry," he says, looking, I must admit, miserable. But not miserable enough.

"You'll have to do better than that," I say. I've wasted three days on this crisis.

"Sometimes I get a little out of hand," he admits.

"I'll say," I spit.

"But I can control it. I really can," he says. "I was dehydrated from the flight, and I hadn't eaten anything, and well, I was just stupid. But I promise it won't happen again."

"How can I be sure?" I say. "I mean, you left me at a party to go home and rent porn, for godsakes."

"Because I'll do whatever it takes to be with you," he says. This time he's looking me straight in the eyes. I can tell from his pleading look that he means it.

"Why should I believe you?" I ask. I am starting to believe him but taking advantage of my unusual position of power.

He doesn't say anything for a minute, while he searches my eyes.

"Because I love you, Bella," he whispers, for the first time.

Well, that's pretty good! My anger starts to subside. He loves me. I've broken my cowboy. It's the first step toward happily riding off into the sunset together.

"I love you too," I say as we embrace. "And I will help you. I really think you need to consider AA."

"I'm not an alcoholic, Bella," he promises me. "It's just that sometimes I overdo it. I promise to never get so out of control again." We compromise with some ground rules: no drinking until five, and a glass of water between each drink.

I decide to believe him, and I'm glad.

Months go by without any drunken incidents, and with Pete's drinking in check, the only thing standing between engagement and us is his career. I know from our conversations that he wants to get to the next step of his profession before proposing. I wish he'd stop taking so many accounts and continue to work on his plan, which is the only thing that's going to get him his own shop. I tell myself I have to be patient.

By the time our one-year anniversary rolls around, things are going pretty well. Pete books a room at the American Hotel, where we spent our first weekend as a legitimate couple. We're hanging out in his apartment making our plans when the phone rings. Pete answers it, then motions for me to get his assignment book and a pen.

"Well, Bella the beautiful," he says, hanging up the phone, "I have good news and bad news. Take your pick."

"Bad first," I say.

"I can't go to the American Hotel," he says. "The good news is I just got the Nissan account. We're going to shoot a car commerical in Hawaii."

"Congratulations! That's great," I say, really trying to be cheerful, although I'm disappointed that once again our plans are wrecked. And for more Grey work, not to work on his exit strategy.

"Come fly with me!" he says, lifting me out of my chair and waltzing me around the studio. "We'll use my frequent flier points. Meet me after the shoot in Hawaii, and we'll keep going to Bali."

Bali—the honeymoon I never had! I'm sure he'll propose!

I realize I have to introduce him to my family before this happens. I don't want my parents disapproving of the relationship when I've finally found The One. And he's preppy and Protestant. Close enough.

To make it easy for Pete, I arrange a dinner party at my place instead of making him schlep out to the folks' house. I shop and chop and cook recipes from *The Silver Palate Cookbook* all day long. I spic and span my entire apartment, carefully hiding any clues that Pete practically lives with me.

Six on the dot my family arrives. "Pete is so looking forward to meeting everyone," I say, passing the shrimp cocktail.

Six fifteen, and no Pete. Traffic, I tell myself. Six thirty. Six forty-five.

"Punctuality must not be important in his profession," says my father, tapping his Notre Dame watch.

"Traffic, I'm sure," I say.

Seven o'clock. Seven fifteen. The organic pork tenderloin is starting to burn, and Bobby is starting to rock in his chair, which means that time is almost up before a meltdown.

"Shake-shake-shake, shake-shake-shake, shake your booty!" says Bobby and the Sunshine Band.

Good idea, I think to myself. "Forgot an ingredient. I'll be right back!" I say, grabbing my bag and bolting out the door.

I pay the taxi double to speed to Rebar. And that's exactly where I find Pete, perched on a stool surrounded by his advertising buddies. I drag him by the earlobe out into the street and let him have it in the cab as we whiz back uptown to my apartment.

"How could you do this to me?" I say, a lump coming up in my throat.

"Bella, I was just having one with the guys before meeting your folks. What's the big deal?" he says.

"The big deal is you are an hour and a half late!" I scream at him as we get out of the cab and walk into my building. "And you have *not* been drinking water between each drink."

Pete hiccups the whole time up in the elevator.

"Please try to sober up," I beg. "For me?"

Pete flings open the door to my apartment and says, "Helllll-llo, Newman."

"Look who I found in the lobby!" I announce to my family. "Turns out, um, his flight was late."

Pete hiccups again.

"Dad, this is Pete," I say as he shakes my father's hand.

"Hello, Pete," my dad says, eyeing him.

"Nizetomeet you," Pete slurs.

"This is my mom," I say, and Pete kisses her hand.

"How charming!" she says, and I think, hope, in fact she thinks he is.

And then I introduce him to Bobby, who is wearing his navy pajamas.

"Dressed for bed, dude?" Pete says. "I'm not that late, am I?"

"Ehhh, what's up, Doc?" says Bobby, looking at him suspiciously out of the corner of his eye.

"Bugs Bunny is the balls!" says Pete, hiccuping again. "I'm a huge fan too!"

My mother catches my eye. Pete has misunderstood. Bobby hates Bugs, and that's his way of saying he doesn't like Pete. Perhaps he can smell the alcohol on his breath. Pete smells like a tequila distillery.

As everyone gets seated at the table, I serve the meal and pour my parents extra-big glasses of wine. I try to give Pete ice water, but he helps himself to the vino. Ugh.

"So, Pete, are you a college football fan?" my father asks, looking for some common ground.

"More of a rugby man," Pete slurs.

"Bella tells us you shoot car commercials," my father says, trying again.

"Yup," says Pete. "They pay me the biiiig bucks."

Everyone is silent as they chew, and chew, and chew the organic shoe leather that I bought for fifteen dollars a pound.

"How is everything?" I ask.

Pete emits a loud burp, cracking himself up.

To cover up the sound, I immediately raise a toast. "To friends and family," I say. As everyone is politely clinking glasses, Pete chugs his wine. Then he gets down onto one knee and serenades my mother.

> "Mary Ann Barnes is the queen of all the acrobats;
>   she can do tricks that will give a man the shits.
>   She can shoot green peas from her fundamental orifice,
>   do a double somersault, and catch 'em on her tits."

Before I can stop him, he launches into the next verse.

> "She's a great big fat shit, twice the size of me,
>   hair on her ass like the branches in a tree.
>   She can swim, fight, shoot, fuck,
>   climb a tree, or drive a truck.
>   She's the kind of girl that's gonna marry me!"

Looking completely horrified, my mother looks at my father and says, "Robert, perhaps we should go—"

"Calm down, Beavis. You're going to soil your drawers. Heh heh heh eh heh heh heh," Bobby says, straight-faced. " 'Uh, I have

an injury.' 'You do?' 'Yeah, I have this great big crack in my butt!'
Heh, heh, heh."

Stimulated by Pete's loud singing, Bobby has taken this opportunity to regale us with his favorite Beavis and Butthead ex-
cerpts.

I put a call into Kate Capshaw Positive Self Talk, but her line
is busy. I'm going down in flames all alone on this one.

"I'm sorry," I say to my parents. "Pete is dehydrated. He just
got off a long flight and didn't realize the effect alcohol would
have on him."

"Bella, we understand, but it's late, and your father has an
early morning tomorrow," says my mother. She almost looks
sorry for me.

Pete wanders off toward the bathroom, and I walk my family
to the door. After all the work I've done, the night is a complete
and total disaster.

"Sure you're okay, honey?" my dad says, looking toward the
bathroom door, from behind which are loud retching sounds.

"He's got a lot of food allergies," I lie. "We'll be fine, don't
worry."

As soon as my family goes down in the elevator, I fling open
the bathroom door and launch into Pete. He is sitting on the bathroom floor with his forehead resting on the porcelain bus. Hands
on hips I repeat for him the raunchy rugby song he sang for my
mother at the dinner table.

"She can do tricks that will give a man the shits?" I say. "Did
you think she would find that charming?"

We sit there in silence. This is the end, it's over.

"My mother's never been Rugby Queen before," I say.
"Thanks for the honor."

"I'm sorry," he says.

"That's not good enough," I say. I love you is not going to
work this time, either.

"I need you, Bella," he says, lifting his head to look at me. "I have a problem, and you can help me."

The words cut right through me—because they're true. He *does* need me. He's a mess, and he needs to change. It's as simple as that, and I can change him.

"Well, you need to admit that you are an alcoholic, not just have a dehydration problem," I say.

He nods.

"Will you go to AA?" I ask.

"No, I want to handle this on my own," he says, clearly sobering up. "But I promise to control myself."

"Will you quit hanging out with those advertising guys after work?" I ask. "They are the worst influence on you."

"Yes, for you, I will," he says. "For you, I will do anything."

He gives me a look that almost breaks my heart and says, "And I will because you make me a better person."

I'm not perfect, and neither is anyone else. Everyone deserves a second chance.

For a while, everything goes back to normal. Even better than normal. Pete even offers to come along on the weekly excursions Bobby and I take together. This is perfect, because the day of the *Virtuosity* premiere, I run into a snag. My morning Julia Roberts interview is pushed to late afternoon. I decide to call Pete and ask him for help, for a change. If I can help him, then he can help me, right?

"You want me to meet Bobby at Grand Central Station *without* you?" Pete says into the phone. I can't see his face, but I can hear the hesitation in his voice.

"Please? I don't have the heart to cancel on him," I say. "Just take him to get something to eat first, and I'll meet you both in front of the theater."

"Pajama Man's not going to freak out, right?" asks Pete.

"No, his new drug, Tofanil, is working out great," I say. "Just remember, no touching and no loud noises. I'll put on my cell phone when the interview's over."

As soon as I finish with Julia, I race to the Ziegfeld Theater. I see paparazzi galore, but no Pete or Bobby. I check my cell phone—no messages. When I'm the last person standing on the red carpet, I start to panic. I'm just about to call my parents when my phone rings.

"Bella, you better get here fast!" says Pete. "Pajama Man's going postal!"

"Where are you?" I scream into the phone.

"Uh, Scores," he says.

"You took him to a *strip club*?" I say in disbelief.

"I decided to bring some work friends with me to meet your brother. They thought it'd be funny," he says, slurring. "But you better hurry. He's under the table in a fetal position."

I jump into a cab and promise to pay the driver double if he runs the red lights. I am so angry I feel like a cartoon character with smoke coming out of my ears. I feel like screaming and crying at the same time.

I charge into the club to discover Bobby crouched down in a ball saying, "Well, isn't that special?" over and over again. By the Dana Carvey catchphrase I can tell he's regressed to the eighties.

"What the hell happened?" I say over the disco version of "I Touch Myself." Pete's friends look away embarrassed. One glance at Pete, with his hooded eyes and dime-slot mouth, and I realize he's too trashed to even be chagrined. He's all the way over on the Dark Side.

"The guys wanted to watch him get a lap dance," he slurs.

"Bobby, who can't stand human touch, got a lap dance?" I say incredulously.

"I'm sorry," Pete says. "I didn't mean to hurt him. Let me help you."

"You've helped enough," I spit. "Get the hell away from us."

I spatula up my brother off the floor and drag him out of the club.

"I'm so sorry, Bobby. I'm so sorry," I say to him.

"Well, isn't that special?" he repeats Dana Carvey's Church Lady line quietly.

I hail a cab, and tell the driver to take us all the way to Westchester. I watch Bobby watching the lights as we whiz along. The highway seems to calm him.

"I know, I'm sorry," I say, trying to put calming thoughts in his head. "Space, the final frontier. These are the voyages of the Starship *Enterprise*. Its five-year mission—"

He picks it up from there: "—to explore strange new worlds, to seek out new life and new civilizations, to boldly go where no man has gone before."

"Well, Bobby, you've boldly gone where plenty of men have gone before," I say. "Not that their wives or girlfriends have known about it."

After a forty-five-minute drive, the cab pulls into our driveway.

"You can keep the meter running," I tell the driver. "I'll be out in about fifteen minutes."

I manage to get Bobby up to bed, and he's completely silent with a weird look on his face.

My mother, dressed in her bathrobe, appears in the hallway. "Bella, is everything all right?" she asks.

"Yeah, Ma, it's under control. Just thought I should tuck Bobby in myself tonight," I say. "But I've got to head back into the city."

"Did you two kids have a nice time at the movies?" she asks.

"Well, I think Bobby might be a little worn-out," I say. "Do me a favor and let me know if he acts weird tomorrow, okay?"

"Okay, sweetie. Sure you can't stay the night?" she says, kissing me on the cheek. "You're so good to your brother—do you know that?"

If you only knew, I think.

"Thanks, Mom. We'll talk tomorrow, okay?" I say. "Meter's running, gotta go."

The entire way back I rage at Pete in my head. How *could he*? That's it. This is the last straw! I could *kill* him! The volume of the screaming in my skull is so loud, I get a crushing headache.

Letting myself in to my apartment, I see a trail of Pete's clothes leading to the Bali tickets and a note on my pillow. "I love you. I'm sorry. The truth is, I got scared," it reads.

I slide into bed next to him and toss and turn. I can see our perfect future so clearly. It's just that the present is such a mess. I wish for a sign.

An hour or so later, I am awakened by a sign there is no way to misinterpret.

First I think I'm dreaming, when the cold, wet feeling starts sopping the sheet beneath me. As I awaken I am saturated with disgust. Pete peed the bed.

"Gross," I mutter, jumping out of the bed as Pete snores it off.

The only bright spot is imagining Pete waking up to his own mess, with me gone, which I explain to Joyce at my early morning therapy session.

"What a coincidence, right?" I say. "I asked for a sign. The Universe is telling me clearly that this is not someone I can Depends on. Pun intended."

"There are no accidents, Bella," Joyce says, who firmly believes that everything in life is connected.

"It's just that he'd be so great, if he'd just get this one problem under control. I feel like I have to help him," I say. "But I don't know how."

"Feel familiar?" she says.

"Yes," I say as I put my finger on the feeling. "It's the Gray Cloud."

With Joyce's gentle coaching, I push my way deeper into the Gray Cloud.

"Tell me when the Gray Cloud started," she says.

"It was there before I can even remember, raining inside my house, on me, Bobby, and our parents, who are helpless," I explain.

"Sounds like there is a problem in the Gray Cloud," she murmurs.

"But there are no words for the problem, just a nameless, faceless dread," I continue to explain. "I'm trying as hard as I can to be a good girl to make up for something that's broken, but I don't know how to fix him."

"Fix him?" she asks.

"Him," I say.

"Him, Pete?" she asks.

"No. Him, my brother," I say, the tears making their way through my closed eyes.

"Yes, Bella, that's right. You can't 'fix' an alcoholic any more than you can 'fix' an autistic," she says gently. "Are you ready to face the truth?"

"The truth about Pete, and the fact that it's over?" I say.

"The truth about yourself," she says carefully.

I'm not sure how to answer, so I don't.

15

Year: 1996
Age: 31
Idol: Oprah
Favorite Song: "You Oughta Know" (Alanis Morissette,
a cappella version)
Prized Possession: my shrink
Best Shoes: Gucci loafers

O prah Winfrey is running in circles. Literally. It's pitch-black outside, not even 6 A.M., and I am watching her work out. What makes Oprah run? That's the focus of the cover story I'm doing on the TV powerhouse.

"What makes me run is the *thwap, thwap, thwap* sound of my fat ass hitting the backs of my thighs as I take each step," she says. We are settled on a terra-cotta leather couch in her plush Harpo office, later that day. Winfrey is radiating calm and control. She is wearing a long, black Jil Sander apron dress with matching sandals, an elegant Bulgari watch, enormous diamond drop earrings, and tortoiseshell eyeglasses.

Winfrey is literally the most powerful woman in the country. But that's not why she feels *all that* today. Oprah's on top of the world because she has finally gained control over *herself*. No one knows better than me that if you can say no to a Krispy Kreme donut, you can conquer the world.

"I just lost thirty pounds," I mention halfway through the interview.

"*Really?* You just did?" Oprah says. I watch her eyes slide around my body, taking inventory. The once-over. People can't resist when you tell them you've lost weight.

"Well, re-lost I should say. I've had a thirty-pound weight swing my entire life," I explain. "And I've tried every fad diet there is. But this time I'm doing something really different."

"What?" she asks.

(How much do you love this, me giving diet tips to the big O?)

"Psychotherapy," I explain. "Until I could get control over my emotions, I could not get control over my food. Those mint Milanos can be so bossy! But the key, for me, was asking for help."

Oprah's nodding so fast she looks like one of the bobble-head things in the back of a car. "*Uh-huh, uh-huh!* Last year I asked God for freedom. Did I not come out of myself in a *big* way, breaking out of that fat shell?" she says with a proud smile. "And this year I asked for clarity. I have become more clear about my purpose in television and this show."

"So how do you find out what your purpose is?" I ask.

"Every day I wake up and ask myself, What do I want? and What am I willing to sacrifice to get it?" she explains.

"Sacrifice, that's the part most people want to skip over," I say. "So is this what gets you up before five a.m. and makes you run?" I ask.

"Running is the greatest metaphor for life, because you get out of it what you put into it," she says. "Nothing is harder for me, but this is what I have to do to get the kind of mental and physical sharpness that I want."

"But how does a person know when they've discovered their real purpose in life?" I ask.

"Let me ask you this, Bella," she says, leaning toward me and looking me straight in the eyes. The intensity of her gaze almost makes me sweat. "What are you doing when you feel *true joy*?"

I know the answer immediately.

"This!" I say. "I love interviewing people. I love long, late-night conversations on the phone with close friends, and of course, I love pillow talk. That's the best part of being a couple. That's what gives me true joy. Truly, deeply connecting."

"Well, Bella, then that's your purpose in life," she says with a nod.

Amazing! For as long as I can remember, I thought I had two alternating purposes in life, my selfish wish, to meet my soulmate and get married, and my unselfish wish, to make up for my brother somehow. But the way Oprah phrased the question, my truth popped out! It's interesting that I have always been so goal oriented, but my purpose is more of a means than an end in and of itself. I'm so surprised that I literally get chills.

Our interview goes on for another couple hours as we cover the Steadman question ("The reason I'm not married is because there really is no reason to be"), the biological clock question ("So, yes, it's ticking, *so what?*"), and her best stress-busting tip ("I hide in the closet with the shoes and *breathe*"). By the end, we have such a fabulous give-and-take rapport that it's more girl talk than an official interview. I am in my stride, and I'm joyful.

"So are you married?" she asks as I'm packing up my tape recorders and notebooks.

"Hardly!" I say, tears starting to well. As I sit here interviewing Oprah, Pete is moving his stuff out of my apartment. I give her the quick recap of the two-year on-again-off-again Pete roller coaster ride, ending with the summation that, after a lot of first, second, and third chances, in the end I was less attractive to him than alcohol. Even after getting peed on, it took me a few more episodes before I was ready to quit him completely. Like he was my addiction.

"Mmmm, mmmm, mmm, let me give you some advice, girl-friend," Oprah says, pursing her lips and shaking her head. "The first time a man shows you who he is, believe him."

She was right. I was refusing to see Pete for who he really is, because I was so invested in the man I believed he had the potential to become. But time after time, he let me down. Move over, Cleopatra. I'm the Queen of Denial. If Zack was a sustitute for comfort, Project Pete was a substitute for fixing Bobby.

"So I guess you're free for dinner next week?" she says.

Fulfilling Oprah's lifelong fantasy, we've hired Francesco Scavullo, the photographer famous for his super sexy *Cosmopolitan* covers, to shoot Oprah sexpot-style for our cover. Proves that even Oprah isn't immune to the fantasy of being a *Cosmo* girl.

"Let me check my book," I say sarcastically. "Yup, I'm free for the rest of my life, actually."

"Well, you're not next Thursday night, girlfriend, 'cause we're going out on the town," says Oprah. We say our good-byes, and immediately I'm plagued with the question, "What does one wear when going out to dinner with the most powerful woman in the world?"

The following week when I tell Joyce during our session that I am going out to dinner with Oprah that evening, her mask slips.

"You're kidding!" she says giddily before composing herself. In a calm voice she adds, "Breathe, Bella, and tell me how that makes you feel."

"Breathe, that's what Oprah does in her shoe closet when she's stressed," I say. "Why do you always tell me to do that?"

"Because when you breathe, it brings you back to yourself," she says. "I can always tell when my clients don't want to feel something, because they take really shallow breaths."

"That's exactly right. I don't feel anything, really," I explain. "When really good stuff happens to me, I'm just sort of numb to it. I *know* it's great in my head, but I just can't *feel* it."

"Take your time," Joyce says. "Breathe into the numbness. Ask the numbness what its purpose is."

It's through these visualization techniques that I've learned to talk directly to my feelings, or even in this case, my lack of feelings. As kooky as this sounds, I go with the flow. Eventually the vagueness forms itself into words.

Live, reporting from the Numbness, it's Bella Grandelli standing by.

Slowly, the words come. "The numbness is telling me 'Don't feel happy,'" I say.

"Why are the words saying 'Don't feel happy'?" Joyce prods.

I wait until the new words form. "It's saying 'Because you don't deserve to,'" I say.

"Why don't you deserve to feel your joy?" Joyce asks quietly.

The Gray Cloud darts out from behind a corner in my mind. "Because it's not fair," I say.

"Why isn't it fair?" she asks, not missing a beat.

I stumble around in my imagination like a paleontologist on a dig, trying to find this answer. Finally the words surface in my brain, as ancient and permanent as a fossil.

"I don't deserve happiness," I say, "when my brother is so miserable."

"So you need to feel miserable too?" she asks.

"Yes," I say. "Misery loves company."

My eyes blink open. It is an Aha Moment. "Joyce, do I make myself miserable so I can feel a connection to my brother?" I ask.

"Let's look at the way you don't let yourself savor your achievements, or how you periodically sabotage yourself with food," she says. "Do you see a connection?"

"They are both a direct link back to my brother," I say. "On one hand, I've been driven by the need to compensate for him, yet my successes feel hollow because I feel guilty," I explain. "It's like I'm stuck on a hamster wheel. I keep running and running, but I never get anywhere."

"Guilt is just a smoke screen for something you don't want to see," Joyce explains. "What don't you want to see?"

She waits for me to see what's beneath the guilt. What's beneath the guilt is something even more painful than the guilt. No wonder I avoid it.

"Helplessness," I eventually blurt out. "I'm helpless at helping him."

"That's right," she says gently. "You are."

"I would give him half my health and happiness, if I could just find a way for him to take it," I say. "It's not fair."

"Life isn't fair, Bella," Joyce says. "But you can't change Bobby. You can only change the way you feel about him."

"But I have to help him," I say. "He needs me."

"Bella, you are the one with the buy-in to this victim-rescuer relationship, not him," she says. "Inside every rescuer there's a victim. By taking care of him, you're avoiding taking care of yourself."

I can see what's coming next. "So the question is What am I *really* avoiding," I ask rhetorically.

I fumble around in the Gray Cloud to find what I'm avoiding. Ugh, this is so uncomfortable. "Looking for something you're avoiding is an oxymoron," I say, throwing up my hands, frustrated. "I'm lost."

"Exactly," she confirms.

"If I'm not helping him, I don't know who I am," I continue.

Joyce sits back and smiles.

"You can never know yourself if it's only in relation to someone else," she says.

Taking Bobby out of the equation, I suddenly feel scared, and very, very alone.

"Who am I?" I whisper.

"Exactly," Joyce says as if I've just won the Daily Double. "Time's up. Nice work today."

That night, I'm making my way through the bar of the Cub Room when I spot Oprah, looking like a queen in a long white dress and those jumbo diamond earrings. There's a gentleman seated to her right.

"This is Raymond, my bodyguard," Oprah says. "You can speak freely in front of him."

Banishing the bread basket, we order Chardonnay and grilled fish.

"So what did you think of the shoot?" I ask. "Did you feel as sexy as you looked?" Am I flirting with Oprah?

"I feel good these days, there's no doubt about that," she says, radiating confidence.

I take a few sips of Chard for courage and ask her what I really want to know.

"But how did you talk yourself through all the bad times? The real stuff, being born poor, getting sexually molested, trying to make it as a black woman in TV during the eighties," I say. "How did you get through all that?"

"Whenever something bad happens, I always ask myself, 'What can I *learn* from this?'" she explains. "There's a lesson in everything. Even that jerk you dated."

That makes me giggle. "You're right about that," I say. "I learned that you can't change another person, no matter how hard you try, or how badly you want to."

"Mmmmm, hmmmm, girlfriend," says Oprah. "The only person you can change is yourself."

Apparently, Oprah and Joyce got the same memo on that.

"Yeah, but here's what I'm starting to realize," I tell her. "When you change the way you look at things, the things you look at change."

Analyzing my relationship with Pete, and how it connects to Bobby, has been making me realize that by taking care of them, I'm avoiding taking care of myself. As Joyce says, inside of every rescuer there is a victim. My fear is if I don't take care of someone else, I'll be left all alone.

"You are pretty wise for a girl your age," she says. "I didn't start really getting it until I was deep into my thirties," she says.

"Thanks, but I'm not sure this wisdom will help me avoid my biggest fear, which is becoming one of those obese spinsters you read about in *The National Enquirer*," I say. "You know, one of those shut-ins who gets so fat they have to saw the house in half to get them out."

"Now I am going to tell you something, Bella. I am *not* worried about you," she says, fire and brimstone simmering in her voice. "You are a very charismatic person. Raymond, have I ever had dinner with a journalist *before* reading the story?"

"No, ma'am," Raymond says.

"That's right!" she continues. "Girl, you have a bright light in you, but you just need to let it shine out! Stop getting in your own way. Step into your God-given potential and shine!"

Wow! Let me tell you about getting a pep talk from Oprah Winfrey. It makes you hot. I mean, like temperature hot. When she turns her attention on you, it's like being surrounded by helicopters with searchlights emitting megawatts of white light. Well, if Oprah likes me, eventually I'll find some guy that will too. The weird thing is, in the meantime, I think I have a crush on Oprah.

Oprah drops me off in her two-block-long, white stretch limo. I realize that this date has so filled me up that I'm not even tempted by my usual frozen yogurt nightcap.

As I drift off to sleep that night, somewhere between being awake and asleep, a comforting thought comes to hug me. Perhaps, I think, Joyce and Oprah are right: Things happen for a reason. If I hadn't just gotten ejected from the Pete roller coaster, I wouldn't have been so vulnerable during our interview. Then, I'm convinced, the interview would not have become so intimate. Oprah and I really *did* connect, or she never would have invited me to dinner, and I never would have heard her words of wisdom or gotten that incredible pep talk.

It's like the domino effect of fate. You can never know what's going to tip that first one over. But thanks to tonight, I know from Oprah that at least you can learn from the things that happen to you.

16

Year: 1998
Age: 33
Idol: Audrey Hepburn
Favorite Song: "The Bright Side of the Road" (Van Morrison)
Prized Possession: autographed copy of
Women Who Run with the Wolves
Best Shoes: Barneys New York high-heel mary janes

I can smell the Giorgio even before Blanche's stripe appears in my doorway. "Bella, we need you for a TV segment," says the Skunk, barging into my office.

"Uh, sure, Blanche," I say. "When?"

"Right now," she says, pulling me out of my chair. "I can't do it, so you'll have to go on *Wake Up New York* in my place."

Oh, no! I'm interviewing Bette Midler this afternoon. I skipped this morning's shower to force myself to take a spinning class at lunch, so I'd be pumped for my Bette. Let's just say my Jennifer Aniston 'do is looking more like a Bozo the Clown don't.

"The topic?" I ask as the Skunk power walks me to the elevator.

"When Your Husband Is a Slob," she says, eyeing me. "Although you're one to talk. You look like you're going to the gym."

Busted. Not to mention the fact that I don't have a husband, sloppy or otherwise, nor have I had a boyfriend in years. Remember that seventies John Travolta movie *The Boy in the Plastic Bubble?* Well, I feel like the Girl in the Plastic Bubble, unable to get up close and personal with anyone. Since Pete, my most interesting dates have been with Joyce at $150 an hour.

"Read this on the way. There's a car waiting for you downstairs," she says. "And don't forget to say *Style* magazine at least three times during your appearance. The whole point is to promote the magazine."

On the way, I use the car phone to call Zack and tell him to tune in.

"Dude, *très* cool!" he says. "I'd watch, but je suis on my way to the l'aeroport."

"Ou etes vous going?" I say.

"To Newport with Meredith," he says. "She has a romantic weekend planned."

"Is she the Multiple Orgasm Chick, or the one whose father owns the Jets?" I ask. I can't keep up with the heavy rotation of women in and out of Zack's life.

"Neither!" he says, laughing. "Meredith is great. You'll like her. We should do a foursome sometime."

"I'll let you know when I can scrounge up a fourth," I say. Why does it seem that when you are not part of a couple, the whole world is Coupledom? I know I shouldn't complain. At least Zack still makes time for me between his booty call partners.

"Bon chance!" he says. "Break une jambe!"

"Merci!" I say, hanging up.

Next I call my mother. But I regret my spontaneity the second she picks up.

"Hello," she says weakly, the No Makeup screaming from her voice.

"What's wrong, Mom?" I say. I always dread this second, between knowing something's wrong and hearing how wrong it is. The panic starts rising from the pit of my stomach, accompanied by the rest of the anxiety about going on live TV for the very first time.

"Bobby isn't doing so well," she says. "The new meds aren't

working, and he's been rocking and stimming," she says, referring to the violent hand flapping he does to relieve stress. What
usually comes next is a full-blown temper tantrum, where he can
really hurt himself. The last time he bashed his head into the wall
so many times he wound up in the emergency room with seven
stitches. After a certain amount of self-destruction, the doctors
always decide to institutionalize him until he stabilizes.

My insides start to gurgle.

"Did you put his helmet on?" I ask.

"I tried, but he won't let me near him," she says. "I can't seem
to track down your father at his CPA convention."

The car pulls up to the studio, and the driver opens my door.

"Mom, I'm really, really sorry I can't be there right now, but
I've got to go," I say. "I promise I'll come home tonight. I'll take
the train right after my Bette Midler interview."

So much for the mother-daughter-wow-you're-on-TV moment, I think as they rush me through hair and makeup. As the
sound tech guy mikes me, I have a sudden panic attack—*this is
live TV!*—and ask to see the segment producer.

"You're on in three minutes," says a frazzled woman wearing
one of those Madonna-type headsets. She is leading me into the
refrigerator of a studio, which instantly gives me a case of nip-
plitis.

"I just wanted to clarify that I'm actually the entertainment
editor, not a relationship editor," I explain. "As long as the host
sticks to the story, I'll be fine."

"One minute and counting," she says into her headset, ignoring me, and then bellows, "Where's Sam?"

With thirty seconds until countdown, Sam Fox (celebrity
look-alike: younger, not-as-cute Dennis Quaid or perhaps a Bald-
win brother) strides in with an entourage of hair and makeup
people in his wake. Sitting down next to me, he ruffles a copy of
the Slob article and says, "So, Dr. Grandelli, I understand you

have a Ph.D. in relationships. Instead of sloppy husbands, let's discuss, oh, I don't know . . ."

Frazzled Producer is counting, "Five, four, three, two . . ."

"What to do when Bad Party Hats happen to Good Guests?" he smirks, nodding toward my breasts, which are, let's just say, standing at attention.

My jaw drops, but before I can comment, Frazzled Producer says, *"And we're live!"*

The camera light blinks on.

Oprah's voice pops into my head: "What can I learn from this?" Uh, to never wear a white T-shirt in a cold location again? To always shower before leaving the house? That women with curly hair should not attempt the Jennifer Aniston? To kill myself so I never have to do live TV again? Focus, Bella, focus.

"I'd like to welcome our special guest today, Bella Grandelli," says Sam, his smirk disappearing, as he smoothly glides into the sound bite lead-in I had prepared for him. He whisks me gracefully through the five-minute segment—he's the Matt to my Katie. Sticking to the script, we hit all the main points, and before I know it, the producer is smiling broadly, twirling her hand around, motioning for Sam to wrap it up.

"Last question. Bella, what's your personal guerilla tactic for getting the special slob in your life to clean up his act?" he says, cocking his head.

"When my boyfriend is sloppy," I say, "I just, well, delay gratification."

There's a beat. Sam is just looking at me stunned.

"Withholding what a man wants most can really motivate him to clean up all the party hats, *or whatever*, that he's left around the house," I add, smirking.

"Whoa, that's illegal in some countries!" Sam says, guffawing like a frat boy into the camera. "Bella Grandelli, *Style* magazine, thanks for being with us today."

"Bet that boyfriend's neat as a pin," says Sam as soon as we are off camera.

I smile and focus on disentangling myself from the mike. "Yes, and he's waiting for me right now," I fib. "Taking me to a party. Good thing I have my hats on."

I get up to leave, fold my arms across my chest for protection, and stomp out of the studio.

"Thanks for coming!" Sam yells after me. "Give my best to your slob!"

Jerk. But once I'm in the car on the way back to the office, I feel elated! Not only did I survive the TV appearance, but the producer says she wants me to come back and do another segment. I want to share the news, so I dial Carrie on the car phone to check if her flight came in yet. She and Rich, her investment banker boyfriend, have been trekking in Nepal.

"Namaste," she says serenely.

"You're back!" I say. "How was it?"

"Engaging," she says, deeply sighing. "Literally."

I get stabbed with that Ugh feeling in the pit of my stomach.

"You got engaged?" I say, forcing "thrilled" and "excited" into my voice.

"It was the most romantic thing ever, Bella," she swoons. "At the summit, Rich dropped to one knee and pulled a ring out of his fanny pack."

"Details, please," I say. I know for a fact, because we go over it at least once a week, that Carrie has her heart set on a pillow-cut canary diamond in a Cartier setting. There's no way a person with a penis is going to get all those details right. Now I know this makes me a horrible person, but can I admit that a teeny, tiny part of me hopes he doesn't?

"Pillow-cut canary diamond in a Cartier setting," Carrie says, sighing again. "It's perfect. He took my mother shopping with him, after taking my parents to the 21 Club for lunch, where he asked my father for my hand. All behind my back. How cute is that?"

"He's the best, and you deserve it," I say. "I am so happy for you."

Well, one lie isn't too bad. It's not like I'm *not* happy for her; it's just that things in life are so easy for skinny blondes with perfect families. Carrie's had her choice of men ever since I met her freshman year. As for this Girl in the Plastic Bubble, I'm starting to think that I'll never meet The One. Maybe I should go on a starvation diet and get some control over my life, before I'm forty and it's too late. Wait, I know that doesn't work.

"Want to celebrate with us tonight?" she says. "We've got an extra pair of tickets to a black tie at the Met. You could call Zack or someone and we could double date?"

Another thing about being single is you are constantly being punished for it. No black tie for you, young lady, until you straighten up and get yourself a date.

"Thanks, but Zack's busy," I say. "I was sort of thinking of going out and spending time with Bobby tonight anyway. He's having a rough time of it."

"Oh," she says. This is a refrain she's heard before.

"Yeah, oh," I say, sighing. "But promise me you'll have a blowout wedding and invite tons of cute, eligible, funny guys. Preferably out of the most recent J.Crew catalogue."

"You got it!" she says, laughing, before hanging up. "Just e-mail what pages you want."

The driver drops me off, and I rush into the office to gather my things for the Bette interview. When I get to my office, however, the Skunk is waiting for me with her feet propped up on my desk, giving me a beaver shot that I really don't need. Still, it's nice of her to congratulate me on my TV debut.

"So, what did you think?" I say brightly.

"What do you think I think?" she says. "You blew it!"

"What?" I say, dumbfounded. "But the producer told me she was thrilled with the segment. She wants to have me back . . ." I add, my voice trailing off.

Suddenly I feel like a very, very bad girl. An inexcusable show-off who's been caught in the act.

"She might have been thrilled that it was good TV, but what was in it for me?" she demands. "You only mentioned the magazine twice, not three times. How do you think that's supposed to help us on the newsstand?"

"I'm sorry," I stammer, feeling exactly like I did when I got waitlisted for N.D., when trying my hardest still wasn't good enough. Considering everything that was going through my mind—my brother's vulnerable helmetless head, my own vulnerable party hat situation—it's a wonder I got any sound bites about sloppy husbands out of my mouth at all.

"I did the best I could," I add tentatively.

"Well, you looked like shit," she says. "Your clothes were horrible and you really need to get your hair straightened."

Sartorial harassment! From a bitch who chucks beaver shots at unsuspecting editors! Remind me to call my lawyer . . .

"I'll think about it," I say, patting down the puffs on the sides of my head. "In the meantime, I'm going to be late for the Bette interview. I'd better get going."

"Midler's a has-been," says Blanche, waving her hand at me. "I bet she's one of the worst-selling covers of the year, I can't even think of a question for you to ask her that will get us on Page Six. We really need to have a talk, you and I."

It's been increasingly harder to book the covers. All of the A-list stars Blanche wants, Julia, Meg, Jennifer, would rather be on *Rolling Stone* and *Vanity Fair* than some frumpy woman's magazine. Some months we've really gotten down to the wire, but so far we haven't gone to press with a blank cover, thank God.

And I'm excited about Midler. She's an icon for godsakes! And she told me to trust my female intuition and be myself when I saw her in *The Rose.*

Shake it off, shake it off, I tell myself as I walk into Sarabeth's Kitchen, a cute place by Midler's Fifth Avenue apartment. I do my best to block the first half of my day out of my mind and concentrate. I've got to find a way to make Midler interesting to Blanche.

We finish discussing all Midler's projects, and it occurs to me that the Skunk didn't bother to give me one of her classic Interview Ending questions. So I decide to ask Midler the question I personally want to know the answer to: What was it like growing up with a mentally handicapped brother?

Most people don't know that about Midler. What I'm curious about is how she didn't let it get in her way. Maybe I could learn to do the same.

"Well, we were really poor," she says, her focus turning inward, as if she's recalling a dim memory. "My parents raised him at home, and that was a real struggle. When you have that as an example, you never really forget it."

"So your work ethic came from watching your parents," I say. There's no doubt that Midler's drive got her where she is today.

"All these articles in magazines about self-esteem," she says, waving her hand. "The only way people learn self-esteem is by working hard. People have an obligation to live up to their potential."

"I agree," I say. But it occurs to me that there is a difference between living up to your own potential and trying to compensate for someone else's. Perhaps that's where I'm tripping myself up.

Midler looks at her watch and throws her Prada tote over her shoulder. As I thank her for her time, I decide to share with her how her strong sense of self came through loud and clear and made an indelible impression on me when I was growing up.

"By the way, it's thanks to you that I first heard my female intuition."

"Me, why?" she asks. The Prada goes back to the floor.

"It was in tenth grade, and I smoked a lot of pot and went to see *The Rose*," I explain. "And at the end of the movie, I heard this voice. It was *you* talking, but in *my* head. I was really high, so I wasn't quite sure what was happening."

"What did I say?" she asks, riveted.

I pause, savoring the moment of my close-up. "You said," I say, a little dramatically, " 'Be yourself.' "

Midler smiles. "You know what Linda Ronstadt once told me?" she says. " 'You don't need to be original—you just need to be authentic.' "

"Authentic," I repeat. "As in, be true to yourself?"

"Exactly," Midler says. "By the way, you shouldn't smoke marijuana. I really don't approve of that."

"I know," I say. "You already told me, in 1980."

That evening I take the train home to check on Bobby. People always ask me if it's hard to interview celebrities. It's a breeze compared to trying to make conversation with an autistic.

"Hi, Mom. How's he doing?" I ask my mother as I walk through the large Gray Cloud in our kitchen. She looks exhausted, flipping through a Lillian Vernon catalogue.

"Better," she says simply, in a thin papery voice. "He's upstairs watching TV. How are you, honey?"

I desperately want to ask her a zillion questions—How long did the tantrum last? Did she call the doctor? Are they going to change the medicine?—but I can see by her pursed, Ziploc lips that she's not in the mood to deal with another needy child.

"Fine," I say, instead. "Where's Dad?"

"In the basement, working on a model," she says, returning to the pages of discount tchotchkes. I should have guessed. It's easier to get a ship into a bottle than getting this family's ship through the latest Hurricane Bobby.

As I walk down the steps, I can hear the marching band music on my dad's transistor radio. Its jolliness is as out of place in the gloom of our household as a kid telling fart jokes at a funeral.

"Bella, you're home!" he says as he puts down his wire cutters and turns to offer me a kiss on the cheek. "And to what do I owe the honor?"

"I came home to help," I say.

"Help what, honey?" he says quizzically.

I feel like a fool. The crisis is clearly over, and even if I was there for it, what could I have done anyway? The question hangs like a banner on the Gray Cloud, while the Pink Elephant sneers at me from the corner. Short of discovering a pill to cure Asperger's syndrome, Bobby's latest diagnosis, I'm starting to accept not good for much in this situation.

"Oh, I don't know, offer moral support," I say lamely, heading back up the stairs.

"Honey, we're always happy to see you," he says. "And you've come at the perfect moment. Can you hand me the pliers?"

"Scalpel, Dr. Grandelli," I joke, putting the pliers in his hand.

"Okay, now we're all set," he says, fidgeting with his tool. "Ready to raise the main sail, Bella?"

"Dad, this is so corny," I say. The trick to raising the mast is a thread. Out of the neck of the bottle, you pull the thread, and lo and behold, Dar She Blows.

"The first time I showed you this, you clapped your hands like you were at the circus," he says. "In fact, you were so excited that you said it was okay that we never got you a pony for Christmas."

"Let you off the hook that easy, did I? Well, for old times' sake," I say, taking the tiny thread and giving it a pull. Sure enough, up she goes. My dad looks as thrilled as if he's doing this for the first time. In a way I'm jealous that something that simple can give him so much pleasure.

I hug him. "Dad, you're like a skit on *Saturday Night Live*—you know that?" I say.

He kisses the top of my head, shrugs, and says, "All Parental Units are to their children, aren't they?"

I guess in some ways our family is more normal than I thought. For some reason this comforts me.

"Thanks, Parental Unit," I say, giving him another hug.

"For what, honey?" he says.

"For being you," I answer. "I'm going to go say hi to Bobby."

I take the stairs two at a time up from the basement to Bobby's room and see that he has wedged himself between the box spring and the mattress, like in the old days. It saddens me that he's so clearly regressed, but on the other hand, at least he has found a way to comfort himself. That's something I'm still trying to do without eating so much fat-free frozen yogurt that I risk hypothermia.

He's watching reruns of *Batman* on Nick at Nite. Catwoman is the villain, but it's Eartha Kitt, not Julie Newmar, whom I've always preferred, because she's skinnier and prettier.

"Holy sloppy husbands, Batman," Bobby says, addressing me without taking his eyes from the TV. "Sister's starring on *Wake Up New York*."

"You saw that, Bobby?" I say, shocked. Out of all of the people in my family that I expected to tune in to my television debut, I can't believe that Bobby did, in the middle of a temper tantrum.

"Affirmative, Captain," he says.

I lie down on the mattress on top of him, remembering from high school how much he likes the weight of the extra pressure on his body. For the life of me, I can't think of one single subject to start a conversation, so we just lie there in silence watching together.

The Brady Bunch comes on next. The reason people my age are still obsessed with this show is because it's the comfort food version of television. No matter what problem the Bradys faced, they were able to solve it in exactly thirty minutes. I bet there could be a study correlating a Brady fan's ardor with the dysfunction of their childhood.

It's the classic episode where Marcia Brady joins a million clubs in order to be popular, and Peter's volcano spews lava all over her new friends. The Universe's way of showing her to stop trying so hard and just be herself.

Hmm, that's exactly what Midler told me today.

"Hey, Bobby," I call down to him. "Did you ever notice that Mom has Carol Brady hair?"

He doesn't answer. I lean over the side of the mattress and look at him. He's sound asleep, his jaw slack and his face completely at peace beneath his Notre Dame football helmet. On his lips plays just the hint of a smile.

17

Year: 1998
Age: 33
Idol: Dalai Lama
Favorite Song: "Torn" (Natalie Imbruglia)
Prized Possession: sense of humor
Best Shoes: dyed-to-match teal slides

Now, I love weddings as much as the next girl. The strains of Pachelbel's Canon, the ubiquitous "Love Shall Not Be Jealous" reading, and eating the icing off of everyone else's cake while they're out on the dance floor doing the White Man's Overbite.

Still, of the fourteen weddings I've been in since graduation—there's enough taffeta in my closet to decorate a Rose Bowl Parade float—never once have I gotten wedding nookie. The teal, iridescent, poufy-sleeved Laura Ashley brides-maid dress that Carrie's mother picked out, with dyed-to-match slides, practically ensures that there won't be a status change this weekend either.

I knew that Carrie's family was loaded, but I had no idea to what extent until I arrived at her grandparents' compound on Shelter Island, a small island off the coast of Long Island, New York. I mean, Robin Leach could pop out any minute and do a *Lifestyles of the Rich and Famous*. Not one, but two, huge clifftop estates, with property reaching all the way down to acres of sandy beach. Carrie's expecting three hundred and fifty guests, and some of her father's clients, Japanese businessmen, are coming via helicopter that will land on their private beach. Lester Lanin and

His Orchestra are being imported on the ferry, along with a Calypso band and *two* jazz trios.

"Sorry about the dresses, but hopefully the groomsmen will make up for it. Rich has some hot college roommates," Carrie whispers. "Speak of the devil! Sam, come over here and give me a big ol' hug, you dog! Meet Bella."

Uh! It's Sam Fox, morning TV moron!

"Actually, we already know each other," I say, wrapping myself tightly in my pashmina, just in case a breeze comes through. Don't want to expose my party hats to this guy again.

"Bella Grandelli, relationship editor *impostor*," Sam says, smirking.

"How do you two know each other?" asks Carrie, looking surprised.

"I was a guest on his show six months ago," I explain. "I guess it was when you were otherwise engaged in Nepal."

"What a coincidence!" says Carrie. "You're paired up to go down the aisle together."

Oh, *great*. Bring on the iridescent muumuu. I guess I only have to dance with him once to fulfill my bridesmaid obligation.

Too soon, the moment is upon us.

"Will the wedding party please join the newlyweds on the dance floor?" says the bandleader, striking up "Fly Me to the Moon."

"C'mon, Bella, you can't hate me forever," says Sam, escorting me into the tent. "Where's your sense of humor?"

"It's off in search of its party hat," I say.

"Touché!" he says, dipping me.

"Sarcasm," I say. "It's just another service I provide."

Sam rolls his eyes.

But before I realize it, I'm having a good time despite myself. Turns out Sam and I have a zillion things to talk about. We dish on the different celebrities we've both interviewed, discuss our mutual love for single malt scotches, and discover that we've both plunked down $750 for the Robert McKee screenwriting course, an intensive three-day session led by a notorious Hollywood guru.

"That's a coinky-dink," he says. "Are you going in with an idea?"

"I want to write a romantic comedy," I say. "It's my dream to write like Nora Ephron."

"Well, if I can help you with any research for your sex scene," he says, putting his face close to mine and waggling his eyebrows as if he were Groucho Marx, "have your girl call my girl."

"What about you?" I ask, ignoring his joke.

"I have a dark comedy idea about a confirmed bachelor," he says. "A subject I know something about."

"Confirmed bachelors just haven't met the right person yet," I proclaim.

"That's what all women think," he says. "Confirmed bachelors, however, know better. That's what my screenplay will explore."

"Yeah, I'm just wondering, has anyone ever told Claudia Schiffer, 'Sorry, Claud, I'm a confirmed bachelor'?" I say. "Doubtful."

As we're doing the conga line around the tent, Sam, whose hands are on my waist, gives me a squeeze.

"Turn this way," he says, steering me to the right. Our conga-line-for-two heads down the driveway and into the four-car garage. The next thing you know, Sam has commandeered the red Chevy pickup truck. It's got to be vintage.

"Hop in," he says, flinging open the passenger door. "There's only so many investment bankers I can take in an evening."

We blast country music on the a.m. radio as we bump around on the island's pebbly roads. Sam pulls in to the Chequit, the only bar in town. When we walk in, everyone stops and stares. Let me explain: He's in a full morning suit, tails and all, and I'm still in my teal extravaganza. The rest of the clientele is, well, let's just say there may not be a dentist on Shelter Island.

"This round's on us," Sam announces to the entire bar, taking control of the situation.

The bartender rings a bell, and the entire bar starts clapping.

Two large fishermen types approach us with pool sticks. "How about the next game?" says one of them.

"I don't really know how to play," I admit.

"It's fun," says Sam, handing me a stick. "I'll show you."

We shoot pool and listen to tales of adventures on the seas with the locals until last call. Then we drive back to the compound, Sam and I still talking a mile a minute.

"Walk on the beach?" says Sam, extending his arm.

Last time I checked, the literal translation of "Walk on the beach?" was "Care for some nookie?"

"I hear there's some great submarine racing tonight," I say.

We follow what's left of the little tea lights flickering the way down the steps to the water's edge. The moon is full, and its light is glinting on something in the distance.

"What's that?" I ask.

"Must be the judge's station for the submarine races," Sam says, deadpan.

Holding hands and skipping, we make our way in the dark over to the contraption.

"It's a trampoline!" I say, sliding off my slides. "C'mon!"

At first we jump carefully. Now that we're in our thirties, we don't want to break a hip or anything. But then Sam double bounces me, which sends me flying up into the stars. It's a good thing I'm wearing my very best La Perla underwear set, because every bounce causes my dress to fly up over my head. Note to self: Remember to tell Oprah about revision of true joy. The ingredients are a trampoline, a funny guy, and a full moon.

"Whoa!" I say, when one bounce almost sends me flying into the water.

Sam catches me and pulls me toward him. I think he's going to kiss me, but he just looks at me tentatively. And then I get it. Sam's shy. All of his stand-up comic bravado act is a front. Beneath it, he's like a bashful little kid.

I step toward him. We kiss. We make out and crack up and roll around on the trampoline until the early morning, when the invasion starts.

"Uh-oh," Sam says.

"What-oh?" I ask.

"The brisk walkers, coming right toward us," he murmurs.

"Oh, no!" I say, eyeing the pair of track-suited blue hairs. "That's Carrie's mother and one of her society friends. What are we going to do?"

"Can I hide under your dress?" he says, diving under the taffeta.

"And leave me here all alone? Let's scoot!" I say, pulling Sam by the hand off the trampoline and back toward the house.

Once safely inside, we whisper good night and head to our respective Girls and Boys bedrooms.

A scant few hours later, I spot Sam downstairs at the brunch. The morning after Wedding Nookie can be terribly awkward, so I busy myself at the bar with a mimosa.

"Did you hear?" Sam says, coming up behind me.

"Hear what?" I say, trying to keep the relief out of my voice.

"Scandal with the Submarine Races," he says in a low voice, pointing in the direction of Carrie's mother. She is holding up two pairs of familiar-looking shoes and asking around to see who might be missing them.

"Discovered near the Judging Station?" I ask, giggling.

"Apparently," he says.

"Such corruption," I say. "This is worse than the Olympics."

We goof around all day, and the entire way back on the jitney to the city. When it's my turn to get off the bus, I'm wondering if I should write down my number, play it cool, or what.

"Well," I say.

"I know where to find you," Sam says, as if reading my mind. "We need to discuss how we're going to do a reconnoiter for our shoes. I hear they are being held hostage in a secret location."

I laugh and remain happily amused about our encounter as I walk back to my apartment. I can't wait to tell Carrie about this, when she gets home from her honeymoon. I may never wear that dress again, but that was the best bridesmaid favor I've ever received!

The following Monday morning, I tune in to *Wake Up New York,* and Sam is talking about our trampoline jaunt, on national TV! Actually, he's getting teased about it from his cohost, who's commenting about "the twinkle in his eye." As I sip Starbucks in my bed, I realize I'm totally having a New York Moment.

It's the first of many. Within a month, Sam and I slip into a relationship that feels as comfortable as a pair of college sweats. Fellow journalists, out to conquer the world. We go to events together and help each other work the room. At the *Stepmom* premiere, I introduce him to Julia Roberts, and at the NBC holiday party at the Rainbow Room, he introduces me to Katie Couric. I open my Rolodex of celebrities, and he punches up the rough drafts of my profiles with his humor. He surprises me with copies of scripts from *When Harry Met Sally* and *Sleepless in Seattle*.

One Sunday we're hanging out at his apartment reading *The New York Times*. Everything, for the first time in my personal life, is perfect. Except for the fact that I feel absolutely miserable. Sometimes when everything's great, it's almost like I can't take it, and I have to do something to ruin it. My brain just fixates on some vague unhappiness until it becomes real.

"What's wrong?" he says over the top of Arts and Leisure. "Is the pressure of Blanche getting to you?"

It's true that the Skunk has been torturing me lately. Nothing I do seems to be good enough for her. But that's not what's bothering me today. It's that vague Gray Cloud of depression again. In the past, when the Gray Cloud of depression has descended, I've never bothered to explain it. Even to Beau. I'd just go back to my apartment and wait it out, like it was a migraine headache or something. I consider doing the same today, but a little Bette Midler voice inside me says, "What the hell, just be yourself."

So I do. "Dingo ate my mojo," I say, doing my best Meryl Streep Outback accent.

"Come again?" he says.

"You've heard of a bad hair day?" I explain. "I'm having a fat day."

"What do you mean? You wore your skinny jeans last night," he says. "You zipped 'em up and danced around for half an hour."

"Yeah, but I'm fat on the inside," I say. And then a vision pops into my head. "My inner child is obese."

"Should we take her for a play date with Jenny Craig?" he jokes.

"Diets don't work for me," I explain. "I mean, they work on the outside, but I still feel fat on the inside. You know that expression, 'Inside every fat person there's a thin one trying to get out'?"

"Yeah," he says, putting down his paper and giving me his full attention.

"Well, for me it's the opposite. Even though I'm thin right now, inside me there's a big, huge fat person trying to bust out. Like an airbag in a Volvo, she'll inflate at the scent of a Cinnabon."

Sam is laughing, as I am pantomiming the transformation.

"My shrink, Joyce, says I just need to *be* with her," I say. "Well,

I've *been* with her as long as I can remember, and I *still* can't stand her. In fact, I hate her."

"I have an idea," he says, jumping up. "Get dressed."

Next thing you know, we're in a taxi headed to the suburbs of New Jersey. Our destination: Wal-Mart. You've heard of Trainspotting? We're going Fattywatching.

"I think your inner child is lonely," says Sam. "Let's get her with her peeps."

There are virtually no fat people in Manhattan. The Fat Police must secure the perimeter. But Sam's right. They can be found en masse at Wal-Mart in New Jersey.

We get a cart and pretend to shop.

"Inner child heading down the snack aisle," he says in hushed tones. We zip our cart there, and sure enough, I spot someone who looks like how I feel.

I watch as the size 22 places three cases of SnackWell's in her cart. The fact that they are SnackWell's almost breaks my heart. Hasn't she been warned about fat-free food's nefarious, all-U-can-eat false promise?

I almost well up as I watch her open one of the packages to snack as she shops. She gobbles down about six cookies so fast it's clear she couldn't have enjoyed them. I see myself in her. I want to sit her down, take her hands in mine, and ask her what's eating her, instead of what she's eating.

But I can't because Sam is serenading me with *The Partridge Family* theme song, "C'mon Every-Fat-body! Get Hap-py!" and steering me off in search of another inner child.

Within an hour, we have spotted eight inner children, and thanks to Sam's running commentary, I have laughed so hard that my abs are killing me. No one has ever taken my inner child out on a date! I'm so touched by Sam's gesture that I decide to scooch out on a limb. I invite him home for Thanksgiving.

He looks at me suspiciously.

"This is not about meeting my family," I say, fibbing. "It's just that all your relatives live in California. I don't want you having Thanksgiving in a restaurant."

"All right, as long as this isn't a Meet the Parents trap," he says.

"It's casual," I say, trying to sound nonchalant. "Promise."

Thanksgiving morning, on the train ride out, I prepare Sam for my family. I'm counting on his sense of humor for this one.

"So, I can guarantee that my dad will be wearing at least three to five Notre Dame–related items, since today's the big game," I say. "My mom will try to ply you with food while discerning your religion and net worth. And I've already told you about Bobby."

"Rainman," he says. "I can't believe your twin's an idiot savant."

"Well, his latest diagnosis is Asperger's syndrome, which is at the higher functioning end of the autistic spectrum," I explain. "It's a disability that affects his sensory input. He either overreacts or underreacts."

"So all the info comes in confused, like he's got a computer virus?" he says.

"Sort of. So don't be surprised if he's wearing his wet suit with the inflatable vest," I explain. "He blows it up, and the feeling of pressure relaxes him. Big loud family gatherings can be overstimulating, and his invention has definitely fended off some head banging tantrums."

"An inflatable vest—do you think he'd let me borrow it for a segment?" Sam jokes.

"You laugh, but despite his deficiencies, he can do some amazing stuff. You should see him with a computer. Scary."

"Really?" Sam says. "Can he count cards like Rainman too? Should we take him to Vegas?"

"No, and he doesn't actually really understand the concept of money," I say. "Or humor, for that matter."

"So your bad sense of humor is genetic?" he says.

I laugh.

When we get to my house, Bobby opens the door wearing his orange neon vest. He looks at Sam out of the corner of his eye and blows into the vest. Then in a loud voice that sounds like Joe Pesci being channeled by a robot says, "You laughing at me? I amuse you? What the fuck is so funny about me?"

"Bobby, you know you shouldn't use the F-word," says my mother, whose head appears over my brother's shoulder. "Sorry, Sam. He's been watching *GoodFellas* on cable."

"Everyone! Bella's boyfriend's here!" announces my father, the Notre Dame fight song going off on his tie as if on cue. "It's the big TV star! Bella has us watch every day, and you are so funny!"

I cringe. I promised Sam this was no big deal.

"You laughing at me? I amuse you?" says Sam, impersonating Bobby impersonating Pesci.

Everyone laughs. I could kiss Sam for breaking the tension.

Bobby leads Sam over to the life-size Mr. Spock bust that he puts on the mantel for all special occasions.

"And I thought your sister had a nice bust," says Sam, inspecting Spock.

"Captain, I don't think that insults are within your prerogative as my commanding officer," says Bobby, quoting Spock.

Sam laughs. And, actually, I even laugh at the Spock bust, a painful reminder of loves past. In fact, Sam is witty and funny and totally entertains my entire family. My aunts are giving me the wink-wink, nudge-nudge thing every time they can catch my eye.

"*Sooooo?*" my mother says hopefully while we do the dishes together. She still has eyes in the back of her head. I peek around the corner into the den where Sam is patiently making conversation with Bobby, who is puffing into his vest. I can hear Bobby saying, "Beuller? Beuller?" every time Sam tries to make a joke.

"*Mo-om,*" I say, trying to keep the exasperation from my voice. "Sam's a confirmed bachelor, and we've only been together a couple months, so how am I supposed to know?" One thing I've never been able to handle is my mother's disappointment about my love life on top of my own. To this day we have not spoken once about Beau. In her eyes no one else will ever measure up.

"Well, Sam's being awfully nice to your brother," she says in a singsong voice, as if there's a direct correlation between that and an engagement ring. "He's out there telling Bobby jokes."

"He can't help himself," I say. "He used to be a stand-up comic."

"I know, honey. I watch the show," she says. "He's funnier than Regis when he talks about what you two did the night before."

"Yeah, I'm material these days," I say. It's true, he does mention me a lot on TV. I had to give him an Atomic Wedgie until he swore to God he wouldn't mention our Wal-Mart field trip.

Mom sneaks another look at Sam and Bobby and squeals, "Honey, wouldn't it be nice if Santa Claus brought you a nice big engagement ring?"

"Shh, Mom! Besides, I'm still waiting for the Barbie camper," I say. "Not to mention the pony I've been asking for."

As Sam and I take the train back into the city, I can't help myself. The visit went so well that I flash-forward to the big Vows picture in *The New York Times* Style section. The screenwriting, media Power Couple. Our life will be filled with humor, laughter, banter. There's just one little nagging voice. It's Oprah's and it's saying, *When a man tells you who he is, believe him the first time.* I change the channel, thinking Oprah must not have gotten my memo about true joy involving a funny guy and a trampoline.

"What were you and Bobby talking about?" I ask him, snuggling into his shoulder.

"You mean while you and your mother were drafting your deliverables for Santa?" he says, lifting one eyebrow.

Busted!

"I'll be asking Santa for a new mother," I say. "I'm so sorry. But did you get a response out of Bobby?"

"He's a tough audience," he says.

"Don't take it personally. Autistics don't have normal senses of humor," I say.

"Well, Tom Cruise got Dustin Hoffman to laugh in *Rainman*," he says. "Remember the scene in the diner with the maple syrup?"

"Yeah, well, that's a movie," I say. "Besides, don't hang your esteem on that one. I've gotten every celebrity in Hollywood to Open Kimono, but I *still* can't find a way to connect with my own twin. It's been my life's quest, my holy grail."

"Want to know an old stand-up trick?" he says. "The harder you try to make someone laugh, and they don't, the funnier it makes you in the situation, if you're on the outside looking in."

"So?" I say.

"So laugh at yourself," he explains. "It's ridiculously good material if you think about it."

"That's like what Nora Ephron once told me," I say. "She said the bad stuff that happens to you makes great material later on."

The wisdom of what he's saying, focus on my reaction to the situation instead of Bobby's, strikes me. I can't help myself, I start laughing. At me, watching Sam trying out his new material on Bobby, who is furiously blowing into his wet suit.

"*Beuller? Beuller?* Preposterous. A stand-up comic trying to get his girlfriend's autistic brother to laugh," I say between bursts of laughter. "It's like a *Seinfeld* episode!" I laugh so hard it happens. I fart! *Oops.*

"Oh, my God!" says Sam, his eyes wide. "Did I really just hear that?"

"Excuse me," I manage. "Sometimes it happens when I laugh really hard."

"You use the word 'girlfriend' when you laugh really hard?" he says. Apparently that word was more offensive than my staccato gas attack.

"Is Tourette's related to Asperger's?" he asks and immediately goes into a Rainman routine with lots of foul words.

I'm still laughing when our train pulls in to Grand Central. We walk to the taxi stand and he says, "Bella, would you mind if I don't stay over tonight? I'm really beat."

I'm surprised, especially because I was feeling so close to him. "Oh, okay," I say. "And thanks for tonight. You were hilarious."

The next day, I leave Sam a message, but don't hear back from him. Ditto the following day. On the third, I miss Sam's call, but he leaves a message that he's been on deadline. I decide not to read into it. Guys hate when girls overreact. I'm just going to play it cool.

The following week I'm just getting back from my morning yoga class when my mother calls, looking for her Sam update. The only time she's in constant touch with me is when I'm making progress on my love life.

"Hi, hon," she says excitedly into the phone. "I didn't know you were taking ballroom dancing."

"I'm not," I say. "Why?"

"Oh," she says, her voice clipped. Before I can ask her what the heck she's talking about, she changes the subject.

I don't give it much thought until I get to the office and I'm cornered by the Skunk. "Why don't you write about your dance lessons for our Couple Time section?" she says. "Since your cover stories seem to be tanking lately."

"I'm not taking ballroom dancing lessons," I say, utterly confused.

"Well, Sam is. He talked all about it this morning," she says, lifting an eyebrow. "We all thought you were his 'beautiful dance partner, with more moves than Madonna,' quote unquote."

My cheeks burn! He two-times me on national television? And I thought he was "really busy." I call him immediately. This time I get him.

"Hi. It's Madonna," I say. *"Not."*

"Bella, she's just a friend . . ." he starts.

"I thought last night was poker night, not Poke Her Night," I say. Even if that "just a friend" line is the truth, I know this is the beginning of the end. I can just hear it in Sam's voice.

He doesn't say anything for a while.

"This is what I do," he mumbles eventually.

"What is what you do?" I ask.

"I self-destruct every time I find myself in a halfway decent relationship," he admits.

"Wow, that's honest," I say.

"Well, you've got to wonder why I'm still a confirmed bachelor at the age of forty-five," he says.

"I thought you were waiting for the right girl, The One," I say. "Naïve, I guess."

"No, Bella. I meant what I said on our first date about never seeing myself as married," he says. "Even though you thought you could change my mind."

"Save the 'It's not you—it's me' speech. It's going to give me flashbacks," I say.

" 'Nam?" he says.

"Yeah, I was in the shit in '87." I laugh. "Left at the altar for a bimbo with a fake tan and frosted nails. I wish you weren't so funny," I say. "It would be easier to toss you into the discard pile."

* * *

Alone again. This is not the life I signed up for.

I don't know where to begin at my next session with Joyce.

"Breathe," she says. "And see where your breath takes you."

"I laughed at the Bobby situation," I say. "I mean, I laughed so hard I farted!"

"Ah, and who gave you permission to laugh?" she asks.

"Sam did," I say. "He showed me how to see the humor in the situation, and it was a total release. Like putting down a heavy package after a really long haul."

"Close your eyes and breathe, Bella," she says. "Tell me about this release, this good feeling."

"It made me feel really close to him," I say.

"Close to whom?" she asks.

"Close to—" I open my eyes. "I was going to say Sam, but the reason I feel so good is because I felt the closeness with Bobby. That closeness I've wanted to feel with him my whole life. And he wasn't even there!"

"Slow down, Bella," she says. "Stay with the closeness."

"I don't know, the laughter, it softened the barrier between me and my brother," I say. "It let me accept things."

"Accept what things?" she says.

"Accept the fact that I can't change Bobby, but I can change the way I feel about him," I say. "That whole jumbled-up knot of feelings I've carried around my whole life, like he's been a monkey on my back, those feelings are my Frankenstein creation, not Bobby's."

"That's right, Bella," she says. "Bobby has had an effect on you, but you are finally taking responsibility for yourself."

"This superachiever mode I go into, trying to bag the next celebrity, trying to bag a husband—it's like I'm still trying to make my parents proud," I say. "But being able to laugh at myself, it's the loophole to feeling like I have to be perfect."

"And who showed you this loophole? Sam? The guy who took you Fattyspotting?" she says.

"Fattywatching, right," I say. "But that was before he dumped me. And the worst part is he's the only guy who I think ever truly got me. He taught me how to laugh at myself, even my obese inner child. It's just that . . ."

"It's just that what?" she says patiently. She's supposed to be neutral, but the lines of concern creasing her forehead tip me over the edge. Suddenly I'm crying.

"It's just that I thought he was The One," I say, weeping. "But the Gray Cloud scared him off. I *hate* this cloud of depression and anxiety! It follows me everywhere and ruins everything."

"Close your eyes and breathe," she says soothingly. "Go into the Gray Cloud and ask it why it follows you everywhere."

I do as she says but have a hard time concentrating.

"Take your time," Joyce says patiently.

I go into the Gray Cloud. As silly as I feel, I ask it the question: "Why don't you leave me alone?"

Slowly, the words form in my mind. For the first time ever, the Gray Cloud speaks. *Exclusive! The Gray Cloud talks to Bella Grandelli!*

"I don't leave you alone because you are ready to know," I say, on behalf of the Gray Cloud.

"Know what?" I ask Joyce.

"Don't ask me, ask the Gray Cloud," she says.

"The truth about The One," I say, answering for the Gray Cloud.

I swallow.

"Who is The One?" I ask.

I wait, but no words come. I keep waiting, and slowly a face materializes in my imagination.

"It's him," I cry.

"I know," she says quietly.

"It's him," I repeat.

"I know," she says.

"It hurts," I say.

"I know," she says.

"It's Bobby," I say finally. "And I will never, ever be able to connect with him in the way that I need to."

The sadness of this realization crashes over me like a wave. It's a bittersweet breakthrough. No matter how hard I've tried to become Bobby's mirror image, the Gray Cloud has been trying to tell me that I've spent my entire life living in his shadow.

"So the man I have been so desperate to connect with—'The One'—is my own twin?" I say.

"What do you think?" Joyce asks.

"I think I want a refund." I laugh weakly. " 'My other half,' literally."

18

Year: 2002
Age: 37
Idol: Carrie Bradshaw in Sex and the City
Favorite Song: "At Last" (Etta James)
Prized Possession: Mel Gibson's cigar
Best Shoes: maroon suede Manolo Blahnik stiletto pumps

The Skunk is going to just flip! Meg Ryan just pulled out from doing this month's cover. She got an offer from *Vanity Fair,* and they're demanding an exclusive. Immediately, I deliver Blanche the bad news and start working the phones, the fax, and the e-mail. I try Christie Brinkley, I try Calista Flockhart, I try all three respective female *Friends,* I try Katie Couric, Helen Hunt, I *beg* Cher, sending her publicist a letter swearing I am her number-one fan. I put in fourteen formal requests over the course of the next week and get nuked each and every time.

Uh-oh. I can smell Giorgio wafting down the hall. Sure enough, the Skunk's stripe appears in my doorway.

"Any news?" she says sulkily, refusing to make eye contact with me.

"Not yet, but I've put in six more requests," I say, forcing the brightness into my voice. I feel as if I'm suddenly Shirley Temple singing and tap-dancing as fast as I can. "And I'm trying—"

"It's not about *trying*, Bella. It's about *delivering*," she says, cutting me right off. "I could give a rat's ass how hard you try—the cover's still blank! You're on probation. If you don't get a cover within the next week, and I mean A-list, you're fired." Blanche turns on her kitten heel and disappears, leaving her nauseating, eighties stench in her wake.

Gulp. My head feels like it's in a vise. I'm caught. I'm being held fully responsible for something I have no control over.

Over the next few days, I spend fifteen-hour days in the office, phoning, waiting for news. The pressure becomes so intense—you can't go to press with a blank cover—that I stop sleeping at night. When I do nod off, I have nightmares I'm back in eighth grade, throwing rocks at the 'tard bus. But I'm on the 'tard bus at the same time, so I'm throwing rocks at myself. Dreams are weird.

By the last day of my probation, I receive seven more formal turndowns. At this point I'm so desperate I'm even trying celebs Blanche considers has-beens with no sell power: Joan Lunden, Fran Drescher, Reba McEntire. And the big no-no for a woman's magazine, male celebrities: Tom Hanks and Mel Gibson.

Blanche is so disgusted that she refuses to speak to me at all when I pass her in the hall or run into her in the ladies' room. She knows as well as anyone that I have no control over Meg Ryan's publicist breaking a promise, yet she still acts like it's all my fault. I'm stuck, and there is no one to help me.

"Feel familiar?" says Joyce at our weekly session. "This feeling of being responsible for something you have no control over?"

"Yes," I say. "I've felt it my whole life."

As we've peeled back the years together, Joyce has helped me understand how I have made it my mission to be Bobby's opposite, to be perfect.

"That's right, Bella," she says gently. "Your unspoken marching orders were to be mature and perfect, never make a demand or have a difficulty."

"I was hardly a perfect child," I start. It's hard not to get defensive about my parents.

"Bella, you got the message early on to solve all your problems yourself because your parents were too overwhelmed with your brother," she says. "That doesn't make them bad parents, but clearly it made an impression on you."

"I guess," I say.

"Anger turned inside is depression, or what you refer to as the Gray Cloud," she says. "Let's go into the Gray Cloud."

I want to jump up, run outside to Madison Avenue, eat a huge frozen yogurt, and then go on a big diet so I can get some control over my life. Oh right, I keep trying that over and over but it doesn't work. I force myself to do the alternative. Closing my eyes, I follow Joyce into that abyss of fear, anxiety, depression, and guilt.

"Bella, tell me about what you are feeling in the Gray Cloud," she prods. "The pressure to be perfect."

"I have to fix the problem," I say. "But I can't."

"What problem?" she says gently.

"All of them! The blank cover, the fact that I'm the Girl in the Plastic Bubble and I can't find a husband," I say. "And *him*. The main problem. The Gray Cloud's telling me to fix him."

I'm not crying. It's just the tension leaking out of my eyes.

"There's something else that's even scarier," I say, the fingers of my mind plumbing a depth that feels like putting your hand down the garbage disposal.

"The not knowing," I say. "For me, that's the worst."

"Good," she says. "Let's stay with the 'not knowing,' Bella."

I hate when she does this. She finds the emotion I most want to avoid, and she forces me to stay with it. It's excruciating. I feel like any minute, someone is going to flip the garbage disposal switch and grind my hand into hamburger meat.

"What's painful about the not knowing, Bella?" she continues in a soft voice.

"Why did it happen to him, and not me?" I say, the tears spilling down my shirt. "And something else."

"What else?" she says.

"What if I'm just like him after all, a big failure for everyone to reject?" I say. "It's like the dream I keep having about the 'tard bus in eighth grade."

"Bella, who's throwing rocks at the 'tard bus?" she says gently.

"Blanche," I say. "I've let her down. She wants to fire me."

"Who else?" Joyce asks.

The heaviness in my chest is so painful I can barely stand to say it.

"My parents," I say between sobs. "They won't love me if I'm not perfect."

There, it's out. For me, excelling is not an option—it's the umbilical cord connecting me to my parents. Without it, I'll choke off and die. They don't have enough love for two problem children.

Joyce waits a while. Then she asks, "Who else is throwing rocks at the 'tard bus?" she says.

"I am," I whisper. "I hate myself."

"Why do you hate yourself?" she says.

"Because I'm selfish," I say. "Making up for Bobby is simply a way to get what I need most: my parents' love. That's why I don't really deserve it."

Seeing this in myself is unbearable. Joyce lets me cry for a full five minutes, even though I can hear her next patient outside the door.

"Beautiful work today," says Joyce gently, checking her watch and handing me another tissue. "Same time next week?"

"Same Fat Time, same Fat Channel," I say, blowing my nose.

Leaving Joyce's office, I don't make a beeline to the frozen yogurt shop. I feel sad but, in a weird way, relieved. Gathering up all these little shoved-under-the-mat parts of myself, even if I don't like them, is making me feel more, well, together. There's a shift. I'm aware of feeling more whole, rather than feeling *the* hole that is always screaming to be filled.

The next morning I'm cleaning off my hard drive and packing up my office preparing to get fired when my phone rings. My hopes soar. Maybe Christie Brinkley is coming through for me after all.

"Bonjour, Bella," says Zack.

"It's so nice to hear a friendly voice," I say. "Je suis getting beaten up *ici*."

"Le cover, still?" he says.

"Oui, I think they are going to sack me tomorrow," I say. "But how's your life? Let's talk about something happy."

"Well, actually, I wanted to tell you this in person," he says. "But I'm in Miami."

"You're in Miami?" I ask, noticing that his last sentence did not have one word of franglais.

"Yeah, anyway, I wanted to be the one to tell you the news," he continues, all in English.

"News?" I say. But it's too late. A lump the size of a Granny Smith has lodged in my throat.

"I'm engaged, pal!" he says. "Happened last night. Meredith popped the question."

"Wow, that's liberated," I manage. "I am *so* thrilled for you."

"No, you're not," he says.

This is why I love Zack and will always be forever grateful that at least we got our friendship back.

"You're right," I admit. The truth is I feel awful. Even if Zack's not The One, I took comfort in us leading the bachelor life together. And, yeah, maybe part of me did think there was still a slight chance that, at the end of the day, I would fall in love with my best friend. After all, it happened at the end of *When Harry Met Sally*.

Here come the tears again. Zack doesn't say anything but waits for me to compose myself. Chivalrously he plays dumb to my loud, snotty sniffing.

"Vagina?" he asks, finally.

"Yeah," I say. "Happy for you, sad for me."

"How 'bout dinner tomorrow night?" he says. "I'll take you anywhere you want to go."

"Can't. I'm on Bobby Watch," I say. "I promised my parents I'd stay out in Westchester while they go to that ridiculous ships in a bottle convention in Arizona."

"Your dad is a total character," says Zack, chuckling.

"I know," I say. "But tell Meredith I'll give her a shower in New York, and I promise I won't mention the ones we used to take together. Remember, avec le baby oil—"

"That's enough, Bella," he says, laughing. "Je t'aime, babe."

"Moi aussi," I answer. "Better hop. Telephonez when you retournez."

I hang up the phone and realize that just about everything in my life sucks right now. Oprah's voice floats into my head: "When something bad happens, ask yourself what you can learn from it."

Well, Oprah, I hate my job, for one thing. The interviews are cake, but working for the Skunk might not be worth the pressure anymore. If I'm hard on myself, she's downright masochistic. Joyce would say that it's "no accident" that I've chosen her for a boss. Why abuse yourself when you can get someone else to do it for you? So, Oprah, to answer your question, I guess I've learned that I've been pushed to my limit. Maybe getting fired, as scary as it is, is going to help me.

That's when I notice the red dot indicating that I have voice mail. Two voice mails, in fact. One is Blanche summoning me to her office, and the other, to my relief, is some cover news.

I knock on Blanche's door. She has armed herself with the Human Resources manager. Bad sign.

"Your basic inability to perform your job has put this magazine in real peril," she says. "So we have no choice but to terminate you."

I clear my throat and take a minute to get ready for my close-up. "Would you like to terminate me *before* or *after* I interview Mel Gibson?" I say. "Because he just said yes."

Blanche's jaw drops. "Mel Gibson?" she gasps. "But he's turned our interview requests down for five straight years."

"Right," I say. "But this time I didn't request an interview. I requested smoking a cigar with him."

"Hmm," says the Skunk, her beady little eyes boring into me like dentist drills. She almost looks disappointed that I've come through with an A-list star. "Well, I guess we don't have a choice," Blanche says. "But you'd better come back with something newsworthy, because this is your last chance."

"What did you have in mind?" I ask. How easy it is for her to have someone else do her dirty work. For once I'd like to see her summon the nerve to ask her stupid Embarrassing Question.

"Ask Mel if he would prefer a smoke to a woman," she says. "A man like that could have any woman he wants. How could he possibly be faithful? Maybe start with that and see if you can incite him."

"I'll do my best," I say, fuming. The man's got seven kids with the woman he's been married to for twenty-two years. And his publicist, Jeff, has set up this interview as a personal favor to me.

As I'm walking back to my office, I'm hit with the worst thought ever. Bobby. How could I have forgotten about him? How am I supposed to be in Westchester with Bobby and in L.A. with Mel Gibson at the same time? Let down my parents, or let down my boss? Super choice.

I decide to call my mom.

"Honey!" she says so sunnily I wonder if I've gotten the right number. "Your father and I are so thrilled about this trip! We haven't been away on our own since our honeymoon, and Talbots was having this great sale, so I got these cute twin sets . . ."

Okay, so that's clearly not an option.

"Right, Mom. What time do you need me home tomorrow?" I ask.

"We need to leave for the airport by three," she says. "I know you'll have to leave work early. I hope it's not too much trouble."

"No trouble," I say. "I'll be there. See you tomorrow."

The following afternoon, Bobby and I are in the driveway, seeing our parents off.

"Bobby, are you sure you are going to be okay with your sister?" Mom says. "We'll be back in just a few days."

"Get down. Boogie oogie oogie," he says robotically.

"Okay, champ," says my father, who hasn't looked this excited since Notre Dame won the Cotton Bowl in 1994. "Bella, thank you for this. We could never go without your help."

"No prob," I say. "Don't think about a thing. Just have fun."

"Fly the friendly skies," says Bobby as they drive off.

"Yup," I say, my thoughts turning toward dinner. Maybe I should eat my pasta one strand at a time with tweezers like my brother. That would slow me down.

"Fly the friendly skies, fly the friendly skies," he continues saying as we walk into the house.

Not for the first time I wish Bobby had a volume button.

"Fly the friendly skies! Fly the friendly skies!" he keeps repeating, louder and louder and louder. Oh, my God. Is he going to have a meltdown before my parents even make it to the airport?

"Fly the friendly skies!" he yells, right in my face, although he's looking to the side.

Then it dawns on me. *He* wants to fly the friendly skies. Unlike Rainman, Bobby adores airplanes. He loves transportation of all types. Why didn't I think of this before?

"Bobby, you want to go on an airplane like Mom and Dad?" I ask him.

He nods.

The Grand Plan clicks in my brain. Thanks to all these celeb interviews in L.A., I have plenty of frequent flier miles, and, well, I don't really have any other option. Hollywood, here we come!

I spend the weekend getting us both ready. A sexy outfit and new Prada mules for me, since this is the closest thing I've had to a date in years, and comfortable travel pajamas for Bobby. I arrange for Zack's sister, Jaimie, to stay with Bobby at the hotel while I do the interview. We pack up his favorite *Star Trek* figurines and take the Monday morning flight to Los Angeles.

I rent a Miata convertible so Bobby can feel the wind in his face the way he likes to. We're on the 405 freeway, headed toward the Four Seasons Hotel, and I sneak a peek at Bobby. He is strapped in tight but has craned his neck as far as possible into the wind.

"I'm the King of the World!" he says robotically, the wind blowing back his hair like he is Leo on the *Titanic*.

"Yes, you are, Bobby, because this bright idea of yours has saved my hide," I say.

I'm tuning in the radio when I come upon "Me & Bobby McGee," our favorite song when we were little. Janis is belting it out. I steal glances at Bobby. His eyes are closed, squinting against the sun, which is shining on his face. He's singing along with Janis in his tone-deaf, robotic monotone.

So what if Bobby's not normal? In his own way, he's awfully cute. I can't help it—I love him. I reach over and pat him on the arm. He jerks his arm away as if I have poked him with a cattle prod. He glares at me.

"Sorry," I say, glaring back sarcastically. I broke the no-touching rule. But my feelings aren't hurt. Even if we'll never have the closeness I've yearned for my whole life, and despite the fact that I'll never have a clue how he feels about me, in this moment it's okay. It's enough for me to simply love him, without all the other complicated feelings getting in the way.

In some ways, I'm coming to accept that my own twin will always be a stranger to me. Oprah's voice floats into my mind:

". . . what can you learn from it?" Then it hits me loud and clear. My difficulty in accepting this sad fact has led me on a journey right back to the one I really needed to get to know: myself. Accepting the things I have no control over, instead of fighting the fight day in and day out, and soothing the battle wounds with food, is a relief.

We check into the Four Seasons, and there's a message waiting for me. Gibson's publicist, Jeff. We get to the room and I call him immediately.

"Bad news. I tried to reach you this morning," Jeff says. "Mel quit smoking over the weekend. Interview's canceled."

"But you can't! I just flew across the country!" I say. "We don't have to smoke! We can do whatever he wants, but I can't go back without the interview."

"You don't understand. Mel's going through withdrawals. He doesn't want to do anything," Jeff says. "Even talk to me."

Now I'm *really* going to get fired.

"We don't need to go anywhere near a cigar," I say. "I just need an hour or two to interview him."

"Bella, he's in such a foul mood," says Jeff. "The man's an addict."

"Look, Jeff, I know you arranged this as a favor because I didn't out Rosie O'Donnell even though Blanche was pressuring me to," I plead, "but I've got four million women in my back pocket. Please don't make me write about Mel Gibson standing us *all* up!"

A few frantic phone calls later, Jeff works his magic and Gibson decides to stick with the original plan. So I slip on my new outfit, splurge on a professional blow-dry so my frizzball hair is silky smooth, and wait for Jaimie to arrive and watch Bobby.

Right on time, there's a knock on the door.

"Jaimie!" "Bella!" we say at the same time as we hug hello.

"It's been forever!" I say to Zack's sister. Her bed was our favorite place to Get Comfortable. "Thanks so much for doing this for me. I just couldn't leave him with one of the hotel sitters," I say. "You know why."

"Happy to help," she says. "So, are you okay about Zack's big news? I probably shouldn't say this, but my family all sort of hoped it'd be you. Your wedding song could have been 'My Sharona.'"

I put up my hand. I can't even go there now, right before this interview. I manage a shrug. "If Zack's happy, I'm happy," I say. "Now, let me fill you in on Bobby."

After giving Jaimie the blow-by-blows of Bobby's complicated rituals, I take a deep breath and drive the Miata to the Grand Havana Room, L.A.'s most exclusive cigar bar. It's in the middle of Beverly Hills, tucked away on the second floor of a ritzy mall. The only way to get in is up through a bouncer-chaperoned elevator.

"Bella Grandelli," I say. "I'm a guest of Mel Gibson's." (I've got to admit—it's a little fun to say that.)

"Yes, we've been expecting you," says the bouncer. "Right this way."

He leads me up and over to a private velvet settee by the bar. Fifteen minutes early, I survey the scene—an art deco room filled with tanned, important-looking men, all double-fisting stogies and cell phones. Suddenly, who comes strolling in but Gibson, with an entourage of about five guys. Now I've always considered myself more of a John Cusack girl, but *holy smokes*! His eyes are like swimming pools! Bright blue and crystal clear, and so nicely set off by his . . . tight black jeans! Without a moment's hesitation, I dive in off the high board.

Now, I've probably interviewed a hundred celebrities, so why is my heart beating so fast, and what, exactly, am I supposed to do next? Tap his toned shoulder and introduce myself? I pluck out my cell phone and call Carrie.

"You're the girl, he's the boy. Let him come to you," she advises. I've read *The Rules* too, so I do wait for his cue. Finally Jeff spots me, introductions are made, and we get down to business.

Whether it's because I usually interview women, or the fact that I've been so male deprived, I'm not sure, but the Mexican jumping beans are doing the Pee-Wee Herman tequila dance in my stomach.

"Bella, you are now entering the inner sanctum," says Gibson, leading the way into the enormous, glass-enclosed humidor. I lift my eyes from his butt to check out all the wooden lockers, each with a brass nameplate. Gibson's locker is to the left of Arnold Schwarzenegger's and up from Tony Danza's.

"Aren't these lovely for a rainy day?" he says, pulling out box after box of cigars and taking in each aroma.

Gibson's waxing rhapsodic when I suddenly notice steam blasting out from a ceiling vent. I panic, realizing that *duh!* it's *humid* in a *humidor*. "We've got to get out of here," I say, yanking his sleeve.

He squints at me in confusion.

"I've got curly hair," I admit. "It's allergic to water. And we've got to do a photo shoot after this."

"Let's go, Shirley Temple," he teases, walking me over to the snippers. I've chosen a pre-Castro Dunhill double corona, which Gibson says is older than me (37), but younger than him (46). Since Cuban cigars are the best but can no longer be imported legally, it is quite a luxury to be smoking this impossible-to-get $100 cigar.

As he slices off the tip, he starts to make noises like a baby yowling, followed by a blur of Yiddish. I realize he is circumcising the cigar and choke back a laugh. I don't want him to see that his boyish humor is working on me.

"Mel, I really have to congratulate you on your bravery—being interviewed in a cigar club, just three days after going cold turkey," I say. "I would never do an interview in a bakery if I were on a diet."

"You could have someone else eat the donuts. There is a certain degree of vicarious satisfaction in watching you smoke the cigar," he says, seeming impressed with my smoke rings. "I like it."

I like him liking it so much that the reality of his Australian wife of twenty-two years and their seven children is starting to depress me. Enough about them, I decide after I've heard my fill. "What's the proper time to tap my ash?" I ask, changing the subject.

"Anytime you want," he says, looking longingly at my cigar. "You know, you should really inhale that." Right as he says this, he inhales the matchstick he is chewing on. He chokes for a minute, coughs the matchstick up, and it dinks me right in the forehead!

I wipe Mel's spit from my brow. "Serves you right for giving me that advice," I say.

"I'm sorry, but it's very difficult to focus," he says, suddenly jumping up and grabbing my notebook and doodling like a madman. "It takes ten days to get over the physiological addiction. My brain is shooting all over the room."

"You've been through worse, though," I say. "I heard that when you were making *Mad Max Beyond Thunderdome*, you were getting drunk all the time and your costar Tina Turner took one of your glossy head shots and wrote over your face, 'Don't fuck this up,' then handed it to you. You totally quit drinking. How does this compare?"

"That was a snap," he says. "People say when you drink, you're who you really are. That's a bunch of bull. It just turns you into an obnoxious idiot. Believe me, I've had practice."

"Actually, I think you face who you really are when you deprive yourself of your vices," I say.

At Joyce's suggestion, I've been trying to get through my depressions without bingeing, by staying with my uncomfortable, yucky feelings. As torturous as this is, I have to admit, I usually learn something I would have missed if I would have anesthetized myself with food.

"That's absolutely right," says Mel, seeming to be genuinely interested. "I've learned a lot about myself by giving up alcohol."

"Oprah once told me that when something bad happens, you should ask, 'What can I learn from this?' It sounds like you've really done that," I say.

"No one has ever put it like that—" starts Mel.

"Excuse me, guys, but we're out of time," says Jeff, cutting him off.

"No, Jeff. I'm enjoying this," says Mel. "This interview is actually interesting, for a change."

"You were supposed to be at the looping session half an hour ago, and we still have to do the photo shoot," he says. "Sorry, Bella. This is your last question."

I really, really want to ask him what giving up drinking taught him about himself. But I am here for the Skunk, so I have to ask her stupid question.

"You know that expression, 'A woman is only a woman, but a good cigar is a smoke'?" I say, feeling like a total idiot. "If you had to pick one over the other, which would it be?"

Gibson cocks his head and looks at me, as if he's disappointed in my question. But I'm sure he's been asked a lot of dumb questions, so maybe I'm projecting. Maybe I'm just disappointed in myself for caving in to the Skunk.

"I never really understood that saying," he says.

"But if you had to pick," I press, feeling like Dumb and Dumber in the same person.

"If I had to choose between a woman and cigar, I'd take the woman," he says. "I've been asked a lot of questions before, but that one's really stupid. Interview's over. Let's go, Jeff."

The entourage leaves, and I sit there feeling like I've been dumped from a blind date. I hate myself for not following my instincts and doing what Blanche wanted instead. Despite asking the Embarrassing Question, I don't really have a story. That means I've got a lot more work ahead of me in order to make this profile interesting. Tick tock, tick tock. I've got three measly days before we go to press.

Things get worse when I stand up to leave and catch a glimpse of my hair in the mirrored bar. I guess we spent more time in the humidor than I thought. Standing under those little jets of watery air totally destroyed the straightness, but only on one side! To my horror it looks as if a baby raccoon has nestled on the right side of my head. This has got to be the hair equivalent to walking out of the bathroom with toilet paper stuck to your shoe. Or tucking the back of your skirt into your panty hose.

Despite my deadline, I decide to spend the next day taking Bobby to the L.A. attractions, since I can't imagine the next time we'll be able to come out here. We do all the tourist things: visit the Hollywood sign, do the driving tour of where the stars live, and Bobby's favorite, Universal City's Theme Park, where we go on all the rides, which I can't stand.

"Show me the money!" he says giddily while we are in the gift shop. The walls of brightly colored plastic toys stimulate him even more than the Back to the Future ride. He could stare happily at this crap forever.

"Pick whatever you want," I say. "But then we've got to catch the flight."

Bobby picks a blue plastic replica of the *Star Trek* phaser, I pay for it along with my *Vogue,* and we bolt to LAX. I return the car, make sure Bobby has all his belongings, including his beloved *Murder, She Wrote* lunchbox, and we make our way to the gate.

By the time we settle into our seats, I'm totally exhausted. But I also feel good. Talk about multitasking! In two short days I've pulled at least some quotes out of one of Hollywood's most reluctant interviewees, managed to save my job, and taken my brother on a mini-vacation. It may not be "fixing" him, but at least I hope I've made him happy.

He certainly looks content, fiddling with the buttons on his armrest and rearranging the contents of his lunchbox in that perfect, exact way that he likes.

"So, ready to fly the friendly skies again?" I ask, tucking into my *Vogue*.

But before he can answer, four men in black suits with earpieces burst into the cabin and charge right at us. They grab Bobby—one on each arm and leg—and yank him out of his seat. Roughly, they muscle him facedown onto the floor.

"Eeee eee eee," Bobby screeches in an earsplitting tone.

"Let go of him! What's going on?" I yell, the adrenaline coursing through my veins.

"Leggo my Eggo! Leggo my Eggo!" screams Bobby.

Everyone around us is starting to panic. Especially me.

"Stand back, miss!" says the black suit whose knee is grinding into my brother's back. "This man's got a gun!"

"No, he doesn't!" I scream. "This is a mistake!"

They rip the lunchbox from Bobby's grip and open it to reveal the phaser.

Oh, my God! Bobby must have been waving the phaser around while I was busily looking at my magazine and congratulating myself for being such a power-multitasker. How could he be so stupid? How could I?

"It's plastic!" I scream. "He's a Trekkie!"

"Everyone stand back," says one of the suits, while the three others drag Bobby along the cabin floor toward the door.

"Help, I've fallen and I can't get up!" Bobby's shrieking at the top of his lungs. "Beam me up, Scotty! The aliens are attacking!" Bobby yells.

I run out after him, and the nightmare begins.

It's like the domino effect of misunderstandings. A flight attendant spotted the phaser when Bobby opened his lunchbox and immediately reported it. The FBI watched him for a few minutes and recognized the stereotypical body language of a criminal— hunched-over posture and suspicious lack of eye contact. Then they put one and one together and got twelve. No one will listen to a word I say.

"Uh, Dad, I'm sorry to wreck your trip, but I have some bad news," I tell him over the phone when the authorities refuse to release Bobby to anyone except his legal guardian. By this point, they've realized his plastic piece of shit couldn't hurt anyone. Anyone but Bobby, as it turns out. But the rules are the rules, no loopholes for autistics.

By the time my parents fly from their convention in Arizona to meet me at the L.A. County jail, Bobby's been in custody for more than twenty-four hours. Waiting for them is torture, imagining how scared Bobby must be in his cell behind bars.

Finally, I hear the familiar click of my mother's Pappagallo pumps coming down the hall, and she and my father are standing before me. Judgment Day. My mother's eyes are faraway, her mouth tight, and my father is nervously jiggling the change in his pocket nonstop.

"I'm so sorry!" I say, bursting into tears. I had kept my cool up until this point. But seeing my parents before me, looking as scared and anxious as I feel, cracks my composure.

"I know, honey," my mother says. But her scared eyes say something else.

After my parents deal with a mountain of paperwork, the officer leads the three of us through an electronic gate and down a long, dark corridor. We are walking single file, with me sniveling in the rear.

"Pull it together, pull it together," I tell myself harshly, but the tears won't stop.

As a matter of fact, the closer we get to Bobby, the more hysterical I become.

It's as if the Gray Cloud finally has me where it wants me, in a stranglehold, choking the life out of me. My brother is incarcerated, thanks to me, as if his autistic world has not been a lifelong prison sentence in and of itself.

But when we round the corner and come upon Bobby's cell, we discover that he is completely . . . calm. He's sitting on his bunk, arranging his *Finding Nemo* figurines in size order, softly singing something.

"Just sit right back and you'll hear a tale, a tale of a fateful trip, that started from this tropic port aboard this tiny ship," he drones tunelessly.

Are you fucking kidding me? He's singing the theme from *Gilligan's Island*. The theme song puts me absolutely over the edge. Right before everyone's eyes, I have a complete and utter meltdown.

"Oh, my God, he's *fine*!" I sputter, my voice escalating. "He doesn't even know enough to not be fine! *I can't handle this!*" I scream.

The officer takes a step back from me, his jaw dropped. My parents look at me in a stunned silence.

"A three-hour tour," Bobby continues, dropping his voice just like on the TV show.

"It's just like when we were little and he didn't know enough to wish before blowing out the candles on our birthday cake. I just can't do it anymore! I can't handle *him*, I can't handle *myself*, and I can't handle the two of you! You don't say anything. You just let this go on, and on and on! But I know what you're doing. You're hoping!" I say, feeling like I am accusing them of Nazi war crimes. "You're secretly wishing!"

I know that I'm completely out of control, but I can't stop myself. I feel like Peter's volcano in that *Brady Bunch* episode. I just can't keep myself from spewing out what's been brewing inside of me for thirty-seven years.

"Our whole lives we have been held hostage to the Pink Elephant!" I scream. "Can't you see it, either of you? Let me describe it to you—Bobby is *not* normal! And he is *never* going to grow out of it! So stop hoping, because it's killing me! You wish for it all the time, I know you do, but there's *nothing* I can do. I *can't* make your wish come true. I can't. I can't!"

I crumple to the floor, sobbing. "And guess what? I'm not normal either," I tell them. "Because it's not normal for me, the lucky one, to be jealous of him, the misfit. But I am! I'm jealous because you love him just as he is, and I'll never be good enough to deserve that. I'm so tired of trying to deserve it, but I can't help him. I can't make up for him. I can't even help myself," I cry, looking up at them. "You've got it all wrong. *I'm* the one who's really the freak. It's me. Me."

I can tell by the officer's face that he agrees with me, but I don't care. Sobbing into my hands, I curl into a ball against the bars of Bobby's cell. For a minute, no one moves, and I listen to my sobs echo through the corridor. They sound surreal, as if I'm in a dream.

Then I hear Bobby get up from his bunk and, in his short staccato steps, shuffle toward me. I lift my face from my hands and blurrily face him. Through the bars he looks back at me for a moment with his peripheral vision. He clears his throat and says, "Drop the chalupa, Bella."

He repeats himself, a robotic version of the Taco Bell Chihuahua. "Drop the chalupa. Drop the chalupa."

I wipe my eyes and look at my brother, and realize he's called it exactly. I *do* need to drop the chalupa—and the whole proverbial enchilada while I'm at it. The jig is up.

The truth is I'm as needy, demanding, and difficult as my twin, more than I'd ever let anyone know. My goal in life was to be as different from Bobby as possible. But with the Pink Elephant looming over me, it's time for me to face the truth. I'm a fucking failure.

As I weep into my hands, I feel arms around me. It's my parents, kneeling on either side of me, hugging me in an awkward embrace.

"We're sorry, Bella," my mother tenderly whispers into my hair. "We've let you down, honey, not the other way around. We love you so much."

My father is jiggling change with one hand and patting my back gently with the other. "We've always been proud of you. We just thought you knew, that's all." He stops jiggling for a minute to wipe a tear from his eye. "We've been doing the best that we could," he says.

And that, my friends, is the ultimate heartbreaker.

Everyone in my family is doing the best he or she can, and it never changes a damn thing. It strikes me that the things that bug me so much about my parents are really things I can't stand in myself. My father's ships in a bottle obsession is really no different than my dieting. Both are a convenient substitute, an attempt to control something, anything, in an otherwise out-of-control world. My mother's No Makeup voice disgusts me because I can't stand facing in her what I feel inside, the helplessness of not being able to help someone you love so much. And then there's our family pet, the Pink Elephant, our silent, secret, collective wish that somehow, someway Bobby will change.

Meanwhile, Bobby is completely oblivious to the pain his mere presence causes. Compared to us, he's positively free. Except for the fact that he's currently in a jail cell, of course.

"*Yo quiero* Taco Bell," he says, shoving his Nemo figurine through the bars toward me.

I accept his gift.

Life goes on. Eventually, the four of us make it home. I pull an all-nighter and file the Gibson story on time. While it's not my best work, some of the quotes do get picked up in Page Six, and I am summoned to Blanche's office. This would normally make me nervous, but today it does not.

I seat myself in Giorgioland, and she levels her gaze on me.

"So what if you got on Page Six," she says dismissively. "What are you going to do for next month? Our newsstand sales are slipping."

"Actually, nothing," I say. I made my decision on the way back from L.A. I'm finished beating myself up, and I'm relieving the Skunk of her responsibility of doing that job too.

"Bella, if you want this job—" she says, formulating her threat.

"That's just it," I say. "I don't. You're on your own. I quit."

I get up to leave, enjoying the shocked look on her BOTOXed, skunk-framed face. "Oh, and by the way, I've been meaning to tell you," I say, holding my nose against the aroma of Giorgio, "working for you? It stinks."

19

Year: 2002
Age: 37
Idol: Cher
Favorite Song: "Crash" (Dave Matthews Band)
Prized Possession: pink Vespa with matching helmet
Best Shoes: Kate Spade slingbacks

Two twenty-something girls with spiky magenta hair and multiple piercings are giving Bobby the eye. No, make that *star-ing*. He's oblivious, of course.

"So what do you think of this one?" I ask Bobby, pointing to a particularly abstract painting. We're at a gallery opening on the Lower East Side, and it's more star-studded than a movie premiere. So far we've spotted Susan Sarandon, Tim Robbins, and their kids, and Robert De Niro and Leonardo DiCaprio.

Bobby surveys the paint-splotched canvas.

"Madness has no purpose. Or reason. But it may have a goal," he says, quoting Spock with utter and complete confidence.

"That's *so* deep," says Spiky Magenta Hair.

"And he's soooo cute. Look at the way he's dressed—a total individual," agrees Multiple Piercings. "I think he's *famous*."

I bite my lip to keep from laughing. Bobby's non sequiturs, when applied to art, or wine for that matter, have an uncanny way of impressing even the aficionados. Especially down here in the East Village. Even if my parents say that this entire area reminds them of the bar scene from *Star Wars*, I have to say I'm glad I moved here. I love living downtown. In fact *we* do. We're room-mates on the weekends, Bobby and I. Mel Gibson quit drinking and smoking. I quit my addiction to avoiding myself by trying to make up for my twin.

Oprah really was right—when something bad happens, you can learn from it. Not that it's easy. It's, no, *I'm*, a work in progress, and of course I have lapses now and then. But slowly I'm finding a way to *be* with my twin, rather than feel compelled to *do* something for him. And through that, I'm finding a way to be with myself, the real person I've been needing to get jiggy with all these years.

In his screenwriting class, Robert McKee says that once a character changes, so does the world around them. I had no clue what he was talking about at the time, but I see now that the guy had a point. After that jail cell meltdown with my parents, I decided to smoke out the rest of the Pink Elephants in my life.

Quitting my job was a risk. But the longer I allowed the Skunk to abuse me, the longer I was putting off the real work I've always wanted to do. It's always been my dream to write a romantic comedy, and now I have the time to do it. With Sam. Even if we weren't meant to be a love match, he's the funniest guy I know. We meet twice a week to write, and as soon as we finish a treatment, I'm going to pitch Nora Ephron, aka, the Queen of Romantic Comedies.

Here's the kicker—I still get to write *Style* magazine cover stories, or the ones I want to, anyway. A week after I quit, the Skunk called and offered me a contributing editor's contract. The deal: a whopping six thousand a cover story. Blanche's groveling: priceless. So I get to do the part of the job I love but skip all of the pressure of the bookings.

Life is good. It's sort of like I'm starring in my own episode of *Sex and the City;* although, admittedly, there's a lot more city than sex. I'm totally open to love, don't get me wrong, but there is a big difference between being open and being empty. Mr. Right might be around the corner, but for the time being *I'm* Miss Right Now.

My yoga teacher calls it "being present," so I did—buy myself a big present, that is. I decided to celebrate my independence by giving myself a pink Vespa—the perfect daily reminder to "enjoy the ride."

"Drive safely, Bella," says Ron, my doorman, and I strap on my helmet, hop on Pinky, and head uptown to the David Letterman show's studio, where I'm finally interviewing Cher. Well, I don't have an interview, per se, but the request I had put in nine months ago finally came through, sort of. Lulu, Cher's publicist, told the star that I'm her biggest fan, and she's granting me an introduction in the green room before her act on *Late Night with David Letterman*. It's a start.

Locking up Pinky, I make my way through the crowd of bewigged drag queens and rabid fans brandishing "You Got Me, Babe!" signs. I flash my press credentials to the bouncer, and he directs me up the back stairs.

Following the studio's labyrinth, I pass a door that says GOO GOO DOLLS—tonight's opening act—and find the one that says CHER. Tingles! Pathetic, I know, but I feel like the eight-year-old who used to count down the minutes to *The Sonny and Cher Comedy Hour*, on the edge of my seat to see her opening outfit, and watch her try to clap with her long glamorous fingernails.

I take a minute to compose myself. Whether I get to interview her or not, I want to appreciate the fact that at least I'll get the chance to meet the star whose confidence had such an effect on me growing up.

Deep breath.

I knock.

Nothing happens. Am I in the right place? Am I too late?

I knock louder.

Suddenly the door flings open and a beefcake of a guy wearing nothing but a black leather vest—chest fur flying—and black leather pants looks at me like I have three heads. I recognize him from his pictures; he's Cher's manager.

"Can I help you?" he says, giving me the hairy eyeball.

Luckily, Lulu spots me and waves me in. She taps the seat on the banquette next to her, and I amble through the swirl of frenzied activity to sit down beside her.

"Wow," I say, catching my first glimpse of Cher in the makeup mirror. It's a shocker. She's bald. And she has blue eyes.

"Contact lenses, and she's wearing a skullcap for her wigs," Lulu explains. "You better go over there. She's on in five minutes."

I'm nervous. I take a minute to think of the best tactic to get her to do the interview.

"It's now or never, toots," Lulu says, prodding me off the couch.

Summoning all my courage, I rise and cross the room toward the Survivor Icon. I hear Bette Midler's voice in my head: "Be yourself." Well, what have I got to lose?

I smile and crouch down next to Cher as the hair stylist attaches a long black wig with Cleopatra bangs. We are side-by-side, and Cher is eyeing me suspiciously in the makeup mirror.

Taking a deep breath, I launch into my story. "In 1974, there was an eight-year-old girl whose world was imploding. Her brother was in and out of hospitals, a dog bit her eyeball—"

"Her eyeball?" Cher says, cringing.

"Yeah, her eyeball, and her grandmother died," I continue. "So, anyway, this girl felt so lost that the only thing that made her feel better was writing her idol a letter."

Suddenly Cher swivels in her chair to look directly at me.

"So I just wanted to tell you—" I say, pausing.

"Yeah?" she says, one eyebrow arched, the body language of interest.

"Thanks for writing back," I finish.

I pull from my bag a dog-eared purple postcard of Cher wearing nothing but two strategically placed pieces of glitter (a little inappropriate for a child, but whatever).

I flip it over, hand it to Cher, and she reads: " 'Dear Bella, Hang in there! Love, Cher.' "

"That, for me, was a sequined sign from heaven that everything was going to be okay," I say, straight from my heart. "I'll always be grateful you took the time to be kind."

It was a moment, let me tell you! Cher wipes a tear from her eye, and so do I. I feel like the nerve accumulated from every single Embarrassing Question I've ever had to ask just paid off, because I had the nerve to be myself. I may not be perfect, but at least I'm authentic.

"It's time!" says Cher's manager.

"Oh, shit!" she roars, turning to the mirror and inspecting her runny eyeliner. "Makeup!"

I scoot out of the way as the damage control team swoops in to repair the eyeliner. Mere seconds later, she's whisked onstage to perform "Believe."

"Well, kid," says Lulu, "I think you got your interview."

I coast on the thrill all the way until the next afternoon, when I head to her penthouse suite at the Four Seasons Hotel.

Cher answers the door wearing a pink cashmere sweater and faded Levi's. No wig, no contacts. She has a Tootsie Pop sticking out of her mouth. In one way, she's exactly like I expected—straightforward, down to earth, with a hint of biker girl rebellion. Still, beneath the I-don't-care pose, a vulnerable middle-aged woman peeks out.

Talk about being a survivor! When I was doing research I read a clip that said that if the world were destroyed by a nuclear holocaust, the only things left alive would be "cockroaches and Cher." Surviving that criticism alone makes her extraordinary.

"Your confidence, I think that's what I responded to when I

was little," I say. "There weren't a lot of great role models for brunettes in the seventies. Mary Ann on *Gilligan's Island* doesn't exactly count."

To my surprise, Cher says that she felt like an outsider growing up too. "In the Walt Disney cartoons, all the witches and evil queens were really dark," she explains. "There was nobody I could look at and think, 'That's who I'm like.'"

"Well, at least I had you," I say. "What did you do?"

"I went to the movies a lot. And then I saw Audrey Hepburn in *Breakfast at Tiffany's,* and I *became* Holly Golightly," she says with a laugh. "I went to school with sunglasses, and they said, 'Take them off.' I said no."

"So that rebel streak, is that what made you take up with Sonny when you were sixteen?" I say.

Cher nods. "He had this long hair, and we were always getting thrown out of places because I didn't wear dresses," she says. "We were the first hippies."

"I believe that you learn at least one significant thing in a relationship before moving on," I tell her. "What's the one lesson you learned from Sonny?"

"Hmm," she says, taking the Tootsie Pop out of her mouth and closing her eyes to think.

I take the opportunity to review my boyfriend highlight reel too. Chandler taught me about the power of my own beauty. Mush taught me that you have to respect yourself before you expect anyone else to. Grant taught me about the importance of living life and having adventures, even if they don't directly lead to marriage. From Niles Whitford, ugh, I learned that you can abuse yourself with men as easily as you can with food or alcohol. Johnner showed me that perspective is everything. Zack has taught me about the power of friendship (plus without him I never would have gotten on the Joycemobile, which led to a whole lot of other learning). From Pete I learned that you can't fix other people, only yourself. And Sam taught me that having a sense of humor can help you accept the unacceptable. No marriage proposals, but all and all, these experiences have helped me figure out who I am.

Cher clears her throat. "Sonny taught me the power of telling the truth," she says. "It's a great weapon, because people don't expect you to."

The truth. The hardest thing I've ever done was tell my parents how I felt about them, Bobby, and myself. But it was what I had to do in order to start living my own life honestly. It strikes me that we all play hard to get with that one.

"So tell *me* the truth," I say to Cher. "Is it hard being alone?"

"There are so few men that attract me, and I would rather be alone than with someone I wasn't crazy about," she says. "Besides, you can't go looking for that kind of stuff—it happens *to* you. You have to be open, but you can't be desperate."

"I know exactly what you mean. But I do feel like people judge me because I'm still single," I say. "It's got to be ten times harder being in the public eye."

"People get confused if you give them too much information," she says, shrugging. "You do *Silkwood* with no makeup and then get plastic surgery. You do *Mask* and then you do infomercials. You sing and dance half naked and then you win an Academy Award for *Moonstruck*."

"Which one is the real you?" I ask.

"They all are," she says. "It's like therapy, exploring them all, but it sometimes gets me into trouble."

It strikes me that boyfriends for me are like outfit changes for Cher. They both help you "try on" different parts of yourself.

"So how do you make peace with that?" I ask.

"Even with all the mistakes I've made, I still respect who I am," she says. "I know everything about myself, and I still think I'm okay."

It's just like what Mush tried to teach me a million years ago:

The first rule of the road is self-respect. Just like Cher, I'm finally coming to a place where I think I'm okay too, despite my mistakes. I love the fact that Cher doesn't have all the answers, and she doesn't pretend to, either. It strikes me that maybe life is about asking the questions, not necessarily having the answers.

"Okay, last question," I say. "What do you like best about yourself?"

"That I don't give up, and I don't have airs. I don't need to," she says, without even having to think. "—I'm *Cher*!"

I can't help it—I jump up and hug her. Cher looks surprised but hugs me back anyway. Cher's saving grace, it turns out, is the same as mine: having a sense of humor about yourself. Thanks to Sam, I've learned that no matter how bad things can get, laughing at myself is like Dorothy tapping her ruby red slippers together— it always brings me home. Not the home I grew up in, but the little place I've created inside myself where everything really is going to be okay.

Scooting home, I decide that I was smart to pick Cher as an idol nearly thirty years ago. Because I now have a new wish. It's to know and accept myself as much as this woman who has been to hair care infomercial land and back, and has lived to laugh about it.

Year: 2004
Age: 39
Idol: me
Favorite Song: "My Favorite Things," Bella's version
Prized Possession: yoga mat
Best Shoes: Dr. Scholl's, hand-painted with martini glasses

"Y̶ou know that Julie Andrews song 'My Favorite Things' from *The Sound of Music*?" I ask Nora Ephron. We are tucked into a corner booth at Pastis, a trendy Frenchy-French bistro in the meatpacking district. I'm about to pitch her the screenplay that Sam and I have been working on together for the last year.

She nods her head yes, keeping an eye on Ralph Fiennes, who is being seated at the booth across the way.

"I've written my own version," I tell her.

"Well, let's hear it," she says, turning her full attention to me.

"I'm tone deaf. Are you sure you don't want me to e-mail it to you?" I say, losing my nerve.

"C'mon," she says, egging me on. "Let's hear it."

"Okay, here goes," I say, taking a deep breath and putting my head close to hers so the table next to us doesn't have to suffer.

"Cartier watches and dirty martinis
Tiffany blue boxes and sipping Bellinis
Hanging with Bobby and the giggles it brings
These are a few of my fa-vor-ite things!

Strolling in Soho and ditching the scale
Bagels and baubles and Seventh on Sale
Getting the perk, pulling some strings
These are a few of my fa-vor-ite things!

An outdoor table at La Ga-lou
A mani and pedi, all shiny and new
Central Park winters that melt into spring
These are a few of my fa-vor-ite things!

When the rents hike—
When the cabs strike—
When the Gray Cloud makes me sad,
I cruise my pink Vespa down Fifth Av-e-nue
And then I don't feeeeel so-oooooo bad!"

"Bravo!" says Nora, clapping. "What brought this on?"

"Well, I've met someone," I say proudly.

"I thought so," she says. "Do tell."

"He's been in my life forever, but I'd never noticed him like *that* before. Every night he comes up with something exciting to do, movie premieres, gallery openings, and new restaurants, and Bobby is always invited. I don't even have to ask."

"Well?" she says impatiently.

"The love of my life is," I say, pausing to add drama, "New York City!"

It's true. When I faced the final Pink Elephant in my life, that I'll only be happy if I could meet a husband, something magical happened. Hello?! I finally got it. My life is full and fun and sexy as is, without Insert-a-Groom.

Nora does not look impressed, however. "So, what *is* going on with Sam?" she asks, raising an eyebrow. "You said you had something to tell me about you and him."

"Yes, but it is not romantic. I think fate put us together to write this screenplay," I say, steering the conversation to the pitch. "Now let me give you the basic outline." I launch into the idea: a bachelor TV reporter and a magazine columnist who can't stand each other but fall in love, pandemonium ensues, yadda, yadda, yadda, and against all odds they wind up in each other's arms right in time for Celine Dion's corny-but-commercial number-one hit. Roll the credits, please.

"Nora?" I say. She is staring off at Ralph Fiennes again. Somehow, I don't think she really got the pitch.

"Bella, your life is much more interesting than your work," she says bluntly. "Your version of the Julie Andrews song, and that whole relationship you have with your brother, it's fascinating," she says. "Seems to me that you're missing the obvious."

I chew on that food for thought as I drive Pinky home. I've got to admit, I'm totally disappointed. Sam does really bug me at times, but I put up with him because I was convinced even if our idea wasn't the most original, it would sell. Well, says Kate Capshaw Positive Voice interrupting, at least Nora thinks my life is interesting, even if my screenplay idea sucks.

I'm going to have to break the news to Sam. Just as I get into my apartment, the phone is ringing.

"Honey?" says my mother's voice. Here we go again with the No Makeup.

"What's wrong with Bobby?" I say. I'm light-years from where I used to be about this, but I'm still not altogether immune to the stomach pains brought on by anticipating the bad news about my brother.

"It's not Bobby," she says.

Phew. My whole body relaxes.

"It's Beau," she continues. "He's dead."

"What?" I say. The words roll off me like rain on a car hood, completely unable to penetrate. I can't believe this. He's a father and husband. How could he possibly be dead?

"He rolled his SUV on the way to pick up his kids from soccer yesterday," she says. "I just heard the news."

"The kids?" I say, gasping.

"The kids and Janice are fine," she says. "They weren't in the car."

"Oh, my God," I say.

I am just in shock. I haven't seen Beau since we broke up. But I still think of him at least once a day. How can Beau be dead? We sit there in silence for a moment.

"Bella, I'm sorry to even bring this up to you, but actually I am worried about your brother," she says.

"Why? Does Bobby even remember Beau?" I ask, confused. Not only does Bobby never display emotion about other people, but Beau? It's been years.

"He was close to Beau, Bella," she says.

"What?" I say. The first shock hasn't even set in. This is just too much information to take at one time. I sit down.

"Bella, I'm going to tell you something that you didn't know," she says. "After the two of you broke up, Beau used to call him. He's even stopped by the house to visit him a couple times."

"You've *got* to be kidding me," I say. This is as hard to digest as Beau's death. To quote my brother, this does not compute. My mind starts lurching. If Beau cared about Bobby, then . . . surely . . . he still cared about . . . me.

"Why didn't you ever tell me?" I ask, swallowing.

"Because it would have only given you hope," she says quietly. "Beau had gotten on with his life, and you needed to get on with yours."

She is right. I am beginning to see that my mother is not as clueless as I had thought. She kept this from me to protect me from my own misguided wishes.

"Bobby keeps repeating Beau's name and catchphrases from the early eighties," she says. "He's really regressing."

As if to underscore her point, Bobby grabs the phone and says in a plaintive, Dana Carvey voice, "Read my lips—no new taxes. Isn't that special?"

"I know, Bobby. I'm sad too," I say.

My mother takes back the phone. "Janice has set the date for his memorial service, to be held at St. Ignatius Loyola on Park Avenue," my mother says.

"Of course I'll take him," I say.

"Thanks for not making me have to ask," she says.

I used to feel like I had to do things like this, but now I feel like I want to. That's the difference.

"Why don't I come home tonight?" I say. "Not that I can do anything to help Bobby, but it might be nice to just be together."

"Great, honey," she says. "Let us know which train, and we'll pick you up."

That night, after a tweeze-a-thon spaghetti dinner, I tuck Bobby between his mattress and box spring in front of his TV, turning it to his favorite programming, Nick at Nite, and go up to the attic and dig out a box that I shoved there almost fifteen years ago.

When Beau and I first got engaged, Mrs. Callahan gave me a crate of all Beau's memorabilia, his baby book, photos of him as a kid, and even stuff like his kindergarten artwork and high school yearbooks.

But what Mrs. Callahan didn't realize is that the box also contained the special letters he'd saved over the years. Most of them from Janice. At the time, I was so happy that I was the one who got him, that I didn't really notice how odd it was that Janice's letters were the only ones he'd kept. Hindsight being what it is, it's clear that Beau and Janice had a bond that I was too judgmental to see.

Opening the box, however, I don't even feel like looking through his stuff, which surprises me. I wrap it back up and start poking around in the other boxes up there. I open an old trunk by the window and catch my breath. It's my grandmother's wedding dress! Italian lace from the forties, still in pristine condition.

I slip my arms through the sleeves, hold up the dress to my body, and look at myself in the reflection of the window. The cut flatters me way better than the Vera Wang gown I was going to wear. Again, I'm struck by my difference in taste between now and then. I had turned up my nose to something ethnic and vintage, preferring a status symbol instead. As I look at my reflection, that familiar, dull ache of wanting to be in love thuds in the pit of my stomach. I don't run down to the kitchen to apply hot fudge, but instead just let the feeling linger.

My grandmother's voice comes into my head. "You have a good heart," she tells me, and I get an idea. I decide to write Janice a long letter and send the box of Beau's stuff to her. I had been hanging on to it to avoid facing the facts. He's not mine anymore, and neither is his stuff. It may not be much in the way of consolation, but it's the best I can do.

The day of the memorial, I'm waiting in the lobby of my apartment for my parents to drop off my brother. My father double-parks, and my mother walks Bobby into my building. I notice he's wearing my father's Notre Dame fight song tie. I wonder if this day is going to be a disaster.

"Sweetie, I know this will be hard," my mother says, giving me a hug. "But you're doing the right thing."

Bobby and I wave good-bye to my parents, and I try to hail a cab. Ten, twenty, thirty minutes and still no luck. The stress is mounting. We are going to be late, or miss the mass entirely, if we don't do something fast.

"We are on a mission from God," says Bobby in an impatient Dan Aykroyd robot voice. "Let's roll."

"Okay, okay," I say. "Plan B."

My doorman hands me the helmets to my Vespa. I take off my belt and strap my brother to me, careful to keep the *New York Times* between us. We take off.

Luckily, we get there just in time to join the mourners milling into the church. I make sure we are positioned near the door, in case Bobby starts fiddling with his tie and we need to make a hasty exit. Surprisingly, however, he's uncharacteristically calm as he stares at the light coming through the stained glass windows. With the exception of a few loud sniffs, he doesn't make a peep the entire service. I wonder if he even knows what it means that Beau is gone.

After the recessional hymn, "Amazing Grace," Bobby and I head to the reception, which is around the corner at one of Beau and Janice's friend's apartments. We go up in the elevator and we get on the receiving line. I brace myself to face Janice and her fatherless twelve- and thirteen-year-old children.

As I watch the three of them, it's weird to realize that those kids could have been mine, and I could be standing at the receiving line instead of Janice. My life turned out so differently than it would have had Beau married me instead of Janice. I think about the men I wouldn't have dated, the experiences I wouldn't have had, the lessons I wouldn't have learned. Instead, I'd be standing here today in Janice's shoes. I can't even imagine that.

It's my turn, and Janice hugs me warmly. I introduce her to Bobby.

"Hi, Bobby. I've heard all about you from Beau," says Janice, her voice warm.

This gives me a stomach twinge.

"Bella, thank you for your sweet letter and that box," she continues. "It's like you gave me a part of him that I didn't have."

"It belongs to you," I say, shrugging. "*He* belonged to you. He always did, and he always will." It was true, after all.

"You know, Beau had something that belonged to you," she says, reaching into her pocket and producing an envelope that says *Beulah* in Beau's handwriting. "He brought this to the jewelers right before, well, right before it happened."

"Wow," I say as I open the envelope and my grandmother's heart-shaped locket slips into my palm. I try the clasp. As always, it won't open. Then I notice a note from the jeweler: "Mr. Callahan: Edwardian oddity circa 1921. This is not broken. It's a solid gold charm and was never designed to open. Very valuable."

Unbelievable. All those times I wanted to put a boyfriend's picture in there, but it was already full and complete just as it was. I feel a sudden sense of warmth and calm, as if I've finally gotten the closure I needed. I gave Janice a part of Beau that belonged to her, and she's given me back a part of myself that never belonged to him in the first place. It's like a really weird version of "The Gift of the Magi."

"It's beautiful," Janice says, as we look at the gold heart.

"Thanks. It was my grandmother's," I say. "I'm very happy to have it back. Thank you."

"Sure. Bella, maybe we could get together sometime," Janice says. "You know, to talk about him."

This makes me start to tear up. That Janice and I are reaching toward each other over the deceased person we used to war over touches me deeply.

"Whenever you're ready, I'm here," I say. I hug her, then realize that Bobby's wandered off.

I do a lap and find my brother staring into the ice bucket in the bar, transfixed. This is a sign that he's bordering on stimulation overload, and he's not wearing his inflatable vest, so I hurry us to the elevator before it's meltdown city.

"Hold the door, please," I say, and we jostle in. It's crowded, a testament to how many lives Beau touched. As we descend, Bobby leans into the broad-shouldered armpit of the navy suit in front of us and starts sniffing.

I am mortified.

"Bobby, stop that," I whisper. "You know that's not polite." My mother's right—he really *is* regressing. He hasn't sniffed someone since high school.

Suddenly, in a loud, clear voice, Bobby yells, *"No good bushwackin' barracuda! Prepare to defend yourself, rabbit, 'cause I'm boardin' your ship!"*

This is horrifying. We are leaving a memorial, for godsakes! Just when I think I get the hang of things with my brother, he does something like this, and I feel like I'm in high school again.

Everyone in the elevator stares at us. Who can blame them? To make things worse, Bobby starts squeezing his tie and the Notre Dame fight song goes off.

"I'm sorry," I say to everyone. "He gets a little overexcited."

But I am drowned out by Bobby who, at this point, is bellowing, *"Now I gotcha, ya fir bearin' critter! Now quit stallin' and start roastin'!"* at the top of his lungs, while doing yoga deep breathing in this poor stranger's armpit.

Suddenly the guy in the navy suit spins around. He's tall with a chiseled jaw and dimples. His face is sort of familiar, but I can't quite place him. Is he an old friend of Beau's? As I search his blue eyes, something about them makes me feel safe, protected. I look down and realize he's wearing motorcycle boots.

"Bella?" he says.

"Mush?" I say.

Bobby is suddenly quiet. You can hear a pin drop, quiet.

I am shocked. I think about Mush from time to time, especially when the self-respect issue comes up during sessions with Joyce. But I never thought I'd see him again.

"What are you doing here?" I finally manage. "Are you a friend of Janice's?"

"Yeah, but through Beau. He was my mentor," he says. "Nearly fifteen years ago he helped me start my life over."

"You're *Jim*?" I say. I put the pieces together. Jim Mucelli, Mush. The guy Beau used to talk about all the time right after we got engaged.

"Yeah," Mush says. "How did you know him?"

"Tell you in a minute," I say, nodding to the crowd around us. I am still amazed that I am standing next to Mush in an elevator on Park Avenue.

What feels like fifty years later, the elevator makes it to the ground floor. The doors open, and we all spill out into the hallway. "I used to be engaged to him," I whisper. "But we shouldn't talk about that here."

"You're—Oh, my God," he says, hitting his forehead. "You're *Beulah*?"

Beulah! Like it said on the jeweler's package, but I haven't heard that name out loud in almost fifteen years.

"I *was*," I say, the tears starting again. This day is harder than I even thought it would be.

"Great horny toads, I'm up North!" Bobby says robotically, pointing to Mush's forearm. "Gotta burn my boots. They touched Yankee soil!"

"He even remembers your tattoo," I say, laughing through my tears.

"Okay, big guy," Mush says, unbuttoning his cuff and pushing up his sleeve to reveal Yosemite Sam. Bobby sneaks a peek with his peripheral vision. A smile spreads across his face.

"Bella, Beau used to talk about you," says Mush. "A lot."

I swallow. He *did* care.

"So you stayed in touch with him?" I say.

"After he helped me start my own construction business," he explains, "I partnered with him to fund-raise for the mentoring program. When my company went public, I decided to do the mentoring full-time. Beau was a huge supporter."

Mush, retired and a full-time philanthropist. If he has half the patience with the wayward boys of New York City as he did teaching me how to parallel park, we'll see a definite drop in the crime rate. Two of the Mexican jumping beans start doing a Fred and Ginger routine in the pit of my stomach.

"You had me at hello! You had me at hello!" Bobby yells, in what must be the oddest Renée Zellweger impersonation ever to be uttered.

We look over at my brother, who has helped himself to the back of Mush's Harley and has even put on Mush's helmet.

"I guess he didn't forget about your Chopper," I say. "That ride, what was it, twenty-three years ago? I think it was one of the happiest times of his life."

"Why don't I spin him back to your place?" Mush offers.

"Sure you don't mind?" I say.

I give Mush our address and take my time cruising down Fifth Avenue. I go fast enough that I can enjoy the wind in my hair, and slowly enough that I can people-watch as I go by. It occurs to me that inside unhappiness sometimes you can stumble upon pockets of happiness. But they're easy to miss, because your eyes are peeled for something else.

Just as I pull up to my street, however, I notice a fire truck, cop cars, and an ambulance blocking the way.

It's my nightmare come true.

Mush rushes over to me.

"What happened?" I say, suddenly feeling a cold tingling sensation.

"I don't know. As soon as we pulled up in front of your apartment, he just slumped against me," says Mush, frantically pushing buttons on his cell phone. "I called 911, and he kept mumbling, 'You had me at hello.'"

There, in front of my apartment, is my brother's body, sprawled on the sidewalk like an oddly contorted action figure. His hand clutches a McDonald's *Finding Nemo* figurine, as if he were hanging on to life itself.

"Oh, my God!" I shriek, running toward my brother.

I barge through the crowd of onlookers, and watch the paramedics start working on his unconscious body.

"He's not breathing!" yells one of the paramedics.

"Bobby!" I scream, dropping to my knees at his side.

The other paramedic, a woman, pushes me out of the way to strap an oxygen mask to Bobby's face.

"Yo, Ron, gimme the ambubag. I'll start ventilating him," she says, attaching a gray bag to the oxygen mask and squeezing it at four-second intervals.

"I'm having trouble finding a pulse," says Ron, whose hand is resting on Bobby's neck. "I'm gonna tube him and start the IV."

As she sticks a needle in Bobby's arm, his whole body convulses. His eyes open for a second and roll back into his head.

"He's seizing! Now there is no pulse! Let's start CPR," she says to the fireman next to her.

"Miss, is he allergic to anything? History of heart attacks? Strokes?" says Ron, injecting the first drug into Bobby's IV.

"It's complicated—" I stammer.

I don't know where to begin to explain about my twin. The years of shock treatments, wrong medications, and institutionalization roil in my mind like a sinister kaleidoscope.

"Still no pulse," yells Ron, cutting me off. "We're gonna lose this guy if we don't act fast. Let's get him in the bus!"

How can I lose him now that I've finally found him? My entire life has been a quest for my other half, someone to complete me. My search for a soulmate—which has lead me into intimacy with trust-fund babies, "It" boys, and celebrities—has led me right back to the first guy I ever loved, my twin brother. But life isn't always champagne wishes and caviar dreams when your brother has Asperger's syndrome.

"Get these people back!" says Ron, helping lift Bobby's lifeless body onto the gurney. "Careful, don't pull out the IV. Let's work together!"

I stand there helpless, as usual. The Rainman disease was finally his diagnosis, but what's mine? My ultimate goal was to be as different from Bobby as possible, yet only recently have I realized that I've been living in the shadow of my dysfunctional twin.

"Can I be with him?" I ask, running alongside the gurney.

"You can ride up front," a paramedic says. "What can you tell us about his medical history? Who's his doctor?"

They say that some amputees can still feel the ache where the limb used to be. That's sort of how I felt that horrible, horrible day when I found Bobby on the pavement. I guess that's what it's like when you face losing someone you love so much that they are a part of you.

Not that there weren't times when I wished my own twin were dead. Growing up, I used to pretend that I wasn't related to him, guilty that I had a normal life, envious that nothing was expected of him, and relieved that I wasn't the loser, ostracized by society. Look how far I've come.

In some ways Bobby has always been like a Buddha, truthful, honest, living in the moment, without a shred of self-consciousness or malice. In a word, he was always *himself*. Instead of fixing him, changing him, or making him better, I might have simply accepted him, or at least accepted myself for my lifelong struggle to do just that.

As my twin, he was, in effect, holding up a giant mirror for me. All the things I couldn't stand about him—like never being in control, never fitting in, always embarrassing himself—were really things I hated about myself. Accepting his imperfections eventually enabled me to accept myself, flaws and all.

"Hold on," says Mush. I cling tightly to his waist as we roar off on the chopper. Mush has been by my side ever since they took away Bobby in the ambulance. The weird part is how normal it's felt to spend every waking moment with him, as if we are family. And what's even weirder is I never in a million years would be with him right now if my brother hadn't literally sniffed him out for me. Bobby's acute sense of smell, that odd Asperger's symptom, which brought me so much stress in my life, also brought me back into the arms of a really great guy.

I recently caught the *E! True Hollywood Story* on Henry Winkler, and he admitted something shocking. Not once, in his entire life, has he ever ridden a motorcycle. Ironic, considering that it was his role as the biker Fonzie that made him famous. But I can relate. Now that it's finally my turn to get married, the traditional role of bride no longer fits.

Mush and I are on our way to exchange vows in a barefoot blue jeans ceremony on the beach at Manor Park. The only bridal thing about me is Grandina's lace veil, which is dancing in the wind behind me, looking more celestial than the plastic bag scene in *American Beauty*.

But the real proof of God is riding in the sidecar next to me.

"Mind that I'm leaving you for another guy?" I yell over the wind to my brother.

"You're fired!" he says, giving me the Donald Trump hand gesture.

Ever since Bobby's stroke, he's been in physical therapy learning to walk again. But that's okay with him, as long as he can ride shotgun with Mush and me. This may not be a perfect Martha Stewart procession, but at least it's authentic.

We pass the Red Hook Bakery, and I realize something important—we are about to go over the train tracks. Half a block until Wish Time.

"Wait, Mush. Slow down!" I say.

Quickly, quickly, I zero in on exactly what I want: a wish stronger than any of the ones I made over those joint birthday cakes growing up. I squeeze my arms tightly around Mush's waist.

The One isn't some guy, or even Bobby for that matter. The One, Bobby's been trying to show me the entire time, is *me*. The love lesson he was trying to teach me was simply to love myself, flaws and all.

Not that confronting the ultimate Pink Elephant was easy. I was born the normal one. My twin was not. But finding a way to accept this has led me on an incredible journey of self-discovery, one that I never would have embarked on otherwise.

"Hey, Bobby!" I yell back happily. "You're fired too!"

"Shock and awe, baby," says Bobby with a smile. "Shock and awe. Da-da-dat's all, folks!"

Right as the bike's tires bump over the tracks, I close my eyes, cross my fingers, and lift my feet. And, for the first time in my life, I don't hold my breath. I . . . just . . . *wish*.

Photo by Tiff Pemberton

Melina Gerosa Bellows is the Editor-in-Chief of *National Geographic KIDS*. Previously, Bellows was a Senior Editor at *Ladies' Home Journal* magazine, where she wrote and negotiated the monthly celebrity cover stories. Her subjects included Oprah Winfrey, Mel Gibson, Julia Roberts, Jodie Foster and Michelle Pfeiffer among others. Bellows has also been a staff writer for *Entertainment Weekly* and *Premiere* magazine, and has freelanced for the *New York Times*, *National Geographic Traveler*, *Glamour*, *Cosmopolitan*, *Family Life*, *Parenting*, *Elle* and *The Washingtonian*. Bellows is the author of *The Fun Book* (Simon & Schuster, 2000), *The Fun Book for Couples* (Andrews McMeel Publishing, 2003), and *Wish* (New American Library, 2005). She lives in Washington, D.C., with her husband, Keith, the Editor-in-Chief of *National Geographic Traveler*, their son, and their cat Chiang Mai.

*wish

MELINA GEROSA BELLOWS

A CONVERSATION WITH MELINA GEROSA BELLOWS

Q. How much of this novel came from your own experience?

A. Well, this is certainly not a memoir because I do not have an autistic twin brother. But a lot of the "greatest hits" of my love life, and those of my friends, make up the composite of Bella's experience. What is absolutely true to me is Bella's reaction to everything that happens to her. And all that longing, wishing, and avoiding the main issues in her life, and the feeling that she's always five pounds away from accepting herself. Also, almost all of the celebrity stuff is verbatim from interviews that I did during my years as an entertainment journalist. I was always asking Julia Roberts, Jodie Foster, Nicole Kidman, Oprah, and all these stars questions about things I found personally interesting at the time, whether it was diet tips, love life advice, good books, places to go on vacation, or whatever. And let me tell you something. When Oprah gives you advice, you take it.

Q. Why did you decide to write this book?

A. I didn't decide to write this book. This book decided for me to write it. I have a day job (as editor in chief of *National Geographic Kids Magazine*) and I would have preferred to continue sleeping past six a.m. every morning. *Wish* was very bossy, though; it would compel me out of bed and down the hall to where my computer would beckon. I'd sit there bleary-eyed, coffee in hand, and suddenly this movie footage would start in my head. The book literally came to me in scenes, which I would transcribe. Then I'd wait, and I'd get another scene, and I'd write that down. Of course there were a lot of days when I'd sit there and see nothing. Nothing, nothing, nothing. And it'd be five thirty a.m., and I'd be sitting there listening to my husband and cat snoring loudly from the other room. I was recently reading *The Shadow of the Wind* [by Carlos Ruiz Zafon], and there was a great line: "A story is a letter the author writes to himself, to tell himself things that he would be unable to discover otherwise." Maybe I was trying to tell myself something. Like enjoy the adventure that is your life.

Q. What is the significance of the Bobby character?

A. Bobby is a mirror for Bella. You can tell exactly where she is in her own development by how she feels about him. It is only when she finally accepts him that she accepts herself, warts and all. At one point in the original draft, Bobby was an angel who was sort of a special-ops agent sent down from heaven to help Bella. That subplot wound up on the cutting room floor, but if you pay attention you realize that Bobby really helps her at every crucial point in her life. He gets her kicked out of The Clique in eighth grade, which is a good thing, even if it is devastating at the time. He gets her out of a suicidal slump when he visits her in London during her year abroad. And he's even responsible for hooking her up with the love of her life. Bella thinks she's taking care of Bobby her whole life, but really it's the other way around.

Q. Were there any themes or ideas that you wanted to get across to readers while you were writing the novel?

A. There were a few "truths" I wanted to tell. First of all, there is this belief that siblings are just born close. Best friends from birth. And while some families are lucky like that, with others the brothers and sisters need to put some effort into that closeness. I have an older brother and younger sister and we are all opposites. But the older we get, the closer we get, which is really, really nice. We're great friends now, and so love to have fun together. Another "truth" I used to believe was that I wasn't complete until I had a boyfriend or later, a husband. The older I got, the more focused I became on this, until my love life became one huge Sahara Desert dry spell. Meanwhile, all my friends were getting married right and left. Then the craziest thing happened. I accepted that I was going to be a spinster for the rest of my life, with a big hump on my back and a bunch of cats, and I started to have a really good time. And that's when it happened. Keith rode in on his white steed and Prince Charming never looked so damn good. But here's the ironic part: All those disastrous relationships, and the dog years I spent waiting by the phone, and the pints of Ben and Jerry's I downed in the meantime—that was all really good stuff looking back! And I learned a ton. I learned something significant from each relationship I was in, and that's what I want women to come away from *Wish* with: Everything that happens is an opportunity to learn. That's really the key to life. Oprah taught me that when I had dinner with her one time after I was totally dumped.

Q. Why did you decide to structure the novel as you have, spanning Bella's entire life? Why did you choose to revisit past decades?

A. Two reasons. First, I wanted the little time capsules at the beginning of each chapter to invite readers to the party. I thought they would help the reader really relate to Bella. Those little entries before *Bridget Jones's Diary* were funny, but all about Bridget. These, I hope, are all about the reader, and going down memory lane to those Dorothy Hamill haircuts and leg warmers. Second, I wanted the readers to watch Bella grow, and the best way to do that was to show a progression in her choice of boyfriends, not to mention footwear. But the real growth you can see is in how she relates to her twin. In the first chapter she loves him. She knows there's something wrong, but it's a pure love. Then in junior high she's so embarrassed by him she pretends he's not related. Then in high school she starts tolerating him, but not as he is. She wants to change him or fix him. This goes on for decades, until she accepts the fact that she's actually jealous of him in a way. Finally, when she accepts him, and her inability to change the fact that he's autistic, she is able to free herself from their codependent relationship. It's like in *The Wizard of Oz* when Dorothy clicks her red slippers, she's home.

Q. What books have you loved? What authors have influenced or inspired you?

A. I love *A Confederacy of the Dunces*, *The Shipping News*, *A Prayer for Owen Meany*, and *The Life of Pi*, stories that have unforgettable characters who make you laugh. I also love reading books that take you to another world, like *The Poisonwood Bible*. And I am a total sucker for stories with strong first-person narrators, *The Kite Runner*, *The Shadow of the Wind*, and *A Girl Named Zippy*.

QUESTIONS
FOR DISCUSSION

1. Discuss Bella's complex relationship with men, her intense desire to find "the one", and how it all eventually ties into her relationship with her autistic brother. Why does her sibling have such an effect over her and her relationships, in particular?

2. What does Bella learn from each romantic relationship? What do you think men and women can take away from relationships in order to help in subsequent relationships?

3. There is an assumption in society that all siblings are close, but in some cases they are more like strangers born to the same parents. Discuss this dynamic in general. Also, despite Bella's and Bobby's glaring differences, can you see any similarities?

4. What advice would you give Bella? Are there things you wish she had handled differently? Is she someone you could be friends with?

5. Many of Bella's problems—including those involving her relationship with men—stem from her inability to control the circumstances of her life. What do you think is the turning point in the novel when Bella is finally able to feel comfortable in her own skin?

6. How much should the family you grew up with affect your personal plans for the future? In what ways does a childhood shape one's adulthood?

7. The ending to *Wish* is a happy one, but if this were not fiction, Bella might have had to take full responsibility for her sick brother in the event that her parents no longer could. Discuss the responsibility that siblings have when it comes to caring for family members who cannot take care of themselves. What are the long-term effects of living with someone with a disability?